Triple Play

The Battle of Cell Tower Hill

Dan Kemp

DISCLAIMER

This is a work of fiction. Names, characters, businesses, places, events, locales, military operations, and incidents are all either products of the author's imagination or used in a fictitious manner. Any resemblance to actual persons, living or dead, or actual events is purely coincidental or are fictionalizations derived from recorded history.

Chapter One

S taying in one of the Presidential Suites at the Venetian in Las Vegas is one of those 'Look at me, Mom! I made it!' kind of things, and it gave me a perverse sense of accomplishment. I chose to focus on that part. I was ignoring the fact that my mom would actually be pissed off at me for spending this kind of money on a hotel room. I could tell myself it was the company's money and it was part of the job, and honestly, that kept me from wanting to puke at the price involved. It was in the middling four figures per night, and the total was what I once would have called life-altering money. Lemme put it this way, when you figure in taxes, catering, and tips, it was running about five grand a night, so our bill for the week would have paid for four of the five cars I had owned since I got my license at age seventeen. That was just *our* room. The company had over two dozen people out here, but... like, I said, this was work.

All right, for those of you who didn't read the first two books, either go back now or try to keep up. Let's start with me. Don't worry about what it says on my driver's license- no, not that one. Put that down. I mean my real one that's locked up back at the office. People in the business just call me the Professor. I think of it as the old call sign that had eaten the rest of my life. I'd gone over into the dark side of the business because at the time, I really needed the money. Now? Most days I didn't think I'd ever find a way out except getting carried feet first with a tag on my toe. That cheerful thought in mind, I rolled off the king-sized bed. My left knee buckled a little, but at least my back wasn't screaming all that badly today as I stumbled into the suite's palatial marble bathroom.

After the necessary morning drainage, I resolved to let the girls sleep and wandered into the game room to get a Mountain Dew out of the bar refrigerator. I don't know why this place had a game room. Past that, trying to decide what to do with myself at this hour of the morning was difficult. Go downstairs and gamble more? Play with the half million or whatever ridiculous number of TV channels that were out on the living room's big screen? What I needed to be doing was waking the girls up so we could start packing. Mentally, I was delaying that as long as I could because, to be quite honest, I just didn't fuckin' want to. It was going to be unpleasant. Instead, I figured I'd kill a few minutes and shoot one last game of eight-ball against myself on the I-don't-know-why-this-stupid-thing-is-here pool table.

While I was busy selecting a cue and getting the balls racked up, let me explain a bit more. Look, loading up to come home from what I'll euphemistically call a 'work trip' is always more physically and mentally taxing than it was loading up to get there. You're fuckin' tired and emotionally drained from the operations you've conducted. Your stuff is scattered, probably dirty, and sometimes broken because you've been using it. You never seem to have enough time to pack everything as prettily and compactly as you did on the way there, so it feels sloppy and improvised. Then when you do finally get home, you have to unpack, clean everything again, put it all away, and at the same time be ready to load it all up and go back out again. You're doing that when you're exhausted and just want to do nothing but sleep in your own bed for a couple of days.

In that respect, Athenaeum, Incorporated was very much like the real military in which most of us had, professionally speaking, cut our teeth. A very niche contractor to the intelligence community, or anyone else of acceptable morals who'd pay our prices, the roots of the company ran back to the earliest days of the Cold War, though time's scythe had robbed us of most anyone going back much before Vietnam or so. Most of the really old-timers still on this side of the grass had settled into sinecures on the Board of Directors or various part-time contracts with the firm.

Even with the old timers mostly dead or pastured, we still had a strong collective memory of the old ways. That got results few others could, and was one reason we could charge our clients what we did. Sometimes, following those old ways, you need to get out and gather intelligence face-to-face, like talking to people and picking up rumors in bars. There's a lot of that at the Shooting, Hunting, and Outdoor Trade Show, usually just known as SHOT, in Vegas. Anyway, it had been a busy week-plus out here. SHOT had started Tuesday and ended Friday as always, and then not all of us made it over to the *Adult Video News* porn industry convention that ran on until Saturday afternoon.

A defense contractor called ArmEx decided to piggyback their own convention in front of SHOT, the so-called 'Mercenaries' Ball.' I had gone, since I had business with ArmEx's CEO that had gone well enough. But then ArmEx's 'Tactical Models Mixer' strip club party had ended with at least a dozen dead when *someone* shot it up. Some of the fifteen or so wounded in the hospital weren't guaranteed to make it either. Vegas PD was still sorting that shit out and thankfully wasn't looking our direction yet. We had our suspicions there, but more on that as we go, since we were going to be following those rabbit holes for a while.

Sinking a solid on the break, I went first against myself. But just as my second ball clacked into the far-left corner pocket, Morgan rushed in. The Indianapolis-born Dene Indian had been my longtime left hand in matters of IT, cryptography, and petty crime even before I'd come to work at Athenaeum, and he'd really shone on this trip as the acting 'first sergeant' despite his lack of formal military experience. After all, we needed to leave enough of the company home in Tennessee to make the rest of our operations work, so my usual deputies were minding the store back there. The rest of the company dealt with the rest of the world while we handled this.

Anyway, Morgan showing up in here wasn't odd, since he was staying in the suite's other bedroom. What was odd was him looking panicked. Usually,

3

Morgan was nearly unflappable, but he was looking distinctly, uh, *flapped.* "Boss, we got a big fuckin' problem."

I sighed, grabbing that half-empty Dew off the bar's marble top and channeling the late Donald Sutherland. "Morgan, don't hit me with them negative waves this early in the morning. I've been shot at and beat up on this trip already. What the fuck is wrong now?" I drained the can dramatically while waiting for Morgan's answer.

He cut right to it. "One of my commo girls got bounced by two Chinese guys in the hallway outside the headquarters suite about five minutes ago."

Adrenaline spiked. *Jesus, that shook me out of my morning stupor faster than the caffeine.* "Fuck. She okay?"

"Yeah, she stabbed one and one of the UAV guys shot the other one."

Well, fuck. "Let's go." I threw my now-empty in the wet bar's sink, grabbed another can from the fridge, and out we went.

We had a second two-room suite one floor down that was functioning as the headquarters for this little 'Las Vegas Expeditionary Force,' and while no one was usually sleeping in there, it was full of folding tables, laptops, a portable satellite receiver, one of the control boxes for the UAVs, and the rest of the technological bullshit you need to practice discretionary warfare in the modern age. We had a lot of people who were good at making that shit work. I sure as shit wasn't smart enough to do it all by myself.

As much as I wanted more information about what happened, I sure as shit didn't want to try talking about it in the open in an unsecured hallway in one of the largest hotels in the country. Voices carry, you know. We hit the end of the hallway and went down the fire stairs, then popped out of the stairs on the next floor down.

One thought jumped to mind, and I couldn't stifle it. "How the fuck did we not mess up the hallway?"

Morgan waved at the broad expanse of cream-colored marble floor as we walked, his voice pitched low. "You know how many rolls of paper towels it takes to clean that up? I do now." He knocked on the door before unlocking it with his card. "Don't want to spook the kid inside."

"What kid insi — oh." Yeah, one of Morgan's kids was sitting on a chair inside the door with a pistol out and ready — a suppressed Ruger .22. Odd choice for most serious work, but at across-the-hallway distances when you don't want to bother the neighbors, it did quite well. We had a dozen of them leftover from the Eighties in the company arms room back in Tennessee. Obviously one of them had made the trip out here with all the other goodies. It was definitely older than the kid using it. "You the one who took the shot?" I asked him.

I'd think of his name in a minute. He was on our books as a UAV operator, I remembered that much. A stocky dark-haired white kid, well-dressed as all of us were trying to be out here, who had the calm, almost sleepy look you see a lot of in the back-rank squads of infantry platoons. They're the sort of guys who are usually kinda bored unless they've got a gunfight on their hands. If they don't find enough excitement in the Army, they wander into being cops or criminals. In this case, he was working for me, which could be a little bit of both. "Yessir," he drawled a bit.

"What the fuck happened?"

"One of the intel girls was going back to her room, then five or ten seconds later there's yelling in the hallway. I go out to check on her, and two Chinese guys are grabbing on her. She's already got a knife in the one guy's neck, and the other one was fucking around under his jacket, probably going for his gun, so I shot him. I was suppressed already, built onto the gun as you know, and I jammed my thumb on the cocking knob to seal the breech. Sounded like fingers barely snapping, so nobody else heard shit."

I had to chuckle a little. "How bad'd ya shoot him?"

He sighed. "It was maybe twenty feet, so I just popped him in the thigh and dropped him. Well, popped him twice. Figured we might want him to talk. Couldn't get that if I shot him in the head."

I shrugged. "Bad doctrine, good result. I'll allow it," I grimly chuckled some more. It was hard work shooting someone just a little. "What about the other one?"

Morgan tugged me. "He's back here. Come on." Waving at the kid, I followed Morgan into the left-hand bedroom of the suite and on into its bathroom.

"Now where's she?"

"In the far side bedroom we weren't using, with a nice shot of midazolam in her system already. She's taking a bit of a nap and has got a couple of the other girls sitting with her. Don't bother her right now acting like an authority figure."

Now call me softhearted if you want, but one of my people had just almost gotten kidnapped and instead had unlocked the rare, coveted, and envied 'CONUS KNIFE KILL' achievement. I don't think wanting to check on them under those circumstances counted as a bother, but I'd defer to his opinion anyway. "Remind me to throw a few grand in that kid's Christmas bonus. Hers too," I told Morgan. "Who's slinging the meds for you?" He didn't answer before we made it into the bathroom, a twin of my overdone marble one upstairs. I was somehow hoping Morgan wasn't hauling that sort of controlled substance around on his own hook... but then I also knew the guy.

It was a bit of a relief to find Jimmy in there with an open aid bag, and working on the right leg of a familiar-looking gray-haired Chinese guy while two more of our guys pulled security. Well, that answered the 'where did the drugs come from?' question. Between the several professional medical gigs he juggled when he wasn't working for me, I supposed there were ways to carry those sorts of things around. Some of them might actually have been legal.

Jimmy had cut off the right pants leg and had a CAT tourniquet clamped down up by the guy's hip. He was busy packing gauze into the entrance wound. Not to fall on the trope of 'all Chinese look alike', but I would have bet next month's mortgage check that he'd been one of the former People's Liberation

Army noncoms who'd been in Lin's suite at the MGM when that shit went sideways two nights ago. Long story. Look it up if you care.

"Where's the other guy?"

Morgan pointed wordlessly to the shower stall. I looked in, and yeah, there was a dead fuckin' Chinaman in there who could pass for this one's cousin. A non-metallic knife shaped out of black composite was jammed into his neck with blood still dripping toward the drain. Revenant Corps out of Oklahoma, probably. They made good stuff. I had a couple of theirs myself.

Well, fuck. The biggest thing on the list, if not necessarily the first thing, was gonna be getting rid of this goddamn body. There are a small number of really upscale boutique hotels where Room Service and the concierge will help you get rid of an inconvenient corpse. To the best of my knowledge, every one of them was run by some tastefully dressed fellow with a foreign accent, worked on gold coins, and, this was the really unfortunate bit, only existed in the Keanu Reeves gunfight movie franchise. Pretty unfortunate, that. Even with gold prices being worth what they are now as the post-1913 US dollar edges toward worthlessness, I'd still happily give up the equivalent of a twenty-dollar Saint Gaudens double eagle gold piece or two to get rid of the dead guy in the shower with no strings attached. Now I'm sure there's people in Vegas who will do that kind of shit. The Mob roots of this place aren't entirely forgotten, but I also figured you have to know somebody or be somebody connected, and we just didn't know the right people.

"So then what? Your guy makes the shot, you grab the girl and these two, and then what?"

Morgan shrugged. "Remember that entire tough box full of paper towels we had with the headquarters supplies?"

"Not really."

"Just as well. Like I said, used most of 'em with all the spray cleaner cleaning up the hall before anyone saw shit. We're lucky it's so fuckin' early by Vegas standards and no one else on this floor is awake yet. Bagged 'em all up, and we'll pack them out ourselves so Housekeeping doesn't find them."

I supposed it wasn't a bad idea to have brought them. You didn't want to be using up the expensive bath towels or whatever for spilled drinks at the work tables or, as had happened, blood on the floors. Speaking of blood, the Chinese guy winced, gritting his teeth as Jimmy was slowly threading gauze in the hole. Yeah, it's never happened to me, but I've had to do wound packing on other people. I'm told it hurts like shit. "Jimmy, you just happened to be hanging out over here?"

"Came over to talk about the load-out for home with Morgan. Figured you were still sleeping, and instead I get to liven up my morning with a gunshot wound."

"Shit, man, you know that's a fucking joke. Except one night, I think slept as badly out here as I do at home despite drinking a good bit more." I shifted my attention to the guy on the floor. "You speak English?"

He snorted. "Probably better than you speak Mandarin." His accent wasn't terrible, but he sure wasn't from here.

"Well, in my case, you would not be wrong. English is fine then."

This was actually a huge plus. Angel wasn't our only Chinese linguist. I knew at least one of the intel staff spoke it, which was probably just as well. If I had to go pull my beloved out of bed to quickly come do an interrogation, it would probably go really sideways really fast. While being way calmer and less bloodthirsty than Cash, she can be kinda grumpy first thing in the morning. She wouldn't take it out on me, since that would violate her ideals for our relationship, but she'd hesitate less than a nanosecond before taking it out on this guy instead. That could possibly end up with us having another body to hide.

"You know who I am?" He nodded. "Good. What do I call you then?"

He shrugged. "David is fine." He then switched to some flavor of Chinese to cuss as Jimmy shoved more gauze in. A .22 didn't make much of a hole so it was a tight fit.

Jimmy wasn't having it. "Hold still, goddamn it." He looked up at me. "I don't know how the hell that kid managed to miss the bone and most of the major blood vessels. Both damn bullets are in the hamstring somewhere since they were subsonics, and I'm debating looking for 'em until we decide what we're doing with this guy."

"Is it even worth packing a .22 hole?"

He shrugged. "It's a coin flip and I know I'm being unreasonably fussy for trying. It's a real skinny hole that is kinda two slugs down the same track, but I don't want him popping a leak the second someone takes that TQ off of him either."

Well, the latest revision of the Tactical Casualty Care Committee book said you had two hours to get a TQ off at the next level of care, so we still had plenty of time to chat. I turned my attention back to our guest. "So, first things first, did we meet the other night over at the MGM?"

He shook his head. "You mean when you met with that traitor Lin. No, I'm not one of his dogs."

Well, this is gonna be some drama. Ignoring the fact I would have lost that hypothetical bet, I continued. Maybe not all Chinese looked alike, but whatever PLA special operations detachment was cranking these dudes out, they definitely had a type after their years of service. "So what makes you say Lin is a traitor?"

"Despite his bloodline's long service, he resigned his commission to become a sell-sword. He extorts coin for his services to our nation. That should have been done for regular pay out of duty, and most of the personnel of our former command traveling with him are money-hungry scum like him. None still wear a regular uniform." *Okay, cool, definitely some resentment there.*

"By which you mean you still do." He just scowled at me, not giving me much to work with. I didn't even want to touch the political fallout of a dead Chinese regular and one wounded one in a Las Vegas hotel suite. Well, metaphorically speaking, it was time to play a card I'd picked off the table when I met Lin for lunch. "So you were with the other element that shot up the convention center?"

He took a long moment before answering. "No, but I know which team did it. We had more than two pieces on this chessboard."

Interesting. "Did you now? Feel like telling us?"

He waved, the action making him wince. "They have left town. Their actions were sloppy and ill-considered, and they also missed their intended target which might have seen them forgiven. There will be ramifications."

"Yeah, ramifications past thirty counts or so of murder or attempted murder?"

"Not your concern. You're no policeman."

He had a point there. "No, but I almost got my ass shot, and I really try to avoid that kind of shit."

"Find another line of work then."

"Says the guy with a couple of .22s in his leg."

He considered that for a moment before speaking, then I suppose he lost his patience. Pain and meds can do that to you. "Putting it in American terms, fuck you."

"Hey, I'm not the one who went trying to capture one of my people and got hisself shot fucking it up, man. Some of this is on you."

"So what happens now? Geneva rules do not apply in this war."

I sighed and shrugged, and it wasn't theatrical pretense. This was genuinely not the way this shit was supposed to go. "Look, I'm gonna display a rare bit of honesty here, man. You need to go do what you do, and we need to do home and do what we do, and then we need to stay the Hell out of each other's way. It's bad for business otherwise."

"It is not business for us, it is duty."

Well, there was no give in this one. "So, turning it back around, was it your duty to go grabbing one of my people?"

He was still annoyed and started revving up. "Our duty is to find out what is going on. Your kind traffics with Lin, and with many other kinds of filth whose doings are not necessarily in the interest of the Party and of the People's Republic. We came to grab one of your people to determine what you knew, and therefore what threat you might pose to our operations here and elsewhere."

"That worked out real well for ya now, didn't it?"

He nodded tightly. "The outcome was... regrettable."

"Yeah, it was. You could have just knocked on the fuckin' door and we could have discussed business like civilized people, you know."

"As if you would do so from a place of honesty," he sneered.

"What reason do we have to lie to you? We aren't your enemy, and conflict is bad for business."

David *harrumph*ed "We've been enemies since your kind funded Chiang's bandits and that demon MacArthur pushed your troops to the Yalu River frontier in 1950."

Well, that was a grim way of looking at it. "And you're mistaking us for the United States government."

David shrugged. "What master do you serve?" I looked at Morgan, convinced he would go for the Chris Pratt Marvel-movie quote. He wasn't paying any attention to me at all.

Instead, Morgan basically rolled his eyes at the guy. "We're not a government agency. We work for whoever pays us."

David turned to look at him gravely. "Which our research indicates is mostly your government. We are not without eyes of our own in your intelligence services. You are Athenaeum, Incorporated, and you are known."

I sighed and nodded respectfully. He did have us there, and 'game recognize game' as Bun Bun once said when sitting around in happier times. "You did a lot of research quickly."

He waved dismissively, "Again, we had the resources." Yeah, and his were apparently the resources of a top-tier nation-state's intelligence services, not us bottom-feeding orphans. "We followed a few of your cell phones around the town as you no doubt did for us." He read the wince of regret that put on my face. "No one can afford to be off the air and unreachable in this business."

He had a point there. I was mostly concerned that the bigger things out there in the shark tank knew who and what we were. "To be continued," I told David. I needed to think, and not in front of him.

Chapter Two

I went back out into the main living room. A few of the staff looked up at me, but most were head-down in their laptops or phones doing other things. Morgan followed me out as I cracked that next can of Dew I had carried up with me and nearly forgotten about. "We got a problem now, don't we?" I asked him. I took a long sip, hoping the caffeine would finally hit and sharpen things for me.

Morgan just looked at me, shaking his head. "Dude, I fuckin' told you we did."

"You weren't lying." I took another nervous gulp of the sugary green stuff, deriving whatever fuel I could from it. "First, we need to get the fuck out of here, and I mean in a hurry. And we need to get *that* the fuck out of here." I pointed toward the bathroom as Jimmy walked into the room and joined us.

"Our guest is having a little nap with about five milligrams of mido stuck in his ass. Still got the bullets in his thigh, but those can wait. I can smell the cig smoke on him, so lung cancer will probably still get him before the lead poisoning will. So what part are we up to now?"

"The part where I said we need to start breaking down and getting the fuck out of here. I don't care that we paid extra for late checkout on these monster suites. Now."

Morgan and Jimmy looked at me, and each other. Jimmy was the first to answer. "Yeah, we do. And you," Jimmy pointed at me, "need to go be seen somewhere else in the building. Be conspicuous and take your time. Anyone looking for us will hopefully focus on you and then not be watching us while we make these packages go away."

Shit, shit, shit. "Any suggestions that will make me not feel like I'm leaving you hanging?"

Morgan waved it off. "Man, you're just the diversion. That's critical. We got this. You grab your girls and go get seen somewhere expensive spending money. The crew upstairs in surveillance will watch that shit more than they do the fire stairs."

"Wait, wasn't there a camera on that hallway?"

Morgan snorted. "Like we didn't handle that shit ten minutes after we got here. It sees what we want it to."

Never mind, I didn't even want to know. Odds are I was too technologically illiterate to understand it anyway. "Now what are you two going to do?"

Jimmy *hmmmm'd.* "I got a really good idea, but I need thirty grand in cash. Maybe more, but my team's emergency roll is back over in our rooms at Caesar's." Yeah, and across the street and up a bit might as well be on Mars at this hour of the morning. Fuck it, we had more.

"I cannot believe I'm saying this, but yeah, that's easy. Lemme go raid my girlfriend's purse." I had to chuckle at the unreality. "Then what?"

"I go buy a used panel van or box truck for cash off an indie lot, then go to Home Depot for a little two-kay generator, either a Honda or a knockoff with decent surge capacity, and a chest freezer. Old boy in the shower there," he jerked his thumb toward the corpse, "rides home in the frozen food section and we dump him later."

Okay, really cool idea, pardon the pun. But then I thought of a major snag between the Here and the There. "You can't bring the freezer all the way up here. How do we get him down twenty-odd floors to the van and into the freezer without anyone noticing? And what do we do with the live one?"

Morgan waved me off. "You go get the fuckin' money. We'll keep working on that part." They shoved me back toward the door and I headed back upstairs.

14

It was gonna be okay, I told myself. *This wasn't that bad.* We'd planned on leaving today anyway. We'd planned that even before we wanted to be 'out of sight, out of mind' to the Vegas cops while their homicide detectives were working the shooting in the Convention Center and our shooting minutes later in the country club parking lot. This latest emergency one floor down was going to make this way fucking harder.

That was the sort of weird anxiety shit floating around the surface of my brain as I went back into the bedroom to gently shake the ladies awake. Speaking of weird shit. Yeah, the ladies, plural. Give me a minute on the backstory, I'm a little busy right now.

"Cash?" Next to her, Angel quietly snored a tiny bit. Wasn't even gonna try budging her yet.

Silence.

I shook her awake, and she tried curling back under the blankets. "Five more minutes, sir?" Sometimes she's not a morning person either, and we had been living the nocturnal life out here.

"Babe, you got forty, maybe fifty grand in cash?" I know we had a lot more than that in a lockbox that looked like another road case in the closet, but she'd been really busy winning in the poker room this trip, and hitting her up was faster than unlocking and digging.

"Izzit a work problem or you going to the craps table?" the lump of blankets mumbled from beneath her pillow fortress.

"Work problem. Serious fucking work problem."

An arm came out from under the expensive bed linens and waved vaguely. "Purse," she slurred.

I rummaged, and *damn*! The bank straps of hundreds were one hundred bills each, and marked as such. Ten thousand dollars. I shook off thoughts of the past when this sort of thing would have been a fever dream. I grabbed five of them just to be on the safe side. "Ladies, start getting moving. The day's off to an especially ugly start." Not wanting to take the time to fill them in, thereby

15

slowing Jimmy and Morgan, I headed for the door. I didn't linger and make sure they heard the order, let alone followed through on it.

Okay, while I'm moving around again, let me explain those two. Angel was originally my massage therapist for my ongoing chronic back problems, and then we dated a little, maybe ten, no, twelve years ago, after the first wife was gone but before I met the second one. She and I got back together after that second one went bad. From there, she evolved into my slightly warped manic-pixie live-in girlfriend. Taiwanese-American, five foot three, and disproportionately busty from growing up on American food her Chinese DNA wasn't prepared for, I hired her at Athenaeum years later after my boss died of cancer, more or less, when I got promoted into a dead man's office and needed the help. Since then, she's turned into my adjutant, my primary Chinese intercept linguist, and has been my backup shooter three times now because Fate likes to have shit kick off when I don't have any of my professional gunmen in the right place at the right time. Would the Dungeon Master of Life roll the dice then let one of my former Green Berets or SEALs do the job? Nah, Professor. Let's play 'Bet Your Life' and see how good your ex-theater major girlfriend *really* is with a pistol.

She was good enough when it mattered. I was still on this side of the grass.

Anyway, the manic pixie was lightly snoring, sleeping the sleep of the truly unbothered. I was kind of jealous. I never sleep that well even when the situation wasn't completely fucked the way it was now. Curled in next to her, the talking pile of blankets, the one with the Prada bag of money that also had a custom Glock in it, was... my other girlfriend? My girlfriend's girlfriend? Anyway, Angel and I had a third in the mix. It had been really accidental, and I don't really understand it either. Shit, I don't know. That would involve us communicating about our relationships like functional adults, only we were usually too busy living in wartime mode for shit like that to actually happen. When we stop getting shot at for more than a week, maybe we will finally relax and emotionally unpack. Yeah, no. There was a better chance of me hitting big on one of the slot machines downstairs than there was of the three of us taking the time and rationalizing this chaos we lived. And I don't fuck with slot machines.

Regardless of her actual title, she went by the nickname Cash, and she was... a story. While she had a collection of fake IDs, her real name was one of our deep secrets since she still had warrants out on her. The five foot zero lookalike of a couple sex-doll Korean pop singers, we'd basically kidnapped her out of New York City two, no, three years ago now, just before the FBI kicked her door in. See, she'd been a nice, quiet 'Establishment Bookish' sort of girl. Graduated *summa cum laude* at Princeton, then she went on to an MBA at Harvard, also *summa.* And this is where she went off Life's metaphorical rails, as they say, and only so much of it could fairly be pinned on me no matter how much I blamed myself.

See, that stellar academic history had gotten her hired at a major Wall Street investment bank, where she bumped into somebody's rather ramshackle laundering setup buried in the bank's accounts. Giving into temptation for once in her life, she used that formidable intellect to skim about seventeen million of drug cartel money. Since she was new at this and didn't quite cover her tracks well enough, the Feds subsequently wanted her on bank fraud, wire fraud, and enough other 'included felonies' that it would have impressed the late Myer Lansky. We at Athenaeum heard about all this, and decided this made her a potential blue-chip recruit that season. We swooped in and picked her up before the FBI could. Since then, in hiding with us, she'd remade herself physically (breast implants, some wild hairstyles, never mind the clothes) and emotionally. These days she was a whole lot of smart and, to be extremely honest, please don't tell her I said so, a *whole* lot of crazy.

How crazy, you ask? Try this. She had a quite nice Marine Recon tattoo on glass in her office. Yeah, I mean the actual inked skin. She'd gotten annoyed at its former owner for showing up at our house and staging a somewhat clumsy assassination attempt in our front yard. Rather than start small in attempts to get the prisoner to talk, Cash had skipped ahead to the drastic solution. She did warn him, and then she'd cut the tattoo off him with a box cutter and kept it for a souvenir, just as she promised. Yeah. I know you're probably cringing or thinking I made it up, but nope, I saw it happen and very much wish I hadn't. She was *not* a book you could judge by its cover.

Shit, I didn't have real clothes on, just a T-shirt and old black PT shorts, and my copy of the headquarters suite's key card was upstairs in my jacket pocket. I didn't even have my fucking phone on me. *Sigh*. Instead, I knocked on the door and waited for my UAV operator with the .22 to open the door. He just grinned. "Thought you had a key, boss."

"In my other pants," I grumbled. I patted him on the shoulder as I passed. I was grateful for the job he'd done, even if I couldn't think of his goddamned name, and I wouldn't forget it. The rest of the suite was as busy as a kicked anthill as the packing process was already underway. Jake, my usual security 'platoon sergeant', had some nasty bruises from fighting that Russian the other night and squeaking out a draw, but the two-time Afghan vet from the 173rd Airborne was still directing traffic as the headquarters was rapidly disassembling. He merely waved at me.

I found Jimmy in the bathroom, eyeing our now-unconscious guest. "Shit, never mind the dead guy, what are you gonna do with this one?"

Jimmy was a study in contradictions. Looked Korean, more or less, but he was from *Noo Yawk* so he sounded like he should have been in the cast of a *Godfather* sequel. The former SEAL corpsman and sometime SWAT medic waved off my concern. "Not your problem, brother. You go be the distraction. We got this."

"You sure?"

He looked at me sideways as I passed over the money. "Of course I'm not sure. Look at all the trouble this SEAL bullshit has gotten me into for thirty-plus years, and I haven't even worn the uniform in fifteen. Fuck, I should have just stayed in 1st MarDiv doing VD inspections."

"Jimmy, love ya, bro, but even you got tired of looking at that many dicks." The father of... uh, five, I think, maybe six, just gave me the finger.

"Look, we'll deal with the two Chinese assholes first. Then we'll deal with the stabber. She's out cold in the back, but we'll get her moved too.' He held up the strap of bills. "I got shit to do now," and he waved around the suite. "Morgan's other people got this. You go be the distraction and you need stay the fuck out of here. Either him or me'll text you, and then you get out of your room. We'll be out of here mostly in accordance with the original movement order, only you go last now."

I nodded in assent. "If I'm the distraction, I may have my hands full of cards or dice, so text the girls too." I looked around. "Where's Morgan, anyway?"

"Stealing a laundry cart, I think. Don't ask and just get the fuck out of here, will ya?" He made to smack me upside the head like he was Joe Pesci. We had a good laugh, and I got out of there.

I stopped at the door. "Man, help me out. You know I'm awful with names and it's not like we wear tags so I forgot yours."

"Griffin. Bill Griffin." We shook hands.

"Nice work earlier. If I blank on your name again later, I'm sorry, but I'm kinda having a day right now and some things might not sink in well." He just laughed at that. Admitting to my several weaknesses seemed to go further with the troops than denying them. Honesty can be a leadership tactic. People seemed to prefer that to me bullshitting them.

Chapter Three

We had a plan to get out of here. It was a good plan, and I'd miss it as it went out the window in metaphorical chunks. We weren't going to conspicuously stage a vehicle convoy home. A sharp eye would notice our clump of vehicles, and there were a lot of sharp eyes in this town. With the goal of going unnoticed, we planned for a staggered start from the three hotels we'd used. The eight-man heavy team that had been down on the Strip's south end at the Silverton originally under Jake and now with Ruiz filling in as lead would move out first with their two trucks.

The four in the Caesar's Palace backup team would roll next, originally under Jimmy's command, and I don't know what would happen now. Jimmy would probably send them on ahead while he moved the inconvenient package. Then all the headquarters would dribble out of the Venetian in chunks with our trucks and vans, and only then would the people flying back to Nashville get themselves to the airport and go home.

The several troop elements we had here at the Venetian were the biggest pieces of that puzzle. We had two armored Yukons and a pair of the even bigger armored Suburbans here. Yes, the armored SUVs were the same ones we'd gotten surplus from the State Department motor pool where they'd been sitting for years, even if they didn't look like it anymore. I knew a guy with a paint shop, so they'd all been redone from Generic Government White into various civilian soccer-mom jobs. So far it had worked out. Behind them, we had two Dodge vans full of the unmanned aerial vehicles and electronic warfare gear. With this revision to the plan, I was now nine of ninth in the movement order, not counting whatever Jimmy bought to move bodies, so it was time to go be the distraction.

Going back upstairs, I let myself into my suite. Angel hadn't budged at all, and Cash had rolled back over. I got them awake enough to explain the problem, and that had the same 'startle them into full consciousness' effect that it had on me. We all got into the bathroom, and quickly got ourselves put together since there was more than enough floor space in that opulent marble cavern to do what needed to be done all at once.

Angel grumbled as she did her eye makeup. "I didn't get to stab anybody. Why did they grab her? I could have done it."

I had to sigh. "Because you never went anywhere alone after the shit at Lin's, so that made you a poor target. Besides, you got what, three pistol kills this trip?"

"Four counting a stiletto heel. Does that count as a stabbing?" Yeah, don't ask me to retell that part. It was pretty disgusting to watch.

Cash snapped off the hair dryer and piped up "You got three! The last one was mine!" Okay, fine. I'll tell you this much. Cash had come in to bat cleanup and finished off what Angel started in the Las Vegas Country Club's parking lot. I mean 'double-tapped the wounded dude in the head execution-style with a nine-millimeter' kind of finished off.

Angel laughed. "He was gonna be dead in a minute anyway." I squirmed a little bit at the memory from a few nights ago. Yeah, I could see that, but for the sake of my own domestic tranquility, I was not gonna pick sides in this dispute either.

Cash glared. "Still my kill. Work faster next time."

Speaking of faster, we had to get moving. "Ladies, we have a long way home to argue about that, but I wish you wouldn't. Meanwhile, we quickly need to go be seen somewhere conspicuous."

Angel said "Wherever 'conspicuous' is, it better have food, sir. I'm hungry."

Cash laughed. "Babe, you're always hungry."

21

Angel stretched and twirled. "That's because I have to keep these curves properly inflated. I didn't buy mine." *Ouch.* That was brutal.

Cash took that jibe with surprisingly good grace, teasingly running an expensively manicured dark red fingertip over her augmentations. "I was short-changed genetically in that department, so store-bought had to do." And yeah, they did do. *Damn.*

Moving back into the bedroom for clothes, and when it came to being a distraction, they understood the assignment. Their heels were too high, the skirts too short, and the tops too tight, all with a little too much sparkle to work anywhere else in the country. Their big leather work-trip purses were knockoffs from a discreet holster shop outside Houston that catered to gunslinging Texas girls. Each had a lot of custom Glock in there right now.

'Welcome to Fabulous Las Vegas,' dammit.

While Angel pulled on an emerald-green party dress, Cash twirled, her black leather skirt barely covering her ass. "This ought to get some eyes on us and keep the surveillance staff from looking upstairs too much. Yeah, the unbuttoned crimson silk blouse was showing off a truly excessive amount of enhanced cleavage, but again, we were looking for attention. Me, I was actually throwing a suit on at this unholy hour of the morning. I'd packed several, so why the hell not? Excess is a way of life out here.

Clothes handled, except for the tie I was still fucking with, the ladies grabbed The Book and started checking the restaurant listings. It took them less than a minute to decide we were going to Bouchon for brunch. Cash shrugged. "I have a whole bunch of casino chips left to spend, so we might as well go wild with them," she announced in her slightly nasal *Haaahvaad* accent. Fine. It was Thomas Keller's place, and the late Anthony Bourdain once claimed Keller ran the best restaurants in the world. I suppose I could deal with that, even if Keller himself had been retired from the kitchens for a decade. It's Vegas. This town thrives on selling you the chance to do weird shit one time just so you can say you did. Helicopter rides, rental machine guns, strip clubs, losing money at the craps table... at least the expensive food was usually less of a gamble. With all our troubles out here, I think we had used up enough luck for one year. Too bad it was only January so it would be eleven months for that cosmic account to refill.

A winter morning in the high desert is too cold to even joke about eating on the patio, even if the ladies hadn't been showing a Vegas party-mode amount of skin. We sat inside. Ordering country fried steak and scrambled eggs *avec fromage* in French was amusing. Cash took her eggs the same way, but her steak unbreaded. Hers was a Wagyu ribeye so it also cost way more. Angel, being a Maryland girl but much less of an insane crabcake snob than I am, went for the *Bénédicte au Crabe.* She and I had eyed the seafood 'grand platter,' but I was not paying those prices for just one lobster and a lousy eighteen oysters. I didn't care how many more of the black hundred-dollar chips Cash was looking to burn before we left.

Why am I such an asshole about buying seafood? It was a matter of upbringing. Blame it all on my roots like the man once sang. Next time we went up to Maryland, I could get a whole bushel of much better oysters right out of the Wicomico River for less money than that since Dad knew somebody with the right kind of boat. Doing some mental math past that, yeah, the lobster was going a hundred bucks a pound on the plate. Nope. Knew a guy for that, too. A whole lot of allegedly Maine lobster comes out of Long Island Sound anyway, just like all those off-season 'Maryland' crabs are trucked up from Louisiana or Texas. Same species, different zip code.

After we ordered, I slid my phone out to text another of our players. Bradley was an old Army buddy who'd come up from Huachuca in Arizona to help out. Since he was on the cusp of medical retirement, I figured putting him to work this week was a good opportunity to recruit him for my full-time roster. I just hoped I hadn't scared him off.

"You up yet?"

Buzz-buzz. "Not really. Got back here late last night, remember. I gotta work tomorrow? I'm not done retiring yet."

23

"Roger. You still wanna play?"

"Fuck, man, ask me later. It was a wild fucking week and I need sleep. Though I think Morgan's got my next girlfriend already working for him." I chuckled at that. Nobody ever said recruiting was completely ethical. I put my phone away as the waiter approached with our plates.

Now for all my bitching about the ordering process, the food was truly on point, even if I still quietly quailed at the amount of money involved. No place is truly cheap eats anymore, especially not in Vegas, and I told myself it wasn't like we were going to be back here any time soon. The point wasn't just to be fed, the point was to be seen in one of the highest profile spots on the property. I was quietly panicking inside about what Morgan and Jimmy had to do while trying really hard not to show it. We made a point of lingering at the table a bit. When the bill came, Cash waved for it. She looked at it, then ostentatiously handed the server a purple $500 chip. "Keep the change. Thank you." *Damn, they'd remember that one. Probably why she did it.* With that, we headed back down to the casino floor.

In the elevator, Cash handed me a big handful of black and yellow chips. "That's about twelve thousand, sir. Try not to blow it all at one table. I'm going to go cash out nine grand of mine so I'm still below the IRS notification total, then go look for some opportunities to be seen."

Angel patted her own bag. "Shopping for me. Never too early to start looking for Christmas bargains."

I groaned. "There are no bargains here."

Angel shrugged. "That's not the point right now. The point is to get seen wandering in and out of high dollar shops and the clerks remembering the pretty Asian girls with the big tits."

I nodded. She wasn't wrong. "Okay, I'll go get seen somewhere too." Knowing it would get me on camera, I found a blackjack table, put the pile of chips down, and spent a very tense hour nearly losing all of it before the cards turned back my way. To be honest, I just wasn't concentrating on the game. I should have gone and shot craps instead. That was chaotic and random. There was too much else on my mind to be any good at blackjack right now. The key to being good at that is to empty your brain and just execute the strategy chart.

It was an ugly hour. The haggard-looking guy playing twenty-five a hand at the other end of the table wasn't doing great either and finally wandered off. He'd gone hard, whoever he was. He looked like he'd gone too hard for too long. Finally, he pushed his luck one time too many, doubling on a twelve against a three while loudly announcing "Mama didn't raise no bitch!" He then drew a queen and lost, because the game's not called twenty-two.

That just left the dealer and me. But after a good run of luck for which I was tipping well, I was back up to playing five hundred a hand when Cash slid an arm around my shoulders. She delicately nibbled at my earlobe to make it look good if nothing else, then whispered "Morgan says we're clear to move out and get going, sir." Huh, hadn't really noticed my phone buzz or anything.

Just with that, I drew a pair of aces. *Well, shit. Every time I'm getting ready to walk. Gotta split them.* Remember, you always split aces or eights. This just became a thousand-dollar hand, never mind the fact the dealer had a nine showing. Parting my fingers to signal a split and laying out five more black chips, I got an eight, making nineteen. I waved off. The second ace got, shit, a third ace. My gut clenched as I signaled to split again. The first ace got a king, the second a lousy six. The house will hit to a hard seventeen, so you probably should too. Figuring fuck it, I signaled for one more card. Two. *Thank you, miss, I'll take that nineteen.*

I felt Cash tremble with excitement as she pushed against me. She liked this shit a little too much, so it's a damn good thing we lived so far away from Vegas. Adrenaline and money were two of her addictions, and she might develop bad habits if she got to indulge more often. I waved off, so the dealer, a tired-looking blonde, flipped her nine, revealing a five for fourteen. She then drew a two, sixteen, so she had to hit again and pulled a seven. 23. *Boom!* My fifteen hundred became three thousand as I won on all three hands. *Triple play. Time to go.* I slid one stack of the chips across the table. "For the dealers," and she smiled. Cash and I then walked past the cashier's cage and turned another nine grand of black chips into crisp hundred-dollar bills, and I kept another handful of chips for tipping on the way out. The bell staff will take those as fast as they will paper money.

Getting back upstairs, we checking the far side of the suite, Morgan's stuff was all gone, but he'd packed way lighter than we had. I suppose he'd either ducked in or had one of his minions do it while we were off trying to get seen.

The ladies took a moment to change out of their sorta-party clothes into loose and comfortable outfits that would be much warmer outside. To be honest, it looked like gym wear. I used that opportunity to ditch my suit and look like more a normal version of me again as well.

From there, it was packing. Hanging clothes from the closet went into the garment bags they'd come in. Loose stuff went into suitcases. Important things like guns and knives and the night vision goggles I hadn't actually used this trip were already in their padlocked cases. We also brought out all the snacks and drinks the Venetian's catering department had already billed us for when they'd stocked our suite. I was definitely taking the retro-recipe Mountain Dew they'd brought in for me. It bumped my stockpile at home up by half a dozen packs. Definitely the most I'd ever paid for some, I'm sure, but it was so damn hard to find these days and it would get written off on the company taxes anyway.

I left most of the remaining chips on the stripped-out bar top. Most of the suite gratuities had gone on the bill which went on one of the company cards, but I wanted to leave something off the books for whoever came in first. I scribbled "THANKS!" on a napkin and set the chips on it. Looking around, I had to sigh a bit. It cost like hell, but I'd kind of enjoyed living like this for a few days. I'd be damned if I was in a hurry to do it again.

We had everything packed up inside of thirty minutes. What we really needed help with was getting all this shit downstairs. The bell staffers were definitely hustling for tip money on a day like this, and I kept up my end of the unspoken bargain. I sure as shit didn't want to move all of it myself. I had back problems as it was. Two guys and two carts, so two black chips each. Nodding their gratitude, they got it all downstairs as and to the curb where I said the hell with it and gave them each one more. Once down there as it edged up on noon, we were just the part of the traffic jam as everyone else from the SHOT week was also trying to go home at the same time we were. Apparently paying extra for late checkout was a really popular choice, and there were still a lot of hung-over looking people. That left me one chip for the valet parking driver.

So, we stood there at the curb for a moment, wondering where our truck was. We had a royal blue Yukon. Not my personal truck, of course, as that was back home in Tennessee. It was another of the ex-State Department armored ones. We waited, we waited, and we thought about it as other people got their rides and left. Then Angel's role in our relationship as 'The Responsible Adult' kicked in. "Babe, you didn't park valet, remember?"

"Fuuuuuuck." I meant it as a snarl, but it came out as a whine. I hadn't touched that truck since we got here, so to be honest I'd quite forgotten. She giggled as I patted my pockets and found the Yukon keys. It took me ten minutes to retreat back through the casino to the parking garage, find the blue SUV, and another five to make it back around to the entry area. One of the bell staff helped me get everything off the carts and into the back end, and he got the last hundred-dollar chip. Angel slid into the driver's seat instead and silently beckoned for the keys. Knowing it was futile to argue, I handed them over, and we pulled out onto Las Vegas Boulevard.

Chapter Four

I t was now one in the afternoon. That was at least two hours before we'd originally planned to be out of the hotel. Angel looked at the fuel gauge and said "I want to fill this up before we get out on the Interstate." We were still creeping red light to red light down Las Vegas Boulevard as I was texting people trying to keep track of what was going on.

Moving, boss.

On the way.

See you back home.

Rolled out two hours ago.

At the airport already.

The person you are texting has SmartDriving Mode engaged and cannot be disturbed. I laughed at that one. Texting while driving was about the least dangerous thing any of us did. And nobody was rolling alone, so somebody could have fucking answered.

Tell you later. That from Jimmy.

Stop fucking worrying about shit and get your own ass home. That from Morgan.

I just shrugged. Okay, I guess everyone in the ground echelon was in front of us. We passed the airport, the Luxor, the Mandalay Bay, and the rest, and actually had to go far enough south under 215 that we technically missed our exit before we found a gas station. *Shit, maybe we should have looped north to catch the new Interstate 11/15 spur instead.*

I had planned on driving first. Note that I said 'had planned.' You see how that worked out so far. Coming out of the convenience store with a couple road drinks since the stuff from the suite was buried, I nudged her as she was still pumping gas. "Babe, I can drive."

She shook her head. "Uh, sir, I love you, but fuckin' no."

"I can —"

"Your back is already a mess, and I saw you gritting your teeth just to get out of the truck. Get in the back seat. Now."

"Yes, Mistress," I flippantly answered. Talk about role reversal.

"Good boy," Angel calmly replied. Cash giggled hard at that.

Cash reached into her massive black leather Prada-knockoff holster bag, retrieving a pill bottle. "Here. Take two, no, three of these."

I looked at them suspiciously. "Do I want to know?"

"Really good muscle relaxers," Angel answered.

"Where'd you find them?"

Cash giggled a little more. "One of the SHOT Show guys I cleaned out in the poker room is an orthopedic surgeon in his day job, and we discussed you and your damage pretty thoroughly. I got his business card too, but he gave me a partial bottle of these for you as a 'no hard feelings about the twenty thousand dollars' gift."

I looked at the pills even more suspiciously. "If you took twenty grand off him, I ought to throw these fucking things down a storm drain. They'll probably kill me."

Angel cut in. "The NIH alphanumeric codes on the pills check out, and we saw him pop a few out of the bottle too. I think you're safe." I had already been shot at this trip, so I knew my paranoia was cranked way up. I gave in and washed them down with some decidedly mediocre fountain lemonade that tasted as chemical-laden as the pills. I'd gotten spoiled living at the high end with fresh-squeezed this and made-to-order that. *Welcome back to reality,* said the noise of passing traffic.

Angel looked satisfied. "Now maybe you'll relax, your back will unknot itself, and you'll sleep into Arizona." She was in charge of medical-ish decisions like that for me because again, she started as my massage therapist. Those back problems were definitely a result of my military career even if the VA hasn't stamped 'service connected' on that line of my records yet. That would be nice someday, even if I didn't need the money so much anymore. We got onto 215 heading east, which got us to Interstate 11, which then magically became US 93 again at the Arizona border. The pills didn't put me all the way out, but my back did feel better and I was definitely mellowed

I still had some scraps of a plan. I figured that we'd go twelve hours at most between the three of us, maybe stop somewhere around Amarillo, rest some, and then do the last fifteen hours or so back into the Nashville area. Sure, we could punch it straight through and stumble home, at the price of getting there with most of us all sleepy and fucked up. We needed to be capable of sustained operations when we got back in the office, and not waste days stumbling around at one-quarter speed recovering from the trip. That went double for me, and I was already fucked up. The pills had me not minding that part so much though.

Kicked sideways across the back seat, I was reading, something I love to do but rarely have time for any more. I was trying to finish Scott Huggins' second 'flintlock fantasy' *Wishkiller* novel on my phone screen, since I'd loved *A Cold and Mortal Spring*, but I was still thinking out loud. "You know dear, I mean Angel dear, in the last two years you've killed more people than I have."

In the rear view mirror, I could see her smile with just the barest hint of bloodthirst. "I can't let them get to you, sir. You may be the king piece on the board, but I'm the queen and that's her job."

I often had to specify which one of my dears and darlings I was addressing. The other darling, the company's lovely and demented chief financial officer, was stretched out in the passenger seat and smiled lazily over at Angel. "Our job, babe. Our job. And remember, at least I got one on the board so far." *Oh no, not this argument again.*

As for the drive home, since we aren't complete morons, we'd checked the weather forecast before we left Vegas. Yeah, there was a large mass of wet Pacific air coming on the jet stream across from southern California, and hitting freezing mountain air up here in the high desert before blowing over northeasterly into the Rockies. Still, it didn't seem a huge problem. We guessed there was a minimal risk of the weather catching us and things going to shit. All we had to go was make it four hours and get past Flagstaff, Arizona so we'd further east and probably out of the storm's way. Unfortunately, somewhere up in front of us there was one hell of a wreck and Interstate 40 turned into a massive parking lot eastbound.

We're in the information business. Sometimes we produce, sometimes we consume. While we sat parked, Cash was already pulling up a handheld digital scanner radio from the storage compartment under the front seat and looking for the Arizona highway patrol channel. In the back, I figured it was time to 'E.T. Phone Home', so I called back to the Hole.

For you first-time readers, our company office is inside a leftover 1950s bunker complex that goes down eight stories under a smallish mountain north of Nashville, Tennessee. Don't ask me where we got it. I wasn't born yet. Going by real estate records at the county land deed office, the company had it sixty years before I came to work here. As for how we got it? I'm sure it involved government dishonesty on someone's part. The secret ingredient is almost always some form of crime.

"Hello?" It was one of the girls in the Intel section. Usually, the phones were answered in Intel since it was manned 24-7. Except for one line that was in the phone book as our overt front and sister company Archive Associates, all our phones were answered anonymously. No sense giving anything away we didn't have to. If you were calling us, you knew who the hell you were looking for, or at least you should. "It's Prof. Is Dave in?"

"Yes, sir. He's right here." While we didn't formally run on military lines, when you hire enough younger military vets, particularly Southerners or wannabe Southerners looking to stay in the area, you end up getting called 'sir' a lot. Never mind Cash or Angel's idea of relationship dynamics.

Dave came on the line in moments, but I cut him off. "Dude, what are you doing in there on a Sunday?"

"Because you're still out west fucking off and Kara's working nights." He sounded completely done with this shit. Then again, I'd known the guy twenty-five years before I'd pulled him in as my intel chief and all-round deputy even before I inherited 'command' here at Athenaeum, and 'done with this shit' wasn't new for him. Even going back to our infantry school class or his time as a new private in the 75th Rangers back before 9/11, he was not famed for the virtue of patience. Kara, the tall blonde deputy intel chief, was a refugee from a really big intelligence agency at Fort Meade, Maryland. I originally met her at a sci-fi convention in Atlanta when we were both in *Battlestar Galactica* uniforms. No shit. Talent is where you find it, especially the intellectual sort, and most of the people I needed to make this shit work over the long haul were thoroughly marinated in nerd culture. That included me, as if you couldn't tell.

"Yeah, well, we're at least trying to get back, but we're having some hiccups. Can you have one of the kids get into the Arizona 911 dispatch records and figure out what's got I-40 East blocked this side of Flagstaff?"

"Pfffft. Ask for something hard next time... wait a sec, it's loading, yeah, you've got an eighteen-wheeler laid over, waiting on haz-mat response for a tanker full of... shit, I can't even pronounce that. Something-hexa-something tetrafloride? Yeah, I have no idea what the fuck that is, but that doesn't sound good for your health."

I groaned. "Great, and we aren't close enough to an exit to get off easily, either."

Dave snorted. "Sucks to be you, man. You got a snowstorm coming right up your ass too."

I had to cringe. "Phrasing, man, phrasing."

He cackled in sudden amusement. "What? You got a blizzard about to pound you from the backside. That storm's moving almost due east instead of the originally predicted northerly track."

Well, now I was laughing. "Thanks for the good news, brother. Anyway, anything big going on back there?"

"Nothing new since you asked Kara the same thing last night and she told you nothing."

"All right. We're just going to have to learn to like being stuck for a little bit."

"Just get home safe. And I'm taking a couple days off after you get finally back here whether you like it or not." We both had a good laugh at that too, and I hung up the phone.

We sat, and sat, all of us impatiently reading and playing on our phones, then half an hour later with the road still blocked, the snow started. To be honest, I debated taking over, putting it in four-wheel drive, making an illegal U-turn across the grassy gully of the median strip, and just going the four hours back to Vegas. But... no. The snow was coming from the west, so what was behind us was likely to be worse than what was out front. We gave it another five minutes, then Angel and I swapped seats. The pills had worn off, and if anyone was going to wreck us, it was gonna be me. I made a brief and unethical burst of speed up the shoulder for a mile and got off at Exit 191 by the relocated US Naval Observatory.

Angel looked at the sign in confusion. "Wha'? That can't be right. The Observatory is in DC. It's right down Wisconsin Avenue from my parents' house."

My beloved was partly right. I shook my head, and this is where my junior high school astronomy nerd got to come in clutch. "The Observatory there only has one telescope left, and it's an antique for kids to play with on school field trips. The Observatory's astronomy department moved everything else out here in the 1950s because the skies around DC kept getting brighter and more polluted. That ruined the actual astronomy work. They put it here because

Lowell Observatory is up the street and this is one of the last really good dark-sky valleys in America, well, at least in the Lower 48."

The legacy facility in DC is not just an observatory. The Vice President lives on the grounds in what used to be the Chief of Naval Operations' official residence until the CNO moved over to the former superintendent's quarters on the Washington Navy Yard in 1977. Nuclear clocks, the GPS office, and all that other stuff for the Navy navigation offices stayed there. And really the DC facility we both remembered from growing up in the suburbs was a block east of Wisconsin Avenue. Its eastern edge was right off Massachusetts Avenue instead, but I wasn't going to get that pedantic with her. Even I have my limits.

As a further historical note on the subject, the one out in Bethesda was the third Naval Observatory building. The first two had been downtown. The original site more or less has the current State Department building on top of it, and the second one is on the old Navy Hill facility north of the Lincoln Memorial. It later became one of the OSS buildings during the war, then got surplused around the Federal bureaucracy from there. I think DHS is in part of it now.

Meanwhile, we went on every back road my phone's map could find until we dog-legged around the couple miles of backed-up traffic and the wreck itself. It took us nearly an hour and took us far enough southwest we actually hit Interstate 17 a good bit south of Flagstaff. Cash looked around as we stopped at the intersection. "It's only two hours down to Phoenix. Do we want to go see anybody while we're out here?"

I thought about it for a second. It was already past two. "It's Sunday afternoon. I think Gabriel finished moving to Houston already, and Melody won't be working again until Wednesday. As much as I'd like to, we gotta get moving and we're still gonna be racing the snow eastbound until New Mexico if it keeps tracking east-ish."

Cash sighed sadly. She had a long-distance girl-crush on a somewhat famous half-Japanese cosplayer with whom we were distantly acquainted. Since Melody part-timed at a well-known Phoenix strip club named for a predatory cat, Cash wasn't the only one tempted, but... no. Duty called us home. We took 17 back north, and rejoined I-40 eastbound. We couldn't go terribly fast because the visibility sucked and I didn't want to hit a slick patch. This heavy-armored fucker would turn into a hockey puck on the right kind of ice, and you never know what's under the snow.

Angel was playing on her phone. "How far do you think we're going to make it tonight?"

I was feeling for everything the steering wheel would tell me. I was trying to read every bump, every bit of slip, and the snow was definitely coming down faster. With a sigh, I told her "I don't know." Flagstaff to Albuquerque is just under five hours in good conditions, and you can make Amarillo in about nine. Throw in a dinner stop somewhere along the way, and we could have been in Amarillo by midnight.

That was then, this was now. 'Could have' was doing some really heavy lifting but couldn't handle the weight. Yeah, I had plenty of practice driving in weather like this when I had to, but most of that was a long time ago. Being more risk-averse in middle age, I was simply questioning if I actually had to. These conditions were just shitty and getting even worse. Maybe it was just from me getting old, but I was kinda losing my nerve for this sort of thing. It wasn't worth losing the CEO and the CFO in one wreck and decapitating the company if I fucked up out here driving in shit that I shouldn't have.

A stressful hour later, I was thinking that even 'Amarillo by morning' was wishful goddamned thinking. We had a hard time getting above thirty miles an hour, and were usually lucky to keep it at twenty. We had plenty of traction in this heavy fucker, but the visibility kind of sucked as the snow kept coming down. I did not want to have to stop short and, like I said, turn this thing into an uncontrolled projectile. As it was, the storm was still tracking south of expectations and was staying on top of us. Also, nobody else still on the road was going any faster than we were. We were barely going to be in Albuquerque by the time the restaurants would be closing up on a normal night, so with the snow still coming down, we decided that was it.

Angel jumped on her phone and booked a hotel room. That took some work as everything near the Interstate was already full of stranded travelers. She had to go further off the Interstate and up a couple price points. We found a to-go Chinese place in a strip mall that was still open, so we took it to the hotel and got checked in.

Digging in the combination *lo mein*, I called back to the Hole. When I called, Kara answered personally. "Hey, I see the weather has got you pinned in."

I sighed. "Lemme guess, watching the satellite?"

"I was watching your cell phones ping towers along the highway until you stopped, but yeah, I think you were probably on a satellite pass just now if we look close enough."

"You tracking the other teams?"

"Not so much, really. Most of them are way the hell in front of you. Two of the trucks are to Memphis already so they'll be back here this afternoon even if they stop for barbecue. I should call them and ask them to bring me some."

"Lack of dry rub ribs aside, how are you holding up?"

She yawned in my ear from three states away. "I am having my usual love-hate dynamic with ongoing night shifts. I hate getting up early in the mornings, but I also hate being the one on shift when the other side of the world is awake and making their problems my problems."

"Anything serious?"

"Not really. I'm watching a Chinese aerial navigation exercise that's deliberately calculated to piss the Taiwanese off. It just makes me waste my valuable time keeping an eye on them just in case it goes bad. It's an annoyance, but I wouldn't call it serious."

That was kind of a relief. "All right, we'll be back as soon as we can."

I could just imagine The Look. "No, you'll get back here as *safely* as you can. If you go getting yourself killed on the road pushing your luck, I get even worse hours in this job until we sort things out without you." She hung up on me.

Up the next morning by nine-ish, we had a lovely breakfast at the lobby's restaurant. Their Belgian waffles were top-tier, but we were looking out the window at close to a foot of snow on the ground. Shit. We could try... nope, New Mexico's governor was on the dining room TV, already having closed the roads and declared an emergency. It wasn't worth getting pulled over on a closed road by some state trooper then having to explain who the hell we were and why we were in such a hurry to get home. I tried to wave our various fake IDs in front of as few real cops as possible. There was always the possibility of them getting too curious and digging into who we really weren't. A particularly diligent soul might then instead wander down a trail toward who we really were. That was one of the last things I wanted.

Since we were stuck for at least a day until the plows could get the Interstate open, I called a couple Army buddies who lived in Albuquerque. The first one had been my roommate from later on in the Iraq invasion, you know, after we actually had rooms by way of capturing a couple buildings and setting up what we called semi-seriously called 'The US Army School for Advanced Homelessness' in a couple of abandoned warehouses.

"'Sup, playa?" Well, Matt, not to be confused with our usual charter pilot Matt, sounded happy. That was good. Sometimes he could be kinda sullen. That was even before the deployments knocked the smile off him.

"Passing through your hometown on business, stuck in the snow now. Fig-ured I'd check in and be sociable while I was here."

Matt started laughing hysterically. "Sucks to be you, brother. I'm down in Florida about two hundred yards off Pine Key and the fish are biting. Call me later." He hung up. The Keys? Even in January, that was a lot of sunlight for him. I suppose at some point in the last twenty years he'd finally outgrown his Goth-kid vampire phase.

The next one was my buddy Heidi, one of the big clump of West Point grads I knew from the mid-war years. She was a New Mexico Statie these days, I think, though with inter-agency this and joint task force that, people were always getting passed around like a joint at a Grateful Dead concert — shit, am I showing my age with that reference or what? Anyway, it was hard to keep track of who actually worked for who when everyone was on loan to someone else. Figuring she might be busy, I texted rather than calling.

The response was quick. *Buzz-buzz. "Which hotel?"*

I told her. *"And the hotel restaurant is jammed up. Any decent taco trucks still open?"*

"I know a guy. I got you."

Within an hour, Heidi showed up with lunch. Her crew-cab Silverado was nearly new, bright red, and massively lifted.

"Nice truck. Where'd you get it on what you make?" I know a bit about truck modifications, and the chassis work and chromed-out suspension was most of thirty thousand by itself. I hadn't even looked under the hood. That truck had to be most of two hundred grand, easy. None of the local departments or the Staties paid that well. I didn't think she'd gone Fed or we'd have to bump her retainer fee.

She smiled, nearly dimpling. "It was a drug seizure, of course. Previous owner is doing ten to fifteen downstate after he got caught with ten kilos of uncut in that pretty chrome tool box. The task force runs it around sometimes."

I sighed. "It's not exactly subtle."

Heidi shrugged. "I just signed it out from the undercover pool to run you guys lunch. My usual stakeout shitbox would never make it up here even after the plows had hit the main roads. Come on, let's get inside and eat before the tortillas get soggy."

Heidi was a fountain of good gossip on the dark side of life down in this corner of these United States. I took notes on everything from cartel traffic to the latest tricks for ID fraud scams. And these steak tacos were God-tier. See, this is why you have to identify talent and keep up close personal ties in this game. But more than a few hours passed, and the Styrofoam trays emptied, so it was time to say our goodbyes so she could get back to work and maybe we get back on the road in the morning. We had eaten so much lunch that we didn't even think about dinner.

In the hopes we hadn't left all our luck in Vegas, we got on the road after breakfast the next morning. The twenty-four-hour pause had given the road crews time to get some plowing done and the Interstate was at least somewhat passable. We were so far behind schedule it wasn't even funny.

In the back seat, playing on her phone, Cash didn't really worry about it. "Since we're running late anyway, we can go look at Las Vegas, New Mexico so we see them both on this trip. They filmed *Red Dawn* there, you know."

That I did know. I had that movie largely memorized before she was born.

"The real one or the heretical remake?" Angel asked.

"The real one," I said. Not to knock Chris Hemsworth, but I don't know why that movie got remade. Much like the Jason Mamoa version of *Conan the Barbarian,* I think John Milius did it right the first time. "But driving an hour north into the mountains to go sightseeing in this shit is a terrible idea, even by my lax standards for terrible ideas." Too bad. A buddy of mine had been through there and told me there was a great restaurant next to the railroad tracks in the former 'Soviet Headquarters' building. I'd look it up sometime, but fuck knew when I was going to get this way again, even flying over it.

It was horribly slow going out there as everyone tried getting back out on the road at once. The one truly cleared lane was badly clogged with a bunch of eighteen-wheelers, so it wasn't like we could move too quickly either. There were few places to pass trucks that were struggling to make forty miles an hour on the uphill stretches. We weren't going to make it all that far today. The only good news was that the road finally cleared as we came down out of the mountains onto the plains and into the flatness of the Texas panhandle.

Chapter Five

"$\mathcal{M}$*eat! Meat! We crave sustenance!"*

~ *the late Philip Seymour Hoffman as Dusty in "Twister"*

About seventy miles outside Amarillo, we started seeing billboards for The Big Texan Steak Ranch. This is one of those lunatic regional restaurants that also managed to make it onto some critics' lists of the ten best steak places in the entire country. Style and substance combined into a tourist trap for carnivores of all species. Seriously. A zoo tiger had eaten a takeout order in the parking lot on live TV, and the stunt proved popular enough it had been done more than once since then. Anyway, since it had been slow going and we were hungry, we could afford to dawdle on the way home in a way we couldn't when hammering westward not even two weeks ago. Once we accepted that, stopping for a last ridiculous vacation dinner seemed like a marvelous idea.

As we pulled into the parking lot around five, I saw a familiar set of wheels. The big maroon Suburban with the Tennessee tags and the Alabama 'Crimson Tide' stickers was another of our repurposed diplomatic security trucks. Ruiz's team had been using it, and they had even given us a ride across town in it, but they were also supposed to be well ahead of us now. They'd allegedly left first, so they should have been home by now. Anyway, we went inside the bright yellow building and got through the process of getting a table. En route to our table, guess who we saw?

I looked at the girls, and waved for them to keep following our waitress to our spots. They knew I'd catch up. Meanwhile, Ruiz spotted me spotting him, and he knew he was busted as I walked over to where he was sitting with two other guys. He slouched and shrugged. "Hey, boss."

I wasn't upset. "Relax, man. Don't worry about it. I did figure you guys would be a good ways further ahead though. And didn't you have four guys?"

Ruiz looked slightly askance. "We had eight, sir."

"Only saw one of our trucks." Figured I'd let him sweat just a little.

"Well, Jake's half of the team left on time. Us, well, not so much. I got one guy in the shitter, but we did have to reclaim one missing person before we got on the road for home. That took a while. Then there was the snow."

I sighed. "Define 'missing'?"

One of the other kids raised his hand. "That's on me, sir. I fell asleep at this girl's room over at the Hard Rock after, uh, we, uh, and I wasn't back to the Silverton on time."

"Okay, so you got found and you're all headed the right direction. Good enough." I wasn't going to get upset about it. Take guys in that demographic to Vegas and they do shit like that. "I do have to ask though. Was she at least hot?"

They all grinned conspiratorially. "Hell yes, she was. I dunno how he did it. Shit, I think he's gonna be in her next movie."

Oh no. "Movie?" I laughed. "What, you meet her at AVN?"

He blushed a little. "Yeah. Her girlfriend was filming —"

I cut him off there with a wave to the throat. Not a story for in public, I was sure. "Good enough. Which one of you was Johnston again?"

The one who wasn't Ruiz and also not our AWOL case raised his hand. "Here, sir."

I chuckled. "Heard you wiped out the tomahawk ribeye for two back at the Silverton. You gonna try this one?"

He stood and stretched like he was limbering up for an athletic event. "Thinking about it."

"Might as well, kid. Gonna be a long time before we get out this way again on business, I suppose, so this might be your only shot for a while." I looked in my wallet and grinned a bit. I After that last run at the blackjack table yesterday morning, I way more cash left on me than I usually carry, so I flicked a hundred onto the table. "Go for it, my treat." I rummaged and pulled a couple of twenties. "And a couple appetizers for the spectators there."

Johnston held Ben Franklin up. "You want this back if I win?"

I waved it off. "Nah, spend it on snacks for the drive back. We still got a long way to get home to the office."

As was their custom, when Johnston ordered the seventy-two-ounce challenge, they moved their party up to a central table in the main dining room where the whole thing could be broadcast on the Internet. That was another reason I'd never try it. I tend to be camera-shy these days.

Moving to where Cash and Angel had already been seated, I started looking at the menu. Like I said, I wasn't up for the seventy-two-ounce challenge. I couldn't eat like that after about age twenty. Having thought about it a while in the truck, we quickly ordered. I took a ribeye, grilled medium rare, as did Angel, while Cash had to be different and went for the roast prime rib.

Cash snickered a bit. "So, our naughty children were off playing and didn't get out of Vegas in time?"

I nodded. "One of them apparently hooked up with some of the female talent over at the AVN show."

Angel sighed, in full Mom Mode. "God, I hope he bagged it up. Blood tests or no, some things you just can't fix with antibiotics, especially not anymore."

"Making it more fun, some of it may go up on the Internet."

Angel pondered that a second. "Okay, that's not so much our problem. It's not like he has the company logo tattooed on his ass to make it a security issue."

"At least I hope he doesn't," Cash replied. "Even by my standards, that would be really weird."

That got me thinking. "Do we even *have* a company logo? It's not like we advertise."

About the time we finished some forty minutes later, Johnston had completed his challenge. He'd even ordered a second dessert to go. Ruiz was right. That little fucker could *eat*. Then the waitress told him about a professional competition eater, a female even smaller than he was, who put down *three* of the seventy-twos in the allotted hour. That knocked the bloom off his rose.

There was a hotel behind the restaurant, and besides conventional rooms, they offered log cabins, trailers, and even fancy wood-framed tents built like reproduction covered wagons. It was a comedown from the Venetian, but then most things are. Besides, this wasn't Vegas, this was *Texas*, goddamn it. They don't care how you do it in the forty-nine lesser states. Just ask 'em if you don't believe me. I learned that doing a six-week TDY with a kid from A&M about thirty years ago, and he was so militantly Texan that I still remembered the words to *The Aggie War Hymn*.

Angel voted for the wood-framed covered wagon because she thought it would be nice and cuddly, while being so radically different from the suite we'd been in or even the upscale room in Albuquerque that it would be more of an adventure and not so much of a disappointment. She's remarkably perceptive and clever about things like that. Cash wasn't thinking much. She had put down a piece of prime rib about the size of her head and was leaning on me in a daze. Me, I was so full I just wanted to have a nice coma. I was just sleepy and waddling. *I shouldn't have ordered the big one,* I told myself. Fuck, I would have slept in the truck if I had to.

We woke up around nine-thirty-ish the next morning, and I felt like I should lay there and digest that steak like an anaconda for another day or two. Naturally, Angel was looking at menus on her phone. You'd think I didn't feed that girl or something.

"They stop doing breakfast at ten, and," she looked at her watch then at the motionless lump of Cash, "we ain't gonna make it." Okay, fine, an early, early lunch would accomplish the same task. See, I figured we might as well eat a little something before we got going. No sense stopping again after an hour or two of driving just to eat when we could do it now with much better food. As if he'd read my mind, Ruiz texted me. *Lunch and then we roll out in formation, boss?*

Since we had to drive, and not lie about bloated and sleepy afterward as we had last night, it was a light lunch, relatively speaking. I was thinking about the fajitas, but I could get those back home easily enough. Maybe the lunch cut of prime rib? That sounded good. I waved at Ruiz's crew as they came in. Meanwhile, looking at her copy of the menu, Cash went slightly pale in disbelief at the idea of a one-pound cheeseburger. "My God, I like meat more than most girls —" She cut herself off and blushed a bit as she realized her indelicate phrasing. Sometimes she was more like her original self and that actually made her shy, so that was amusing.

Angel found this hilarious and nearly spit her drink. "Slut."

"Bitch."

"Don't make me hurt you," Angel playfully growled.

Cash nearly purred, fluttering her eyelashes. "Please? We've been so busy this last week that I'm feeling neglected."

We all snickered at that, but stifled it as the waitress showed up. Angel got the sirloin steak sandwich and an order of fried mushrooms. Cash took the prime rib-stuffed potato skins and the country fried steak sandwich. Me, should I have ordered that much prime rib knowing I had to drive? No. I did it anyway though, knowing I'd regret it eventually.

About an hour later, heading for our back corner of the parking lot, we were mostly thinking about the drive when another SUV pulled up and four angry Chinese guys quickly piled out of it. I recognized one of them, walking/limping with a cane in his left hand as to keep his gun hand free. Just to look like I wasn't bothered, I grinned broadly and half-yelled "Hi, David!" To be honest, I wasn't expecting to run into him again. Seeing him here was not a pleasant fucking surprise, to say the least, and so I was wondering how the fuck that had happened. I was kinda hoping Jimmy and the others had merely offed him and dumped him someplace.

David didn't say anything, and merely scowled. He was probably still pissed off about the bullet holes in his leg, even if they were only .22s, but that was completely understandable so I couldn't hold that against him. Another one of them said something in some form of Chinese, and Angel laughed and answered. Even David and the other guy broke character and chuckled. Only the one who appeared senior remained inexpressive. I don't speak any form of Chinese worth a damn, as you know, so I had to ask Angel. "What did he say, dear?"

Angel was grinning in a feral 'I'm going to get to shoot somebody again' kind of way. "He'd said shoot the big one with the glasses first, meaning you, and I told him until he had more experience than just sucking the senior lieutenant's dick in the shower after curfew, he should shut his whore mouth." Everybody laughed at that one, even me. Jokes aside, I didn't want to get shot first, last, or ever again. It hurts.

The oldest one up front waved for quiet, as that West Texas wind kept blowing. This shit was already taking too damn long though, and it had to be blowing twenty-five to thirty knots across that big flat space. That shit was cutting right through me. I cut him off before he could say anything. "Gentlemen, it's fucking cold out here. I think we either need to go back inside where it's a lot warmer or we need to quickly get to the point."

Their leader took a long moment, considering my words, then nodded once. "Here's the point then. You made the wrong sort of enemies, Professor."

What the fuck did I do? "Hey, I was minding my own business at the meeting when that fat Russian couldn't handle his liquor and shot up the place. How the hell is that my fault? Blame your boss's big-titted girlfriend who kept pouring him triples." Never mind the fact after Lin ran out the back door, the blonde told me she was working for the Canadian Secret Intelligence Service before she ran off too.

David piped up. "I told you that Lin is not our boss, you *something in Mandarin that sounded rude*."

Angel shot back with something else in Mandarin, but then their leader waved for quiet and shrugged. "That doesn't matter. The Russian is not an issue. Neither is Lin. You are. You know too much. We have much business in many places that does not concern you, and you are in a position to become a problem for us."

"Unfortunately for you, knowing too much is my business."

"Agreed, but since you aren't an actual criminal, we cannot buy you off as simply as we could find and buy off the others at the meeting. Criminals are predictable, you are not. That's why you are a problem that needs to be solved quickly and finally."

I looked at him, looked at his friends, then back to him. "Okay, so I'm *that* kind of a problem. Are we just gonna do this here in the parking lot in broad daylight? I didn't bring a Colt single action with me, so tradition is out, but I suppose we can improvise."

None of us were more than ten yards apart, and there was no cover at all to start with. Angel's hand was already in her purse. So was Cash's. My hand was sliding back to my own holstered Glock. My 1911 was cased in the truck. Just as well, this wasn't an art piece occasion. To quote a buddy of mine who'd been up the street from me at 5th SF Group while I was still in the One-oh-One a long time ago, "What's easier after eight shots, doing a slick reload or just pulling the trigger ten more times?" I had eighteen in the gun. The spare mag was a Magpul twenty-one rounder. I wasn't sure how many bullets this might *take*, but I knew how many I was gonna *use*. Mentally I was rehearsing getting my coat out of the way, my hand on my gun, then it out in time to not get killed.

Then the dice turned a good bit. Ruiz and his team of three more picked that moment to come walking up. "Hey, boss. We got some new friends to play with?" he asked cheerfully.

Johnston laughed a little, waving his phone around. "We got time to pick something off the music playlist before we get started?" His other two guys just looked eager.

Now instead of being on the wrong side of the odds, there were seven of us and four of them, and one of them was still injured. Our guys were already spacing and adjusting to stay out of each other's sector of fire. Hands were going into pockets and under jackets. If somebody moved wrong, all four of them were gonna get famous real fast. Those guys had been around the block enough times to realize they were on the wrong side of the firepower slope, and after about thirty seconds of eyeballing each other, their leader finally waved it off. His two guys relaxed, though David didn't, and they stepped backwards, showing hands. The leader nodded as they moved off into the parking lot. "This is not the end, Professor." Angel just gave him the finger as they piled into their SUV and screeched off.

Ruiz edged up on me as they left. "Think we ought to follow them and whack them?"

I laughed. "Whack them? You been binging *The Sopranos* or something?"

He nodded solemnly. "Not lately, but I'm still in that Vegas wiseguy frame of mind. And let's not forget that *Casino* is right up there with *Goodfellas* and *The Godfather* as great pieces of American cinematic history."

I shook my head. "Get in the goddamn car, Henry Hill. It's fucking cold out here and we got a long way to go until we get home."

After that, Angel drove for a while, getting us eastbound and into Oklahoma,

Chapter Six

"*On some nights, I still believe a car with the gas needle on empty can run about fifty more miles if you have the right music very loud on the radio.*"

~ Hunter S. Thompson

I was in the passenger seat with Angel driving when my phone rang. It was Ruiz. That was a bit unexpected, so of course I answered. "Yeah?"

"Hey, sir."

"What's up, Ruiz?"

"Remember our friends from lunch?"

"The Army buddies from way the hell out of town?" Ruiz didn't have one of the encrypted phones since we didn't have enough of the damn things to go around. I think we needed to fix that since the kid was obviously bucking to move ahead in the world. Shit, we still needed new phones anyway That had been a problem even before all this. One more unfinished project.

"Realizing we're all stuck going the same way, they've still been hanging around three cars behind me since not long after we left the Texan."

"They doing anything else suspicious or just driving the same way you are?"

"Well, just going the same way we are. I think we're only a mile in back of you. Johnston climbed in back and unpacked the 240 just in case they feel froggy." *Well, communications security was right out the fucking window.*

For those of you who don't keep track of such things, let me recap a little bit. A 7.62mm belt-fed medium machine gun is perfectly legal with the right paperwork from the Bureau of Alcohol, Tobacco, and Firearms. After the Hughes Amendment and the ATF's bullshit interpretation of it in 1986, there may be less than a dozen legally transferable 240s on the registry, and a few more of its internationally flavored but mechanically compatible cousins, but they do exist along with a lot of other things in the caliber. Ownership is just one piece of the legal paperwork. It's a separate form if you want to cross a state line with one. Considering I'd bought three of them without serial numbers, including this one, from a probably-CIA arms dealer out of the back of a truck, I had none of that legal paperwork, so right now it was just one more portable felony. The gun, and some other illegal ones in the trucks, needed to stay the fuck out of sight absent a very serious emergency.

"Ah, shit. Don't go getting pulled over with that thing visible." I needed to talk to a firearms lawyer buddy of mine and maybe dummy up some ATF paperwork that would pass a cursory inspection at a traffic stop. With all the other felonies the company committed on a daily basis, what the fuck was a little forgery?

Ruiz was blind to my inner turmoil since he was in another truck. "We're cool, boss."

I sighed, the tension starting to bubble up. "Yeah, keep it that way. Keep an eye on them, no sudden moves unless they make one." We hung up.

I still had my Glock on me, of course. That wouldn't be my first choice in case of trouble. Never use a pistol when a rifle is available- they kill things better. "Cash, we need an AR out." She turned and went for one of the cases in the back, but I was too preoccupied to scope out her ass as she did.

"Shorty one or long one?"

"Shorty. This is gonna be a fucking knife fight if it happens at all."

"Got it." There was the noise of latches and Velcro. "Eleven-five barrel, red dot?"

"Perfect." Great close-quarters gun. Unlike a bunch of the company guns, this one was completely legal and actually one of my personal ones. It was a semiauto only 'braced pistol' I'd built out of a pile of parts on a legally purchased lower receiver housing. Still worked just the same except for the lack of the 'giggle switch.' She passed it forward along with two loaded Pmags. The exposed steel tips told me it was current-issue Army stuff we probably weren't supposed to have. *Ooopsie.* Wonderful stuff for fighting around cars though.

"You want the can?" she asked.

The suppressor would make shooting it less obnoxious, but it would give me about seven extra inches of length, making the gun worse in a truck interior. It would also be hot enough to fry food on after half a magazine so it would be an instant burn hazard in the cramped space. "No, but get your ears handy. Ours too."

Cash pulled her Peltor electronic earmuffs on, recognizable by the black-with-pink-lining cat ears Velcroed onto their headband (yes, the girls shop at Weapon Outfitters too). She handed ours up to Angel and myself. I held the wheel while Angel pulled hers on, those having Multicam kitty ears on the headband. Cash then announced "That prime rib is still kicking my ass. Wake me up when the shooting starts." She then flopped back out. An hour later, she woke up in the back seat. Stretching and yawning, she then announced, "I have to pee, sir."

Texting Ruiz, we met up at the truck stop in Erick. While Cash scurried inside to hit the ladies' room and grab us few snacks and drinks, the rest of us quickly huddled in the parking lot.

"Any sign of them?" we all asked each other. I hadn't seen shit, of course.

Ruiz shook his head. "Negative. They just fell back. Maybe they stopped to take a shit somewhere."

"Fuckin' where?" Johnston wondered. "There wasn't but two or three gas stations since Amarillo. This is asshole nowhere out here."

Ruiz shrugged. "There was that Indian place in Groom I saw the billboard for, but I don't know why the fuck there is an Indian restaurant out here where there aren't any Indians."

"There's plenty of Indians once you get into Oklahoma," Matthews said. "My dad used to be stationed at Tinker Air Force Base in Oklahoma City, but there's a shitload of reservations around there."

Johnston naturally had the answer. "He means tech support call center Indians, man, not the 'We stole their land then they built a casino' Indians. *Tikka masala* Indians, not venison jerky —"

I cut him off, despite chuckling. "Yeah, yeah, we get it, Johnston."

"So did we lose them?" Matthews asked.

Ruiz laughed explosively. "Man, don't even say that. Except for banging that porn chick and her friend back at the Hard Rock, you ain't got that kind of luck. And after getting laid like that, you ain't got any luck left for a good long while." We all had a good laugh at that one.

"At least I didn't lose a thousand bucks at the Silverton sports book betting on the Romanian booty slap championships," Matthews shot back. That made it even funnier.

Angel had been quiet, merely scanning the parking lot as an unlikely-looking sentry, but she just stared. "What the fuck, is that really a thing?"

Ruiz answered around his laughter. "Sure is. We were watching the livestream. Don't listen to him, I only lost five hundred of the two grand I was playing with, and I'd won most of that shooting dice. Now what I need to do is get a planeload of Colombian or Venezuelan hotties over there and show them Eurotrash sluts how Latinas do it."

I had to sigh. The world just gets more and more insane as we go. Snapping back to reality, I leaned into my truck and pulled a Motorola handheld out of one of the gear bags. "Ruiz, if it looks like it's going to get tense, bag up your phones. We don't want to get our shit geo-located to a crime scene and get hemmed up on any of this later. Talk to me on this instead."

Ruiz nodded and handed the radio over to Matthews. "You're on RTO, I'm driving."

"Who's on the gun?"

51

Johnston raised his hand. "You gotta ask, boss? Shit, I haven't stir-fried a car since Second Fallujah."

"That was what, 2007? Damn, I didn't think you were that old." Angel wondered aloud.

"Oh four," he corrected her. "That's what I get for getting out then going back in every few years. Keeps you young."

"Marines let you back in?"

Johnston laughed. "That was my first hitch, right out of high school, yeah. 3-5 Marines, Darkhorse. Got out after that one, got lucky going back in, tail end of 2010." He jerked a thumb at Ruiz. "You're right. The Corps is bad about letting you back in if you were ever disloyal enough to leave. Met that fucker after that when we were in Afghanistan. Got out again after that, swore I was going to college, ended up going Army Guard. Did that all through college, then I fucked up my knee real bad at SFAS with 20th Group, and that was that. Back to Tennessee, back to college, then Jake found me and I found you Ruiz."

I shook my head. "You needed a steadier career, man. That junior enlisted shit wears on you real quick after you turn thirty." Believe me, I learned that one when I was on Career 2.1 or whatever. Keeping up with nineteen year olds even at twenty-six or twenty-seven was hard some days.

"Fuck, boss, why do you think I work here now?" Johnston laughed.

Their fourth, a scrawny white kid who barely looked old enough to be here, asked "What do I do?"

The others just looked at him. "Just pass ammo, Williams."

Hours later, we'd passed Oklahoma City and darkness had fallen pretty thoroughly by the time the Chinese team finally made their move. I hadn't wasted the time. I'd gotten out of my comfy old Sperry boat shoes and into a decent pair of boots before we even left Erick. Other gear got adjusted as we rolled onward. At nightfall, when we'd pulled off and eaten, Cash had gotten into my night vision gear case and I'd set up for that as well. Rather than just playing a waiting game, you gotta use every moment to improve your hand of cards.

We were just crossing the Arkansas River and approaching both midnight and the state line at Fort Smith when Ruiz came up on the Motorola.

"Good thing we got that thing out. They're edging up on us, looking to pass us."

"You sure it's them?"

"Damn sure. The one guy who was walking with a cane recognized the truck, saw us looking, and made a point of giving us the finger."

"Let them pass you then speed up some. Pace them right up in back of us so I can play blocker. Then you get next to them and if they give you a reason, let that thing eat."

"Roger that, boss." It didn't take long. "Dude's got a Kalashnikov!" Ruiz called. *Why the hell would you use an AK in a country awash in ARs?* Oh well, foreigners think like foreigners, and a man is entitled to a preference in his tools, even if I personally thought that preference was fucking stupid. Not my problem, really.

I handed the radio off to Angel while I concentrated on driving. "Get that gun up and ready," she told him.

I could hear a bit of manic glee as Ruiz answered. "You got it!"

This was not gonna go well. Johnston's hyperactive narration was audible in the background. Somebody was holding the button down so we could keep listening for our entertainment. Well, that's one way of shutting the boss up. "Hey, all you crazy bastards out there, this is Marty J coming at you live. Before we get started, I wanna thank our sponsors *Raid: Shadow Legends* and our good friends at *Fabrique Nationale,* USA, now let's see what Spotify has for this occasion..." A couple seconds later, Sabaton's "To Hell And Back" started up. We got about ten seconds of it before the channel went clear.

Cash was only slightly horrified. "Tell me that dumbfuck kid isn't streaming this?" It came out as a nervous screech. Her 'icy calm' switch hadn't flipped on yet.

"Christ, I fucking hope not!" Angel agreed. She hit the button. "Ruiz, he better not be streaming!"

Johnston called back with a laugh. "Nah, I got too many Twitch followers to go getting my account banned for streaming an actual shooting. I make good money on that one sometimes."

"Not to mention putting the evidence out on the Internet!" Angel yelled back. Mama Bear was working up to her full roar.

Johnston replied. "I'd be a legend though! Come on, Mommy!" We could hear the rest of their crew laughing in the background.

Angel was having none of that. "And we'd all go to the serious kind of prison, so no! Fuck no! I'm sure an Oklahoma jail has terrible food!"

When the east and west lanes of the Interstate diverged with thick woods between, and there were no lights in sight, I figured they'd make their move. When it did, it happened quick. I was watching in the rear view as Ruiz blocked their passing attempt, hit the brakes, and slid into a perfect broadside firing position on the target's left side. Muzzle flash lit up the night and tracers streaked as Johnston dumped what looked like the entire two-hundred round ammo can into their car. There was no radio traffic, but Angel faintly growled "Eat shit, you Commie fucks." Taiwanese, remember? She dislikes mainland Chinese Communists more than anyone I know.

Their SUV missed the front edge of the guardrail, but flipped down off the side of the road into the gully and might well have made it all the way into the creek.

I got on the radio. "You guys keep going. Don't stop for shit, see you back home."

"Where you goin', boss?" Ruiz asked.

"Don't you fuckin' worry about it. I'm gonna go pay the insurance."

"Boss..." Ruiz sounded like he doubted my abilities.

"Just fucking go. Keep going, don't argue."

We pulled off at the next exit, 297, and eased onto a gravel lot in the dark, south of the intersection. Checking the map, I was about a third of a mile from the crash site in the creek, with just a field and woods between me and it. "Cash, pull out another radio." I made sure my cell phone was still off and bagged. She handed it over in silence, exchanging glances with Angel.

Okay, just because I was the CEO, I was old, and it wasn't normally my job to go out in harm's way didn't mean I didn't have the gear on hand to do so. Sometimes you still gotta be the one to take the risk, and well, I wasn't that old yet. Going around to the back of the Yukon, I popped the tailgate and retrieved another of my rolling gear cases then quickly closing the tailgate. Just in case of something like this, I could put everything on in here with my eyes closed. I stayed away from the truck, working in shadow. My jacket came off, and I threw on a 'war belt' with a pistol holster, med pouch, pistol magazines, and a few emergency bits. I swapped the Glock out of my concealment holster and put it into the belt holster, re-rigging a bit. A pair of light suspenders would take up some of the belt's weight. Over that, I pulled on the plate carrier, tapping all the magazines (four for the AR) to make sure nothing had shaken loose in transit.

While Cash grabbed her Glock and moved over to stand as lookout, Angel stood close while I was still gearing up. "Sir, what the fuck are you doing?"

Since it was literally freezing, I pulled my jacket back on over the plate carrier. "Like I told Ruiz, I'm gonna go pay the insurance on those four." I pulled on my helmet setup and clicked the dual-tube PVS-31 night vision goggles on. While my pair was a few years old and not the bleeding edge of the art, the binocular-style white-image device still turned darkness into light with nearly Hollywood perfection. They damn well should. The things had a price tag in the low five digits even with the package deal we'd gotten buying twenty pairs straight from the factory. The helmet on the other hand, was a forty-dollar ProTec skateboard helmet I'd cut and taped and painted and Velcroed the way I wanted it. Fuck, it was good enough for the Fort Bragg cool kids in the 1990s.

I wasn't gonna pay most of a thousand bucks for what got likes on the tacticool side of the 'Gram now.

"What, go check the bodies?"

"Yep. Gonna go make sure all four of them are thoroughly fucking dead." I then pulled on a pair of mechanic's gloves I frequently shot in. Not just because it was cold as shit, but why make it easy for the crime lab where what was left of that car was inevitably going to when they found four bodies in it? "If you don't hear from me in fifteen minutes, or you hear gunfire, you guys get the fuck out of here."

Angel just stared at me. "No."

Cash had edged over close enough that she could still play lookout but hear what was going on. I looked over at her and she shrugged. "Don't expect me to take your side on this one, sir."

I sighed. "If I get shot by one of those fuckers who might still be alive, or the cops get there before I get out, you two need to get away because you two gotta the ones to retrieve me. You're the only friendly element for hundreds of miles."

"Because you sent Ruiz and his kids onward. This is their job."

"They were the shooters. I had to get them and that gun gone. And if this goes wrong, you can't go getting pinched at the same time." I slung the shorty AR I hadn't needed yet and locked on the suppressor can that I'd done without earlier. It might have been unnecessary, but for all I knew there were four live guys back there still able to fight. Now I doubted it, but I'd seen machine gun fire do weird shit with cars before, both for better and worse.

Angel nodded tightly, right on the ragged edge of rebellion. "That doesn't mean we're leaving you here. If we don't hear anything in fifteen minutes, we'll displace north of the Interstate to that Subway over there by the truck stop, go get ourselves a sandwich, then you use the creek bed to take that dirt road running parallel to the north side of the Interstate. That becomes this street that comes east to a block north of the truck stop." I just stared at her. "What? I looked at the fucking map while you were dicking with your helmet and your NODs."

"You unbagged your phone?"

Cash smiled. "I had one of my burners out."

God, I love those girls.

There was decent ambient light, and the half moon helped. That was amplified by the 31s into really nice visibility. Nice night for a walk in the woods, except it was also cold as shit out there. It took me less than ten minutes for me to make it the half-mile back to where the creek bed crossed under the Interstate. Just keeping the road on my right side, 'hand-railing' as we call it in military land navigation, got me there. Yeah, it had been a minute since I'd had to do a cross-country movement under goggles on unfamiliar ground, but I'd done it so often over three decades that old habits kicked in and got me through. The Mercedes hadn't burned, which was good, since that would have attracted attention. Overhead, the concrete bridge echoed with *whooshes* as traffic kept whipping by.

I pulled the radio and quickly messaged Angel. "On site. All clear."

"Roger."

Well, at least she and Cash knew to sit tight. Checking the wreckage, all four occupants were dead. I mean really dead. Like 'dozens of holes in each and significant chunks of them were missing' kind of dead. No insurance shots were needed. Cool.

It took me a minute to recognize my old acquaintance, David. His head was in rather poor condition, but he'd managed to maintain what was literally a death grip on that cane. "Fuck you too. See you in Hell, man." Because I'm a movie nerd, the voice of actor Donald Li echoed in my ears from all the times I'd watched *Big Trouble in Little China*. "Chinese got a lot of Hells." Oh, well. Maybe I'd miss him in the confusion down there. Or maybe the Taoists didn't share their Hells with the rest of us. I had a feeling I'd find out sooner or later. You get real skeptical about your own salvation in this business.

Now there were multiple AKs, which meant I could help myself to one, and *oooh*, a Sig Sauer 226. It was a very classic choice, and I actually didn't have one. *Thank you, Mister Dead Chinese Guy.* There was a rolled-up nylon bag on the back left hip of my war belt. They were originally intended as 'dump pouches' for collecting empty magazines, but to be honest, I never took that much time or care with my empties when reloading in a hurry. However, they were also damned handy for throwing loose odds and ends into when foraging or conducting what the cognoscenti referred to as 'site exploitation.' I needed their cell phones, wallets, and anything else of intelligence value, and so the bag was where they went. Yeah, I checked their watches, but none of the four were wearing anything worth looting. And no, I would have voinked an electronically exploitable smartwatch as fast as I would have snatched up a nice Breitling or Omega.

With the corpses searched, I moved on to checking the luggage in back. Mentally, I was counting time on target as I dug for metaphorical gold. No, no, clothes, no, and oh yeah, a laptop case. That was definitely a keeper. And... that was it. With that, I awkwardly clambered up from the wreck and started moving back along the Interstate's south edge to meet my ride out of here. After a couple minutes of hiking, I blipped Cash on the Motorola. "Clear up there?"

"Clear, sir."

I kept retraced my steps eastward through the wooded edge of that field. I opened the passenger door, and climbed in as best I could with all my gear still on. I was doing this in the dark because Angel had taped over all the interior lights while I was gone. *Clever of her.* "First things first, we got any more Faraday bags?" I should have bagged the damn things at the wreck, but I confess I just hadn't thought that far ahead. I hadn't planned on having to do anything like this when I got out of bed this morning. I'd ding myself for it in the after-action review.

Cash rummaged in her enormous purse of... things, and pulled out two more of the signal-blocking bags. I crammed two in each, so now the four dead guys' phones were thus silenced. That done, Angel then wasted no time in mashing the gas pedal and getting us back up onto the Interstate and down the road. I went on and cleared the AK and the Sig. She looked over with a slightly judgy look. "You climbed all the way down there just to steal guns? Don't you have enough of those?"

I laughed. "I know I have enough guns. I'm going to clean this AK up and put it on a plaque and give it to Johnston at the Christmas party this year."

Angel just groaned, certain I was back on my bullshit. From the back seat, Cash piped up. "That's actually really thoughtful. He'll love it."

Me being me, I continued. "Really, I just wanted to make sure they were dead and gather whatever intel off them that I could."

Cash nodded by the dashboard's glow. "It was completely logical to do. It still might have been a better job for those younger and faster guys you sent away."

I grumbled. "Again, I wanted them and that goddamn machine gun as far away from here as possible. Can't afford to lose them." I took my helmet and goggles off, handing them back to Cash to go in the back. With the quick-releases at the shoulders, I undid the cummerbund and got the carrier off, then finally the belt.

Angel nearly grumbled. "We can't afford to lose you either."

"That's what I had you up here, for backing me up."

Cash chuckled. "I feel like a joust squire passing armor around."

Angel chuckled. "And you just wanted to fuck me over and get me driving again." We pulled out of the parking lot, with Mary Kutter singing about her grandfather's moonshining money.

Chapter Seven

Getting across Arkansas and the west half of Tennessee didn't take all that long, relatively speaking, and we got home mid-morning the next day. The first step was to take the armored Yukon and all the work gear to the office and drop it off to deal with tomorrow. My truck had lived in the garage back at my house while we were gone. One of Jake's guard shack kids just dropped us and our luggage off once we were done at the office.

Surprising me, another one of Jake's kids was in a lawn chair in the driveway smoking a cigar next to another forest green Yukon. I recognized it as another one of our dozen-plus ex-State Department trucks. As I got out, I looked at the kid and laughed. "That better not be one of my smokes, man. I don't have that many left."

He was a skinny black kid who'd come out of 1st Brigade up the road at Campbell. As was my mental pattern, I'd think of his name in a minute. "Sir, I've been out in the gazebo with you on break. I know damn well I usually smoke better ones than you do."

That was a matter of individual taste. My stockpile of the long-discontinued Rocky Patel Valedors was running out, but an email to the company told me that they still made them by a different name, so I was buying those. I kept laughing anyway. "Fine. What the hell are you doing out here, anyway? Pet-sitting?"

He blew a good-sized smoke cloud. "Four of us on the house at all times now, sir. I'm the section lead now, and I'm actually on break. One guy's inside on the cameras, and the last two are sweeping through the back woods to calibrate the seismic detectors. We may have to cover some of the other principals' residences in time. Probably gonna need more bodies for that tasking."

Cameras? Seismics? Angel came up next to me. "Yeah, you lost the extra downstairs storeroom off the garage. It's the ready room for the duty section now. It got walled in half to make bunk space, control board is in the other half, and they're getting priority on the basement bathroom too."

I sighed. *Nobody tells me anything.* "Why are we putting a duty section at the house?"

She gave me That Look. "Because someone tried to kill us out here. Obviously, some at-home security is needed."

Nobody had said a thing to me about this. "What the hell?"

Cash smiled. "We ordered the cameras and seismic intrusion stuff the week after our little adventure out here, sir. It just took a while to get all of it delivered, and we scheduled the install to happen while we'd be gone. That way you couldn't complain about it." With that, she and Angel went on inside with the last of their bags.

The kid blew another smoke cloud. "Can't do it all yourself. You gotta sleep sometime, boss. Come on, be realistic."

I was getting lectured by a kid young enough to be *my* kid, assuming I had kids. My dad would love this, if I ever decided to tell him. Again, I was not completely honest with my parents about what I was doing for a living these days. "Yeah, but we hired you guys to guard the office, not my house."

"The point Jake made to us at the briefing before he left town with you is that guard shifts were guard shifts, and that if we let you get yourself killed, we're all out of a damn job."

"Oh, bullshit. Dave could take over for me just fine."

"That's why there's a two-man element rotating on his house. My buddy's team has that one. But past that, we're going to need more bodies. Between twelve of twenty-nine from Security being gone in Vegas for over a week and then picking up the tasking on two houses plus what we already had on rotation for the Hole, we're pretty jammed up right now."

Another snap of inspiration hit. "You got anyone you worked with before who doesn't work here who should be working here?" I stopped, thought about it for a second, re-parsed the sentence in my head a couple times, and then figured it was close enough to intelligible English for as worn out as I felt.

Hawkins. That was the kid's name. Hawkins. Hawkins took another drag on his cigar and nodded. "I can think of a few. Mostly ex-1st Brigade cats since I was in No Slack." For you non-Fort Campbell people, that's the traditional nickname for 2nd Battalion, 327th Infantry. "Four or five of 'em are still around here and still in shape enough that could hang with us."

I nodded. "Good. Think of them, tell your guys to think of more, and I'll pass the word through Jake to have the other team leaders do the same. If we have to grow, I don't want to stick you guys with people you don't want, and the easiest way to do that is bring on people you already know, have served with, and will vouch for."

Hawkins nodded. "Yeah. Staying around here is the hard part. Too many guys went back home to try getting on with their lives." I never tried that part. I knew a lot of other guys who had and more that hadn't. Let's be honest, if home had been all that awesome, most of us never would have left it in the first place. That made me think of Nichols. "That new staff sergeant show up yet?"

"Jacked black dude, used to be 82nd? Yeah. Pretty bad motherfucker. You really find his ass in a Waffle House?" That made me feel better. Growth can be hard, and I needed to do it right.

While I thought about it, I noticed the back of the now-green Yukon had been augmented by at least a dozen big full-color stickers from various gun and gear companies, plus a metallic National Rifle Association Life Member insignia and a 101st Airborne Division license plate frame. I merely pointed and looked over at Hawkins. "We spent a bunch of money repainting them to make these trucks blend in. Why fuck that up with the decals?" As soon as I said it, I realized I'd answered my own question. The Alabama Alumni, Little League Mom-stickered Suburban that Ruiz's team used was its own example of blending in.

Hawkins laughed and blew another smoke cloud. "Bossman, remember, the damn trucks are blending into the Nashville-Clarksville metro area. Every asshole with a DD214 and an AR in the closet around here's gotta have eight or ten stickers about it on the truck. It's a rule. Come on, you've been living here damn near longer than I've been alive."

The kid was right, and I had to admit it. Trucks like that were everywhere from the grocery store to the gun shops. "You got me there. You really do." I stuck my hand out, he stood, and we shook. "Thanks for the effort, man. I'll follow up with you later, but since I'm old, I'm going to go inside and pass out now."

He raised his cigar in salute. "You do that, boss. The dog's been out recently and was asleep on the couch the last I saw."

I went in through the garage, turning, and finding the stair to the main level. Damn, I knew it had only been a few months, but I just wasn't to the point I could get around this place without thinking about it. I really thought Cash and Angel had overbuilt it, but it wasn't like they asked my opinion either.

Odin was asleep on the couch, snoring. I petted him, but didn't want to wake him up. He just made happy rumbly noises from Doggy Dreamland. He farted a little as he shifted around on the cushions, paws gently twitching. For me now, it was just time for a hot shower and a nap. It was good to be back in my own bed, no matter what room it was in now. I didn't give a shit if I was backwards on sleep schedule.

Chapter Eight

"Every saint and sinner in the history of our species lived there—on a mote of dust suspended in a sunbeam."
~ Carl Sagan, American astronomer

At my insistence, everyone who'd been in Vegas was supposed to be taking a few days off. But nope, not me. I was setting a Good Example, goddamn it. I was letting everyone else recover while ignoring myself, as usual. The next morning, I was back in the office. Really, I should have given myself a couple days off. My back felt like shit, I was still about three or four days behind on genuinely restful sleep, and I was more tensed up than normal people are when they're getting shot at. But my own frailties were no reason to fall out of the march when no one else was visibly collapsing.

Angel staunchly refused to stay home when I'd told her take the day off. I was secretly relieved. I was going to need her help explaining what the fuck had gone on with the Chinese guys. Cash had merely smiled a bit and said she needed to get into her office for a couple hours. As for Dave, I'd promised him a whole week off if he just came in for the morning meeting, then he could go home early and take Liz to Paris or some shit for all I cared.

The biggest thing would be meeting Dave. I had to tell my longtime right hand the parts about Vegas and the cross-country killing spree after that he didn't know. Kara was on nights, so I didn't expect her. Petey, the wiry blond IT boss was also supposed to be there. I knew he had questions about how the gear had worked in Vegas and what we needed to upgrade. I wasn't so concerned about that, as that was a 'him and Morgan' problem and it didn't need to happen today.

When I walked into the conference room just before 0930, I was surprised to see Morgan over on Intel's side of the table. "Thought I told you to take a couple days?"

He snorted. "Fuck that. You need me for this part. Let's only tell this story once and tell it right. Then I'm gonna go home and just stare at the walls for a couple days. Gotta reset my focus." He could spend it high as fuck, I didn't care. Whatever he had to do to maintain.

"Wait, before I forget, where's what's her name who did that thing?" I still hadn't laid eyes on her since it happened.

Morgan smiled a little. "We asked Addy where she wanted to go for an extra week off on us, so her and her boyfriend are spending a week down below Miami where it's actually warm. I put them on the plane myself a few hours ago."

Fuck. "Can we trust the boyfriend?" Though he had a point about the warm part. We'd had more snow on the ground than usual and some mornings this week it had been in single digits. The high desert of Nevada hadn't been this fucking cold. This was not a usual Tennessee winter.

He snickered a little. "You tell me. She's paired up with your boy Johnston who did the other thing for us."

All right, I feel like I should have known this. "No shit? I had no idea."

"Ain't your job to have any idea, boss. They're getting some sunshine and an open bar tab to get over the extra work they put in. Got them a nice little all-inclusive place down in the Keys, but they'll be back next week."

Fair enough, I guess. "Speaking of getting home, where's Jimmy? I tried calling him."

"He's still got his phone bagged while he handles that other business."

Dave looked at Morgan and then me quizzically. I shook my head. "Tell you later. It's super dark and should be the tightest of tight holds."

Even as I said it, I know I was probably full of shit. More than one person had been slinging paper towels in a panic to clean up the mess in the hallway outside, since stabbing somebody in the neck is not a tidy process. Everyone who was on duty in the headquarters suite at the time knew what had happened to one of their own, and what had happened to those who'd tried to do it. From there, it wasn't much of a leap that one live body and one dead body had to be dealt with. But one of the rules of working here was that sometimes shit was going to happen that you didn't want to know and sometimes you had to know what not to ask. If you couldn't figure out what not to ask, be prepared to be told. You can do that with employees who were mostly former military. Anyway, we'd have to have a sit-down meeting with all of them, assuming Morgan and Jake hadn't while we were still out there.

Morgan looked up at me. "I know what you're thinking."

"How sure are you of that?"

"Those who were there know what they didn't see. We had a meeting while we were still out there."

Shit. "How the fuck did you do that?"

Morgan chuckled. "Know what you were thinking? I probably had a shaman in the family tree, so I got the sight in my blood sometimes. Besides, man, you're predictable as shit. It's a natural concern for you to have."

Dave was looking back and forth between us. "Can someone please explain what the fuck you two are carefully not talking about?"

Okay, fuck it. If I couldn't trust Dave and I couldn't trust my own office as a secured space, I had even bigger problems than just the risk of a couple of loose murder indictments.

As if to punctuate that thought, Jake picked that moment to walk in. "Ain't you supposed to be off?" I asked him. He gave me the finger and laughed a little, but then he locked my door and started explaining for me.

"We didn't want to try getting rid of a body in Vegas, so Jimmy rigged a freezer and a generator in the back of a van and hauled the body back this way to ditch it."

This didn't faze Dave at all. He'd seen and done worse. "Huh, anybody we know?"

I shrugged. "All I know is he was one of the Chinese guys who tried personnel-snatching one of Morgan's intel girls out of the hallway at the Venetian. She stabbed him and is now having a week off for free."

"Addy's commo, not intel, not that it matters. But she's apparently dating your boy Johnston who machine-gunned that carload of Chinese guys for you. He might actually pop the question while they're in Florida." I just stared at him. "Ruiz told me as soon as he got back, boss. He's my guy, remember?"

I finally sat down. "Yeah, and we gotta figure out who those dead Chinese guys were." I thought about it for a minute. "And speaking of dead Chinese guys, why the fuck did the one guy what's his name from UAVs... Griffin, wounded in the hallway, why the fuck was he still up and limping around with the guys Johnston ended up killing in Oklahoma? I had thought he was a solved problem, but there he was in Amarillo and following us all the way across the country with his buddies Larry, Moe, and Curly."

Morgan grumbled. 'We already had one body to deal with. We drove David off, talked a bit, and then instead of killing him, we let him go."

"That might have been unwise," I observed.

"Yeah, yeah, I get it, and when Jimmy's back you can chew both our asses for it."

Jake actually looked worried. "Fuck, let's just get Jimmy back here. He was supposed to check in this morning, and I don't know where he is."

"He'll be okay. Dude's survived too much shit to go out like this, though his going alone was fucking stupid." I looked over at Dave. "And yeah, we gotta figure out those other three."

Dave leaned back in his chair. "We got their wallets and cell phones you dropped off yesterday, and we already started on those. Huawei phones, not American, so they gotta have a backdoor in them. Chinese won't make a phone that doesn't. Just a matter of finding it."

"I got two techs on them right now," Petey piped up.

I looked back to Morgan. "You get anything worth knowing out of David?"

Morgan shook his head. "He's a pretty hard fucker. Real professional."

I shrugged. "It happens. We can't flip everyone or this job might get too easy." I pulled at my drink to collect my thoughts a moment. "Backing things up to Vegas, Dave, you got any news on the other set of dead guys, the ones from the country club parking lot?"

He shook his head. "Vegas PD has no idea who these guys were. Their fingerprints aren't on the books that anyone's found yet. Their clothes were all brand new and locally bought, but supposedly they're working DNA and dental records —"

"And we stole their wallets."

"No matter," Dave interjected. "The credit cards didn't give up much. They were all new ones from cheap low-end banks, and there were no transactions outside the Las Vegas metro area. The names on them match the IDs, only the IDs were brand new Florida driver's licenses, and they were all fakes"

"You already told me they were fakes when we were still out there."

Dave grinned a bit. "Now we know that they were European-made ones by the work."

"Okay, I'm impressed, but how the fuck can you tell?"

Dave shrugged. "I can't tell, but I know a really good document exploitation guy in the UK. We met on a joint task force in Afghan years ago. I hit him up to pick his brain, and sent him some really high-rez scans. He thinks the work was from a place in Berlin, something about only one source for the holographic tape but there's an error in the line spacing. Plus," he handed me a color printout of an autopsy photo. "Vegas PD might not recognize that tattoo, but I sure as shit do."

Sheeeeiiiiiittttt. I thought, looking at a wild shoulder piece with two sets of jump wings and a coiled Asian dragon between them. "I do too. Looks like older Russian Airborne ink blended into a 2nd French Foreign Parachute commemorative." Wish I had a face to go with that one — that might have been the asshole who busted me in the face that Angel stomped in the head then Cash shot. "Did they get ATF traces on the guns? Wait, never mind, we have the guns, they don't." ATF traces aren't all that wonderful anyway, and my inner anarchist was totally fine with that.

"Your headquarters guys forward had sent all the info on them back to us. There was nothing of significance anyway. It was three Glocks and that one suppressed HK45."

I waved it off. "Most Glocks bore me, even though I have a couple. That HK was pretty fucking cool to find though."

Jake rolled his eyes at me. "We already had half a dozen of them downstairs. You had me buy them, remember?"

"Yeah, but those are the company's guns. I may keep this one just because I got hit in the face with it." Morgan nearly giggled at the memory. I know he had the video.

"Fucking weirdo," Dave grumbled.

"I'm sorry, old buddy, but how much did you spend on that .408 CheyTac that lives in your office so your wife won't find it?" There wasn't much I could rag on Dave about, but I had him there. It was at least an eight-thousand-dollar rifle. Never mind the other custom one he'd bought that got him in trouble at the house and necessitated his taking Liz to NYC for a week of Broadway shows. That was part of why we were there when all these dominoes first started falling. We weren't at the end of that chain reaction yet, either.

Dave wasn't having that discussion right then. "Man, fuck you. Oh, lemme change the subject before I forget. We got lucky on a research monkey about your Chinese buddy."

That perked me up. "Finally some good fucking news. Who?" James Lin, that shady maybe-former Chinese intel officer, had told me at our sit-down meeting that he'd attended private school here in the States, specifically outside DC. The easiest way of confirming whether the back story he'd given me was true or bullshit was to get somebody into the shelves of old yearbooks at the school.

"A former commander of mine is a two-star now. He lives out on the Maryland side because he works downtown in civilian clothes these days, but I finally remembered his kid is at Georgetown Prep."

"Easy to get the kid into the library then. Unlike anyone else we'd find easily, he's actually *supposed* to be there."

The concept of recruiting a penetration agent with access to a Jesuit high school's library as opposed to one who could get into a Russian air force base or something was a ludicrous comparison on its face. On the other hand, the principle was exactly the same. If you're putting someone in somewhere, they need to convincingly belong there or alarms go off. Sometimes literal ones. And since Prep was the sort of school that produced generals, senators, some Kennedy offspring, and two of the current nine Supreme Court justices, their yearbook archives weren't exactly open admission anymore.

Dave grinned. "Exactly. So I asked him to ask his kid if he was willing to make a few bucks in the library looking for an alumnus, but didn't tell him why."

"You knew the kid before this, but does he know what you do?"

"He knows what was doing, and what his dad did when I was working for him out at Meade." It was a long story, but Dave's former unit, the US Army Asymmetric Warfare Group, didn't exist anymore anyway. "I mean I hadn't seen him since he was in elementary school, but he liked unit barbecues and stuff. He knows that secrets are involved."

Morgan looked a little skeptical. "Good, because if this kid has two brain cells to rub together, he's going to realize he's combing yearbook photos from twenty years ago looking for a Chinese guy, and he might decide that's the sort of shit his dad professionally needs to know."

"Yeah, I talked about that with him and his dad. He said he trusted me to back-channel him anything genuinely critical, otherwise he had too many problems over in Europe to give a shit about what we were up to."

"So then what?" Jake piped up.

Dave shrugged. "The kid wants to be a spook when he grows up, so he was more thrilled over this than he would have been over naked cheerleaders. Anyway, I helped him work out a process, so he's going to get in there this week and dig for me."

"He's in high school. There is no way this would excite him more than naked cheerleaders."

"Dude, you're old. People get bored with nudity at a much younger age these days." Yeah, great. No wonder nobody's having kids anymore. Never mind the flat wages and rising housing costs; we're like pandas that won't fuck.

Still, this would take a minute, and there was no guarantee it would work. Lin could have lied his ass off and gone to any number of other schools in the area, assuming he was telling the truth about having grown up around DC at all. Lin being honest would have been way more of a surprise. "What have we got elsewhere in the world?"

Dave shrugged. "Worldwide? Nothing serious you wouldn't have seen on the Internet while you were gone."

They would have been surprised about how little I was playing on my phone during that trip. I was off my phone and living in the moment, as they say. "What do you think the two hotspots are?"

"Overseas? The Russians and Ukrainians are still shoving each other into the meat grinder and refusing to negotiate. It's gonna come down who to who runs out of ammo and-or bodies first." The math on that was kind of unavoidable.

"Chinese air naval assets are poking around Taiwan as always, but they aren't ready to come out and play with the Seventh Fleet yet, so that's gonna simmer a few more years, probably."

I sighed. "Then with our recent change of management, the border may get sporty." I thought for a moment, wondering what linguists we'd have to find and hire for whatever would blow up next, then I cut myself off and pulled back to the here and now. "Find a way to drop a dime with Las Vegas PD. The Russian / Foreign Legion paratrooper tattoo thing, and also that the shooters in the Convention Center were Chinese and no longer in the country."

Morgan, who'd been quiet, piped up. "I can handle that."

Dave nodded. "How do we know about the shooters being Chinese?"

Angel had been quiet, but that got a laugh out of her. "Oh, you hadn't heard this part yet?"

Dave shrugged. "Him and Morgan were kinda jumping around." Yeah, welcome to ADHD Incorporated. The days of ragged sleep weren't helping.

I sighed. "Fuck, okay, let's go back over all this shit from the beginning."
*****

A couple hours and a bite of lunch later, it was quiet. I think Angel and Cash were downstairs in her office, or maybe even napping in Cash's old room, the now-underused Witness Protection Suite. Sensing an opportunity, I pulled my spare poncho liner from my bottom desk drawer, and then I turned out the lights, collapsing on the massive leather sofa. I just needed to take an hour to relax under the lightweight nylon quilt and have an existential crisis. Just an hour, I told myself, as I set my glasses aside and closed my eyes.

Over the laptop speakers, the opening piano chords of Vangelis' *Heaven and Hell* began, the best known bit, the third movement that many astronomy nerds of a certain age recognize from *Cosmos*. Then Carl Sagan's famous narration of the 1990 "Pale Blue Dot" photo from *Voyager I* soon joined in. Spending a little time in the dark contemplating the miniscule pointlessness of the human condition was important to put everything back in its proper perspective after the sensory overload of Las Vegas. I think actually managed to sleep for about twenty minutes out of that hour. Fuck it. I didn't have to micromanage everyone. They knew what to do without me.

I gave myself that hour, and then I forced myself up. I was tired, but I just felt bad about hiding out. The big question on my mind now was 'what the fuck were the Chinese up to and why were they bothering us?' So I did what I did with all of my unanswerable questions. I pulled myself up off the sofa, took a minute to look presentable, and then I went down two floors to the Intel section on the third level. On the white board permanently dedicated to "Pending Questions," I wrote in red. "WHY ARE THE CHINESE FUCKING WITH US? MEETING SOON."

Downstairs, the intel guys were trying to do document exploitation on the four dead Chinese. Well, really it wasn't document exploit, it was tech exploit, but close enough. It wasn't going so well. Yeah, we were into their phones, well, three of them. The fourth had a pair of fat 7.62mm bullet holes in it and was basically trash. Still, everything except the basics of the phones' operating system had secondary encryption on it we hadn't beaten yet. We were fucked if it was biometric. It wasn't like I'd cut their thumbs off to get the prints.

The tech exploit on the laptop was also going nowhere. It was encrypted in Chinese and whatever the fuck software it was using, we were just hitting and bouncing. This needed to be done by somebody better resourced than we were. We wouldn't quit on it until something more important took up the effort, but Petey wasn't hopeful. Then of course there was our continued spying on Vegas PD regarding those shootings. The waiting was the hard part sometimes.

Chapter Nine

A few days later, my desk phone rang. "Hello?"

"Hello, Prof."

Fucking Hell. I recognized the voice. "Hi, Charles. How are you doing?"

"We need to talk. Can you get up here... say the day after tomorrow? I know you've been up here before and know where to park. You'll have a visitor pass at the desk out front."

I sighed. Charles Stevens was, to use his euphemism, a 'senior executive' in the Directorate of Intelligence at Langley. I wouldn't call him a friend, but he was probably an ally. For certain, he was the sort of guy who possessed the connections to really, *really* fuck up both my life and the company's well-being if I crossed him. That unspoken sword of Damocles meant this was not an *'invitation'* I could blow off, nor was it a bridge I could afford to burn. "What time?"

I could hear him think for a minute, and he chuckled. "I know you don't do early mornings well, so aim for ten or ten thirty. That ought to do fine."

"So, ten, the day after tomorrow."

"See you then." He hung up and I set down the phone handset. *Fuck.*

I looked over at Angel. "I gotta run to DC day after tomorrow."

She nodded. "For how long?"

I shook my head. "I don't even want to spend the goddamn night, but probably better to get there the night before. But this is one of those friendly invitations that's more of a command performance."

Angel nodded. "Am I coming with you?"

"No, unless you want to sneak off and go see your parents or something. He didn't mention the invitation covering you or Cash, and I don't want you left cooling your heels at the gate."

Angel thought about it for a minute. "I can live without dealing with Mom right now. And really, I have plenty of stuff to do here." Shit, there were boxes at the house we hadn't touched yet since the move three months ago. We'd just been so goddamned busy.

"I'll fly up commercial. Not worth getting the charter bird." We had a long-standing relationship with a locally owned Lear 60XR and a retired USAF F-16 pilot named Matt who usually flew it. I wasn't going to take a goddamned seven seat private jet for just me. I might have elevated my standard of living to a ridiculous level from my original standards, but I liked to think I had my limits.

"You do that if it will make you feel better, but I'll do the rental car and a hotel since all the business accounts are saved on my computer." Yeah, Angel fancied herself our travel agent.

*****

Maybe it was a subconscious reaction to Vegas, but I was being fucking cheap, so I went in on Southwest. I was always a little unsettled getting on one of their planes. I was pretty sure Ex-Fiancée number two hadn't retired yet, and while I hadn't talked to her in several years, not even Facebook messages, it didn't mean that I wouldn't run into her in the aisle of a 737.

My luck held in this case. The flight attendant working my section was male, which even in these later days was statistically unusual. Red beard, wisecracking sort, and built like a rugby player. Fun guy, really. We traded a few jokes. Might have even grabbed a beer afterward, but that flight had another outbound leg and I wasn't going onward to LaGuardia.

Night had fallen by the time we were on the ground. Ever since my college years when flying home from school, I have enjoyed night flights into Reagan National. First, you get to see downtown DC all lit up. Second, at least for me,

I always think of the movie version of *The Hunt for Red October* when Alec Baldwin's version of Jack Ryan was met at the end of his overnight flight by the two guys from the CIA who gave him a ride out to Langley. Now there was a bit of Hollywood bullshit involved. Really, Ryan would have gone into Dulles where all the big jets go, especially the trans-Atlantic ones, but the scenery isn't as nice going into the bigger airport further west. Nobody met me, which was fine. I wasn't expecting it.

I was traveling pretty light. The only reasons I'd checked a bag was so I could get a gun up here with me and so the one suit I brought for the meeting wouldn't be too mussed in the process. I could have gotten a loaner piece, a couple cigars, and even a free bedroom at a buddy's place over in Fairfax, but I didn't want anyone noticing I was here. I'd see him at the NRA convention in a couple months anyway.

Getting my stuff at baggage claim, I pulled the rolling suitcase into a men's room stall. The locked pistol case was inside the roller, it and a laptop bag pinning the rolled garment bag in place. I opened it and retrieved Mr. Glock, who hadn't had a lot of time off lately. I hadn't had an issue checking it in with the magazines still loaded, which saved me a few minutes getting everything ready. Loading most of forty rounds of 9mm takes a bit. Outside the stall, toilets flushed, water ran, and people talked. Meanwhile, I undid my belt, got the old Raven Phantom holster in the correct spot just behind my right hipbone. I then flushed the toilet to cover the noise of the slide as I chambered a round. No, I didn't just drop the slide — too noisy. I ran it back and forth by hand then checked it was fully in battery. I then dropped the mag, a factory fifteen rounder with a Taran Butler +3 extender I'd had for years, put in a loose one to top it off, and I was at nineteen in the gun. I didn't anticipate needing it, but you can't be too careful. I holstered it, snapped the spare mag carrier into place, closed everything up, and exited the stall.

I knew which rental car booth to go to. I gave them my name, well, one of them, and the twenty-something brunette behind the counter nodded. "Yes, sir. Your PA just called a few hours ago to check on your reservation. Your car is a premium option from our American Muscle collection, and she said you preferred Chevrolet products, so we brought a Camaro SS over from our Dulles location for you." Yeah, that was definitely Angel's work. If it had been Cash calling, there would have been a Mustang GT sitting here instead. I wouldn't have put it past her to have personally bribed the manager to do it, either. We do shit like that, and have done so for less.

She walked me out to the black Camaro. I got settled, taking a few minutes to get the seat and mirrors adjusted and the radio presets where I wanted them. Compared to my Silverado, it felt like I was dragging my ass on the pavement, and I really needed those mirrors to cover the blind spots for me. Even so, I was still shortly on my way with the V-8's roar and DC101, the rock station of my youth, on the radio. Angel and Cash spent too much of the company's money on this, but I suppose that was their call. Stopped at a red light, I texted Angel. *"Nice car."*

Buzz-buzz. "You have a hotel reservation too." I knew she had made one, but to be honest, I'd forgotten to ask her about it. It was probably in my email. The information popped up in the next text to save me the trouble of looking, and I hissed a bit. To my way of thinking, she had overspent on that as well. Why the hell was there a Ritz-Carlton way the hell out in Tyson's fucking Corner, anyway? But despite being dark early as you get in midwinter, it still was too early to hit the hotel and bed down. It wouldn't even be dinner time for another hour. I also had way too nice a car just to drive it ten miles in slow traffic and park it. Temptation crept in.

I turned left to head south down US 1, and took the Beltway on-ramp toward the Wilson Bridge and eventually Baltimore. Halfway up the ramp, the opening guitar riff of "Welcome to the Jungle" slithered out of the speakers. See, even DC101's programming director was telling me to relax and live a little. Within a minute and a half, I was across the bridge and into my native Maryland.

Driving a fifty- or sixty-thousand-dollar car 'back home', blasting the music of my youth... for a few glorious moments the stress went away and I felt better. It was sixty-four miles all the way around the Beltway, a bit of trivia I remembered from high school driver ed. I wouldn't cover more than fifty of it to get to the hotel, and I still had to eat something, *but let's see how fast I can make that fifty miles*. Rush hour was over, traffic was sparse, and some of us still out here on the counter-clockwise Outer Loop were in it for the sport.

The next song on DC101 sucked. I have never cared for the Stone Temple Pilots. I hit the next preset, and got the Boneyard on satellite. Keith was introducing... even more Gn'R. Man, you never hear "Double Talkin' Jive" on the radio, even satellite. I was impressed and hit the volume knob. Even with that banger of a song cranked up, I was still loafing along in the not-quite-left lane doing about sixty when some dickhead in a BMW blinked his headlights and went for the pass, so I smashed down the gas pedal and watched the speedometer needle leap. *Not today, motherfucker.*

*****

One lap of the Beltway turned into two. A few of us were enjoying the ride out there, I'll put it that way. Then I'd eaten too much dinner at the Brazilian steak place across from the Ritz, and I'd slept a little too well as a result. Call it a meat coma. That had me a little sluggish this morning, and it wasn't like I'd flown up here with any of my good kind of Mountain Dew. This gas station Coke just wasn't cutting it, plus I'd skipped breakfast. I was dressed way nicer than usual and was scared shitless of spilling it on myself. I didn't want to show up for... whatever this was gonna be while looking a mess.

I was still parked in the visitor lot twenty minutes early. In an effort to look like a responsible executive type, I wore a nice dark grey suit, another one of the ones Cash insisted I'd acquired while in Hong Kong. I'd brought my dark green silk 7th Gurkha Rifles tie with the little silver kukri knives woven in, since that had a good story to it. I chickened out at the last minute. It was a very good tie, but it was memorable, and I didn't want to be memorable today. I wore my dark blue Royal Scots Dragoon Guards tie instead, since that didn't look like anything in particular. I was sure they'd have me on camera anyway. Still, the only overt case of me being me was the black cowboy boots in place of dress shoes.

I was trying to sit on my nerves. If these guys wanted me dead, they probably wouldn't have invited me up to Headquarters to do it there. *Probably.* That word was gonna be doing a lot of heavy lifting today. I left the Glock and its spare mag in the rented Camaro and went on in to do the visitor check-in bullshit.

For all the alleged glamour of the CIA, ignoring the stuff like the A-12 Oxcart spy plane on display in the backyard, the bronze starred-memorial wall, or that really cool granite lobby floor inlaid with their seal that you see in a bunch of movies, you could change the door labels and sell most of this place to an insurance company. Office work is office work, for the most part. Then again, I saw what I was allowed to see. They could have the drone-strike guys, the torture chambers, an occult altar, and the disembodied head of Adolf Hitler on ice shouting orders at them through a loudspeaker and I wouldn't fuckin' know. To be honest, I wouldn't want to know. I consider myself fairly knowledgeable about our world's many manmade horrors, but even I have my limits. Getting lost thinking about that shit is not helpful when you're just trying to get through the work week.

I was ushered into Charles' office at a couple minutes before ten. He waved me to a comfortable looking chair, still engrossed in his desktop computer screen. "Glad you made it. We're running early, and you really might want to see this." A big sixty-inch flatscreen on the wall jumped to life, showing a UAV-eye view of a mansion. Looked somewhat tropical, with architecture that was fancy to the point of bad taste. Seems to be a recurring theme with some of these people, but I digress.

No sooner had I completed that thought than the screen flashed. The mansion exploded spectacularly, with none of the gasoline fireball you get in the Hollywood version of such things. A bit of black smoke and one hell of a percussive shockwave you could see in the humid air, and that was about it. The house just sort of ceased to exist. I had to chuckle grimly, both at my timing and the result. "Well, good luck with your homeowner's insurance, whoever you were," I wisecracked.

Charles laughed a little too. "As for who, that was *long list of flowery Mexican names*, known to his friends, so much as the rotten bastard had any left, as 'El Bajoon.'"

"Can't say as I know the guy." I probably should have known who he was, but they all kind of blur together after a while. Keeping details like that straight was what I paid other people to do.

"He was the Big Bass because he had kind of a weight problem and I guess nobody was willing to call him Fat Fuck. His dad had been the *Bajito*, the little bass, then his father and his father's father before him back to the 1960s when they were just growing weed in the mountains and running it north into California. Anyway, he'd arguably been in charge of a local-ish cartel down there that still existed as a subsidiary of a larger one. He was a clever fucker though."

"How so?" I figured he had made a breakthrough in body disposal or something.

Charles saw my skepticism. "He really was a smart guy. His dad sent him off to the London School of Economics, for one thing. Apparently, he had an epiphany somewhere along the line. See, he was like those people in the California or Yukon boom towns who realized that selling supplies to gold miners was easier and much more certain money than trying to mine gold themselves. He was still moving product north, but he'd gotten into cash transport southward and providing discreet banking. He used to hide the shipping containers in old barns on farms that had gone bust."

Uh-oh... I think this is where I came into the story. I tried real hard not to show the thought.

Charles kept talking, appearing lost in his own lecture. "Unfortunately for him, going on three years ago, he lost a whole lot of cash from a transshipment point in the southern US. Most of it wasn't his to lose, and that pissed a lot of people off. Apropos of nothing, I'm sure, he and whatever organization remained with him after that misfortune and the resulting violence afterward put a lot of effort into looking for that missing money. They probably would have been really unpleasant to deal with had he ever figured out who really had it."

I shrugged. "Interesting." *I wondered what rumor he thought he'd heard.* "Probably pay some bills off if you found it laying around somewhere."

"Like we have the time to go looking for lost treasure. You'd have better luck looking for that lost Confederate gold stash in north Georgia."

Funny he should mention that particular mystery. I hadn't tried my hand myself, but as I so often do, I knew a guy down there who was looking.

Charles plowed onward. "Anyway, he'd personally killed a couple DEA agents in a fairly ugly manner, and with a classified Presidential Finding from the new administration, we were finally able to get crosshairs on him and stop letting that slide any longer than we had done. We had a really tight timeline to do the job before his wife and kids got home. We do have some morals, you know." He shrugged. "Anyway, I thought you might find that interesting and want to watch if we could time it right. That's one reason why I didn't just call you. Couldn't exactly put this up on YouTube, you know."

"There's plenty of ways to share classified, even streaming video, and you know we're hooked into most of them."

"Most, but not all of them. We wouldn't send this out anyway, except to the White House. This was extremely close-hold, even with the Finding. Plus, the timing was just very opportunity-driven. Good thing you weren't your characteristic ten minutes late."

He had me there. "I see. Neat trick, though. The bomb itself though, that was no small-diameter job like the Reapers carry. That was at least a five hundred, more likely a thousand-pounder. How'd you do it?"

His face perfectly blank, he merely replied "Do what?" He clicked his mouse and the monitor clicked off. "Anyway, that was us eating dessert first. Now talk to me about Las Vegas."

I laughed a bit, mostly as a defense mechanism, while at the same time my guts started to tighten. "In what context? Restaurants? Maybe hotel advice? You want to know the best strippers at the Crazy Horse Three?"

"Yeah, you had the SHOT Show parties, the Presidential Suite, all that good stuff. You probably had a great time and got to expense all of it because you're private sector and get to spend what you like. There seemed to be a really unusual amount of gunfire out there in Vegas that week though. Let's cut to the really important part that interests me, though. Talk to me about four retired Chinese officers with forty or fifty holes in each of them, all in a Swiss-cheesed Mercedes SUV. Car was in a creek-bed gully down off the side of I-40 just west of the Arkansas state line, and yeah, with a couple AKs and a few pistols in it."

One less AK than had been in it, I snickered to myself.

Charles continued, heedless of my internal amusement. "So the ballistics on what hadn't punched out the other side of the Mercedes came back as eighty percent 147 grain FMJs, thirty caliber and twenty percent hollow copper jackets, also thirty caliber, left when the tracers burned out. So obviously 7.62mm NATO link and a whole lot of it."

"I didn't do it."

He didn't give a shit about my cursory denial. "But you know who did. You aren't the only one who can ping cell phones, Prof. Two carloads of cell phones I know are Athenaeum employees, including you, just going off a history of location tracking data were driving down that same piece of road at the time of the shooting. Well, they do appear and disappear their way across I-40. Faraday bags and airplane mode, probably."

"But you don't want to know that, Charles. Or at least not tell the Oklahoma State Police or whoever is running the case that you found that out."

Charles just stared at me in slight disappointment and sighed. "Okay, I get it. I really get it. But you aren't supposed to be whacking people on the highways, man. Not like that at least. I mean two hundred holes. What did you use, a fuckin' 240? Really? You're supposed to be a responsible adult and not be doing shit like that back here in civilization."

I did my best to stay really unexpressive. "First, it wasn't civilization, it was Oklahoma. Second, I'm failing to see how this is your problem."

"In some ways it's not, but let me provide some necessary professional development and education since Big John and Mikey are both dead now and nobody's holding your leash."

"You got me there. I'm listening." Bringing up two deceased members of Athenaeum's board was kind of a low blow, but from where he sat it was probably necessary. *First step in training a mule is getting the mule's attention.*

"I'd even feel better if James hadn't retired out of there. Saw him playing golf at the Army-Navy last week." He had a ghost of a smile as he kept busting my balls on the subject of my missing adult supervision.

"Which one? Arlington or Fairfax?" He merely leaned back in his desk chair, smirking at me. I sighed in frustration. "I get it, Charles, I really do. So please explain what you think I need to be retaught?"

"Okay, one of the really big unspoken rules between intelligence agencies is that we don't gunfight one another on each other's soil. Think of their getting shot up like it was a bad day in Baghdad as a violation of the international rules of hospitality. If intelligence agencies spent all their time killing each others' officers, no one would get any work done, so that's why we don't do it."

I nodded. "I seem to recall that explanation in a Jack Higgins or John LeCarre novel when I was younger. Now here's a question for you, since I was the one they were trying to shoot. Were they actual intelligence agency personnel? They were acting a hell of a lot more like Chinese organized crime. Them trying to kill me isn't exactly them being good guests who can't get shot at in return."

He looked up, contemplating the ceiling. "To be honest, they could have been either one. Maybe both? Maybe neither? But we know who they are. Well, or were. That took a little work since their wallets and cell phones were gone, and someone had tossed all their luggage."

I really, really tried to stay unexpressive, but this was not a happy situation.

Charles continued. "All four were formerly serving officers in the Chinese army, One colonel, two retired lieutenant colonels, one major. Two infantry officers, both with extensive special operations assignments, one guy we thought was a combat engineer, and one guy we're absolutely fucking sure was a cyber warfare specialist."

"Surprised your order of battle book on the Chinese Army goes down to the field grade officer level."

"Some of it is information we got from other people and agencies, not necessarily ours, and it's not like any of the four were the stay-at-home type. They were known above and beyond their peers."

"Even before this?"

"Remember the Chinese officers we caught in the States working as computer science grad students on various campuses about ten years back? Yeah, the lieutenant colonel cyber expert had been one of them. Was working on a PhD at Carnegie-Mellon in Pittsburgh when we figured out he was an active duty major at the time and had deported him for visa fraud. I'm surprised he got back into the country."

That made a few things about Lin's codebreaker gadget make way more sense. *Carnegie-Mellon, though... I wondered how Vivian was doing?* I shoved that thought down. We'd taken her on as a finance intern as favor to the Singapore 'family business' we'd banked with. She had a few months to kill after she'd finished her first master's degree down at Georgia Tech, but I doubted we'd see her back our way again. As she said, her family commitments had unbreakable demands on her life. Getting my concentration back, I knew I had to give up something. "Can I tell you something in absolute confidence?"

He laughed. "In this business? Not fucking likely, but try me."

I sure as shit wasn't going to tell him I knew exactly where this now-dead Mexican guy's missing money was. As I said, much of it was banked in Singapore, and you longtime readers know exactly how it got there. Instead, I had other juicy bits to give up. "Okay, I guess that will have to do. Anyway, we met these guys in Las Vegas..." I then gave him a two-minute recap of the Mercenaries' Ball, the meeting with ex-Lieutenant General Shellington of ArmEx, the shooting at the Convention Center, Lin's codebreaker auction, and the standoff in the Big Texan's parking lot with these now-dead Chinese guys who said they had bad blood with Lin's entourage and therefore with us. "So to wrap up, I close with two points. First, they did wave an AK or two at us. My guy was just quicker on the trigger. Secondly, I need that kid going forward, so I'm not giving him up as a human sacrifice. Oh, and Point 2-A, I don't know where Lin is, but we are working on who he is."

For whatever his other failings, Charles took in information and analyzed on the fly really well. God, I wished I could trust him enough to hire him in a couple more years. "Damn, I know a guy a couple hallways over who would love to hear this part, but he's out of town right now. The conflicting loyalties issue among them rings really true to me though." He really was good at this. Better than me, that's for goddamn sure. Then again, that's what I had the others for.

I continued. "I got another one for you to chew on. The Canadians, of all people, had somebody on Lin embedded in his entourage."

He shrugged and grunted. "Who?"

"If Lindsay was her real name, I'd be shocked, but a five-six blond, maybe a buck thirty-five, ten of it being a good-sized pair of bolt-ons."

"Sure she wasn't just a stripper or something?"

"She was trying to fake the role, but when push came to shove, she told me she was CSIS," I pronounced it 'see-siss,' which I was pretty sure was the insider way, "and that she was working a reciprocity deal for 'us,' by which she probably meant you guys versus the FBI. More interestingly, Lin and her both knew who

85

I was and that she'd been specifically warned about getting too close to me by her boss and her boss's boss."

"Maybe she just didn't want to run the risk of your creepy Korean girlfriend getting jealous and trying to stab her," Charles joked.

I threw my hands up in exasperation and went for a melodramatic reaction. "Why does everyone seem to think Cash is some kind of kill-crazed psychopath?"

He practically rolled his eyes at me. "You've met her, right? Come on, I'm not exactly the undercover cowboy type anymore, but you can look her in the eyes and see there is something seriously, *seriously* damaged with that girl."

I did my best to sound like an offended aristocrat. "That's a base canard. She's got some trauma in her past, but she's hardly that bad. I've met worse." At least I think I had. Maybe. I was still going to stick up for Cash under the circumstances.

"Man, I'm not kidding when I say Laurie really likes her, but if you think Cash is at all normal, I shudder to think about your taste in women."

"Quoting an ex of mine, everyone loves crazy girls. They fuck better."

Charles sighed, very visibly sick of my bullshit. "Okay, getting back on topic, talk to me about this James Lin character." I recapped what he'd told me of his background and the bits we were hoping to confirm from the yearbooks stored up at Georgetown Prep and the University of Virginia down in Charlottesville. "But what we don't have is any kind of access to Chinese military records to figure out who the fuck this guy really became when he grew up."

"And China's a bit out of my usual wheelhouse, let alone this sort of inside-baseball internal drama of theirs. Damn, why didn't somebody try recruiting this guy when he was still at UVa?"

"We talked about that. He says he's a Chinese patriot and it wouldn't have worked."

"Yeah, yeah, everyone says it's their first time right before they start taking their clothes off. A whole bunch of them still end up in bed if you pay 'em."

I had to laugh at that. "Charles, now that we're buddies again, I got a present for you down in my car."

"Oh, Christ, do I want to know?"

"It's the laptop I pulled out of the Chinese guys' SUV."

That stunned him a little. "I'm genuinely surprised you're willing to give that up."

I shrugged. "It's relatively useless to me. We can't get into it. Maybe you know someone who can. I only have a couple of Chinese linguists and whatever kind of crypto this thing speaks isn't something we have the horsepower to fuck with. I'm willing to give it up in exchange for a gentlemanly split of whatever's on it."

Charles chuckled a little. "I know a couple guys downstairs and a buddy out at NSA who could all stand a lesson in humility. Maybe they'll have problems with it too."

"I'd be just as happy if we got into it easy as falling out of bed. I prefer to keep my childhood illusions about how good those guys are."

With that, we stood and exited. Charles followed me down to the parking lot. I handed my visitor badge in at the desk on our way outside. He whistled at the black Camaro SS as we walked up to it. "Nice car."

"Yeah, it's a rental, of course, but somebody decided to treat me. It's not like I had time to drive myself up here so I was going to be renting at the airport anyway. Shit, you've seen what I usually drive." I popped the trunk and handed him the laptop bag. "There you go. All four phones, even the one with bullet holes in it. There's also an envelope in there with their driver's licenses and credit cards too. Maybe your document guys can do more with them than we can. We have too much junk sitting around in file cabinets as it is."

He considered his words for a moment. "I... genuinely owe you one. This may be really helpful."

I looked at my watch. I'd worn my pretty stainless-steel Apollo 11 commemorative Speedmaster just because I figured this was a medium-dressy occasion. "Yeah, and I got a plane home I gotta catch before long."

He jerked his thumb back toward the building. "Got time for lunch? If we weren't in such a rush, I could have gotten us the Director's dining room where the food is genuinely impressive, but even the regular cafeteria is pretty good."

I chuckled. "I appreciate it. Gotta pass, though. I gotta run around a little bit and do some back-home kind of errands before I catch my plane. I'm sure there will be a next time though." I climbed into the Camaro and cranked it, enjoying the V-8 rumble. "And I'll hold you to it on that IOU." We waved, and I made as sporty and spirited a departure of the parking lot as I dared, heading out the George Washington Parkway side of their campus because the view was nicer.

Really, my plane wasn't for a few hours, but I wanted to get a decent lunch somewhere other than the Langley cafeteria before I had to return the car and catch the flight back to Nashville. Part of me wanted to loop the Beltway and hit what I thought was the best pizza place in the world out in Wheaton, Maryland, but there just wasn't time with the potential traffic issues you get. This side of the river still had options. I was barely onto the GW Parkway southbound toward Alexandria when my phone rang. Danny Elfman's "The Little Things" told me it was the office and I didn't even look as I hit the button. It was Dave. "Hey, man."

"What's up?"

He was chuckling. "You want to make some kid's day?"

"Depends what it's gonna cost me."

"You got two grand or so actually on you?"

"You mean in cash? Actually..." I thought about it. "Yeah, I do. Why?"

Dave kept pushing. "Your plane's not for a few hours, right?"

"Yeah, but I gotta get something to eat, take the rental car back, and shit like that."

"Don't care. Move your flight if you have to. Get yourself across the Potomac and meet our research monkey over on the Maryland side over by Georgetown Prep. He says he has good news."

"Does our research monkey have a name?" I never had asked because until about ten seconds ago I hadn't seen a need to waste brain cells on it. I only have so many of those.

"Dustin."

Man, I just wanted to eat and go the fuck home. "Why am I doing this and not you? You're the one who knows him."

"Because I'm eight hundred miles away and you're twenty minutes down the road."

I couldn't argue with that, and admitted it. "Shit, you got me there, but you really want me to hit the Legion Bridge traffic this time of the day and go back up Route 355?"

Dave may be one of my oldest friends, but he still had no mercy since at this point; I was just whining like a bitch. "Call it payback for all the days straight I worked while you were fucking off in Vegas, motherfucker." It's okay, I knew it was a term of endearment. Dave had actually met my parents, and I'd met his the first time at our Benning graduation.

I relented. "Okay, give the kid my cell phone number and have him tell me where to meet him." Cursing, I hung up.

This was going to suck. Contrary to the name, Georgetown Prep had relocated north of the Beltway out in Rockville decades ago. The Pike, which was really just Wisconsin Avenue extended northward, was always a goddamn parking lot. Shit, the next chance I had to get off the Parkway was Route 123, so I just took the Chain Bridge across the Potomac instead of doubling back out to the Beltway and its American Legion Bridge. Last time any of us used that one on was the day one of our teams had killed... never mind, that's another long story. Ask me later.

Huh, I was technically in DC for a few blocks until I broke out to the northwest. My carry permit was no good here. Ridin' dirty now. *Oooopsie.* Right turn, left turn, then scooting out MacArthur Boulevard, my phone buzzed with a text, giving me a restaurant name and address right on the Pike.

"Can you drive south and meet me?"

Buzz-buzz. "I don't have a car. I'm only fifteen."

"Be there in twenty-ish."

Still on MacArthur, I jinked past another collection of intelligence community buildings by Dalecarlia Reservoir at the old Army Mapping Service site. I'd been there with Big John for a couple meetings my first year with the company. Wait, I needed a post office. Why? I couldn't just hand this kid a stack of hundreds for his work in front of God, the world, and everybody. I needed an envelope, and the nice lady in the tiny white-siding Glen Echo post office didn't care that I took one of the free flat-rate ones off her counter with a smile and a wave.

I figured I'd get on and run outward on the I-270 Spur rather than hit every red light on 355. I was only a couple miles from my sister's house, but it wasn't like I had time for family business at the moment. Maybe thinking about it is what jinxed me. Maybe the universe just decided to fuck with me again, I don't know. But while cutting cross-country through the wealthy suburbs, I didn't pay as much attention as I should have when I pulled up on the right of one of dozens of silver SUVs I'd seen prowling the Maryland suburbs in the last twenty minutes.

You fellow Eighties kids, you remember that scene in *Ferris Bueller's Day Off* when he's in the taxi cab, looks at the taxi cab next to him, and is face to face with his dad who didn't know he was cutting school that day? I looked to my left, and my niece was staring at me. Great. My covert wandering of suburban Maryland had just gotten made courtesy of an eight-year-old. Fortunately, the light picked that second to turn green, and I mashed the Camaro's gas pedal like I was street-racing for pink slips. My sister's GMC whatever the fuck it was made the left, and I was heading away cleanly.

Thirty seconds later, my phone rang. My personal one, not my work number, and it was my sister. The stereo was thumping out Metallica, so I muted it and cheerfully answered "Hey!"

She got right to the point. "Where are you right now?"

"I should tell you Hong Kong or Kuwait City to mess with you, but to be honest, I'm in Nashville doing work stuff like usual."

"That was what I thought, but Ellie was absolutely convinced that she just saw Uncle *real name* next to us in a black Camaro that was playing its stereo too loud at the traffic light on River Road."

"Sorry to disappoint her, but no, it wasn't me. How's her lightsaber holding up?"

"She loves it, but those rechargeable batteries don't last anywhere near as well as the ones in her old saber did."

"Well, her old one just had the light, that new one has more LEDs plus the sound system to power. Tell her you gotta give it to get it when it comes to electrical stuff."

In the background, Ellie yelled "HI, UNCLE *REAL NAME*!!!!" so loudly she probably damaged my sister's hearing.

Mollified, my sister said "Hey, I'm going to let you go. We're almost to the soccer field."

"Love ya. Catch you later." I hung up. *Man, it's always the little shit that almost gets you.*

I made it to the restaurant about fifteen minutes later to meet Dustin. Finding him was easy. He was the only one in there dressed to the school's code in a blue blazer, khakis, and a tie. He was a little blond kid, built like a lightweight wrestler, and already had a plate. He was chopsticking away like he hadn't eaten in his entire life. Well, he was a growing boy. They all are at that age.

"You Dustin?"

He put on the worst fake London Cockney accent I have ever heard even with all the Guy Ritchie movie fans I know, and he replied "Aye. You the guvna on this li-ul capah?"

"You're too young to be watching British gangster movies. Why aren't you in class?"

The kid didn't back off. "Don't worry about it. I'm on lunch."

"Okay, good. I don't know your dad, Dave does, but I still don't need a two-star general mad at me for contributing to his kid's delinquency, especially for what tuition costs there."

"Sir, relax, get a plate, and let me show you what I found. I don't have class for another hour and it's a short bus ride back."

"Grab an Uber if you want. I'll cover it." I quickly hit the buffet line, loaded up, and sat back down.

He wiped his hands after tossing down another dozen shrimp. "Okay, so I got into the yearbooks. I figured I might have to cover a twenty-year window. Uncle Dave estimated his age at forty. We then assumed he could really be anything from thirty to fifty because, well, Chinese. So, I started checking the lacrosse team photos first looking for any Asian kids at all, because to be honest we don't have that many of them even now. That gave me a short list of names, then —"

I was eating quickly as I listened. Dustin had to get back to class and I was still hoping to make my plane and get home tonight. Don't get me wrong, I'm a historian at heart and love a good systemic research story, but we were pressed for time. "Dude, cut to the good part. I can congratulate you on your clever methodology later. Do we have his ass or not?"

Dustin handed me a color printout, like he'd physically put the yearbook on the copier and hit the button. A familiar face, much younger, gazed back at me. "I give you Wu Xian Lin, born 1986, graduated with the Georgetown Prep Class of '04. He was a three-year letterman on the lacrosse team, and two on baseball. Anyway, that makes him what, thirty-nine now?"

I sat and nodded silently, slightly overwhelmed. *I'll be damned. That asshole did tell the truth.*

Dustin kept talking. "I e-mailed Uncle Dave the raw high-rez scans of everything on him I could find in his years." He picked up his chopsticks and got back to work.

"You're pretty fast with those for a white kid."

He switched his fake accent to Hollywood Japanese. "Rots of practice, *gai-jin*."

"Fuckin' weeb."

He let the meme-tier insult pass. "Now can I ask what this was about?"

I chewed on some rather good lobster and broccoli, and told him the truth. "You can *ask* all you want. Dave tells me you want to get into this line of work one day. Learn to live with the fact that you're never going to know everything that's going on. I sure as shit don't."

He looked somewhat crestfallen. "I already know I can't go in the military like Dad and all his friends. Three screws and a steel plate in my ankle. Broke it dirt-biking last summer. Missed sophomore year soccer season and wrestling season didn't go that great. So going to the civilian side in intel is my new plan. So, when Uncle Dave gave me this research mission looking for a Chinese guy? It was pretty obvious what I was doing —"

"Kid, look, you did a good job, but it's gonna be a long road to get you where you think you want to go. But, I will throw you a bone and tell you that nobody else could have done for us what you just did. With that in mind..." I delicately kicked him under the table and passed him the envelope. "Don't open it here, goddamn it, or you'll get mugged on the bus."

He tucked it inside his school blazer. "I wasn't born yesterday, sir."

I waved my fork at him, a grilled oyster stuck on its tines. "Good work, Dustin. Stick that somewhere for car shopping or something." Dave had promised him two, but I'd given him four grand of the five I had on me. Call me a softie, but I liked his attitude. Maybe we really could use him when he grew up some.

Dustin looked at his phone. "Oh, shit, I gotta grab the bus."

"You want an Uber like I said?"

He shook his head. "Bus is less conspicuous."

"Get out of here then. I got the check."

"Thanks." He jumped up and hustled out.

I shook my head as I went back to the buffet for more. I might have been that young once, but I'd be damned if I remembered it all that clearly.

Chapter Ten

C ash picked me up at Nashville Airport in her Mustang. "I had to knock the Camaro feel off of you, sir. That's why I came and not Angel."

"Really? Car rivalry made you drive all the way down here?"

She laughed. "No, not really. She's home in the kitchen making a batch of something. Soup dumplings, probably. Looked like mass production. She's got two of the guard crew helping fold and crimp them."

"Either way, it's hard being a Ford girl in a Chevy family, isn't it?"

"I have to do something to stand out besides look hot and be really good at math." As if to underline her point, she shifted and wiggled a bit in her seat. Luckily for her, it was a freakishly warm evening after several weeks of worse-than-usual cold. She'd dressed down a bit, but her top was just a little too tight and her skirt just a little too short to look innocent. Nashville people would recognize the bachelorette party look. "The kitchen at home is a mess, like I said. Shall we grab dinner out instead?"

*****

I was awake before the alarm clock again. From the foot of the bed, down in the dark, there was an angry kitty noise, the *MEOW!* that says "You, human monkey, you have the ability to open cans and feed me. Why are you not doing it?"

I slapped at the bedside lamp. I had modified long ago it so it was a 'touch anywhere' sort. In its dim light, I squinted at the cat while fumbling for my glasses. There were four cats in the house, I think. No, five, my four plus Cash's orange chonker, Rockefeller, who was staying here. Her? Her, maybe? Her face was almost all black and she was half the size of my two male black and whites. Everyone else was an orange or a gray. This one was definitely not any of my cats. "Who the hell are you and how did you get in here?" I asked the cat.

The only answer was more loud and incoherent meowing. Somebody was hungry and annoyed. The commotion was enough to wake Angel up, if not Cash. She looked over at me. "What's going on?" she fuzzily mumbled. I merely pointed at the feline interloper. Angel perked up a bit and fairly squealed in delight. "BABY!" She scooped up the adolescent kitty, hugged it like a plushie, and was asleep again by the time her head hit the pillow.

The cat, now wrapped up, meowed again, glaring at me like this was entirely my fault. Her expression said 'I was just here for the food and now I'm a hostage. Thanks, asshole. I'm definitely shitting in your shoes later.'

I sighed and rolled over, feeling it in my back. I debated trying to sleep that last forty-five minutes or so, but thinking about it, I had to piss. I got up, wandered into the bathroom, did my necessary drainage, but then went downstairs to bullshit with the security detail in their ready room. Though I was unconvinced that I needed a full fire team out here at the house 24/7, it was kind of nice having people around to talk to when I couldn't sleep. Otherwise, my insomnia fueled my addictive patterns of Internet usage that went back thirty-plus years.

Hawkins' team had clocked back around on the rotation and were the ones working tonight. He greeted me as I came into their control room. "Hey, boss. How they hangin'?"

"One below the other, same as always."

"Ain't we all," opined McIntyre, Hawk's second. Pretty sure he was also an ex-Bastogne Brigade kid. It seemed to be a function of the friends and friends-of-friends recruiting process. As the teams split and grew into new teams, alumni of the same units clumped up based on who knew who. It was like the NHL expansion draft, only with guns.

Time to yank their chain a bit. "Anyway, we had an intruder upstairs."

In mild panic, they suddenly looked at me in all seriousness. "It's okay, it was a cat."

"A cat?"

I chuckled. "Seriously. There's a cat in the master bedroom that isn't one of ours. But Angel's got a good hold of it since she thought it needed snuggles, so it's not getting away easily."

One of Hawkins' new guys shrugged. I didn't remember this one's name yet. "Little black and white girl, mostly black?"

"Yeah."

He continued. "It was in the garage about four hours ago. I thought it was escaping, not trying to infiltrate, so I grabbed her. I just gave her a quick bath in the laundry room sink since she was dirty and then dropped her off upstairs."

I had to laugh a little. "You guessed wrong, but no harm done."

Hawkins shrugged. "We don't have ID books on the cats, bossman."

At some point I'd reach out to the neighbors to see if anyone was missing her. Otherwise, it was just Nature's mysterious Cat Distribution System at work. I'd gotten quite a few that way over the years.

Chapter Eleven

C oming into the office, Ruiz's crew was working the shack up front, and Johnston was back from his extra vacation. I looped around to its back door, well, its only door, and had a good chuckle. "Looks like you got some sun, kid. Have a good time?"

Johnston sighed happily. "Too good a time. You can get used to living like that. And the e-girls and online thots of the world are all in mourning, as I am officially off the market."

"What, you pop the question while you were down there?"

He grinned. "Yeah. I'd bought the ring in Vegas. Lots of secondhand jewelry in that town and with what I'm making in this job and some winnings from the trip, it wasn't like I financed it."

"Nice. Well, congratulations. Let us all know what you want to do about the wedding." We'd make a shitty venue for it, but I've heard of weirder things.

"Will do, boss."

*****

Meanwhile, security headaches continued, mostly with everyone else being way more obsessive about it than I was. I've had enough close calls over the decade that they don't bother me so much anymore. When it's my day to go, it'll be my day, and in my experience not much changes that.

The first of the headaches was, as I mentioned, putting more security crews together. We didn't call those four-man elements 'fire teams' since they didn't roll around with 249s and grenade launchers. Not that I'd spend company money on 249s anyway. That gun had a couple major design flaws in my thirty years around them, and they wore out too easily.

I ran into Nichols on my way in the next morning. The muscled-up black guy had left a scout platoon in the 82nd Airborne as a staff sergeant rather than go be a drill sergeant, but hadn't been doing too well in civilian life. We'd met him outside Little Rock, Arkansas while we were on the way to Vegas. His truck was in the shop for a new transmission and he was working security at a particularly raucous Waffle House for pocket money. Me, there's a lot of things I do not do well and I'll admit it, but I can spot, poach, and hoard talent with the best of them. I'd waved a job under his nose. Hearing the money involved, he only asked if, "it smelled like hash browns." On a promise it did not, he'd jumped at the chance.

"Hey, boss!" Nichols certainly looked happier away from the pervasive smell of griddle grease. He'd just come up from downstairs, which surprised me. We generally kept the topside folks separate from those who worked below. But he had the correct badge for downstairs, which meant Dave had signed off on it while I was gone. Obviously, he saw something in Nichols too.

We shook hands. "You get settled in okay?"

He nodded. "Yeah. Dave was mostly 173rd and Regiment, but we still knew some of the same people and so he helped me find temp quarters and all that good shit." Holding up his badge, he continued. "Personnel onboarding here is about the easiest thing I've ever seen." He waved around the bay and back toward the blast door and the elevator that went down under the mountain. "Now this place is fuckin' amazing. I didn't know places like this really existed outside the movies or *GI Joe* comic books."

I got to put on my historical lecturing hat, which I always enjoyed doing. "It's old. Like not long after WWII kind of old. Back in the days when nukes were only as accurate as a human bombardier could make them drop out of an airplane, places like this were way more popular. We know very little about it. Near as I can tell, someone started it then quit when they decided it was surplus to the changing needs of the Missile Age, and then ended up changing hands a few times. And a lot of the work has been done in the eight years since I've worked here, and a lot of it we did ourselves. You gotta be picky about who you bring in to help on a place like this."

"The plumbing looks like the high school in *Back to the Future*." Well, he wasn't wrong.

"Only on the first three floors. Below that? Almost nothing is complete. But that old stuff will probably outlast all of us, tilework and all. Anyway, you busy?" Really, I wanted to sit down and shoot the shit with him to see how he was adapting.

"Actually, yeah. We got a list of names from the team leaders and so Jake and I are about to have range tryouts for about another dozen prospective hires in half an hour. The armorer, that white dude who used to be in the Marines, he ran a four-wheeler full of guns down there about twenty minutes ago. Spencer, I think his name was?"

"Sawyer. Close, but not quite." Hiring Sawyer had been a Christmas present from Angel. She thought me hiding in the arms room was a poor use of my time when I should be doing management stuff. He'd done a hitch in the infantry, then changed MOSs to small arms repair. She never had explained how she found him, and to be honest, I hadn't taken the time to ask.

Jake picked that moment to come up from downstairs. He merely waved as Nichols happily continued. "I also want to run some training days for the downstairs personnel who wanted to sharpen up. The desk types don't get to shoot that often, and I thought that might make a nice break in their routine."

"Well, it's not like we have to share the range with anyone else and schedule for it. I'll try to make it down in a couple hours. I need the trigger time myself."
*****

Jimmy decided we needed a genuine professional to look at the security arrangements for key personnel. He called a buddy of his from twenty years back in the dark side of the SEALs. Willie had left Virginia Beach since then and was now on VIP protection details for the Secret Service. He came down as a favor, and out of deference to the fact he was probably being watched by the security and counterintelligence types, I made a mental note to give him any travel money in straight cash. Mysterious bank transfers to people who guard the nation's most important people make their bosses real nervous.

Willie was tall for a SEAL. He had that college swim-team look, and looked extra pale like he hadn't been getting a lot of daylight lately. He said he'd do some poking around, then meet me for a late lunch tomorrow at that Italian place on Fort Campbell Boulevard so he could give me an informal rollup.

When the time came, Cash was busy in her office, so I had Angel with me for taking notes. He was visibly charmed with her, so I let him admire the scenery for a minute before I asked him "So you've looked around, looked at the house, looked around the office, what do you think?"

He paused for a minute as the waiter ran our salads out, and he got a big bite of Caesar first. "Look, man, I'll call this one straight since Jimmy says you're a no-bullshit kind of a guy. You're pathetically easy to kill if someone serious wants to take a run at you."

I wasn't expecting that. "Armored vehicles, a security team at the house..."

He was too polite to sneer, but the look on his face was clear. "Come on, you were on the raid side of the Army for a while. What's the easiest time to hit someone? In transit. You're still driving yourself around. All three of you are usually in one vehicle. You can get hit between here and there way too easily. No matter how many ways you want to pick to get from home to the office, you only have one driveway into the house and one driveway into the office. That makes you vulnerable at one end of the trip or another since that's a known point you have to pass."

"That's depressing." The calamari came and I started stress-eating my emotions. Angel waved at the waiter, pointed at the platter, and held up two fingers to get us more.

Willie wasn't backing off. "Hell, they can get you most places on your routes, even in the grocery store."

I confess, my hackles were up and it got me defensive. "I like grocery shopping. I like cooking at home. I still try to have something resembling a normal life when I can."

He shook his head at me in disapproval. "Dude, you could do that when no one knew who you were. You don't have anonymity as a shield anymore. Sure, the locals don't know who you are, or you're just one more old-man vet in a town fuckin' full of them, but anyone putting serious effort to track you down and kill you knows they can follow you and tag you in the parking lot. They're gonna wait until your hands are full pushing your buggy in the Kroger parking lot and shoot you before you even get your groceries into the car."

"That's kind of conspicuous now, innit?" I shaded a little bit of Guy Ritchie movie or *Peaky Blinders* into my voice just for my own amusement. I blamed Dustin up in Maryland for putting that idea in my head a couple weeks ago.

Not waiting for the next two platters to show up, he and Angel both reached over and dug into the calamari I admit I was kind of hogging. "Look, with the kind of people you apparently piss off for a living, some of them might not want to be subtle. They might want to make a public example out of your ass."

Angel popped down a bite, then loyally answered "They'd still have to get past me." Queen piece, indeed. No matter what, I had to have someone in life I could trust the way I did her. Murderous devotion is a beautiful thing. I trusted Jake and the fire teams to be loyal to their salt if pushing came to shoving, but... she was my queen.

Willie just looked at her and shrugged before hitting her with the honesty we were paying him for. "You're good, but you're not that good. I know how hard we gotta work at this on the Detail, and it's not your full-time job so it's just not humanly possible for you to be at that level. Plus, there's a whole lot of us on the job running a couple layers plus the local support we get, and there's just one of you. Whoever wants to make a move on your boss here, they probably ain't going to come solo and they'll just pop you at the same time. Keep that in mind." He turned his attention to the food as the next two platters came out. "This is damn good calamari for this far inland."

"Guy who runs the place used to manage a restaurant in Little Italy in NYC. Moved out here to get out of the City and cut his overhead. I imagine he still knows a supplier or two for the good stuff."

"Worth it, and cheaper than the City. Anyway, your grocery shopping is hardly your only weakness, but it's a conspicuous one. Your house isn't as hard as you think. You don't own a 360-degree perimeter around your house, so you have vulnerabilities around you. Yeah, you have a crew at the house, and the IR and seismics are a nice touch, so that's good. Bad side, you could probably still get sniped off your balcony from your back woods if they beat your sensors. Or grab your neighbors' places and snipe from one of them. And unless you wire up the woods across the street from you that you don't own, it's even easier for a sniper to hide over there without tripping any of your alarms or fighting your neighbors. You do have a bunch of scary backwoods combat vet types out there around you though. No wonder you like it."

We kept talking as the entrees came out. We went back and forth as we ate, and he could see I was struggling with the idea of changing my life even more than I already had. "Look, I can tell you're a nice normal guy who still thinks he can live like he used to. You can't. I've been doing VIP security since my element was detailed off to keep the President of Afghanistan from getting killed. We did that in rotations for a while before the State Department made it a contractor gig."

"You get out in time to cash in on that?"

He grinned. "Yeah, it gave me something to do while my Secret Service application went through the machinery. Took most of a year to get through the hiring pipeline, and that was with my clearances already done by DOD."

"Shit, I knew a guy who went FBI and it took him most of two to get on."

Willie fairly sneered at that. "I'd rather get fucked to death working overtime on the graveyard shift at a glory hole than go in the FBI."

Angel just laughed. "Inter-agency rivalry is real, huh?"

"Nah, I'm too old and too sensible for that. I'm looking at it practically. I am not putting up with the Fed bullshit just for my first assignment out of their academy to be sitting on my ass in Boise, Idaho waiting for some asshole to rob a bank or to have someone come up in the system getting busted for kiddie porn. You know how many single chicks are working in DC?"

"Lots," Angel piped up. Remember, it was originally her hometown too.

"Yeah, and as my marriage didn't survive my time in the Navy, my gym is full of hot late-twentysomethings with degrees in poli sci or public relations or some other skill for the local industry, which is government. They're making jack shit out of grad school as interns on Capitol Hill or the think-tanks while they're trying to get a nice GS-13 job somewhere, oh, and also hook a guy who makes more money."

"You ain't making that much more than them."

"Base pay? True, but then we absolutely kill it on night differential, overtime, and travel money. So, again, I make more than them, more than enough so I can pop for a nice dinner or two, but I'm not trying to get remarried either. Once was enough for me, man." That casual approach worked for some people. Never quite did for me. He looked at his watch, a Sangin. I was impressed. "Anyway, I gotta get out of here. I got to get down the road and catch a plane home. I'm on shift tomorrow night."

I stood and we shook. "Appreciate the help."

Willie nodded, and happily took a hug from Angel. "Look, I'll send you a more formal roll-up and I can design the patches for some of your holes, but a lot of it is gonna be lifestyle changes for you, and I don't know you well enough to realistically assess your threat profile. I've known Jimmy since he got back from Somalia and I know when that motherfucker's not telling me shit."

I handed him one of the Archive Associates business cards. "Secrets are kind of our thing. Stay in touch, lemme know when you come up on retiring. Even if you want to stay around DC, we have interesting piecework for friends."

*****

My own security issues were a side show compared to all the other irons we had in the fire. Europe, the Pacific, the Middle East, plus the Vegas shootings. We were trying to look over the shoulders of other people who were trying to solve mysteries, since the answers affected us. We needed to know who'd shot up the Convention Center, we needed to know who was in that parking lot, and we were completely screwed knowing either unless someone somewhere else got lucky. At the same time, we needed the Oklahoma state cops to not get lucky and have brilliant ideas on solving the shooting that could rightfully be pinned on us.

I was as stressed as anyone, and I was trying to put some of the stress downrange one afternoon when my antique bullseye 1911, the 1918 Colt, made an embarrassing *click*ing noise instead of its next *BANG*. Checking, the one hundred and seven year old hammer was flopping loose. Something had finally sheared off inside, one part or another finally dying of old age. Well, fuck. I didn't have time to pull it apart and fix it, let alone doing all the hand-fitting work involved in getting the trigger back to where it had been. I'd have to call Pat Sleem down outside what might be Fort Benning again, or maybe Tori George up in Indiana. It would just be a matter of who wasn't busy. Meanwhile I had other pistols to shoot. Believe me, I had plenty.

Chapter Twelve

T hings went on for a few weeks, and except for the ongoing annoyance of not finding Lin's trail, it wasn't too bad a time since our other work was going well. Surprising me, I got an old-fashioned paper letter from Shellington at ArmEx detailing their efforts at poking into the separate-but-maybe-related deaths of his guys Eicher and Castleman that had precipitated our little meeting in Las Vegas where so much of this shit had gone off the rails. I didn't want to reciprocally tip our hand for what we'd developed on Castleman's murder though. I didn't trust Shellington or anyone else at ArmEx that much.

I did call him back to thank him for what they had on Eicher, which wasn't much. It seems the coroner had found what 'looked like' a self-inflicted gunshot wound from before the fire ruined the scene. What started the fire was still something of a mystery. Was it the suicide of a troubled, crippled vet, or was it someone tidying up loose ends just as Eicher had apparently been the cleanup shooter in New York? Who the hell knew? We'd figure it out someday, well, maybe. Quoting Wayne Gretzky, we were going where the puck was going, not where it had been. The past usually unfolds in enough time.

The biggest problem was going on here at home. We had made some improvements to the Hole's air delivery over the years. UV sterilization, HEPA filters, a slight overpressure... we'd gotten paranoid in the early days of COVID when the world locked down and the initial reports made it out to be deadlier than it was. Our other issues since had made us somewhat militant on the subject of being able to breathe safely down there.

But none of us lived there full time, not even Cash. She had put in enough effort getting my house built that she was... *a much more frequent guest,* to put it discreetly. That meant we were always spending time out and about, getting exposed to whatever was making the rest of the world sniffle and sneeze. This time, the late winter into early spring flu season was kicking the region's ass. It was one of those years where what became the dominant strain wasn't in the best-guess cocktail mixture of that year's flu shot, and now everyone was passing it around. We had roster holes in every shift. The reduced manning made the old military 'I'm okay, I can gut through without calling out' mentality kick in for everyone who was still up on their feet and moving around. Unfortunately, that basically kept them in the office sneezing on each other while still trying to work productively.

As you the reader have noticed from him dealing with gunshot wounds in Vegas, Jimmy was the closest thing we had to a full-time medical expert. I had to call him since he was also home, busily tending to his sick wife and their three sick kids. He'd started out as a Navy corpsman to the Marines, and then been a medic in the SEALs. That meant in addition to all the SEAL shit like underwater demolition, he'd been to most of the same courses as the fabled Army Special Forces medics. After getting out of the Navy a second time and a few career detours, he had been working for an air ambulance outfit as a trauma-specialist flight medic when I finally pulled my old buddy in.

He cut me off real quick when I started asking questions. "I have been thinking about this for a minute. Short term, I'll set up upstairs in the garage. Better ventilation. Long term, what we need is to use that dead space at the front of the fourth floor where somebody probably was going to put in office space decades back, and then put in a two or three cubicle miniature urgent care. That way our people can get seen and treated at work, and we cut costs to outside providers. Cool idea. Okay, sure, I can do it. Can I do it great? No. I specialize in car crashes, bullet holes, and the occasional really messy industrial or construction accident. This problem doesn't involve bleeding."

I snorted derisively. "Yet, you mean."

Jimmy brushed it off. "One crisis at a time, man. I can plan for that later. Right now, you need somebody with bedside manner to take temps, shoot IVs if needed, and sling OTC medications. Call around, hire a couple civilian RNs, preferably ex-military ones because eventually they're going to be downstairs and legally they're gonna need clearances." As we'd handwaved Morgan's security clearance for years, there were ways around that, but I didn't interrupt.

Jimmy continued. "I'll just help, well, need help, on setting up the clinic space since if it ever comes to us managing battle casualties in-house, that's my lane. Hell, if we get a licensed NP or PA, we can do some prescriptions in-house and keep an inventory of some. Not worth doing our own lab though. We can set up a subscription to one of the central ones in Nashville like Path —" Then I heard one of his kids start puking in the background. "Yeah, gotta go." He hung up.

Okay, great. We now had a plan. But since my probably mutant immune system was doing its job and keeping me okay, I was doubling on night shifts in Intel for Kara, who was also home puking her guts out. Cash, while kinda sick herself, was still playing the market at about two-thirds speed. She was also trying to cover day shifts in Intel for Dave. He was missing all this fun since he was in London and points east of there meeting more of our European friends.

As I have noted, Dave is the one with the foreign language skills and the tasteful Brooks Brothers wardrobe, so he handles way more of that than I do. He was maintaining our relationships with Mikey's surviving networks across the continent. He also had a long list of his own professional contacts among the special operations alumni of a dozen European militaries from his fifteen-plus war years, mostly in Afghanistan. Those NATO social circles intersected at multiple points, so he had that covered. For me, foreign chess games could wait. The immediate crisis was driving the bus. I turned to Angel and told her "Dear, find us a couple nurses to hire." She merely threw up her hands in annoyance.

Eventually Angel and Cash went home for the night. Somebody besides the security detail there had to look after the house. Me, I was too keyed up to sleep, so I went into Intel. The night shift crew had some different screens up, including some sports channels. Weird sports channels. Yeah, the weird stuff that caters to the two in the morning, living-on-vampire-hours crowd of uppers-addled gambling addicts. Bikini ping-pong. Florida lawnmower racing. Wheelchair boxing from Thailand, you know, that kind of weird. Yeah, wheelchair boxing. I swear to God I didn't make that up. Look it up if you don't believe me. Eventually I got bored of shooting the shit in there, and I went down to Cash's old room and slept in there for a couple hours since it was easier on my back than the office sofa.

The next day, I went upstairs into the parking lot around 0800 to meet Angel when she pulled up in her Camaro. We hugged, then I noticed she was alone. "Where's Cash?"

She shook her head. "Home puking."

I sighed. "Wonderful. Hope she doesn't get the security detail sick." We'd swapped some bodily fluids recently, enough that I was worried I'd get it. My eyes wandered around as I thought for a minute, then I noticed there was a different car in the usual mix. It was a familiar gray Honda, and I recognized the various stickers. I then turned back to Angel. "What's River's car doing here?"

"She's the first nurse I hired, sir."

I sighed. Twice. "And this happened how?"

"Because I don't know a goddamn thing about hiring nurses, babe, so after I talked to Jimmy yesterday looking for details and not getting too many, I called her for help. She asked what it was paying, I told her, and she volunteered for the job and said she could be here this morning. I can then leverage her to get the rest of the hiring done and help Jimmy get the clinic setup done since unlike me, she knows what she's doing."

At one level this made sense. River Lafitte was a longtime friend of ours, a bubbly, *extremely* extroverted fortyish blonde who was what happened when

109

the Cajun French wandered far enough north to intermarry with the remnants of the Cherokee. She'd started out as a cop in Louisiana. Getting her cruiser rammed by a drunk driver outside Baton Rouge hurt her just badly enough that she'd quit that and gone to nursing school on the vocational rehab money. She eventually drifted to Nashville. She was an outstanding nurse. She had a mind like an encyclopedia, she was deeply empathic... it was one of the reasons she burned out then changed specialties every few years. But on another level, this was a hell of a violation of the personal rule I had about 'keeping our civilian friends away from our work stuff.' I wasn't one hundred percent sure how I felt about that.

River was still in her car playing on her phone while waiting on Angel to show up. Angel hadn't told her I was there and had been working all night. She bounced out of her car when she saw us, and the hugs were ferocious. "Hey, babes! How are you two?" She was *way* too perky for this hour of the morning, but it was just the way she was.

I shrugged. "Been up all night covering for sick people. She's," and I pointed at Angel, "just getting here."

She turned toward me with an instantly cold stare. "And when are you going to be sleeping?"

I snorted. "We're shorthanded. It's going to be some extra work for all of us who are still on our feet."

River shook her head. "No wonder y'all are sick. We gotta do some wellness classes or something. People can't abuse themselves like they're twenty years old anymore." She then looked at the can of Dew in my off hand. "And we definitely need to watch your consumption on that." She and Angel nodded in unison. *Well, this was going to be a joy. Need to draw some blood? Would you like to do my colonoscopy while you're here?*

We got her a visitor pass from the guard shack and led her into the garage bay. Five minutes later she was pacing out her temporary clinic layout, counting electrical outlets, and writing notes to herself. I left Angel with her to keep her out of trouble. River didn't know what was going on downstairs here. To be honest, River wouldn't care. River now had a medical management project to happily hyper-fixate on and I had probably just doubled her take-home pay, so if I had to simply tell her she was getting paid to not ask questions, she would roll with it. The clinical setup issues were mostly for her and Jimmy to fuck with.

I was back downstairs working at my desk when Angel came in with a large steaming bowl. She set it down and handed me a spoon. Her *won ton* soup tends to be amazing. I looked at the dozen dumplings floating in the broth. "Thanks, dear. Yours?" Her dumpling recipe was a closely guarded secret even from me, until I finally spent a long Saturday in the kitchen at the old house helping her make them. She'd tell you how she does them, but then she'd most likely kill you. Dead men do not give up the secret ingredients.

Angel shook her head. "I ran a big batch of them while you were gone in DC, but with everyone being sick. I'm out already. These are store-bought from a place down off Nolensville Road, but they're still a lot better than the ones at that buffet place you insist on eating at."

She had a point there. Just because their Mongolian pork was excellent and I was seriously addicted to their salt and pepper shrimp didn't mean everything on the steam tables was ideal. The soup dumplings were at least good enough, in my opinion. Angel disagreed. She'd actually talked about buying it and getting a couple of her relatives to move down and manage it for us.

Cash naturally thought the idea of owning a restaurant through a shell company was an excellent idea. She saw the Fort Campbell Boulevard lunch rush as yet another excellent opportunity to launder money. I sighed at the thought. We were all going to end up in jail someday if we 'delved too greedily and too deep.' Restraint was not exactly Cash's strong point. And I'd rather deal with an actual Balrog than have the IRS wrist-deep in our shit looking for our secrets.

"Where's River?" Meanwhile I figured I could sneak down to Cash's old room and get a nap after this. I wasn't sure if I was technically on shift right now or not.

"My having fed them first, she's got one of the Suburbans, and a guard shack guy to do the heavy lifting, they're picking up the first set of stuff she ordered at some medical supply warehouse down in Nashville. Jimmy sounds like he's setting up for battle casualties as much as he is flu patients."

I shrugged. "World being what it is, that might not be a bad idea."

The next day, Jimmy surprised me by walking into the office. "I got us an actual doctor, too."

"Where'd you find him? And nice to see you, by the way. Family doing okay?"

He nodded. "They're fine. At least on the downhill slope of it. Me, I just needed to get out of the house to get more Gatorade if nothing else. Wife's got it handled for a while." He sat down and leaned back. "As for Mickey? Found him on the frogman grapevine. We were platoon medics together at Team Three back after Somalia. He got sick of swimming for practice and rucking in the mountains for work. Tears your knees up, you know. So he got out after another Afghanistan trip, finished college on the GI Bill, and went to med school. The Army picked up his tuition for that in exchange for a commission."

"Never went back for his long tab?" The club of guys who are dual-qualified as SEALs and Army Special Forces is really, really small, but it does exist.

"Nah. Actual MDs can't jump career fields like that since you still owe the DOD for paying your med school bill. They want to keep a cadaeucus on you, not let you get the crossed arrows on. Either way, he still spent a lot of time deployed in Iraq and Afghan working for a couple different SF groups, and then he finished up his thirty teaching at the schoolhouse. Anyway, he finally just retired, bird colonel, but he can't afford to retire for real with three kids coming up on college. At the same time, he really doesn't want to do three or four overnights a week working an ER someplace or running a doc in a box clinic."

I knew enough doctors to appreciate the difficulties in a career change. Regardless of his military background, he'd be starting from scratch in civilian practice. "I could see that. ERs especially. That's a game for young people who can take the hours."

"Yeah, and little kids are just germ factories, man. You get sick a lot working there no matter what you do. Same reason elementary school teachers either have really good immune systems or they don't make it either." He wasn't kidding. I knew a chick up by Philly who was living proof of that one. She needed a career change at the rate she was going. A dozen different sinus infections a year from her petri dish of a classroom was not a good thing for her.

"You talk out his price yet? Sounds like a guy we're going to want around."

Jimmy shrugged. "Probably a little under 300K a year for tax reasons, plus some stiff bonuses, but what you're going to save in the company's medical bills with running stuff in-house? Money well spent. Totally worth it." Another buddy of mine down by Atlanta had told me the same thing two years ago. I'd tried convincing him to run it for me, but he just didn't want to trade Atlanta for Nashville. He had too many friends and too much of a social calendar down there to walk away from, and I had to respect that. Not everyone is a deranged obsessive with no social life, and the world is probably better off that way.

Jimmy stuck around that afternoon to help with the first wave of clinic setup, and told me his buddy would be there the next day. Then the SUV-load of supplies showed up and within half an hour River and Jimmy were shooting IVs like an assembly line. Anti-nausea meds and vitamin boosters shot into a thousand milliliter bag of saline ripped right into a vein will perk most people right up. Most of us needed it. Even Gatorade or DripDrop mix only gets you so far. Then we cranked up the air handling fans and set up a few more UV lights to try decontaminating the downstairs. We'd be okay before long.

Chapter Thirteen

"Consistent with the logic of both markets and war, competition in the market for force escalates until one market actor emerges victorious with the monopoly of force, eliminating all rivals."

~Sean McFate, in "The Modern Day Mercenary,"

Yay, Mondays. Doc Mickey, our new 'Frogman M.D.,' had just left my office. It had been a productive meeting where we agreed on a few things, including the fact that I was a more than a few years overdue on an in-depth physical. He wanted to do that himself because he decided he didn't trust me not to wallpaper over anything. He'd already insisted on checking my blood pressure right there at my desk. Gee, it was like he'd been talking to Jimmy, or maybe River.

I bounced down the stairs into IT for a minute to find Petey. Addy, Johnston's now-fiancée, was pulling cables for something or another, and I went over to her. "I never did congratulate you on either the knife work or the engagement."

She shrugged. "We're on opposite shifts, mostly, so I know I'm hard to catch."

"I had no idea Johnston had caught you."

That got a laugh. "And I wasn't expecting him to pop the question down in Florida. And thank you for that extra vacation, by the way."

I waved it off. "Morgan's idea, not mine."

"For which you still paid, and that place could not have been cheap."

"Not your problem to worry about what it cost. The important things are you're both healthy and you had a good time."

Addy shuddered. "Healthy now, you mean. Christ, I was out for two weeks when the flu was kicking everyone's asses. Thought I was gonna die."

"Glad you didn't. Petey around?"

She pointed toward the back. "Hiding in his command desk behind the server rack."

"Cool, thanks. Oh, and I'll tell you what I told Johnston. We'd make a shitty wedding venue, but if you guys want the gazebo and a garden wedding over on that side of the grounds, it's yours anyway."

Addy chuckled. "He mentioned that. We might do Florida or something with our families, but we'll keep it in mind. Thank you."

I shrugged. "You're welcome. This company has had more than a few funerals, but never a wedding. It might be nice to celebrate the positive for once." With that, I wandered off to go find Petey.

My tall blond Georgia native, that *Waffen-SS* looking SOB, was head down in his computer, so I lightly kicked his desk chair for attention. He turned. "'Sup?"

"Not much. We gotta stop procrastinating on this 'We need new encrypted phones' issue. The scare we had last year with the Blacks getting hacked doesn't make me super happy, and I know for a fact the CIA has patterned a bunch of ours." The art of reading what phone pings where and when in relation to every other phone's pings. Welcome to the electronic fishbowl.

Petey leaned back in his chair. "There's no way to not get your phone patterned unless you keep it either bagged or turned off every minute of every day, in which you might as well not bother with a phone at all."

"You got a point, but we definitely need more encrypted phones. It's not the Big John era anymore and they can't just be a badge of rank."

"You got a point there. I'll put Spiral on it when he gets back."

"Who the fuck is Spiral?"

Petey sighed. "That was his old hacking nickname, but as his real name is Pete and we have three Petes including me, it's easier to break the nicknames up."

"Well, where is he right now?"

"In jail over by Knoxville."

It wasn't the first time one of our employees got arrested somewhere, but the last time had been a minute. "Fuck. What'd he do?"

"Started a decent-size riot at a home-brewer's convention this past weekend. Banned for life from that one now, that's for damn sure."

I sighed. Most of us were supposed to be too old for that kind of stupid shit. "How the fuck did that happen?"

"Well, he showed up with a keg full of a beer he called 'Actual Horse Urine IPA.' People were drinking it, only they got really mad when he told them it had two pints of actual horse urine in the mix, and that's when the fight broke out."

Okay, that was batshit insane even by our standards. You the reader know by now that our standards for sanity at both Athenaeum and Archive Associates are, to be honest, shamelessly lax. I shrugged, trying to look unflapped and play it off. "Justifiable. I can see how that would piss people off, pardon the pun."

"He said it was their own damn fault for getting upset, because it was right there in the name. They didn't go for that line of reasoning. Really, he thinks what did it was that he was coming in second out of thirty-five in the judging before he told 'em."

Well, great. "Look, I know big boy rules and all that, but somebody go bail his ass out, get him back here, and y'all start working on the phone thing."

Petey nodded. "Two of my guys left hours ago. Way ahead of you, man."

"Good. You're supposed to be smarter than me anyway." I went back upstairs as my phone timer beeped, and reminding me it was morning again. I opened my desk drawer and pulled one of my spare pill bottles out, tossing one down.

River walked in as I did it, and just sort of stared. "Did you just wash a blood sugar pill down with a fucking Mountain Dew?" she asked.

"Hey, it's a 'take it every morning' med and this is what I drink in the morning."

She sighed, shaking her head. "That's like trying to put out a campfire with gasoline."

"Doc said I get two cans of Dew a day. This is one of my two."

"You're going to die. Seriously."

I shot that argument down. "First, we're all going to die eventually. You usually don't get to pick what from, either. Second, I got my A1C down by four and a half points and knocked four hundred off my tri-whatevers by not drinking an entire gallon of milk a day anymore."

"Triglycerides."

"Yeah, those.

"How's your stomach feel without that much milk in your system?"

"Right now? Like I could spit acid and melt a steel plate, but I think that's just the stress."

"Or the amount of hot peppers in dinner."

"Babe, you helped cook dinner last night." She'd come back out to the house since she likes my gumbo recipe. High praise from a Louisiana culinary snob, really.

"Yeah, but I have the Acadian genes for that. You're too New York Irish to handle that much spicy food."

"Says you. You should have seen some of the stuff the Thais fed us."

"That was twenty-five years ago and you don't make a habit of it. It's like drinking. You have to maintain your tolerance."

"You may have me there."

The desk phone rang, saving me from the conversation. The number on Caller ID looked familiar. "Hello?"

"Hey, man, it's Bradley."

"Where you been, man? Figured you would have final-outed by now."

He sounded sheepish. "Yeah... about that. Med retirement got held up ninety days minimum. Apparently, I'm in a shortage MOS so somebody hit the brakes on it. I gotta get another round of physical therapy and the first general officer to sign off, yadda, yadda."

"Well, fuck."

"It sucks. I'm kind of emotionally over it all at this point and was looking forward to coming out there."

"Even after Vegas?"

"You may get me killed, but the money's good and a little excitement is good for me."

"So you say now."

He chuckled. "Save a seat for me, bro. I still want to come play."

"You got it." He clicked off.

Chapter Fourteen

"*I just don't exhibit emotions like everyone else. On the inside, I'm vomiting.*"
~ *Phoebe Spengler, paranormal researcher and amateur nuclear physicist*

A week later, we were on the way back up I-24 from Nashville. We'd picked up some out-of-town guests, and I had to go because there had been a fancy welcoming lunch involved. You know, diplomacy. They were riding with Dave, about three cars behind us in another one of the company Yukons.

My truck was off the road for a day getting some maintenance done. It being a heavy-armored beast now, it was rougher on its systems than it once was, so the brakes were getting done. Rather than squeezing into Angel's Camaro or Cash's Mustang, I'd just borrowed another one of the armored Yukons for the trip instead, and was damn glad I did because the road sort of... exploded.

I felt the front wheel on the driver's side detach, and the Yukon lurched to the left as if chasing it. We skidded onto and across the shoulder and into the ditch at the center of the median while we were still going well over sixty. The change in ground slope was enough to flip the truck, rolling left. Huh. This hadn't happened to me in a while. *Oh, it seems to me as though I've been upon this stage before... CRUNCH.* We made about a half roll before the air bags banged to life, padding us through the rest of the full turnover.

We hadn't even stopped moving yet, sliding along atop the driver's side doors, while I was acting like a good Iraq War truck commander again out of what had once well-drilled habit. "EVERYONE OKAY?" Meanwhile I had one of my knives out and was slashing the air bags trying to get them out of my way.

Angel yelled "GOOD!"

Cash... was screaming. Screaming is good. Screaming means you're breathing. I looked back over my shoulder to where she'd been sitting behind Angel. The heavy polycarbonate windows had kept out the worst of whatever it was that hit us. Finally screaming turned into words. "THIS IS FUCKING BULLSHIT! I WANT TO GO BACK TO MY BASEMENT!"

Then the ground exploded again, right next to us. Somebody had held just a little low and skipped the round.

Dave's truck screeched to a halt next to us. He bailed out with his AR in hand, scanning the west side of the Interstate three lanes over for the firing point. I popped the sunroof as if it were a gunner's hatch and went out first. I joined Dave in trying to figure out where we got hit from while Angel unhooked herself and then Cash. Dave's friends from Warsaw were digging around in the gun cases and cursing in Polish. They actually sounded like they were enjoying themselves, the mad lads.

Dave pointed to a gap in the trees up on the high ground. "Smoke trails looked like it came from there. AT-4, maybe a Goose."

I was surprised the ambush party up there wasn't hosing us down with small arms fire as we got out of the truck, to be honest. It was pretty amateurish of them not to finish us off. Just in case whoever was up there changed their mind, Dave and I had his truck for weak cover, and Angel was getting Cash behind ours. She was okay, but Cash was holding the side of her forehead from where she'd hit the door frame, and was looking a bit concussed. Looking back southeast, I saw blue lights in the distance. I made a real fast decision.

"Angel, get the work phones and the gun case into Dave's truck. Cash, gimme your laptop. Dave, you gotta get the fuck out of here."

The career Ranger was having none of that. "No fucking way. Never shall I leave a fallen —"

"Dave, this ain't Point du Hoc or Objective Rhino. We got three unregistered machine guns counting yours, and Cash's laptop which we also don't need to be holding when those cops get here. Never mind that you gotta take care of our guests too. Grab this shit and fuckin' *get gone now!*" Angel thought about it, tucked her personal phone into her jeans pocket, and threw her whole purse into Dave's passenger seat.

Dave was visibly torn. A second later he agreed. "Fuck, okay, roger that!" He grabbed Cash's laptop bag as she offered it to him, threw the gun case to the former Polish commandoes in his back seat, unironically saluted, and got the fuck out of there. If anything, the Poles seemed kinda pissed off they didn't get to kill anyone.

Cash took a moment to think about it, and then loudly announced "I'm going to pass out now." She neatly slumped into Angel's arms. Angel looked at me, rolled her eyes, and shrugged, still holding onto her.

The Ford Explorer with the gold and black Tennessee State Police paint job damn near locked up its brakes stopping next to us, computer-controlled antilocks or no. A surprisingly small blonde under a big Smokey the Bear campaign hat jumped out, looked at us, and after visibly trying to find her words, gave up and loudly asked "What the fuck happened to y'all?"

*****

Vanderbilt Hospital, sorry, "Vanderbilt University Medical Center," isn't just one hospital — it's at least three if you include the VA building. Eleven blocks by three blocks of nursing school, med school, hospital, children's hospital, and God knows what else, it's also one of the best emergency departments in the Southeast. Yeah, as good as Grady down in Atlanta, though Grady gets more gunshot wounds because 'Tha ATL' keeps it real like that. Anyway, if you're really bad off, you arrive by helicopter and get worked on in the upstairs trauma unit below the chopper pad. We were coming in by ground, which meant we weren't that bad in somebody's professional judgment. That was sort of reassuring.

I was lying in bed, reading Jonathan LaForce's sequel to *Hell's Belles* on my phone, just trying to take my mind off shit, when somebody who looked like hospital management walked in. She was in business semi-casual, not scrubs, and looked ten years older and way more serious than most of the RNs. She introduced herself, but I confess I didn't catch the name at first telling. Then she got to the point, which was of course about money.

"Yes, we're having difficulty pulling up insurance information on you or either of your... companions."

I was expecting this eventually. Unless you come in unconscious and looking 'unhoused,' in which case you may be a charity item, VUMC expects to get paid. That's fair. Most hospitals do. "They're fully covered through their employer on private policies." See, that was the Athenaeum health plan going back as long as I worked here, even before I'd hired Jimmy and Doc Mickey. You got a doctor bill, and we paid it for you in cash, usually using the cash leverage to negotiate a steep discount. We found it was much less trouble than dealing with an actual insurance company.

She looked at me strangely. "Okay... and who's their employer."

"It's a small company, and I'm in charge of it."

"So... how do we bill this? I need contact information, we need —"

I sighed. "No, you don't. Look, how about I just make a phone call, have one of my guys come down here with the company checkbook, or I've got a couple of Visas, an Amex Black, or... hell, I can make that call and do literal cash. No shit." Her eyes got kind of wide at that. I steamrolled into that opening. "But wait, there's more. I even can throw you a better deal. If you want to get ahead on next quarter's fundraising, we can arrange a nice charitable donation to the hospital with a couple digits to the left of the comma in it in exchange for you giving us a whole lot of discretion."

She was looking really lost now. "Discretion..."

"You might have noticed my girlfriend is a multiple shrapnel case, my girlfriend's girlfriend is a multiple shrapnel case with head trauma, and I got cut up too. Someone tried fairly hard to kill us, so we don't need to be on the patient directory as ourselves right now."

Nodding and looking a little dazed, she exited, and Angel came in about ten seconds later. She edged in close, both of us a little achy from the crash. "Cash may be a problem."

"What happened?"

"She got a needle of something before they stitched her forehead up. They were working on her when one of the nurses did the standard 'confirm your patient data' drill and, well, Cash couldn't remember her alleged name."

"Shit, I can't remember the name on her driver's license either."

"Yeah, so now they want to do a full head injury protocol on her and keep her here for at least forty-eight hours for observation."

Damn. "How far away is her room?"

"Surprisingly she's just up the hall. As big as this place is, I'm surprised you're in the same zip code. I got lucky."

I wasn't hooked to an IV or anything, and the nurse wasn't around, so I got up and followed Angel down the hallway. Cash was awake, but she looked somewhat out of it. She looked toward Angel and me as we walked in. I was kinda limping again, to be honest. "Hey, guys." Her voice seemed... off, and her eyes were reddened like she'd been crying.

"Hey, dear. How are you feeling?"

She sighed, staring up at the ceiling. "Off center. Kinda lost. The drugs fucked me up enough that I lost track of who I was for a minute, and I don't really have it wired back together yet. The voices are really, *really* bad right now."

This wasn't good. I moved forward slowly. "So... what do you remember?" Since she'd fit in the bed, Angel just sighed and climbed in with her for comforting cuddles. Part of me wondered what the hell they gave her, but I wasn't exactly a skilled professional at this shit.

"I remember somebody trying to kill us with a rocket launcher or something, passing out, passing out again in the ambulance, waking up here higher than Snoop Dogg, and then Angel found me after I freaked the nurses out."

I sighed. "Better than I expected. So, which one of you am I talking to?"

She chuckled. "I'm still me, sir. I know who I am. Well, I know who I want to be. When I first woke up and people sounded Southern, and one of the doctors mentioned me as a car crash case, I was a little confused and it took a few minutes for everything to snap back into place."

"So, you're not going to quit the job and decide you're J —"

She laughed explosively. "Oh, fuck no. She'll shut up in a couple hours as the drugs wear off. I'm just surprised we're still the innocent victims here and don't have the police looking for us. I'm *way* too pretty to go to prison, especially now."

We all had a laugh at that. "Really, I'm surprised the cops haven't shown up either. But I made an arrangement with the hospital to keep our real names quiet, and in your case, the name on your driver's license."

She shrugged. "If we still know anyone in that office, I may need a new one."

"We'll think of something. We always do."

Short version. Cash's original personality, the Miss 'Establishment Bookish' who embezzled seventeen million of someone else's dirty money, panicked and hid under the metaphorical bed at some point in her escape from impending Federal custody that was organized and led by, well, me. At some level, what's left of the original personality knows it's still hiding under the bed several years later. Sometimes it yells a lot in the background and that makes Cash weirder than usual. As for who Cash really is in relation? Shit, your guess is as good as mine. We've had that discussion, but there are no clear answers and it's not like she wants to talk to a shrink. She naturally thinks that 'the new her' is an improvement.

Eventually we were all herded back to our separate beds, and the staff refused to shift us around to one room because, and I quote, "You're all getting discharged fairly soon." This was not just a lie, but a goddamned lie, as it wasn't until six the next morning that they finally let us go. Because we were on the pending discharge list, we didn't get on the 'feed them' list. Unfortunately, we napped through closing time on the excellent food court downstairs. Fortunately, we had our personal phones and Nashville has no shortage of delivery food. We didn't starve.

That next morning, after ten minutes of haggling to more reasonable cash-discount totals, I paid us off. I threw all three of our hospital bills on the AmEx Black just to make sure I charged enough for the year to be allowed to keep the fucking thing, and Jake had a SUV downstairs to pick us up. We ran to Waffle House for breakfast then it was off to the office. From there, Angel put Cash in her Camaro and they headed for the house.

Me, I wanted that goddamn Yukon back. That took some phone calls. The State Police had it towed, of course. Their towing company was a different one than our insurance company used. Since the damn things weren't stock, the insurance company didn't know what they really were and I knew there was no way in Hell that they'd pay to have the armored monster rebuilt — they'd treat it like a 2013 Yukon, total it, give me a check, and probably try scrapping it. Well, that was unacceptable, since it wasn't like I could get more of the damn things.

Morgan was on one line with the towing company while I was trying to tell the nice lady at my insurance company's call center that no, I didn't want to file a claim for the accident. Shit, the accident report was a good bit imaginary. The trooper did not write anywhere that the front driver's side wheel had been severed by an explosive projectile of some sort. The last thing I wanted was their adjuster actually looking at it up close.

When I got off the phone with her, I called Henry, the Alabama redneck mechanic and part time rocket engineer who had done the rebuild on my personal truck after it got shot to shit a couple years ago. He finally answered. "What's up?"

"You up for another vehicle rebuild job?"

He made a noise somewhere between a chuckle and a snort. "I already have one of yours down here."

"You do?"

"Remember that armored black BMW you sent me a few months ago?"

"You're still working on it?" I mean I hadn't forgotten it was there, but it was just an engine and transmission. I'd sent it down there a good while ago and I refused to believe it would take that long. I would have thought Henry's guys could have put a fucking warp drive in it in six months.

"Well, yeah. The powertrain is out of it and it's still up on a lift, too. It's pretty fucked up, but parts availability is absolute rock-bottom. You still want it?"

"Yeah, I do. I don't care about it authentic; I just want it running. And now I got a wrecked armored Yukon if you and your crew of miscreants want the work."

He sighed. "Work is work, and I know damn well you can afford it these days. Get it on a trailer and get it down here. You better not be in a hurry though."

"Nah, I have other wheels for me and the company, but that Yuke saved my ass plus the girls' asses, so I don't want to lose it."

"Their asses are much nicer than yours. We'll give it our best." He hung up.

Long story short, we got the Yukon back from the towing company and down to Henry's shop west of Huntsville. A week later, the towing company then complained the Yukon had been grossly overweight and they'd damaged a truck, etc, etc. They wanted ten grand. Cash counteroffered with buying the company. They politely refused, probably thinking the slightly slutty looking Korean girl with the fucked-up Yankee accent was just fucking with them, so she gave them the ten and told them it was their loss.

Chapter Fifteen

"I don't mean to sound superior, but I hate the company of robots."
    ~ V.I.N.CENT, "The Black Hole."

A week later, still a little roughed up, we were back in the office. Don't ask what Dave and the Polish shooters were off doing. Not even I knew for sure. Me, I was just digging in file folders when the desk phone beeped. It was the security booth topside letting me know I had a package.

See, there was a sign out at the road gate instructing FedEx, UPS, or whoever to call a number that rang in the guard shack. One of the duty crew would go down in a four-wheeler, sign for the package, and bring it back. This wasn't unusual. Stuff came and went all the time that didn't go through our PO boxes, plural, in Nashville. Not much that came in had one of my names on it specifically, but it happened. But for some reason I asked, "Who's it from?"

"Uhhh, some outfit called ArmEx International. Aren't they the ones —"

Oh, fucking hell. "Set it down, right now, clear the area. Possible IED."

We'd drilled for this contingency, and this was a time when buying quality showed. "Roger, sir." He hung up the phone, and I grabbed the Motorola intercom mike again. *I really did like this silly antique thing.* "Haze to Garage, Haze to Garage. Bring your gear for an IED."

Lee Hazenbury had been a PFC of mine in the brigade recon squadron about twenty years ago, the chemical specialist running the storeroom of gas masks for Headquarters Troop. Boredom drove him onward and upward. Last year, while on leave from the resident explosive ordnance disposal company at Fort Bliss, Texas, where he was the first sergeant, he took a fairly large cash payment from me to build, uh, an 'automated pyrotechnic distraction device.' As a condition of doing the job, he told me he wanted a job with the firm when he retired. He had a year until retirement, and didn't want to stay in and try for battalion sergeant major. At the same time, he still had three young-ish kids to put through college. In return, he would handle my explosives needs, do odd jobs, and also continue to not tell anyone what we'd done down in Mississippi that night. I could handle that.

When he retired early this year, and once he had the wife and kids settled, I gave him a budget and told him he was now the company's IED response element in addition to whatever other jobs I stuck him with. He then amused himself finding a portable magnetometer and X-ray machine, then buying two armored bomb suits before assembling a search robot out of assorted spare parts he'd been hoarding for a decade. He was having fun, which was always nice to see. Now, not knowing if Shellington had both a bombmaker and the desire to try blowing me up, time to let my investment and his effort pay off rather than get anyone killed.

The kid from the guard shack had, without orders, taken the box back outside. "Figured it was safer for us if it was out there, and also away from everyone's cars." It was out in the bigger- than-football-sized field past the parking lot and the picnic gazebo. Gutsy move. I made a mental note to kick him an envelope of bonus money since as civilians, we didn't do medals.

We got back inside the door. If you can see a suspected IED, it can see you, and fragmentation can do the damnedest things. Haze picked that moment to show up with his big rolling toolboxes of goodies. It took him a few minutes to get his toys unpacked and going, and longer for his janky little tank-tracked bomb-bot to make the long trip out to the box. Once it got out there, he offered a running commentary in his vaguely Scandinavian 'Nort-*DahKOH-da*' accent.

"Not enough metal to matter, even for a low signature... X-ray is warming up."

The robot picked that moment to literally fall over and die, its X-ray camera now pointed helplessly up at the sky.

I just looked over at him and sighed. "Dude. Seriously. Dude. All that budget money I gave you and you're using this piece of shit?"

He looked offended. "Hey, I made that bot myself out of three of my best ones. Well, with some replacement parts I pulled out of the trash pile behind the company a couple years back. The Army retired that model and we didn't need them, so the parts were free."

Sigh. "What do you mean your three best ones?"

"Every time I had a robot get blown up on a job, I'd keep the pieces. Eventually I made one that worked out of about half a dozen that didn't, including three of my favorites."

I pointed out the door, where the bot was still laying on its side, one track spinning angrily in the air. "It doesn't look like it's working to me."

"Hey, it's like Johnny Cash said, I got it one piece at a time, man. Cheaper that way."

"After we get through this, figure out what a new robot's going to cost, and give that fucking thing to somebody's kid to play with. Buy an R2D2 clone from the guy at DragonCon. Fuck, call Gary and get one of the *Robot Battles* guys from Chattanooga to do a custom build. I don't care. This," I gestured broadly, "This is just embarrassing."

Haze was barely listening. He was still staring at the box, lost in thought. "Fuck it. I don't think this thing is live. For what you're paying me, since I like the odds, let me get the suit on."

Since we didn't have a full EOD team, I had to be the one to help him into his armor of ceramic plates and Kevlar. I hadn't been around a bomb suit in most of fifteen years, and so it took twice as long as it would have taken if we had a competent assistant to figure out the buckles Lee couldn't reach himself. He then took the long walk over to the box, carrying a briefcase-sized portable digital X-ray machine.

We waited until he walked back. His surplus-store suit helmet didn't have a functioning communications setup put back in it yet. "Looks like cigars. At least four boxes worth. No cardboard. Wood boxes, probably cedar plywood, which means they're the good kind. I can see the little nails in the boxes and that's about it. Nothing dense enough for fragmentation. There was nothing on the explosives sniffer either. Fuck it, I'm declaring this thing officially 'not live.'"

"You sure?"

"I can always bust it open with a water charge and fuck up your smokes."

I shrugged. "It's your ass, bro." He walked back out. A few minutes later, he waved me over then started shucking his suit before I got there. The FedEx box was cardboard scraps in the grass, and Haze was handing me a stack of half a dozen unmarked cedar cigar boxes wrapped in factory cellophane. Well, Shellington did say he bought his off-label. There was also a card-sized white envelope. Setting the boxes aside, I pulled my pocket knife and slit it open. "Hey, fuck it, maybe there's anthrax in here or some shit..." I grumbled. Frustration can breed fatalism.

There was no mysterious white powder, just a note on Shellington's old official stationery, leftovers from before he retired. Heavy cream-colored card stock, three shining silver stars embossed in metallic ink, with a nice raised scrollwork border. It was all very tasteful, and very visibly expensive. I was actually impressed. Unfortunately for him, he had the handwriting of a demented nine-year-old. The pencil scrawl merely said:

THAT ONE WASN'T ME EITHER.

ENJOY THE SMOKES.

BEST WISHES,

JIM

"Well, so much for that shit." I handed Haze the top two boxes. "Still have a humidor at the house?"

Going back downstairs, I repeated my usual process for calling people I didn't trust. I fired up my desk phone, using its caller ID scrambler, and ran it through a computerized redirect function on one of the laptops. Only then did I dial Shellington's cell number. It picked up on the second ring, but it wasn't him. "General Shellington's line, how may I help you, sir?"

Shit, did he hire his old aide and he forget he's a civilian now? "Yes, if the general is available, please tell him it's the Professor calling to thank him for the cigars."

"Just a moment, sir, the nurses just left and he's still awake." *Nurses? What the fuck?*

Shellington came on the line. "Hey, kid." His voice was weak and scratchy.

"Your aide didn't get the memo you retired."

He chuckled weakly. "Don't mind Charlie. He's been with me since my first star at Fort Carson. He's a little stressed right now, so old habits are coming back."

"With all due respect, and I say that merely for old time's sake, you sound like shit."

"Three rounds to the chest will do that to you at my age." *Fucking hell.*

"I confess you got me at a bit of a loss. I hadn't even heard you got hit."

He chuckled again. "Nice to find out that you don't know everything all the time. We did our best to keep it really quiet. Still might be the death of me. My lungs aren't what they were between years of breathing the burn pits in theater and getting a good hit of that Chi-Com lung virus a couple years ago, and the fuckers naturally gunned up enough to beat the vest I had on. I should have been wearing hard plates; that might have helped a little. A damn plate carrier just doesn't look right with a suit jacket in CONUS though. The more I think about it, between Vegas and this, my wife was right. Trying to keep up appearances probably will be the death of me."

Ouch. "They do say vanity is one of the deadly sins. Still, you got any idea who?"

"Only that they were two Asian gentlemen with MP-7s and the *good* armor piercing ammo."

I thought about it, leaning back in my chair. "Well, that rules out a bunch of people."

I could almost hear him shrug. "It doesn't rule out enough of them though."

"And you're lucky they didn't go for the head."

"They were some flavor of Chinese. It's related to that Southeast Asia thing we talked about. Or maybe the Africa thing. China's got their fingers in both pies, so we're trying to settle that. They put up too much of a fight to get taken alive. I got hit, yeah, and so did the two guys with me."

"Too much to think that whoever took that whack at you..." I trailed off.

"You're thinking, kid. Tell me."

"You know somebody took a shot at me too. Can't imagine someone knows us and our history of drama well enough to try to get us at each other's throats and hope we wipe each other out."

He snorted. "Kid, that's a bad novel with lazy writing. Reality doesn't work that way."

Well, so much for that flash of insight. Another idea came to mind, one guaranteed to mess with him. "Or... you got one of your guys to shoot you just so you'd have an alibi for this second hit on me and mine. That would make it look good for most people. And considering who got put in the hospital with me on this one, I'm in a far bloodier mood than I was in Vegas. I'm still cool enough to hide it though."

"Wait, deliberately get myself shot..."

I grinned, though I kept my voice level. "Come on, it's the perfect cover up."

"What the fuck sort of brain-damaged redneck trailer-park psycho shit is that?" Shellington spluttered. *Ha, Got 'em.*

I still managed to keep my voice perfectly calm despite really wanting to laugh. "How is that not the perfect alibi?"

He scoffed, taking a deep breath and coughing some before continuing. "I take back everything I said about offering you a job. I regret even meeting you at this point. You're even crazier than the rumors say you are."

"Focus, sir. Focus. People are trying to kill us both. Oh, and before I forget, and the reason I actually called, thank you for the cigars."

He chuckled then coughed again. "Smoke them in good health, though not all at once."

I had to grin at that. "I gave two of the boxes to my EOD tech. I had him clear the package when it showed up. We got a little nervous."

"You really do have trust issues, kid."

Though he couldn't see it, I reflexively shrugged. "I came by them honestly. The world fucked me like I was Sasha Grey more than once." *This was pre-Adriana Chechik though.* Okay, enough of that line of thought too. Contemplating that industry's Mount Rushmore could wait a while and there were no fixed answers to it.

That got a good laugh out of him, though I could hear a wheeze in it now that even my amateur medical knowledge found alarming. "I see you are a man of culture as well."

"An obscure anime reference from a three-star. This day is full of surprises."

"Nah, one of my guys used the meme template in the slide deck for a Friday briefing and I liked it after he explained it. My taste in anime ended with *Space Battleship Yamato* or the original *Voltron* with the lions. *Cowboy Bebop* was good though."

I snorted. He and I were sort of contemporaries, and I could have said exactly the same thing. "Careful, Jim. At this rate I'd hate to actually have to like you."

His laughing turned to a scary barrage of coughing, and the aide's voice came back on. "I appreciate you cheering him up, but I think he's talked enough. He's got the oxygen mask back on but he is giving me a thumbs-up."

Seemed reasonable. "All right, you guys take care. I'm off." I hung up.

Chapter Sixteen

T hings shifted at ArmEx about a week after that, and not in a good way. The major shareholders, the big venture-capital funds he'd waved his stars at for startup cash and operating money, had figured out Shellington was in the hospital rather than busy in the office making them their money back. They found that unacceptable, and Shellington was forced out as CEO by a hasty shareholder vote. I tried calling him after word leaked out onto the grapevine, but by then his cell number was out of service. I supposed it had been a company phone, not his own. The new CEO was a New Zealander colonel, military intelligence rather than infantry, and a fluent speaker of Chinese. That alone sent up a red flag, as the Kiwi government got really chummy with Beijing a few years back for a few minutes, so much so that a lot of people wondered if they'd stay on the team.

With their change in leadership and the intersection with people from around Beijing who didn't like us very much, ArmEx was no longer 'Neutral, Trending Friendly.' That meant violence was possible, and they had much better resources behind them as the cat's paw of a potentially hostile nation-state. Remember when I said our list of threats started around Venezuela on the list? This was way higher. If ArmEx was a Chinese asset now, this was David and Goliath level stuff, so we needed really good rocks.

Things really got bad at ArmEx from there over the next few weeks. Budgets were cut and personnel churned at their Virginia offices, and then things got really, really unhealthily quiet. Rumor was the company was most of the way shut down as the investors were running for the doors with whatever they could salvage. They still had five battalions in the field in three countries though. I found this whole thing really suspicious, and we resolved not to lose track of keeping an eye on those guys. Meanwhile we had other problems around the world to watch.

*****

That meeting I had put on the board in Intel rolled around. Since we'd gotten back from Vegas, everyone had gone all-out trying to get a handle on the China questions. We'd pulled every string we had and dug into every file farm and data repository we could get into by means fair or foul. We figured out in the first two minutes that it wasn't going all that great. *We just didn't know.* We weren't used to not knowing things. Helpless ignorance was not in our usual way of doing things.

Charles at Langley hadn't given us anything off the laptop, despite his assurance of a gentlemanly split of the data on it. He'd been putting me off with the equivalent of 'the check was in the mail.' Whether that meant he'd screwed me or simply that his buddy at NSA hadn't broken it yet, he was real evasive about it.

We still didn't know if we were dealing with the Chinese government, a faction of the Chinese government, a rogue faction of the Chinese government, Chinese organized crime, or what. See, China pretends to be Communist, like their flags are still red and there's 'People's This' and 'People's That,' but they gave up on literal Communism thirty seconds after Mao died. And Mao was more an emperor than most Chinese emperors had been. The Communism was a new coat of paint on the old system — he just had Marx as the lodestone of the state religion rather than using the sky gods of their old days.

It took us an hour, and we kept going back into circles that we didn't know, and we didn't know anyone else who did either. We got into files of several other government agencies and DOD organizations, and we still couldn't find exactly what we were looking for. That was a goddamned annoyance.

Kara leaned back in her chair. "It's not merely China that's the problem. Let's not think too big and get lost here. It's Chinese overseas operations, and there's a pattern to those. They've got their tentacles deep into Africa, for example, which is where they turned Castleman." Castleman, a retired lieutenant colonel with Africa experience, had been in management at ArmEx and gotten murdered at home. Cell phone tracing had put Lin at the scene the night he died.

"They sign deals with local governments, loan a lot of money that people can't afford to repay, open a lot of their own businesses with 'civilians,' air quotes, who they send in to put the locals out of business, and buy off enough local politicians so the local governments stay bought."

"And that, while interesting, isn't what happened here. So, is this part of Chinese empire-building overseas, their Belt and Road initiative? Or is this organized crime shit?"

"We don't know," I shrugged. "And we know we don't know."

"We can surmise that it's China's ongoing pushback against us, their drive to make the Middle Kingdom the world's preeminent power again."

One of the other intel kids, Erik something, raised his hand with a shrug. "What are the two eternal human desires? Delicious fried food and someone to look down on."

Morgan chuckled. "Tack 'getting some really good head' on that list and I'll go with it."

Erik went on, undaunted. "They want to look down on us. We're an upstart barbarian kingdom compared to four thousand years of The Middle Kingdom."

"So with the Castleman thing, is Africa the intersection of all this?"

At that point, Erik rhetorically ran out of gas. "We don't know, boss. Maybe."

"There's gotta be a connection there. That's where ArmEx draws from, and they went to the trouble of taking over ArmEx," I mused.

Angel objected. "A New Zealander took over ArmEx."

I shook my head. "With somebody else's money when the controlling interest in their stock changed hands, and the Chinese had their hooks into the

New Zealanders bad about five years back when whuzzername was their PM. Assume a bunch of their field grade officers of those year groups are politically compromised, otherwise they wouldn't have been field grade officers in the first place."

Jake was thinking. "They only have what, one big brigade?"

Dave nodded. "And another brigade's worth of headquarters. You can hide a lot of politically connected shitbags in a force structure that lopsided."

Welcome to one of my hot button issues. "Like we have room to talk about being grossly over-officered. We still have more generals for ten divisions than we did for eighty-nine divisions in World War II," I grumbled, wondering how many four-stars and staffers you had to fire to afford reactivating a missing infantry brigade.

Kara started making a 'cut it off' hand signal at her neck. "Shut up, don't get the boss started or we'll fall down some historical rabbit hole and never get to the point of all this."

I looked over at Morgan and Kara. "Now who do we know who's a genuine expert on Chinese infiltration of some of these African militaries?"

Morgan one-upped me. "What the fuck do any of us really know about Africa? I've never been near the place, and I don't think any of us have."

I started thinking over people outside the company that I knew who had been. One retired Army intel officer I know had been doing a UN assignment back during what became the Rwandan genocide, but that was thirty years ago and I don't think he'd left Louisiana since except to pop across the Sabine River into Texas. I couldn't blame him. Seeing some shit like that? I wouldn't want to leave the house again either.

Dave raised a hand halfway. "I knew a couple observer types and SFAB dudes who went over there pretty often, but they were generally on base and working through interpreters."

I shook my head. "Nah, we need some local hacker or journalist types. Supposedly Nigeria and Kenya are some of the most online countries in the world, even if their circles on the Internet don't intersect ours all that often."

Morgan nodded. "I do know one guy. Port Harcourt, Nigeria. Met him when he was trying to scam his way into my inbox claiming to be Sydney Sweeney."

We all had a decent laugh at that. "Sydney Sweeney? Really?"

He shrugged. "Three months before that, it was Taylor Swift, and so on. Whoever the flavor of the month was, he'd target some lonely horndog who posted too many comments on an Instagram thread."

Kara snickered. "I'm surprised you have the time to fall for thirst-trap scams like that."

Morgan gave her the finger. "I don't. But I also log incoming IP addresses and the same guy was a very busy little shit claiming to be famous women online, so I ran him to ground and offered him some work."

"He went for it?"

That got a self-satisfied grin out of Morgan. "Of course he did. Unless you find that one loser out of a hundred who you can get some bank data out of, there's no money in trolling the basement dwellers. Usually, they're trying to troll you back. He was making pennies on the dollar compared to more honest forms of computer crime." My brain screeched to a halt for a second trying to make that last sentence come out logically, it really did, but Morgan didn't notice and was plowing onward. "I use him for reading local news sites, and also for finding translators for all those local languages absolutely zero white people speak since the British Empire broke up and the Oxbridge types stopped learning them."

I nodded. "Pretty goddamned clever way of leveraging the guy."

Morgan shrugged. "And at least he can pay his rent now without having to go back out in the oil fields or whatever. He kinda sucked at that whole 'trying to be a white girl' thing."

I chuckled. "Morgan, try finding your buddy over there and put him to work on it. Maybe something will come of it." It was a weak and skinny thread to pull on, but we weren't exactly blessed with a ton of options, either. Shit. Story of our lives here.

Dave thought about it, then blurted. "We're wasting our fucking time, man. We don't know shit and all we agreed on is that we don't know shit."

He had a point. The only thing worse than a meeting is a meeting that didn't accomplish anything. "All right, everyone get back to work. We know what we don't know, so we all get to work on it now."

Chapter Seventeen

"H*ere is the riddle of steel, boy. Steel is not strong. Flesh is stronger. What is a barbell without the arm that lifts it?"*
~ *My high school football captain's version of Thulsa Doom's monologue from* Conan the Barbarian

Yes, I still work out at my age, even if I don't talk about it in the course of the narrative. I rarely describe brushing my teeth either. Both are just routine things, and while I'll never put up the weight room numbers again that I could in my twenties or thirties, I'm just too damaged, it's still not something I can afford to neglect either. I put in my time in the garage-bay gym as much as anyone, which is probably how I pinched this goddamn nerve in my shoulder.

I have knee trouble. I have back trouble. Thank fuck that I never have had long term chronic shoulder damage, because now having had a sampler of it, I think that might well be as bad or even worse than the lower back. Anything I did with my upper body somehow found a way to annoy the nerve. Sleeping was fucking near impossible. I simply couldn't get to a position that was comfortable, and if I found one, staying there was even harder. Cash and Angel were jamming every throw pillow in the house under me to try keeping me supported and immobilized like the keel blocks under a drydocked battleship. Angel was massaging it, and I was drinking a decent glass of whiskey a night. Sometimes bourbon, sometimes Scotch, occasionally Irish, it was all a bit of gentle anesthesia.

I'd gone to bed early by my standards, and probably been down for six hours. I woke up around three in the morning, and I couldn't feel my legs. They were dead weight, and I couldn't move them at all. Stifling a wave of panic that I'd had a stroke or something, I sat up slowly and painfully, reaching down to feel that they were still there, and I bumped into a sleeping Odin who'd decided to lay his sixty pounds right across my shins and ankles. Normally he was at Cash and Angel's feet since they were shorter and there was that extra foot of clearance between them and the footboard. Nope, not this time. He decided to lay down right on top of me and didn't give a damn. I pulled myself out from under him, and he sort of *harrumph*ed at me in his sleep and rolled a bit. Shifting right, I bumped into a cat, but I couldn't tell which one in the dark.

As I struggled to find a spot in bed that didn't have another living thing already asleep on it, and worse, get comfortable again, it made for a bit of an existential crisis. How much longer could I keep burning the candle at both ends with the work hours, the travel, and the stress of running the company? I could afford to retire. I knew I could, even with what had gotten spent on the new house. Hell, I even wanted to retire. I just couldn't let myself see it as a possibility. Not with all this shit going on. I was just so fucking tired all the time. Somewhere, I dozed off again.

*****

Back in the office, I found the Johnstons had taken a couple weeks off, then headed out of town to get married. Well, that got us off the hook for hosting. Just as well, despite my offer, since having a bunch of curious about-to-be-in-laws looking around our grounds asking why there was a mountain with a garage door in it wasn't exactly on my to-do list. About a dozen people were on leave to go watch. I'd gotten an invitation to the Florida ceremony, even though Johnston knew I couldn't or wouldn't break off from work. Cash RSVP'd our regrets and sent them a nice check instead.

Hours later, I went outside to walk around a while. I figured I might go smoke a cigar at the gazebo and see who from night shift was fucking off out there. I grabbed another can of Dew since it would be a late night anyway and selected a smoke from the office humidor. The Dominicans from Shellington were quite good, but I went for something different. I decided to treat myself and grabbed one of my oddballs, a nice dark Gurkha 'Cellar Reserve,' and went upstairs. Kara was out at the gazebo burning one, as were Hawkins and some of the other usual suspects. There wasn't much talking there in the dark. Instead, they were all looking toward the woodline and listening. Finally there was an angry yowling, which got everyone *aaaaw*ing and clapping for some reason.

I looked over at Hawkins. "Bobcat. Probably a younger one."

He chuckled. "Yeah, adolescent male. We got him on night vision pretty regularly since he was younger and his mama kicked him out. He used to be a lot friendlier in exchange for chicken nuggets, then puberty hit. Now he wants to pretend to be an asshole unless he's hungry enough and he wants his nuggies again. We call him Mister Murderbritches."

Of course we fucking do. Humans will try pet-bonding with anything. "So we have a bobcat now. Sure. I'll roll with that."

Hawkins laughed. "We're too far from Land Between the Lakes to get the Dogman and too far from the Mexican border to get chupacabras. Fuckers got to building more McMansion suburbs and probably scared Bigfoot off. Shit, we need something out here except deer."

I sighed. "We already had bobcats. We got deer, wild turkeys, groundhogs, at least a couple foxes, raccoons, possums, skunks, squirrels, chipmunks, a surprising number of coyotes, one mountain lion on trail camera over by the county dump, and fuck knows what else. Surprised we don't have bears again yet. So I guess this is our bobcat."

"They got bears down in Murfreesboro now. Caught one in a dumpster a few months back," somebody interjected in the dark.

Angel piped up in the dark. "I want a bear. Bears are cute."

"Bears are fuckin' dangerous." I replied.

"If not friend, why is friend-shaped?" Kara piped up.

"That's how I'm gonna die, petting something that didn't want to be petted," someone else commented in the dark.

Well, fuck, I guess the terminally online nature of our business had imprinted us with memes.

Hawkins took another drag on his cigar. "I gotta have something to fuck with my new guys about. Gotta threaten 'em with something that goes bump in the dark and we don't have that mountain lion around. So little Mister Murderbritches is now it."

"I have had housecats bigger than Murderbritches," I replied, scowling in the dark. That was not an exaggeration. Maine Coons can get huge.

Kara giggled at the exchange. "He's just a baby yet. He's growing."

I sighed in resignation. "Kara, I better not find him asleep on the map table in Intel. Cats, and I mean regular cats, are fine, even grumpy ones like your buddy Duncan Idaho was, God rest him. But actual predatory wild animals? No. Fuck no. I gotta draw a line somewhere."

She blew a smoke cloud at me. "I make no promises."

Goddamn guard shack kids were probably going to try taming a coyote next. The long-ago words of one of the Benning NCOs, the ironically named Sergeant First Class Fox of the 2/29th MOUT committee, echoed in my ears. "Do not bother my wildife. It's just like you. It just wants to be left alone to eat, sleep, and fuck." That said, we had chicken nuggets and that had to be better bait to make friends with potentially cuddly animals than MRE scraps. Then of course my own Bad Idea switch flipped. "We could just get a raccoon." The old guy who hosted our regimental reunion barbecues out in Dover had a couple raccoons that had gotten so tame they would take Cheetos right out of your hand. He fed the deer on his place too.

Hawkins answered "Naw, fuck that. They're cute when they're small, but they get big as shit if you keep feedin' 'em. I hit a monster one out by Texarkana one time. Fuckin' thing had to be fifty pounds. Did fifteen hundred bucks worth of damage to the car I was in."

I laughed my ass off at that one. "Fifteen hundred? What the shit? Did it crawl under it with a Sawzall and steal your catalytic converter or something?" You know, just Arkansas things.

"Nah, I was in a Corvette with a lot of custom bodywork up front and it fucked up the air dam and some of the add-on parts. This was before the mid-engined ones, it was a '18. You wanna know the worst part?"

"What?"

"Damn thing just rolled through the hit, got up, looked at me like it wanted to fight, and walked off into the damn woods."

"You go after it?"

"Fuck no. It might have had friends out there."

Part of me wondered what the fuck Hawkins had been doing in a custom Corvette out by Texarkana when he was still in the Army at the time, but that was his own damn business. If he wanted me to know, it would have been included in the story, I'm sure.

Going back downstairs, still faintly vibrating from the nicotine, I cued up a good playlist of music videos for background noise then got back to work. When it got to a particular 2002 BBC broadcast I'd had bookmarked for a long time, I stopped and watched. It was 'live' at the time, from the Royal Albert Hall in London, as the National Youth Symphony of Great Britain did Mahler's Eighth Symphony. I loved this version of it. One, it's a hell of a venue I'd never actually seen in real life. I always told myself I'd do London someday, but it was another of those 'when I had time, I had no money, now that I have the money, I have no time' things I so often complain about. Two, the massed choirs surrounding the kids' orchestra spoke to the effort they'd put on. Three, Simon Rattles' absolutely bonkers conducting style amused the shit out of the long-ago scraps of band geek that still lived on in me. I know I shit on the British occasionally, and they usually deserve it, but some things they still do very well and the performing arts is one of them. You rarely see that sort of effort put in on American television.

Still listening to various classical pieces another four hours later, I kicked my shoes off and flopped out on the couch. I couldn't concentrate anymore, and I knew why. I was preoccupied with the idea that someone was going to take a serious run at us. They'd tried for me, what was to stop them from trying to hit the company itself? As I had told Mikey that day, the main defense of The Hole was that nobody knew where it was. In an age of Google Earth and off-the-shelf recon drones, almost nothing stayed hidden anymore.

Really, I needed to sit down and talk this worry out with some of the primary staff, but everyone had their hands full right now. Angel was working downstairs in Intel helping Kara's people with some Chinese issues, Cash and Dave were on day shift, and Morgan was traveling. Then I think I closed my eyes for a minute and everything blacked out.

Chapter Eighteen

Angel nudged me awake with a giggle. I was still out cold on the couch when she'd come upstairs. "You okay, sir?"

I slowly pulled it together. "Sort of. It's not like I'm sick, but something's bothering me about our vulnerabilities, and it's not something I can completely articulate yet."

She nodded. "Hang on a minute." She ducked out, probably heading for the break room fridge. I slowly sat up, just getting my breathing right, and she came back in with another can of Dew. I looked at my watch before I cracked it open. 3:56 in the morning, so two hours left until shift change. Yeah, there was a while to go yet, so I cracked it open and drank.

I know I throw the terms day shift and night shift around indiscriminately when telling these stories, but really, of all the people in the building, only five people were on a solid twelve on, twelve off rotation. That was the four-man security crew topside and the on-duty watch officer, who at the moment was also me. Everyone else came and went at the whims of their section chiefs, and that partly tied into what specialties were tied into what was going on in the world. If something was happening in the Middle East where we needed the Arabic speakers on deck at a certain time, we scheduled for that. If something was going on in the Taiwan Straits, same with our Chinese military analysts and our best Mandarin speakers.

Making the machinery work was what management was for. Not me, so much, but the department heads and their subordinate leaders. We were also at war with twenty-three other time zones and our own body clocks, which is why with the growth of the company, I'd tried to hire around single points of failure. Nichols was now my spare Jake. We had more security teams, and Cash was now a fully qualified intel watch officer, so much as we formally qualified anything around here. I'd diversified my portfolio of subject matter experts on everything from cartel money laundering to Chinese naval affairs, or at least tried.

But with the growth, and the additional business, we had a brand name that was more recognizable than ever. That wasn't limited to our friends and customers, which was the hard part. The late, unlamented David had told me as much when he was bleeding on the Venetian's bathroom floor. "You are Athenaeum, Incorporated, and you are known."

If you are known, you can be hunted, and if you have a lair, you can be found. All they needed was one asshole inside the Federal government who could get into the contracts database, and they could eventually get the Hole's street address. That was on the physical security inspection log sheets if nothing else.

So, let's get into physical security. We did have a fence at the property line. Except for the bit around the road gate, it wasn't much. Mostly it was just three strands of barbed wire encircling four hundred acres of mostly woods that the part-time Roads and Grounds crew kept up. I might need to make a better department there, looking at who I could trust with some of the secrets of what they were working on. Really, I needed a tame platoon of engineers, mostly combat type, with a couple horizontal and vertical construction sections built in. Of course then I had to ask myself if I really needed forty guys working on this all the time. Half of me had a normalcy bias and thought things would roll along as always. It didn't want to disturb the routine or spend the money. The other half of me was paranoid and it said forty wasn't enough.

See, the people I had weren't always the people I needed. The company had a wide range of people who worked here in The Hole under the mountain. Some were going to be of way more use in an immediate local crisis than others. I

147

needed every one of the security teams and then some. A real emergency was gonna take every shooter in my Rolodex. I would need my UAV crews, and probably extra ones. Some of IT would stay. Meanwhile, I did not need just about any of the intelligence analysts, most of IT, and absolutely none of the linguists. Some of them were too old or too unhealthy to be of any particular utility in a crunch anyway. I'd just keep Angel close if I needed someone to speak Chinese for me.

Kissing Angel quickly to say thanks for the drink, I left her with the file folder she was working on, picked up the book I'd been reading earlier, and headed up the hall to the bathroom.

Making a very long story short, terrain shapes a fight. Ask Robert E. Lee on the third of July, 1863 how that worked out for him over his three previous days. That example was at the forefront of my brain right now. Sitting on the 1950's vintage porcelain throne up the hall, instead of playing on my phone reposting stolen memes, I was instead rereading an actual hardback paper copy of *The US Army War College Guide to the Battle of Gettysburg*. My anxieties about potential threats aside, waste elimination is a biological necessity and I also needed a few minutes alone to keep thinking.

See, the goal wasn't to keep everyone out. With enough people and explosives, you could eventually get into anywhere. The goal was to control where they went once they were in. You use the 'natural lines of drift' that the terrain gives you to steer your unwelcome guests to where you want them. People like to walk downhill. Right-handed people tend to drift right. People will generally walk down a path if one is available.

Now, as then when Buford and his cavalry picked the particular ground the Federals held and upon which the Confederates broke, terrain shapes the fight. As I mentioned, we had been enthusiastically preparing for that. We wanted to make sure any trespassers were correctly channeled to the right spot for their eventual reception.

There hadn't been a real infantry fight with live ammo and spilt blood in Middle Tennessee since late 1864, when Hood's Army of the Tennessee mortally wounded itself trying to get through the Federal earthworks at Franklin before it finished bleeding to death outside Nashville two weeks later. Modern technology had given me a lot of advantages absolutely undreamt of then, or even in the post-Vietnam Cold War Army in which I'd spent my formative years.

See, I'd spent my younger years mostly studying the wars I considered more operationally relevant, like Korea or Vietnam. Desert Storm didn't really count, and then once they started, I'd spent most of two decades distracted with the ones we were actually in. Too many of my formative professional lessons were secondhand ones from Vietnam, and the years I'd spent in Iraq or preparing others to go there, Afghanistan, or a devil's buffet of other shitholes hadn't made me trust technology any more than I had to. That's why I maintained a skeptic's view of things like night vision or GPS, and had also tried having as much of the technological voodoo done in advance. That gives you time to work a backup plan should there be a critical gadget failure at an inopportune moment.

But yes, some of my thinking on this was driven by my midlife rediscovery of Civil War studies. This wasn't merely an older man's folly, since our worst-case scenarios here at home had more in common with Little Round Top or Horseshoe Ridge than the Normandy invasion or the 2003 capture of Baghdad. Our homegrown force would still be built around rifles and the modern versions of light artillery. More capable in some respects than .58 caliber muzzleloaders or 12-pounder cannon, of course, but rifle work is rifle work. Machine guns only change that so much. We couldn't hide behind an air force here, since we didn't have one. There was no wall of heavy modern artillery back behind the horizon.

At the same time, technology had put some cards in my deck. Back when Jackson took the 'foot cavalry' on that long flanking march at Chancellorsville, he didn't know for sure what was in front of him, and Lee could only hope old Stonewall would actually get there to the Yankee rear to blindside the Eleventh Corps. Instead of having to send aides out on horseback to run messages about, we had radios, and if I needed eyes on something, I had UAVs and maybe some satellite coverage. It would take a lot to make me blind, as Stuart had left Lee before Gettysburg.

Of course, all this had not been a one-day sudden interest. A lifetime of study helped, and a lot of other somebodies' lives of study helped even more. Research for this did not stop at 1865. Having a copy of Command Sergeant Major Robert Rush's outstanding book on the battle in my library, and I do miss that old man, I had slowly cribbed every dirty trick I could find from the Hürtgen Forest in '44, then moved on to the A Shau Valley, Hobo Woods, and a dozen other forest fights. Most of the advantages accrue to the defense in such an environment. The slopes and rocks were generally inhospitable, and we did have something of the barrier plan in the woods already. Now for the sake of the wildlife, the pits were covered, and the Claymores weren't set, but there was a plan for all that to go in quickly.

Once we had a firm handle on the historical fundamentals that would be our foundation stones, *then* you could top off the plan with some technological leverage. We'd basically dumped all the lessons the Internet had learned from the Ukraine War and numerous other less publicized dust-ups on the table when it came to defending the acreage. If a neighbor to the east was ever willing to sell, I'd pick up another hundred and fifty or so, but not today. A notch in the north ridge was where the driveway gate came off the paved road, coming southeasterly then breaking back southwesterly to the parking lot in front of the garage doors into the mountain. All the ridges were thickly wooded and full of underbrush except where we'd cut trails. Those trails would be trapped and those traps overwatched by blockhouse-style bunkers. Probably half a dozen would do.

I'd wandered back up at the hall, sat back down at my desk, and Angel set her file aside to work on my neck and shoulders. I got to enjoy a whole ten uninterrupted minutes of that, then my work phone rang. It wasn't even five in the fucking morning yet, and I didn't recognize the number. *This ought to be good*, I thought, so I hit the button, fighting the temptation to snarl in anger. "Hello?"

"Hey, Professor, it's Luke."

I was slightly surprised at that. "Luke as in tried to stab me in Vegas at Shellington's party then went home with the stripper Luke?" Now I really didn't know who he'd gone home with owing to how that party ended and me being in a gunfight elsewhere after, but I wasn't above puffing the man's ego a bit since he'd reached out.

He laughed a little. "Yeah, man, it's your drinking buddy from the Mixer."

"I'm kinda surprised you found this number."

"Well, I got it from a mutual friend of ours." *Well, fuck. Wonder who?*

I decided humor was the way to go. "Wasn't the stripper, was it?"

"No, it was your buddy from the dentist's office."

Double fuck. I didn't realize those two knew each other. "Huh. Thought he wasn't around anymore."

"No, he's just out of town. Way out of town. But we finally talked. I heard what a good job you did for him after getting off to that rocky start. He's still doing well. But after that chat, I was wondering if you had room for someone else who, well, finally grew a conscience."

I tried to consider my next answer real fast. Once upon a time, my mom commented on my habit of collecting both stray animals and stray people. The difference is stray people can and often will bite you worse. I had the scars to prove it. "Where are you at right now?"

"Off I-95 down below Quantico. Just ate at one of the truck stops."

"Head south, then you go west on 64 out to 81, and then on down to 40. It's a long drive to Nashville, relatively speaking. Take you about fourteen hours if you keep it around the speed limit. Once you get there, turn north on I-65, and go up about twenty miles. Call me back when you get there."

"Roger that. And thank you."

I nodded to no one in particular. "Just drive safe and get here in one piece."
I then learned back into Angel as she made the pain go away for a little while.

Chapter Nineteen

I think the mad bastard drove it mostly straight through. Sixteen hours later, a little before midnight, Jake rode over with me when I met Luke at a Waffle House off the Interstate. It was close enough to the office that it was easy for us to get to, but we weren't leading him onto the grounds yet either. You'll recall we didn't let our lawyer Fast Eddie Netherton come inside for a while either. We got a booth off to the side, we all ordered, and only started seriously talking after the food arrived.

Jake hadn't met Luke that night, so the burden of starting and carrying the conversation was on me. "All right, Luke. You wanted to meet up, here we are. First thing, where's our mutual buddy Davidson?"

He chuckled just a little, despite how worn-out he looked. "Recon Marine with a scuba badge, remember? He's working on his buddy's dive boat down in Grand Cayman and lying to people about the scar your girl gave him. He told me to tell you he's staying way the hell away from whatever this turns into, and he warned me stay away from your girlfriends. Said the one just liked to shoot people and the other was Hannibal Lecter with a boob job."

Jake hadn't heard any of this and was just looking at me funny. I side-eyed him. "Tell you later." I then turned my head back to Luke. "That is a grotesque exaggeration."

"Really? Because I'm inclined to believe the guy with a piece cut off him."

"Well, calling her Hannibal Lecter is an exaggeration, at least."

Luke looked real skeptical. "How do you figure?"

"At least to the best of my knowledge, she's never actually eaten anybody."

He just looked at me with a severe *what the fucking fuck* expression. "Man, if you're trying to make me feel better, I don't think that's exactly the tactic to use."

"It's not to reassure you. It's merely a statement of fact that she likes to think of herself as the 'or else' option for people who try to cross us. Just file that away in the back of your mind as we go forward. So, I suspect we're all racing the clock, so let's get back to the point. What went wrong at ArmEx?"

He looked depressed as much as he looked tired, though of course that was going off the one time I'd met him when he was half-drunk and bumping coke while we were watching the strippers. Most days are a comedown when you've been living like that, I'd suppose. And God knew it was a hell of a damn drive. I'd been running that same route back and forth from Maryland for over thirty years and it never gets shorter. Thinking about it, he finally answered "A better question would be 'what *didn't* go wrong at ArmEx?'"

I supposed that was a fair enough question. "Well, give it to us from the beginning then."

"Okay, first of all, the General got eased out quick before he was even out of the hospital and that Anzac comes walking in as the new CEO. The kangaroo fucker starts slashing the numbers right off the bat and talking about profit margins and investor dividends instead of the mission goal and building units. See, we were a military business, emphasis on military. Colonel or no, he just gave a shit about the business side, like the military part was an obstacle."

We at Athenaeum are information brokers, so sometimes you have to be pedantic. "Kangaroo fuckers are Aussies. That guy's a Kiwi."

Luke didn't care, and his face showed it. "Whatever. He's still some condescending dickhead from *Down Undah* who sounded like Crocodile Dundee's gay uncle, so I didn't pay that much attention. I was kinda distracted because he cut my department by two-thirds on an hour's notice. And get this, the renta-cops doing the walk-outs were all Chinese."

Jake looked thoughtful. "Our Chinese or their Chinese?"

Luke shrugged, chewing his hash browns. "Beats me. I speak enough Pashtun to get by, some Dari, and a few scraps of Arabic. That's on top of some Tijuana Spanish from when I was still at Coronado. I don't speak a word of Chinese past *lo mein*, not that these dudes were chatty. Angry, hardened fuckers with whitewall haircuts going gray, looked like their version of SOF retirees."

I looked over at Jake, then back at Luke. He knew what I was thinking, that they sounded just like the rival crews of Chinese veterans either working with or pissed off at James Lin. Four from Column B ended up multiply perforated west of the Arkansas state line, but we didn't know who else from that side was out there making moves on our side of the Pacific.

Jake shrugged, and hit the next question. "How the fuck does that work? ArmEx does most of its work offshore, but there's still some DOD contract stuff in there, and they gotta have cleared spaces same as we do. You can't have a bunch of rented 'Third Country Nationals' wandering in and out of there without a lot of prior clearing and coordination. Even the Kiwi should have gotten cleared in."

"Beats the shit out of me, man. We had about thirty seconds' notice that they were coming in. I wasn't senior enough to be told things like that, and admin shit like clearances and stuff was a whole different chain of command there at the home office."

I thought about it for a second. "Well, they're a bigger company run by an ex-general, so of course they're gonna want a great big complex staff structure and grow it downhill from there. He can hire all his old buddies that way and get everyone a nice paycheck." We'd gone the opposite direction at Athenaeum. I remember when the *entire* firm, and I mean *entire*, totaled maybe twenty-five people from Big John on down to both shifts in Intel.

Jake was head-down, busy on his Black work phone. He showed Luke a picture of the new ArmEx CEO. "That the same guy we're talking about?"

Luke washed that bite of hash browns down with more coffee before he answered. "Yeah, that's him. He had another Kiwi with him, and a dozen Chinese jarhead types for muscle."

"They started slashing the company, and then what?"

"Over fifty people got laid off, in person, with less than an hour's warning. He brings some Canadian in to take over the force generation office while firing half of it, and then announced there would be a new guy overseeing the contract units that were in the field. I think that one was also a kangaroo fucker, and they would be pushing that office offshore 'closer to the action.' Special Projects where our buddy worked? All gone. You know he was gone already, but there were five others in there and they were history, just like that. I was with Training Branch, and most of us are gone too."

Jake made a *huh* noise and commented. "I didn't know you guys had a training branch in the States. I thought it was overseas somewhere."

I cut in. "Yeah, he'd mentioned Florida the night I met him, but I never found anything else after that about it."

Luke shrugged. "Most of Training Branch is offshore. It's in Namibia, where there's a good-sized site for the lower-level contractors. We only hired experienced personnel, but you still gotta do some selection and refresher to make sure you hire the right ones and then you gotta up their skills some. Usually they train up under the cadre they're going to deploy under, so those guys, once they get hired, get to the camp first and do a month of workup together before they host the selection intake, have the tryouts, and do follow-on training."

I nodded. "WWII force generation model all over again."

Luke shrugged. "Probably goes back to the Romans if you go far enough, *Professor.*"

"Yeah, but in this case, I'm thinking it's more like Camp Toccoa, Georgia more than it was the legionary camps along Hadrian's Wall."

We all shut up for a minute while the waitress came over and refilled our drinks. Then he picked up again. "So anyway, the company's got near to a thousand acres down in Florida north of I-10 back in the pinewoods. It was going to be the Stateside training area over the long term, with pretty quick access down 231 to the new container docks at Panama City. Not a very big port, but it's not like we're trying to ship an armored division in or out."

I chuckled. "And close to Panama City Beach so you guys can get in on all that tourist pussy, right?" I was trying to cheer him up a little. He nodded, but he still seemed way more subdued than he did that night in Vegas. I chalked it up to fatigue and a little bit of shock.

"Anyway, the idea the Special Projects assholes came up with was that we were going to have some land in the States where we could train on and generate a genuine US veteran force for the high dollar jobs. What we've got now is for doing riot control in the Solomon Islands or stopping a coup in some African shithole. As for Florida, there's not much down there yet. Some prefab barracks for about fifty guys, a pair of hundred-meter ranges scraped out of the pinewoods, and a decent shitter. It was all pretty basic because we weren't supposed to need it yet. It was mostly in caretaker status. I was down there three weeks a month planning and working on it —"

"You personally?"

"Yeah. I was a Seabee before I went to BUD/S so I do decent carpentry and electrical. Hell, I'm great with a front-end loader and I love plumbing. I was gonna do the shower side of the new shitter building next. I had actually parked my camper down there and was living in it — I just grabbed a hotel whenever I was in Virginia and the company always covered it, but my camper's still down there. It was slow going. We blew the budget just buying the land, so we were waiting for the company to make more money on the jobs we had to fund what we really wanted to do down there."

I snorted. I probably knew more about ArmEx's finances up until a few months ago than he did. This news did make me wonder what was going to happen to that money Shellington had banked overseas and had probably been hiding from his investors. Really, we needed to find Shellington too. Something told me if we found one, we'd find the other.

He continued. "Another month goes by. I do three weeks in Florida, come back up, and then the company card declines for the hotel. I call the number on the back, and their call center tells me that the fuckers at headquarters had turned it off without a word. I'm already there, so I still sit through a couple days of bullshit, half of it in Chinese that they don't translate since I'm one of the last white guys in the room except for the other kangaroo fucker."

Jake found that as weird as I did, and said so. "They didn't translate?"

"Apparently they all speak Chinese, even the white guys. Me, I didn't matter. Anyway, we get to the end, and the Kiwi tells me go back to Florida and keep working on the training site. I do that for another three weeks. I was supposed to come back up for another meeting, but they hadn't gotten me a new company credit card or paid me back for the last trip, so I was already pissed off. Then the more I thought about it, the angrier I got. I didn't make it all the way up 95 when I called you. Something fucking stinks, man, and you're the only other player I know on the field. I sure as shit don't trust the real government."

Well, that was a compliment, I guess. "You know if they have anyone at the Florida place?"

"Nothing popped on my cameras as of an hour ago. My phone will get a notification if anything does set the motion sensors off." I found that pretty fucking funny. Twenty years ago, motion control cameras were the stuff of securing the US Mint or something, and now could now be easily ordered as a boxed kit off Amazon. Welcome to the modern age, I guess.

First things first. "You gonna be able to move your camper with what you're driving?" His truck was a dark blue Silverado 1500, newer than mine, and definitely lacking the engine modifications Henry had made.

"Yeah, it's a little one, not a big fifth wheel or anything stupid."

I nodded. "Okay, it's what, six hours down there? Go back to Florida and move it before they show up and you lose it. Assume you're never going back.

Get back up here when you can, and then we'll find you a place to park that thing and we'll ease you in with us. Fair enough?"

Luke nodded. Really, what he needed was a couple days of sleep rather than another six or seven hours on the road each way. The other team wasn't going to give a fuck, so I couldn't afford to either. "I appreciate the hell out of this. I guess time's a-wasting then."

We stood, walked outside, shook hands, and went our separate ways for a bit.

Chapter Twenty

"When your life and those of your people are the stakes, you don't want to have to depend on strangers."
~ Colonel Charlie Beckwith, US Army counterterrorism pioneer

The first thing I did when I got back downstairs was let myself try to sleep until about six in the morning. That was a much more decent hour of the morning to call what was left of the Board of Directors to let them know what was going on. Yeah, I was Chairman and CEO, and Dave was also a member, but there were a few old guys still hanging on. We were down to five. When I'd started here, there were seven, but we'd had two deaths and a retirement. One of those deaths had been my boss and predecessor. Cancer, mostly, but he'd hastened the exit.

Dave was in around breakfast time. I filled him in on what was going on with the Waffle House meeting. I then blurted out the next thing on my mind. "I gotta call Eric. If I don't invite him to this goddamn fight that's coming, he'll be really pissed off, and if I survive it, he'll kill me."

Eric was the oldest remaining member of Athenaeum's board, and absolutely the scariest. Lemme give you the short version. He was a retired Special Forces sergeant major with a combat record that went back to the early-early days of the Vietnam War, and he hadn't missed one after that, including a few we hadn't officially been in. He'd hunted everyone from the Viet Cong and Khmer Rouge to Pablo Escobar. He'd hung up the uniform after thirty years, but had carried on as a contract asset for a couple Other Government Agencies. Even now he was still playing the occasional road game on the private military circuit. He'd go out on thirty-day trips to assorted foreign shitholes as a visiting troubleshooter for various 'security firms' or 'consultancies'. The math said he had to be past eighty by now, but didn't look all that much past sixty if the light was right. Was it just good genes or had he made a deal with some ancient pagan god he'd met in the jungles of Southeast Asia? I didn't know, but with him, I considered either one entirely possible. When I called him, I got his voice mail. I just told him to call me back and it was important. I also texted him just for the sake of redundancy. Maybe he would, maybe he wouldn't. He could be anywhere from Baja California to Baghdad to Bangkok, wherever the wind blew him and wherever there was a whiff of trouble.

About ten seconds later, my Black phone rang with some weird foreign number. Thinking it was Eric calling me back from West Buttfuck in North Middle Of Fucking Nowhere, I answered though it wasn't showing fully scrambled, either. "Hello?"

They coughed at first, and then I heard "Hey, kid."

Well, this was a goddamned surprise. "General Shellington, sir. This was unexpected." I was actually being extra polite for some reason.

"I bet it was unexpected. You probably thought I died."

I nodded. "None of the phone numbers I had for you worked and nobody knew where you were, so that outcome did come up in the discussions, yeah."

"You paying any attention to what's going on at my former employer?"

"Yeah, that's got to be ugly to see considering you built that damn company."

He snorted. "They can fuckin' have it. The venture funds wanted their profits back all at once up front, and they got them. The price they paid for getting their money out early is it's a Chinese military asset now. Let's see how much they make anymore off that. I cashed out my options already, so fuck 'em. Let the Chinese run it into the goddamn ground and the assholes in New York can see what the paper they still hold is worth then."

"They cut a lot of your former people after they cut you. Without naming names, I have a few of them coming to hide with me right now." Better to be vague.

"Pretty decent of you, all things considered."

I laughed. "My humanitarianism has its limits. I need the info they have though, so playing nice benefited everyone under the circumstances."

He coughed and chuckled. "You're learning, kid."

I pushed a little. "You need a place to hide out?"

He really laughed at that. "Hell, no. Not with what you might have breathing down your neck. I'm too old for gunfights now, particularly dragging an oxygen tank some days. I'm not even in the country anymore."

"Hiding out with your Laotian money in the land of tea and steak kebabs?" I was betting he still had a bunch of that money in Riyadh. The Saudis can keep a secret if you pay them enough that they decide they like you.

"Not a bad guess, but I'm not telling you on a phone line. Our crypto isn't that good, you know. Too many people want me dead and want that stash."

I knew that feeling way too well. Even with El Whoever having eaten a JDAM for lunch, I was convinced there were still Mexican drug cartel guys out there who wanted their money back. I'm sure they were quite grumpy about it, even if they didn't know it was us. "Kind of a reversal of fortunes for you now."

"I'll be okay. I just wanted to let you know I'm alive and warn you that I still have a couple people there in the company. You're absolutely the next name on the hangin' list Beijing sent them."

I nodded. "I might have guessed. Ran into a couple of those particular bastards later that night after you and I talked, and more of them later."

He paused for a long second. "Word is they're coming hard, bringing offshore hitters. You need any help? I can pass the word."

"Unless you have an operational A-10 Warthog outfit with pilots, fuel, and munitions, or maybe a tank company, I think we're doing most of what can be."

He coughed and chuckled. "Roger that, but no. All I got is a borrowed nine mil and a suitcase. Good luck, kid." With that, he abruptly hung up.

You guys ever hear the saying 'the true measure of someone's intelligence is how well they agree with you'? Yeah. Knowing a retired three-star and former defense CEO, even if I still kinda thought he was a blow-dried, face-lifted weasel, confirmed my paranoia made me feel better about the whole thing. I could almost emotionally deal with the knowledge that we were about to get hit. It took the uncertainty out of the process. At least he warned us. Well, shit. Meanwhile there was much to be done.

The next on the list was Little John, a retired naval officer who lived down in Florida. As a two-star admiral, he'd been chief of intelligence for the Pacific Fleet. He'd spent his career being as much of a spook as he was a submariner. We'd had two Johns on the board when I got here, but Big John had been the Chairman and CEO in addition to being four inches taller. His having died hadn't eliminated Little John's nickname though. Anyway, John had pretty serious heart trouble and was only healthy enough to handle his fishing hobby and an on-call consultancy for things in the Asian rim. I felt bad about bothering him, to be honest, but I had to.

John picked up on the second ring. "How's it going?"

I sighed. "Shitty, to be honest. We got some real problems."

"Anything I can help with?"

"Unless you have a back-channel source inside the Chinese military intelligence departments, specifically their land-based special operations forces, most likely not, but I figured you had the right to know what was going on."

I could nearly see the look on his face while he was thinking. "I haven't been cleared for direct HUMINT out of there since a few years after I retired. I still see a lot of their naval stuff, both for you guys and for the squirrels on the Washington Navy Yard and out in the new building at Suitland, but the sources are always scrubbed off since I'm too old to need to know anymore."

"This isn't naval. This is Chinese Army, so far on the dark side of their special operations force that it's practically organized crime."

"Shit, you know that wasn't my thing, but I knew a guy for that once. Too bad it's not 2009 or so."

"What makes you say that?"

"Because he got himself reassigned to the cemetery up at West Point. Cancer finally finished him off about ten years back."

"Goddamn it," I cursed in annoyance. "Why does everyone we always really need for shit like this turn out to be dead?"

"Because we got old but we just ain't died yet," he replied in that Downeaster Maine accent he'd never completely lost. "Give it long enough, and other people will be cussing that we're dead too."

"Might be sooner rather than later if this goes sideways."

John was quiet for a minute. "This one of your little criminal capers?"

"Nope. We have at least elements of a full nation-state intelligence apparatus pissed off at us, and we legitimately didn't start it."

"How pissed?"

"I got a retired Army three-star telling me there's third-party hitters coming in from offshore, and it's not like The Hole is all that hard to find in the satellite age."

"You survived worse."

I shrugged in an empty room. "Yeah, but I was a lot younger then and I got civilized since."

That got a laugh out of him. "You're as bad as Eric."

"Nah, he had a much more distinguished career than me."

"Okay, what can I do to help? I haven't even touched a pistol in six months, and my heart would be just as likely to kill me as the flying lead."

"See if anyone knows anything about Chinese military intel operations going on in the States as far as pushing a direct-action element."

"The Chinese aren't stupid. That would be an act of war."

"Third party hitters? Make it look like something else? 'All warfare is based in deception,' as Sun Tzu eloquently put it."

He scoffed, cursing at me in Mandarin before switching back to English. "It's a good thing you have that cute girlfriend of yours to translate, goddamn it, because you couldn't tell Sun Tzu from General Tso if you had to read it in the original."

"Just because I had to read the translation doesn't mean I didn't read it." Never mind what I'd done on my own, I'd actually had to read the whole thing in back-to-back semesters in grad school. I had fourteen weeks each of "Military Theory and Thought" then "The Asian Way of War."

"Well, the theory isn't your problem right now. Your problem is the real world, and we just don't have the connections there that we used to."

There was one member of the board left. "There's Greg."

"Greg was at Geospatial, and this isn't really his thing."

I grumbled. "A lot of things weren't Greg's thing." Ninety percent of the time, I thought he was kinda useless. Nice guy, but kinda useless.

"Credit where credit is due," Little John continued, "Greg found us a lot of legitimate money compared to a bunch of the other shit we got into through Pete or Big John."

Pete had been on the board when I got here, but I never actually met the guy. He was just another grumbly voice on our encrypted conference calls. When he died, I was voted onto the board as the junior member. I also continued as Big John's adjutant and on-hand whipping boy until his not-so-abrupt passing. "Eric found us a lot of dirty money too, but he's always complaining he outlived most of his contacts. Now legitimate money is great, and I can't argue with it, but we got a much bigger problem breathing down our necks. Legitimate only goes so far."

He sighed. "Well, you do what you gotta do. I'm too old and broken to do you much good. You talk to Eric yet?"

"Got his voice mail and texted him. Hopefully I hear back soon." With that, we said our goodbyes and I got off the phone. I debated calling Greg but there wasn't much point.

Anyway, since I was in charge, I was morally obligated to let everyone else know what the fuck I was thinking, so it was meeting time. I managed to get all the principals together in the conference room within the hour. Dave and Kara, Petey and Morgan, then Jake and Nichols. That gave me the top two each from Intel, IT, and Security. We never had put together a separate admin branch, and I still think we should one of these days, but we just had never gotten around to it.

Cash and Angel sat in as well. That wasn't for eye candy. First, this was gonna cost the proverbial metric fuckton of money, so that meant Cash was going to be highly involved in moving dollars around and getting the pile where we needed it. Angel was there for her common sense and her particular ability to keep me sane. I knew I wasn't doing all that well. That skill of hers might be needed sooner rather than later.

As was my habit, I started without preamble. "Ladies and gentlemen, big shit up front. Some of you may know some of this already, but I'm gonna recap from the top so we're all on the same page. We may have a war on our hands. This place may become a battlefield eventually. I know we talk about it sometimes as a worst-case scenario, but this is the real fucking thing. The serious planning cycle for that begins now."

Several people just looked at me funny, so I explained the conversation with Luke and events at ArmEx, ending with "So we get the people we don't need in a gunfight the fuck out of the way. Damn, I wish there was somewhere to park them so they could keep doing paying work somewhere other than here."

Morgan shrugged. "This would have been a really cool time to have that backup facility we talked about a year ago." He was interrupted by a quietly musical laugh from the end of the table.

Cash was looking over at Petey, then back at me, looking delightfully amused for once. I sighed. "Darling, what's so funny?"

She grinned impishly. "Sir, remember when I once told you that you had the attention span of a hamster for the administrative side of the business?"

I nodded. "Yes, I do recall that conversation, even though it's been a minute." For a girl who claimed she had no sense of humor, she could and did say a lot of genuinely funny shit that lodged in my memory.

Cash looked over at Petey. "Well, I knew you would forget about the idea with one crisis or another, so I used my role as holder of the financial leash to get the signal officer to do signal officer stuff as a hedge against the time there would be a sudden problem."

I leaned back and stared at the ceiling, looking for familiar constellations of pockmarks in the tiles. Yes, I do this often enough I've picked out mental landmarks up there. "Okay, Cash dear, or Petey, I don't care who, somebody skip to the part where you tell me what you either didn't tell me or that you did tell me and I simply failed to retain."

Petey picked up the ball and pushed forward. "We have a backup site."

Morgan looked over at him. "We do?" Okay, if Morgan didn't know either, I didn't feel so bad about being caught lacking.

I perked up. "Missile silo? There was an Atlas-E site in Kansas for sale last year and those are the hard ones to get since they're the horizontal hangar rather than the deep vertical hole."

It was Cash's turn to sigh. "No, sir. Nor an Atlas-F, nor neither iteration of the Titan, or even a Nike SAM site. Those last ones are really hard to come by commercially anyway, no matter how many of them got built."

"Damn, and there were Titan silos in Arkansas, too. Relatively convenient."

Petey shook his head. "And on the wrong side of a river with only three bridge crossings between Dyersburg, Memphis, and down at Helena. Not a lot of options when you're on the run. Why have your exfil route past a choke point at a linear danger area?" I was impressed he'd phrased it that way, but when you work commo support for the infantry or brigade recon for years, you get smarter at the maneuver aspects of warfare than the average signals guy.

"So, what clever bit of fox-like cleverness did you come up with instead?" Yes, that was a deliberate homage to the *Blackadder* finale scene just before where they all die in 1917, but I don't think anyone noticed.

Cash smiled. "Down the road a couple hours in the city of Chattanooga, home of some of the fastest commercial Internet in the country, are several office parks. On the back side of one of those office parks is a smallish space under long-term lease to a nicely anonymous firm called Telecon Systems, Incorporated."

I didn't want to tell Petey that Chattanooga wasn't exactly easy to get into or out of either. There was a whole long and ugly campaign in the Civil War that proved that, and modern road-building had only done so much to rectify the issue. Those mountains and ridges were not significantly changed. Ignoring all that, I continued. "And let me guess, Telecon Systems, Incorporated is a paper company at the end of a trail of other paper companies and subleases that eventually dead-ends in a PO box somewhere belonging to somebody who doesn't actually exist."

Petey shrugged. "Oh, they exist, in that someone put that particular name on a piece of paper. They're as real as all those small companies that were scamming paycheck protection loans from the Feds during the pandemic years." Ah, yes, when Etlanna famously ran out of snow crab legs or whatever. Days of wine and roses for some people.

I waved off his demurral. "Point is, it's a separate front company that we can walk enough people into to keep part of the operation going."

He nodded. "Furniture is there, mostly secondhand junk, some computers are there, and the phones are up and the Internet is on. Unclassified commercial stuff only. No government wiring because they don't know about it, but it's at least a place to run to."

"Caretaker staff?"

"Yep. I hired a couple ex-signals types to keep the lights on. Nobody you'd know, so don't bother asking."

Okay, cool. "Moving on from there to the service and support side of the evacuation. Where do we quarter everybody if we have to surge that way?"

"You know those extended-stay suite hotels?" Petey asked. "They're mostly chains and all have boring names mentioning winds, creeks, or bridges?"

"Yeah. You see them all over the place, but I stayed in a couple of them down there in Nooga for conventions."

"There's one across the street from the office park. For some reason none of the rooms on the fourth floor ever get rented out. That gives us 36 rooms, all en-suite with little kitchens and everything."

"Lemme guess, we own that too." It wasn't a question.

Cash giggled. "Of course we don't own it. A wholly separate legal entity owns it."

"Anything useful stashed there?"

Petey shrugged. "Arms room on the fourth floor. A dozen each of ARs and Glocks, all legal, with a couple cases of ammo and some accessory shit like holsters and mag pouches. Not much, but it beats nothing. I know he's is working on it."

"Who's 'he'? I assume the staff is ours?"

"You remember Mendoza from the guard shack? Used to be a Marine?"

Yeah, I did, though he was no relation to the Mendoza I'd gone to Iraq with twice. Yes, I'd asked. "Didn't he leave and go back to college?"

"Yeah, but he's a business major at UT-Chattanooga, and so he's the assistant manager of the hotel. That makes him the fourth floor's caretaker, and so he also keeps that arms room."

"If he's the assistant, then who is the real hotel manager?"

"None of us knew shit about running a hotel, and neither did he, so we hired a guy and made sure he knew what he was getting paid not to ask while still teaching Mendoza how to run it over the long haul."

This was pretty fucking clever and I was very proud of them for thinking it through and executing the plan. See, this is a time where decentralized leadership actually worked.

Chapter Twenty-One

---

*"A*s of this moment, we are at war."

~ *Commander William Adama, the Colonial Fleet*

This wasn't the first time we thought we may have to go to a wartime footing. This was the first time it felt close enough to make a generalized announcement. Two days later, we pulled everyone in for a meeting, whether they were off duty or not. *Everyone* in the building came upstairs to the garage bay. Even more so than the picnics or parties, when at least somebody was still rotating inside on the phone, the entire company was in the garage bay. There was no massive American flag hanging. I wasn't in Class A uniform, there were no trumpets blowing, and no roll of drums. But this was my George Patton movie moment, I guess. Cash and Angel waved and smiled, trying to be encouraging as I climbed up on top of a workbench to be seen, took a deep breath, and began.

"Ladies and gentlemen," I began, "a bunch of you know what we may be in for here. For those of you who don't, here's the short version. We have a front company controlled by Chinese intelligence pissed off at us. They might well be pissed enough at us to resort to real violence."

Dead silence. A pin dropping would have been thunderous.

"We aren't sure how they're coming at us, though there are some rumors. Some of you remember that shit last year and heard the story of how my house got burned down. They may come at you at home. They may come at you on the road. They might decide to throw caution out the window and come at us in full strength here. We just don't know. But we're planning for as much as we can, and some of it's going to fall on your shoulders. Understood?"

There were some nods and murmurs, but nothing significant.

"Now you know as a company, we're information brokers, not mercenaries. That said, we're at a moment in our history where we may have to engage in some serious self-defense. We may need every finger on a trigger before all's said and done. This mountain fortress of ours can only get us so far. Now I sincerely hope every one of you is willing to participate in that. If not, *he who hath no stomach for this fight, let them depart.*"

There were nods at the Shakespearean reference. One kid from IT tried standing up, but he was sitting next to the newly married Johnstons. Addy grabbed him by the hair and pulled him back down into his seat. "Sit down, you fucking twink, or I'll kill you myself," she sneered, loud enough for everyone to hear it. Sound carries real well in there.

He looked embarrassed and indignant. "Jesus Christ, I was just going to the bathroom."

She wasn't having that either. "Pinch it and hold. The boss is talking."

Normally we'd all have a good chuckle at that bit of interplay, but the mood was just too somber. Too many people knew what was going on, and also had the experience to know it might be a real tough row to hoe. Plus, Addy had that knife kill in Vegas that was still whispered about, so she had too much street cred to be laughed at right now.

I looked around. No one else moved. "All right. Who doesn't own a gun and needs one issued? Standard is 5.56mm, standard AR magazine compatible. Pistols, 'run what you brung,' as the Outlaw class dragstrip guys say, but we have loaners for that too." A few hands went up, mostly IT or Intel. "Fine, tell your supervisors and we'll get into the loaner stuff. We can also cut you loose to go shopping. God knows we live in the right state for it. There will be refresher classes out back on the range complex very soon. Like 'starting later this afternoon' kind of soon."

There were more nods, and a few faces went a little pale, but everyone was holding tight.

"Next thing. Some of you are not staying for this." There were various confused noises, but I continued. "We've got a backup site where some of you will get to relocate. Some of you may have the option to relocate permanently to keep that backup site viable over the long term."

"Criteria for that?" somebody asked.

"Basically 'Do I Need This Person In A Gunfight,' or are you better off behind a computer somewhere else keeping the money coming in," I replied. "Don't worry about that too much. You'll get asked, more like volun-told one way or another. That's gonna be an IT and Intel issue, mostly. Some of you might get to relocate permanently if you prefer it there. Security, your task-org is gonna change somewhat, and you are gonna have a training schedule up. Lemme put it this way, for you Campbell guys, it's Gold Cycle all over again."

There were more quiet nods and those murmurs of assent. Hawkins then chuckled a bit. "Bossman, FYI, they haven't called it that in at least fifteen years."

"But you know what I meant, which is the point. Now, for those who are staying, there's going to be lovely springtime yard work getting ready to host a party with an undetermined number of guests. We're gonna be digging and fencing and doing sandbags and whatnot."

A voice popped up in back. "Sandbags? Fuck that. Can I volunteer to relocate?"

"Maybe. Depends how much I need you here." There was some laughter at that. A few people with the skills for it had already been rotating in and out of the woods prepping for the work to come., At one level, everyone knew we were hardening up for the threat. "Okay, questions?"

Dead silence followed. Everyone was looking at each other, waiting for someone else to talk first. I didn't really have time for that, and knew the questions would bubble up when everyone came out of the shock. There wasn't much else to put out beyond that, so the meeting broke up and everyone got back to work or headed home until it was their turn to get back on duty.

Just then, my cell phone rang. I recognized Luke's number. "Hey, man, I'm coming up 65 to what I think is your exit. Where do you want me to park this thing?

I grinned. "Your timing is perfect. I need some Seabee shit done."

Chapter Twenty-Two

"*When the going gets tough, the tough go feral.*"
~ *John "Conan the Barbarian, Red Dawn" Milius, Hollywood writer and director, co-author of my childhood*

Right now, I wasn't kidding. I needed Luke's Seabee background more than I needed a SEAL. I had SEALs. I had Jimmy and Tommy around for years, and neither of them were doing long swims or shooting people right now either. Jimmy was working medical setups with Doc Mickey for the new sick bay clinic on the fourth floor, and Tommy was doing electrical work on our generator room since that had been his rate in the Navy before BUD/S. He'd voluntarily gone to suffer at Coronado just to get out of the *Eisenhower*'s bowels, but right now, I needed him pulling wire and checking breaker panels. Luke would be living in his camper back by the rifle range and working on the barrier plan.

I'm not a professional combat engineer, but I know a thing or two. The first two steps to a barrier plan are figuring out where you're putting them and what you're making them out of. The third step is having the stuff to make them out of. My usual commercial trucker Steve was only available sometimes as his regular job came into their busy season, and there was no time to send more people to truck driving school for their commercial licenses. That was inconvenient, because I needed multiple flatbeds of stuff and dump truck loads of other stuff.

Within a couple days, Luke was putting in pits, swing gates, and all sorts of other nastiness. I imagine the ghost of Ragnar Benson was riding on his shoulder. None of the traps were live yet, but it was at least prefabbed, and he was obviously having a lot of fun. We were up on the east ridge of the property down past the Party Field, and he was showing me another spiked swing gate setup, pivoting off the trunk of a dead cedar tree. Luke shrugged. "I wanted to put it off an iron pipe post."

"Nah, that will show up weird on thermal. The tree trunk will blend in."

"Yeah, you're probably right. Still, what I really need is a hydraulic auger for your skid steer."

"Go buy one then, I don't give a fuck."

"Will do. But what pisses me off is I already had the goddamn auger for one of these."

"Where'd you get it?"

"Some junkie had stolen the goddamn thing off a construction site somewhere. I traded him a bag of coke for it." Eh, while I didn't approve, he wasn't working for me at the time, so I couldn't bitch about it too much.

"Still got it somewhere?"

He cracked a Gatorade and took a long pull at it. "Fuck, don't I wish. Had it at the Florida camp I was doing for Shellington."

"What did you do with it?"

"It sat around for about four months, and I hadn't used it, so I traded it to some other guy for a bigger bag of coke."

I tried not to be really obvious when I rolled my eyes and sighed. Now I don't mean to make it sound like everyone in the military contracting space is a broken human being with mental health issues, and more than a few of those with substance abuse problems besides. At the same time, there's enough of them that you shouldn't act surprised when you find another one.

Everyone was getting in on at least some piece of the construction. I was outside checking the positioning for six primary bunkers when Cash went rolling by on the backhoe. I had no idea the girl even knew how to run a backhoe. I waved at her to stop, and she did. Cutting the engine, she took off her earmuffs.

176

I noticed they were her cat-eared Peltor electronic ones. Smart girl. Loud engines are as bad for your hearing as gunfire.

"Darling, when did you learn how to drive one of these?"

Her smile was dazzling in a *'Look how proud of me you're going to be'* way I'd seen before, and always appreciated. "I'm still learning, sir. This is actually only my second time driving it.

"First, Luke gave me a tour of what the parts were. Then I speed-read the manual twice, and for everything after that, there was YouTube, sir." Well, she is one of the smartest people I know who isn't a PhD at NASA or something.

"Okay, and we did this why?"

"Despite having a talent I didn't know I had for field interrogation, and proving I learned something from all those pistol lessons, I still think I need useful skills for the company other than investment portfolio management, tax evasion, and money laundering. If I can run a backhoe, I can dig graves quickly. That means the next time I think it's a good idea to kill somebody, I can cross 'I don't have time to dig the hole' off your list of reasons why I can't do it."

Paraphrasing the late Major Moxley Sorrel of Longstreet's staff, at least his movie version, I'll tell you plain — there are days that girl worries me.

Blind to my reservations on the idea, she kept chugging along. "Anyway, I'm helping out on the bunker plan. Gotta go. Love you!" I got a quick but passionate kiss as a parting gift, then her cute little ass bounced back up into the backhoe's cab and she sped off.

Meanwhile, the truckloads of stuff were starting to come in. I needed a dozen concrete T-walls, the big ones, to block the garage gate. Past that, I needed steel-mesh Hesco baskets full of dirt and stuff for overhead cover above that. It took a little time, but we eventually got it all. Where did we get those Hesco baskets? I sent half a dozen guys to buy a couple flatbed eighteen-wheelers' worth of them off the loading dock at the factory down in Louisiana. Like most problems, it could be solved by throwing money at it.

*****

We started slowly kicking out the noncombatants to the backup site at Telcon in Chattanooga. Linguists, IT types, and everyone else we'd decided wasn't going to be super-critical in whatever was coming. Like I said, I was going to ping a few of them about permanently relocating. The backup site was a good enough idea that once it was up, it should stay that way, and dividing like an amoeba was the easiest way of duplicating a smaller version of the company. I made sure Petey sent... what's his name, Spiral, down to 'Nooga and keep working on the new secure phone project. That was a long-term infrastructure thing, and I didn't want him getting distracted from working on it with everything going on here. I told Petey to keep him busy with that and to have some sort of forward leadership there keeping the crazy fucker out of jail.

Thinking further about it, I caught Morgan in the hallway. "We're duplicating the personnel capacity, or trying. What are we doing about backing up the data?"

Morgan nodded. "We've been working on that. It's a rolling hard drive rack with at least a skin and bones copy of the operating files. Basically, it's the size of a big fishing cooler and it'll fit in an airplane door if we go out that way."

"Nah, we're gonna be smart and duplicate and move ahead of time. Hit that shit now. Back up everything you can to Nooga, legally or no. I don't give a shit what it is."

"What about the fourth floor?"

Shit. We had hundreds of dusty decades-old government-issue steel file cabinets down there, jammed full of old stuff someone had taken the time to squirrel away in the 1970s. The cabinets were jammed in so tightly that most of them were inaccessible. It looked like a losing game of *Tetris* in there. We could only easily get into fifty or so on the near row, and had nine or ten times that. There was no discernible filing system to any of it, and we rarely had time to explore it no matter how interesting some of it was. There certainly wasn't time or the resources to easily evacuate them with everything else going on. I could have the missing redacted bits of the Kennedy assassination files in there for all I knew, and if we lost this fight, that whole hoard could be among the casualties. I shook that thought off. *All the more reason to win.*

Meanwhile, Luke was taking to his new job with a cheerful will, which was nice. The weather was even playing along somewhat. That was good, because you couldn't do dirt work in the mud. I went out to check on him, and he had questions. "Boss, you got a backhoe and a skid steer. Cool, I've been using the shit out of them, but the backhoe is too big to get back in the trees and dig some of this."

Really, the guys I usually used for roads and grounds shit brought their own stuff with them. That way I didn't have to own it or maintain it. Well, the situation had changed. "Would a Deere mini-excavator do it, the little baby one they use for digging graves and whatnot?"

"Yeah... they ain't cheap though."

"I don't give a shit about cheap. I ain't digging that shit by hand and we don't have enough people doing nothing that we can use to dig it by hand either. Go get a mini-ex."

He looked kinda skeptical. "You got mini-ex money? I don't."

"At some point, you will notice a gorgeous little five-foot-nothing Korean chick around here. She's the chief financial officer and keeper of the money. And yes, I can afford a mini-ex."

"Boss, there's at least two short Asian chicks around here. I don't know one from the other and don't want to be rude and ask. And I also remember what Davidson told me about one being even more of a psycho-killer than the other.

"Neither one is that bad. Well, usually."

"So you say. I think I'm gonna believe the guy with skin missing."

I sighed but ignored that part. "To be honest, they both have their moments." I thought about it another two seconds. "Shit, let's go find her. She probably wouldn't give you thirty grand just on your own word anyway. Come on."

"You guys just do shit like that? Dump that kind of money on projects?"

I shrugged as we walked. He wasn't getting my point, and I would rather give an in-depth explanation once rather than have to repeat the short version over and over until it sunk in. "Good, fast, cheap, pick any two. Time is what we're always short on, so we just skip to good and fast. We acknowledge that will cost, but that's what it takes to get good and fast done so the mission gets accomplished."

He looked at me like I was nuts. Well, I might be, but that's also beside the point. "You know how many layers of supervisor approval paperwork that would be at ArmEx?"

Remember when I said Texans don't care how us other forty-nine states do it? That's about how many fucks I gave about how ArmEx did things. "Yeah, and look what happened to them."

Luke stopped and thought about it for a second. "Shit, you may be right."

"I sure as shit hope I am, or we all have problems. Me, I believe in a few underlying principles that I hope you let sink in as you journey with us. One, wars cost money. Two, when you're playing the game with someone else's money, you owe them. When you owe them, they in turn own your ass. Look what happened to your old boss when Wall Street called in their marker early. He ends up out on his ass and the company dances on Beijing's puppet strings now. Three, winning wars is expensive, but losing one will cost everything."

"Wasn't that last one Robert Heinlein?"

I laughed. "A SEAL who can read. Shocker. Then again, I do know a few of you who do."

"I probably shouldn't say this, you know, since I'm living in your parking lot like a stray dog, but fuck you."

We both chuckled as we took the elevator down. "It's okay, you didn't mean it personally so I don't take it personally. But yeah, I stole that line somewhere, I just don't remember where. Could have been John Ringo. Back to the point though, and the point is that if you need a piece of gear for this project, be it another bundle of railroad ties, or more chainsaw chains, or a couple fresh chainsaws for that matter, fuckin' tell me or someone else in leadership, and we'll get it for you. I don't care. You need a dozer? You need a six-k forklift? Again, I don't fucking care. We can afford it. If it gets to the point we can't, we'll just go rob somebody else and refill the piggy bank. But we gotta be alive to do that, which means keeping people off our lawn. That's what I need you to be my SME for."

He nodded and turned. "Okay, since you said to ask for shit, I'm gonna ask for shit." I was just about to ask him to formally work for us, but that could wait. I didn't want to interrupt. "I know we have the little skid steer loader, but we're gonna need at least one big front-end loader, which means we're going to need two for when one's broken, and probably a full-time equipment mechanic to keep everything going."

"Okay, get one. Deere 644 good enough?"

He was giving me that look again. "You know those are about a quarter mil each for a good used one, right?"

"Cool. Get two. And get the forks, not just the bucket so you can swap as you need. Or leave one with one and one with the other if that's easier."

"There's only one of me to run the things!"

I shrugged. Smallest problem I'd have all day. "Then get somebody else to help you out. Get a couple somebodies. Ask Jake to see who else we have with heavy equipment experience."

"Are we starting a fucking construction company?"

That actually made me pause and think for a minute. *Not a terrible idea, really.* I'm sure Cash could have thought of a way to bill it to ourselves and write a bunch of it off. I'd have to remember to ask her. "We can always resell whatever equipment we don't need later, but I want the shit right now and I don't want to wait on bank financing. They ask too many questions. I hate answering questions." I wasn't going to come right out and tell Luke that we probably had over thirty million in assorted cash, shrink-wrapped on pallets in the basement vault, and maybe ten times that in various banks where we could

181

probably get at it easily. Never mind what was banked overseas. That didn't count the rest of the company's inherited or stolen multimillions buried in the stock market where it wasn't readily accessible, or never mind the gold bullion and other portable wealth. I found I liked Luke, but I wasn't prepared to fully trust him yet. Very different things, you know.

We stuck our head into Accounting. Cash was off the backhoe and back behind her desk, even if that meant she was dressed much less like the pinup girl she usually played in the office. "Babe, got a job for you. You've met Luke here, right?"

She smiled. "Yes, sir. My backhoe tutor."

"Good. If he needs money to buy equipment, give it to him. Right now, he needs a mini-ex."

She looked at him, looked at me, and nodded. "Easy." She then pursed her lips a bit. "Um, what's a mini-ex?"

Chapter Twenty-Three

A lot of the preparations were outside. Some were downstairs. The guys in IT did a lot more than keep the Internet connections up and running. Sometimes I just paid them and if nothing else was going on, they did whatever the hell they wanted under the vague intent of 'hey, we might need this later.' And because I didn't necessarily have the technical vocabulary to understand what the hell they were talking about, I left them to it. I was usually too busy to try herding them, so that's what I paid Petey and Morgan to worry about.

Ever since the downstairs meeting where I'd given the IT guys the mission of coming up with some defensive systems, junk had been piling up out in the parking lot or the garage bay. Spools of cable, some of them the 'eight feet across' kind of spools. Surplus antennas arrived on trailers. Some of them were big boxy desert tan Army surplus things while others were spherical gray Navy surplus things. Sometimes crates or containers were there, and then they vanished after a few days. I didn't know what the hell was going on. I figured I'd find out.

This was the time where I got to see how my delegation of authority and decentralized operating style actually worked in this context. The situation was going downhill, so now I wondered if I was betting our lives on whatever wizardry my downstairs gang had come up with while I'd been busy doing other things. Some of this was spearheaded by Corey, who'd been one of our more recent hires.

Corey was what happened when you decided to run your company by slightly different rules than most defense contractors. Technically he worked for

Archive Associates, not Athenaeum. Did Corey care? No. Corey was getting paid, which was what Corey cared about. See, Corey began as one of those cases military recruiters pray for, where a then-skinny black kid from the middle of asshole nowhere in Mississippi popped up with a near perfect ASVAB and a genius level IQ back in the late 1990s. Signing his paperwork with the Navy and heading off to Great Lakes, he started his career zig-zags in the Pacific Fleet as a fire control radar tech, mostly on Aegis antennas.

Corey got out of the Navy in four years after one enlistment... well, because he liked smoking weed. Staying in California after his discharge, he'd gone to Cal Tech, but it took him a while to finish because... he liked smoking weed. He'd worked for Lockheed Martin, Raytheon, BAE, L3, and a couple others on the strength of his resume, but never stuck around with any company for long because... well, you see a pattern here? As long as Corey didn't wreck his car coming or going from work or make me smell it while he was here, I didn't really care. The latter wasn't a moral judgment, merely acknowledgement that pot smoke makes me gag. With the trend toward *de facto* legalization if not *de jure*, it makes most concerts these days genuinely unpleasant even when I have the time to go to one anymore.

I put up with all this because Corey was useful. Even when he was still looking a little baked while on the clock, the dude was an absolute genius with antennas and electronic system architecture. Because he'd burned most of his other bridges in the industry, I got him, and more importantly *kept* him fairly cheap. So what if he weighed north of three hundred pounds these days and was seriously lacking in social skills? He called himself the Spectrum King, and some of us figured it wasn't just the electromagnetic one if you know what I mean.

See, much of what we were doing downstairs was the ongoing planning cycle for the defense. You planned the initial defenses, then you planned phases of improvements. You get a little done on everything, then a little more. That keeps you from having all of one thing done super-well but not having shit of anything else. Unfortunately, with some of the guys in the meetings being video gamers or military intel dweebs without sustained ground combat experience, there was a lot of Internet bullshit coming up in the discussion and 'Rule Of Cool' seemed to be a major planning factor.

"Can we build a Killdozer?"

I wanted to cut that shit off at ground level. "No, we are not building a fucking Killdozer. If those guys have the sort of tank-killing UAVs the Ukrainians bought, largely from China I might add, armored vehicles are a resource suck. For us, armored vehicles are a resource suck anyway."

I know I'd fucked with Charles last year about wanting a platoon of surplus Bradleys, but I really hadn't been all that serious unless they were free. I'd almost never turn down free anything. It's a character flaw. But really, for four hundred acres with a lot of woods and not a lot of flat spots, this was poor tank country. Armored vehicles are just expensive mobile bunkers unless they have a place to maneuver, and we didn't. That made them a resource suck. I could build real bunkers for less money and those can be set up to be a lot harder to kill.

Kowalski, one of the intel desk guys, piped up. "We need some Ewoks."

I snorted. "We don't even have the technology for working lightsabers, let alone a hyperdrive. Where the fuck are we going to get Ewoks? Buy a genetics company that makes fake dire wolves? They haven't even brought the wooly mammoth back yet."

Forget it, he was rolling. "Think about it though. Ewoks are simian arboreal predators. Looking at Earth animals, think of an adult chimpanzee. They're roughly the same size as an Ewok, but an Ewok is more stocky. They're like a chimpanzee who's gonna be a nose tackle, not a wide receiver." I took my glasses off and rubbed my eyes as he heedlessly continued. "Now a chimpanzee is roughly ten times stronger than a human pound for pound, and Ewoks are more heavily built than chimps. Getting into hand to hand with one would be a damned nightmare. You saw them easily stabbing through the necks and joints of Stormtrooper armor with sharp sticks. Plus, they use swarming tactics, so you aren't dealing with one 'roided-up cocaine-raging koala bear, you are dealing with a dozen or more."

Sighing, I reached for my wallet. "Kowalski, I am going to give you five hundred bucks right now to not have any more impossible ideas for at least the next hour, okay?"

Chapter Twenty-Four

I t wasn't just the yard outside filling up with engineer junk. The bay was getting more 3-D printers and a second welding rig. Never mind the deliveries of ammo, medical supplies, and other combat-logistical stuff.

I had been downstairs for hours trying to do other paying work, when I'd finally hit my limit. I decided I was going to go topside and get some air. I refilled my water then hit the elevator. Heading out past the blast door and walking through the garage bay, it looked like the Athenaeum Inc. Robotics Club was having a meeting. All half-dozen of the UAV operators had quadcopters unpacked and spread across the expansive concrete floor. The big and expensive sort we used for serious reconnaissance jobs were intact, but at least a dozen lesser ones were being modified. Zoey had come out from behind her map desk and was there with the rest of the drone pilots, waving a Dewalt impact driver at one of her cohorts as they bickered.

There was one familiar face among them who didn't belong there. I'd tried hiring Gilmour a couple years ago when he was getting off active duty, but he packed up and went home to Alabama instead. He did robotics system maintenance at a major car factory down there. Four years in the infantry with a tour in Afghanistan had been a vacation from that, but he had no desire to stick around here working my guard rotation when he could make twice the money at his old job with the contractor who fixed BMW's automatic assembly line welders. Couldn't blame him a bit.

I walked on over. "Hey, man, good to see you. Kind of a surprise."

He stuck his hand out with a grin, and the handshake turned into a bro-hug. "I got a phone call saying you needed robotics work done at a nice day rate, so that was enough to get me burning vacation days to drive up here."

"Who called you?"

Zoey raised her hand, still wielding a screwdriver. "I did. Angel got me into your personnel notebook, and I looked for every robotics person I could get. He was one of three, I was another one, and the third isn't answering his phone. Believe me, I tried."

Yet again, I had *no* idea what was going on. "I didn't even hire *you* to be a robotics tech."

She rolled her eyes at me. "There's no more mapping work to be done right now, and we need everyone who can wire an actuator working on this shit. I made some more calls. We've got three or four more coming from down by Huntsville. Mostly people I knew from the state competition in back in high school, and a couple of my old rocketry club people are coming just in case. Gilmour was looking for a couple more people too, but I think we got a handle on it."

One of the full-time UAV pilots, the redheaded female one who came from 2-17 Cav, laughed a little at that. "Zoey, you're trying to pack five pounds of shit into a two-pound aircraft on some of this. You know robots, we know robots that *fly*. There's a difference."

Zoey wasn't backing off. "And we still need these things to fly with a useful payload and go further than the goddamn parking lot and back. We got literal handfuls of money for this, so we are gonna rebuild 'em til they fuckin' work, dammit." She was definitely in a mood. The angrier she got, the more she cussed and harder she drawled.

I interrupted. "Can I ask what the hell we're doing?"

The Cav tried to answer but Zoey cut her off. "We finally got around to stealing the Ukrainian grenade clamp design off the Internet and we got it successfully adapted for whatever you call the grenades we have."

The Cav sighed. "M67 fragmentation, the baseball style as opposed —"

Zoey looked over at her almost gracefully as she cut her off. "Yeah, those. Thank you." She then turned back to me. "Anyway, we're modifying a dozen of the cheap off the shelf quadcopters as tiny unmanned bombers." Off to our left, the arc welder popped, lighting up the bay for a moment.

I kinda liked this idea. "That's pretty cool. Anti-trespassing devices?"

Cav answered as Zoey stopped to bite off a bit of wire insulation. "Yeah, with one grenade per, and it's droppable, not suicide. Once we get the concept down, we're going to build something bigger that will haul a 60mm mortar round. Enough endurance they could go, drop, return for rearming, and then go right back out to deliver again without battery swaps."

I stopped, sensing a potential problem. "We don't have any 60mm shells. We have 81s. They weigh a lot more. Ten pounds, more or less. 60s are only about four each."

She shrugged. "Too bad some 60s can't fall off the back of a truck."

I supposed I could call Izzy. "Or... we just build a bigger quadcopter?"

Having lost interest in the conversation, Zoey was back to wiring things. I was going nuts trying to remember the redhead's name. "I'll work on it. Now you're gonna have to help me out." *Time to be honest again.* "I'm awful with names and I wasn't the one who hired you so it's just not sticking in my head."

She chuckled. "Britny Fox. Just N-Y. No E in between like Spears spells it."

I just stared at her. "You know that was a band, right?"

Britny sighed. "I know. Believe me, I know. My parents were Eighties kids."

I shrugged. "I was an Eighties kid, mostly."

She continued. "Were you enough of an asshole about making 'Eighties kid' your whole personality to, with the last name Fox, then deliberately name one daughter Britny and the other Samantha? Seriously. Samantha Fox. She's two years older and she caught way more shit about it than I did since Samantha was still way more famous. But Mom and Dad met on a VH-1 theme cruise down to Cancun when they were still in college, so I suppose we were fucked from the very beginning."

Oh, shit. "Yeah, I see your point." Junior High School Me was wondering if the sister was hot enough to pull it off correctly, let alone do the British accent, but I smacked down that line of thought. I had enough relationship issues without borrowing more.

Another memory re-jogged itself again. "Your dad wasn't a sergeant first class in 2nd of the 29th at Benning around '99 or '00, was he?"

"Nope, not at all. Dad went from high school to thirty years doing commercial HVAC installs back home in Pennsylvania." *Oh, well. Not an uncommon last name.* She continued. "Anyway, Angry Map Desk Girl here came up from downstairs waving one of the company credit cards and told us to start ordering parts. Then Morgan started cutting and welding, the EOD guy with the glasses showed up with a couple extra 3-D printers past what we already had set up, and an hour later she was giving orders and taking over the process."

That got her attention again, and Zoey still wasn't backing off. "Hey, I'm the one who went to Accounting and got us the money. 'No bucks, no Buck Rogers' like they said in that old NASA movie."

We were momentarily silenced when somebody went loud with a grinder over at one of the workbenches. That gave me a second for me to I think about it. "She's got a point there. Now Fox, are you senior with the UAV people?" I should know this. I really should. This would ordinarily be a 'ask Dave, maybe ask Kara or even Morgan' question since the UAVs were under Intel. Neither of those two were here right now, and Morgan was busy with a welder. I had to fumble through this by myself.

Fox shrugged. "Maybe? No one's really in charge. We have two teams of three, the two vans, and all the gear, but it's not like the Army where we would have an NCOIC over the two teams. We get told what to do and it gets done. We haven't had both teams out at once since that thing last year anyway." I know

190

what she meant. I also hadn't talked to her since she'd flown top cover for Dave's raid force that night of the heist. We had taken the other team to Vegas.

I thought about it a second. "Okay, follow on question. Do you *need* to have somebody be in charge?" I had known one guy years back who'd be perfect since he actually had been a UAV platoon sergeant in the Division, but cancer finished off my buddy Owen Stinehorten some years back. Ugly way to go, but more cynically, I also really could use him right now.

She shrugged. "Again, maybe? But that's not a today subject. We're busy in the hangar, as you can see. We'll get it done and worry about it later."

I turned to Zoey. "Okay, as long as Dave and Kara don't need you downstairs doing your real job, you can hang out here so long as you aren't pissing anyone off too much. If you need more money, you know who to talk to in Accounting. Good, fast, cheap, pick any two? Go with good and fast. I have a feeling we're going to need this shit sooner rather than later."

I looked back at Fox. "She means well, I promise. You guys just get it done." Then I pulled Gilmour aside for a very quiet word. "Your additional job is to break up any fights when one of the two ladies finally loses their patience and punches the other, got it?" He just grinned and nodded.

A couple days later, walking back through the garage bay, one more UAV project was underway. This one was now topped with a UFO-like top antenna reminiscent of a Navy Hawkeye radar aircraft. "What the hell's that set up for?" I asked.

Fox was turning wrenches, while Morgan looked up from the wiring. "With luck, this is a drone that finds other drones. We've been working on the idea since that night in Vegas."

Shit, I hadn't thought of that. "That's... damn clever."

Morgan nodded. "We're building more than one if we have time. We also have a rotating antenna with the same setup on the cell phone tower above us. We know what freqs to look for drones on, both commercial and military, so we can use these in conjunction with the tower to triangulate anything up there that's not ours. Hopefully we can do this without ending up a hood ornament on a passing aircraft."

He had a point there. The local airspace got really crowded fast, and the higher you go, it only gets worse. Airline corridors in and out of Nashville. News and traffic helicopters. Your neighbor's Cessna. Most of Fort Campbell's air traffic stayed well northwest, but it wasn't impossible to see a passing Blackhawk either. And my worst worry was that these guys would exploit China's position as the world's most prolific maker of commercial UAVs and do unto us before we did unto them. I was glad one antenna was up and running already hooked to an alarm in Intel. I didn't want these guys scouting us ahead of time.

Chapter Twenty-Five

I was back in my office working on other shit when Morgan walked in. "We're getting the in-house industrial base to start building complete UAVs here," he announced.

Huh. "That's pretty cool."

"Yeah, but there's lead time. We gotta find and buy the things we need to make the things we need to start building the things. It's a multi-step industrial process." He held up a black polymer chassis. "Know what this is?"

I looked at it and thought about it for a minute. "I would say an old MOLLE 2 pattern ruck frame, but the slots are wrong and it has too many holes in it."

"That's because it's a UAV quadcopter chassis."

"Where'd you get that?"

"3-D printed it. Took some hours, but it went. Got the idea from an article in the Clarksville paper about what the 101st is doing for their small UAVs." Yeah, I'd seen that one too.

"Does it work?"

"Another one just like it is getting put together right now."

"Remember, ideally we want it to do is pick up ten pounds of mortar shell and fly at least a mile with it. Preferably more, but a mile will do for local defense. Will this do that?"

Morgan shrugged. "That's what flight tests are for."

Oh, no. I quietly invoked the ghosts of Chuck Yeager, Jim Lovell, Bob Hooper, and every other test pilot of the classical era I could think of. We probably wouldn't get anyone killed doing this, not like pile-driving an X-plane into the Mojave Desert at Mach 2, but we also really needed the fucking things to work and didn't have that much time in which to do it. Life comes at you pretty quick.

Half an hour later, I got upstairs just in time to walk out the door and see the test UAV crash in the parking lot. A chunk of cinderblock had stood in for the ten pounds of mortar shell. Near as we could tell what happened, the frame flexed too much under load and the props lost clearance from each other. As the frame bent, the rotors hit the frame and each other, then that was the end of that.

Morgan shrugged and looked over at Fox. "Okay, a polymer frame isn't going to work. It's not stiff enough."

Haze shrugged. "We could just design a new frame with a horizontal truss built in?"

Morgan countered, but I didn't stick around for it. Not my concern.
*****

Two days later, a massive water jet cutting table was being rolled into place in the bay, Morgan supervising carefully.

I walked over and watched them work. "Okay, this is really cool. Lemme ask a stupid question."

"Boss, do you ask any other kind?"

"Fuck you. Anyway, what did this thing cost?"

Morgan shrugged. "We got it used, still cost us about one seventy-five."

I sighed. "I assume that's thousand?"

Morgan shrugged. "It was cheap for what it is."

"Does Cash know?"

"Man, who do you think cut the check for it? I don't walk around with that kind of money." Well, if the CFO had blessed off on it and there was some sort of use for it, whatever. He was grinning with enthusiasm. "We'll be cutting UAV frames out of half-inch aluminum plate by tonight."

"Lemme guess, the plates are coming in next?"

Morgan grinned. "I got guys down in Nashville picking them up now."
*****

That wasn't to say everything went together with no issues. Once we had a UAV sufficient to carry them, we dropped a whole crate's worth of 81mm mortar rounds on the range from two hundred feet in the air. Not one of the fucking things actually blew up. Freddie took one of the duds then shot it out of a mortar, and it worked just fine. He got into his old notes on mortar operations from when he'd been an 18B instructor and realized the fuse had to get 'kicked' by the force of the tube-launch to arm itself. Merely dropping the damn thing nose-first from a UAV wouldn't do, something our badly translated notes from the Ukrainian-speaking Internet hadn't covered in adequate detail.

I considered this a problem. Quoting Robert Stack's excellent movie version of 'Vinegar Joe' Stilwell in Spielberg's *1941,* "You can't have an air raid without bombs!" I told him to fix the problem, so he wandered off with Lee and a couple of our other demolition-minded personnel to work on another solution. Lee thought it was solvable with blasting caps, C-4, and fishing line. I hoped that worked, since that was a lot of net explosive weight to not have available for air ops, and running the shells all the way in with a UAV had a better probability of a good hit than shooting them out of a mortar. I left them to it and just hoped they didn't blow themselves up. I needed them.

Surveilling ArmEx's old training camp in Florida was slightly tricky. The remote cameras were still live, and Luke got the occasional alert on his phone as a raccoon or possum would set off the motion detectors. Then one day weeks later, he got an alert, and came zipping up to me on one of the four-wheelers just in time to show me the cameras around the barracks going dead as angry-faced older Chinese guys started ripping them out, their last broadcasts the scowls of their uninstallers. Behind them, at least fifty African-Africans stood in ranks I was pretty sure there were more where those were coming from.

Well, shit. Here we were in April. Obviously the other team had a plan they were going to train up for, and they were using that site to do it. What I was worried was that we were it. Okay, war was definitely coming now. Reconnaissance and counter-reconnaissance are, when combined, a snake eating its own tail. Collect information on them without letting them recon you. See them, blind them so they can't do the same, etc.

The first thing I wanted to do was push a recon screen as far forward as possible. I grabbed Morgan and Fox. "I need you two and at least four others, shooters, UAV support, whatever, to load up and get a place within UAV range of these guys. I mean I want a Cuban Missile Crisis U-2 overflights level of 'up these people's ass.' Buy a goddamn house up the road from 'em if you have to."

Morgan just stared at me, thinking I was on a level of my bullshit even he hadn't seen before. "Man, you gotta be shittin' me. Buy a house?"

No, I was completely serious. "First, those dudes probably aren't here legally. They're gonna be hunkered down on that camp. Second, I got a real bad feeling that the Chinese intel guys we pissed off are going to use these dudes on us. It matches what Shellington told me before he vanished again. We gotta see what they're doing, and we gotta see if they leave. If they leave, and they're coming this way? Fight's on at that point."

Morgan, Fox, and one of the security teams were out the door four hours later.

Chapter Twenty-Six

As air support and reconnaissance were handled and deployed, the next priority had been fire support prep. Remember how I said the mortars were the equivalent of Civil War light artillery for purposes of our little defense? Yes. We needed things to explode, and making them explode where you want them to is an art, and not one I'd ever been to school for. My reference copy of Field Manual 23-91, *Mortar Gunnery,* was 25 years old and pulled off the Internet, but then our mortars were even older. In my characteristic leadership style, I knew somebody who knew more than I did, and made it their problem at the same time Morgan was spearheading the quadcopter bombers.

Freddie, my retired Special Forces heavy weapons instructor, had the ideal resume to assume that project. A stocky little blond guy that I'd known for over twenty years on and off, he just nodded, took a couple notes, and moved out to look at the issue. Not even an hour later, I was head-down in a file folder dealing with a completely unrelated issue in Europe we were getting paid to look at when Freddie knocked at my door. I looked up, peered at him, rubbed my eyes, and commented "Shit, man, that was fast."

He walked in and sat down. "Well, it wasn't that big a problem, dude."

"Okay, walk me through it like I'm stupid."

"Okay, cool. Covering it from the beginning, overlapping shit I know that you know. Mortars are merely small artillery, optimized for a high parabolic flight of projectile versus a howitzer. Things go up, then gravity brings things back down, and then they explode. You vary that by the elevation and deflection

197

of the tube itself. Up or down, left or right, and then how fast it's going and with it how far is controlled by varying the propellant charge. It's all just physics and math."

"Got ya so far." I had spent two years in a field artillery battalion long, long ago, and I did read a lot of books.

He continued. "The math in the middle is mostly done for you by either handheld ballistic computers, which is basically just a fancy calculator, or the backup plotting board."

"Okay, and we have those. I remember they were in the boxes the night we bought the damn things from Izzy."

"So everything else is just targeting. Knowing where you are and where the target is."

"We're only trying to defend four hundred acres or so, we aren't trying to hold Fulda Gap."

"That makes it easier, yeah."

"Great. You're in charge. If you need more money, tell me."

Freddie being Freddie, he got busy with his characteristically manic enthusiasm. First, he conferred with Zoey at the map desk and digitally charted every inch of the property using Uncle Samuel's reconnaissance satellites. Renting a set of surveyor-grade GPS gear, he borrowed a couple of Jake's kids and cross-checked it on the ground.

The useful outcome of all that effort was that a week later, anyone standing anywhere on the grounds could be at a known point, establish direction and distance to the target, accurately know that point, and call it in to the mortars. From there, so long as the mortar crews dialed it correctly from their equally well-surveyed points, they should be able to drop the first warheads within the kill radius of the enemy's forehead with a minimal need for calling in adjustments.

That having been far too easy, Freddie did what Freddie does. He got bored and started thinking. Usually, the most awkward thing to lug around for a mortar crew, besides enough ammo, is the baseplate. This is, as the name suggests, it's the big heavy steel thing the mortar tube sets on. Because it is big and heavy, it slows down the movement of the mortar crew unless they have vehicle support. I'd rather the crew be carrying ammo. We probably needed carts for that anyway, or even a couple more four-seat ATVs with cargo beds on the back. None of us were exactly young anymore.

Since the firing points, and I mean the primary, alternate, contingency, and emergency (PACE) firing points for each of the four 81mm tubes were known to within a meter, it had been trivial to put nice concrete pads at each, with a steel socket set in the concrete to do the baseplate's work. There were a lot of small machine shops in the region, and we only needed four sets of four. Junkyard truck axles did the trick, and from there it was thirty minutes of lathe work. Those went three feet down, anchored in place by a good bit of concrete. No recoil-setting the baseplate, no mud problems, no fighting the bubbles to level in. You knew where you were. All you had to do was set the tube, snap on your bipod and lock it out, then set the sight and dial in. Aiming stakes and lay data were all hard-set for each of the sixteen (four tubes, four possible points for each) points.

Meanwhile I was working the phones over the weeks looking for a little more help. I wasn't trying to sign anyone up for what my anxiety was telling me was a suicide mission, at the same time there's no such thing as 'enough' when you aren't sure what you're defending against.

Some of the calls for help went great. More guys than I thought were willing to take a few days off work when the time came, show up, and maybe get a few last rifle kills in for a few grand in cash. Some mortar guys were just itching to hang a round one last time since you don't get to do that in civilian life. But some other people? A lot of guys figured they were too damn old or were maybe just annoyed with me. I heard "Fuck you, no" a good bit, which shouldn't have hurt my feelings in most cases, but occasionally did.

See, I was trying to recruit along a narrow band on the graph. I needed 'Really Competent' plus 'Not An Asshole' plus 'Still Healthy Enough To Do This'. That was hard, since the We Invaded Iraq generation was all over forty years old now, if not a decade past it like I was. I also had to include mentally healthy enough. I knew a couple guys who would have been great for this if I could get their twenty-something selves back, but weren't even worth calling anymore most of three decades later. That narrow demographic band made a pretty shallow recruiting pool. I just didn't have that many connections in the younger generation. The security platoon 'kids' did, but we'd also kinda drained that well to make more teams in the first place.

The situation and the demographic weirdness had given us a really uneven distribution of human talent. The younger four-man teams of my full-timers worked out and trained together like it was their job, because it actually fucking was. Those guys would have to do my heavy lifting out in the woods. They'd hold the bunkers and have the linebacker mission behind the bunkers.

Above them, I had guys like Jake, Ben, Jimmy, Tommy, and so on. They were the hard core of my on-call veterans who'd made up the raid force that night in Mississippi. I wasn't worried about them not handling business once they arrived. I just needed six or seven of them to get here before the gate locked. With the recon screen forward in Florida, I would have some warning of that, but I couldn't assume those bad guys were the only lurking threat.

Freddie was going to be busy running the mortars, and Jimmy was going to be busy on the medical side. But one of those formerly more senior NCOs would bolt two fire teams together to make a squad. Once the squads had some exercise, we'd worry about building squads into a platoon after that. I don't think we'd have enough people to build a company, but numbers aside, it wouldn't be impossible. Everyone had done the job before; it was just a matter of rehearsing enough to knock the rust off and make a cohesive team. That's what wins gunfights.

Past that, now I had at least a dozen guys showing up to pinch-hit who hadn't done serious tactical training in some years. Unbuttoned BDU tops were common, since you can't get much of a post-Army gut into a Medium-Regular. Fortunately, most of those guys were former mortar guys who could free up the younger men to fight forward. An 81 needed five guys to crew it by the book. We were doing it with four per. It was still a resource suck, but we also needed the firepower.

Freddie rostered 'his' guys according to condition and skill set. Healthier guys who knew what they were doing would still be hanging rounds or carrying the tube and bipod from point to point, but it didn't take athletic ability to spin knobs on the gunsight or work the plotting table. That didn't mean he wasn't drilling the living fuck out of those skills to knock the rust off of them. 'Charlie school' or the Mortar Leader Operations Course had been a real long time ago for some of them. We actually had a couple excess Intel and IT people slated to pass ammunition for the mortars. More of them would be stepping and fetching for the UAV crews or carrying stretchers if it really went bad.

On the subject of going bad. I wasn't such an optimist as thinking we couldn't have a gunfight without any of our own people getting holes in them. With that in mine, Doc Mickey, Jimmy, and a few other hands were prepping a space in the garage bay for immediate battle casualties. Work tables, medical gear, and all kinds of neat stuff. River was over there with them, wearing one of my spare Glocks in a borrowed holster. She was smiling and happy at the same time she was working as fast as a ferret on Adderall.

Jimmy took the seats out of two of the armored Suburbans and announced they were the designated casualty evacuation trucks in case the medics had to push forward and make a pickup under fire. River had asked if we should put Red Crosses on them, but we patted her on the shoulder and broke the bad news to her that this wasn't that kind of a war.

Then came the real wild cards, the help that was unlooked for but had been trickling in over the last few days anyway. My buddy Andy, retired from his twenty years of active duty, some of them with me at Campbell, took a couple days off work from his new job and just randomly showed up, looking to scratch one last gunfight itch. I could use a combat-experienced platoon sergeant out there, well, another one, but Christ, if he got himself shot, his girlfriend was gonna kill me.

It wasn't just the mortar and survey guys who'd been running hog wild with lethal innovation. Once they'd finished building the fleet of little radio control bombers, the UAV operators kept looking for new things to do now that the funding spigot was wide open. Then one of my online acquaintances on the 'moon's out, goons out' side of paramilitary Twitter had made the observation that racing drones are suicide drones. A smallish UAV moving at a hundred-twenty to a hundred-fifty miles an hour isn't like getting hit by a truck, but it's not something you're walking away from, especially to the head. We did the math. At a hundred-fifty miles an hour, that one pound UAV had five times the kinetic energy of a .45 bullet.

Naturally when the crew of psychos in our UAV section had heard this idea, they ripped off the design of a recent *Guinness Book* drone speed-record holder, and then mass-produced fifty of the things with 3-D printed frames and parts ordered online. Were most of the parts cheap knockoffs from overseas? Yes. But they only had to work once, I suppose. The world record was two hundred fifty-seven miles an hour, but a mere two hundred was good enough, if that slight speed loss allowed for mass production. Tests proved it did, as the prototype clocked at two-twenty-five. Then they built another fifty after that, and a couple of the operators were just terrifyingly eager to see what would happen when they tested it on a live target.

To keep the same thing from being done back to our mortars, lumber canopies had been set at their primary and alternate positions. Not merely overhead cover, either. Each one rolled about on wheels, so it could be adjusted to clear the muzzles of mortar tubes. Then microwave antennas were clamped onto it, angled upward and outward to signal-kill any enemy UAV that got close to it.

When I was down there watching the setup, one of the mortarmen raised his hand. "Are those antennas going to give us cancer later?"

I shrugged. "To be honest, I don't know. But do you want to roll the dice on cancer later or on an enemy UAV sticking a rocket warhead up your ass now?"

He nodded. "I'll go with roll the dice later."

I figured that would be a very popular choice. Everyone had seen enough Ukraine War air-delivered murder videos online to know what we could be dealing with. Yeah, it wouldn't handle the fiber-optic wired versions, but you gotta pick and choose your nightmares.

A couple of the guard shack kids who had worked here then moved on once they'd finished college had somehow heard what was going on, then showed up at the gate telling me they wanted back in for the fight. I damn near cried at that one. Loyalty like that is probably the best gift a commander can get. I wasn't going to let those kids get killed for free, so back on the payroll as temp help they went.

The called-in help did what they were expected to do, and started solving some of my problems for me. Some of them started attacking problems I didn't know I had yet. For one example, a U-Haul truck full of green plastic gear cases was backed up to the garage bay door, and being unloaded by a crew of young-ish, healthy troops in correct Multicam uniforms without insignia. You could see the exposed Velcro where they'd sterilized their issue uniforms before showing up. Doc Mickey, Jimmy, and River were helping them organize stuff as they unloaded. When in doubt, as I was, ask. I pulled Jimmy off to the side. "Who the hell are these guys?"

Before he could even get a word out, one of them walked over to join us, introducing herself. "We're with the advanced life support and battlefield re-suscitation unit out of Nashville."

"Reservists?" I asked.

She nodded. "We heard a rumor from a friend," she eyed River, "about an opportunity to get some free live-tissue training only an hour away from our home armory, so I found a dozen people with clear personal schedules who were due up for... Call it 'recertifications'."

Cool, so that's what we're calling this. "Well, we'll at least pass the hat and cover your gas money up here. Don't want anyone asking questions later." I didn't want to give anyone ethical qualms about getting mercenary-medical money out of this.

*****

The snipers were, subject to the cramped terrain up here, my longest ranged direct fire asset, which was great. I wasn't worried about Troy, Paul, or Nichols either. They would do what needed to be done without bothering me with a lot of questions since they mostly knew more about their art than I did.

Since I'd paid good money for the damn things last year and I didn't want them going to waste, the four nearly antique 82mm Chinese surplus recoilless rifles I'd gotten from Izzy were going to get put somewhere. I had ideas on the subject, but crewing them was going to be interesting since it's not like anyone in the States taught the fucking things. Freddie told me that they weren't even in the base curriculum for the SF weapons sergeants any longer. Oh, well. One of us would think of something.

Now let's consider the next major thing on the list... machine guns. And I mean real machine guns, belt-feds on tripods. Though there's no such thing as too much ammunition until you have to pick it up and walk with all of it, the basic load for a machine gun team in normal combat operations where a three-man team has to carry the gun and goodies is 'only' eight-hundred rounds, four two-hundred-round cans. Of course, each can has two one-hundred-round cardboard boxes in it, but you can combine and recombine. For years, the Army machine qualification test was a single hundred-fifty-four-round belt to fight eleven separate targets. I never did find an explanation nor figure out on my own how the Infantry School arrived at that rather obtuse number. I had seventeen of these. Machine gun ammo I had by the case, damn near the truckload. To shoot that pile of ammo, there were the three freshly checked-over M240s, and then twelve M60s that had been sitting downstairs because I trusted them about as much as I trust most strippers.

Allow me to elaborate. An M60 machine gun was basically Army Ordnance's umpteenth attempt to reverse-engineer the rather revolutionary German MG42 of WWII, only they did a very half-assed job of it. At the same time, as I explained earlier, the rest of the Western world was buying the much superior Belgian MAG-58, and the MAG is what we bought after the Army could no longer ignore the fact the inventory of M60s were dying of old age by the 1990s.

Why were they dying? The receiver design. While the Browning family and their Belgian stepchild are steel plates riveted together, the M60's receiver is a bunch of stamped steel rails welded together that looks something like a box kite's frame. Over time, those rails stretch and warp like a railroad gone bad. Instead of the locomotive jumping the tracks, your bolt assembly then falls out of proper alignment and the gun misfeeds. That stops it from going BANG-BANGBANG when you need it to. It just makes embarrassing *ka-thunking* noises as the bolt assembly drives forward, minisculely out of alignment. The smaller 5.56mm M249 is built the same way and inherited the problem same lifespan problem. But I had still had twelve '60s and they were still too much potential firepower to not put out there. They might accomplish something up there. Down here they'd definitely do nothing.

This was a problem I didn't have to fix myself, since I had people now. Sawyer and some of the security teams hauled the M60s out of the arms room for the first time in decades. Not one of the stolen guns had seen daylight since Eric stored them down there in 1980-whatever. They lubed the hell out of the dust-dry things then ran a thousand rounds through each one for testing. The results were generally acceptable, so I guess Eric had stolen good ones. I still didn't want to put them anywhere super-critical and I didn't have any of them positioned alone. The much more reliable 240s I pushed forward with three of the fire teams.

I grabbed Johnston in the hallway. "Got a job for you. Find Ruiz and meet me in the arms room in half an hour." He nodded.

When they found me half an hour later, I hit them directly. "Okay, this is one of those good news, bad news things."

"Bad news first," Johnston said.

"I'm taking your 240 away from you. Yeah, I know, it's a blood weapon," I raised my hand to cut off his protest, but he barely got his mouth open, "but I got something even cooler for you to fuck with." I pointed toward the two water-cooled Brownings. "I need you to become the world's youngest expert on the fucking things." The two heavy, extremely non-mobile water-cooled guns would be in fixed positions to anchor the defense. Johnston was a proven commodity on a belt-fed, and unlike most anyone else I knew, had gotten it done with one this decade.

Johnston just stared at the Browning like it was Michelangelo's *Pieta*. "Have we always had these?"

"You hadn't noticed?"

He looked beatifically toward the ceiling. "Saint John of Basilone, thank you for the blessing I have been given this day." Marine machine gunners could be weird, but the bastards took their tribal traditions really seriously and I had to respect that. They also tended to have a much better academic grounding in the art of machine gunnery than Army 240 guys, since machine guns are a whole separate MOS for them.

The rest was just rehearsals and planning. I could handle us screwing up in a rehearsal. That's what the fucking things were for. When in doubt, "FUCK IT, WE'RE DOING IT AGAIN!" as I once loudly said in front of my company, battalion, and brigade commander. Yeah, all of them at once. We did it again, too. "Training errors are recorded on paper. Tactical errors are etched on gravestones," as Erwin Rommel supposedly once said, never mind the various quotes on the subject by assorted Romans.

While all this was going on, the UAV-detecting UAV was up and orbiting, trying to make sure we weren't getting scouted. If I were those guys, I would have put a UAV team in somewhere near me well in advance the same way I'd sent Morgan and Fox down to Florida. Time spent in reconnaissance is time seldom wasted, as the British field service regulations once eloquently put it. Some people get arrogant though and just raw-dog the process thinking they can fight through. I hoped these guys were that dumb. The smarter your opponent is, the higher a chance of a fair fight, and that's the last thing you should want.

Not all the preparations were tactical. Some were deep-structural. For those, I had some outside talent. Alex was a convention buddy from Dallas. His day job was in commercial refrigeration and air handling, so he was one of the old friends working on our air handling system. Frank, the former Marine turned former CDC facilities engineer, had also come back up from Marietta to help us out again. If we had to fall back to the mountain, we had to be able to breathe.

Chapter Twenty-Seven

*"*H*ow do you go from this tranquility to that violence?"*
"I usually take the Ferrari."
~ *Detective Sonny Crockett, Miami PD*

Things were blurry as we prepped. It might have been a week or two later when my phone went *buzz-buzz*. It was Morgan. *SOS SOS SOS ENEMY MOVEMENT!*

I called his ass back, and he picked up damn near before it rang. "They're fucking loading up. Brit surplus gear, Chinese rifles. Texting you a pic." Yeah. When it came through, I saw that Morgan had literally taken a picture of the UAV terminal's screen, so the approximate level of detail was as if he'd used a baked potato. Dave and Jimmy eagerly squeezed in to see it anyway.

Lots of black guys, and I mean African black-black, not the wide range of African-American shades, were piling on board a line of five plain white charter-style buses. They were in camouflage uniforms I couldn't make out with rifles at the ready, while others were sliding bulkier loads into the luggage compartments beneath. To be honest, it reminded me a hell of a lot of my college marching band getting it together in the parking lot for a road game. Yeah, I was a band geek since I was too small for Division 1 ball. Not even nineteen-year-old me was dumb enough to try walking on at defensive line when I'd be giving up six inches and a hundred pounds on average, I don't care what I benched then. Even the damn quarterback had two inches and twenty pounds on me.

I told Morgan "Let me call you back on video so I can see this live. A screen-shot isn't cutting it at my end." That took a minute to get reconnected, but the resolution was much better. Now I could tell they were all wearing British style woodland 'disruptive pattern material.' The Brits had gone to Multicam like everyone else, but Africa was still full of their surplus stuff. It would work in a Tennessee springtime just fine just as the old American M81 Woodland we used would. I was looking at their rifles on the phone's screen. I generally dislike bullpup-style rifles regardless of national origin, and here was a model I didn't recognize issued out by the hundreds. "What the fuck are those?"

Jimmy looked up from the oversized aid bag he was rechecking for the third time that morning. "Uh, Chinese QZB... look at the mag. If it's a NATO mag it's a 97 in five five six, that's the export market version, if it looks like an AK mag, it's a 95 in their proprietary 5.8 millimeter."

I shrugged. "Can't tell on camera. Nobody's got a mag in. Why would they use Chinese five eight, anyway?"

He shrugged. "If you're smuggling machine guns, why not bring ammo?"

I sighed. "Smuggling ammo into the US is like shipping coal to Newcastle." They looked at me, not getting the reference. "England's version of West Virginia coal country. You don't ship coal to coal country. It's a metaphor."

Jimmy shook his head. "Fuckin' nerd."

I couldn't argue that, so I kept going. "Anyway, that's why the Chinese bothered making the export version in a way more common caliber. America's only got twenty or thirty billion rounds of five five six tucked away here and there."

Dave snickered. "Speaking of shipping imported ammo, aren't you still wait-ing on a delivery of that Serbian-made .303 British ammo for your damn Enfield collection?"

He had me there. "Yeah, and some 7.7 Japanese too." Old bolt-actions were a weakness of mine for a while because I could afford them in the '90s and early '00s when they were a hundred bucks each. Unlike ARs, AKs, or FALs, they didn't scare my mom. As for the smuggling? It wasn't like people paid much attention to the national borders for a few years there. If you could get twenty-foot containers full of cocaine in, let alone a few million people walking across in daylight, who was going to complain about a shipping container or two of anything else?

Morgan was still on the line, listening as I mused out loud. "Would be nice if we could blow up one of those damn buses early so they start off behind on people..."

I didn't realize he had me on speaker at his end too. In the background, I heard "Blow it up? Weapons release, roger!" from Fox.

Oh, fuck.

One of the now-modified 81mm mortar shells, still recognizable on camera by the fins, fell from the UAV. The camera image shifted as the UAV bounced sharply upward on account of having lost ten pounds. Nose-first after maybe a four-hundred-foot fall, it punched through the sheet metal roof of the lead bus. Silently, the shell detonated, and the bus windows blew outward in clouds of black smoke and broken glass. Morgan was sort of screeching in terror, while Fox happily yelled "BULLSEYE, MOTHERFUCKERS!!"

This wasn't quite the level of fucking up that had the Japanese *Kido Butai* task force bombing Pearl Harbor before the declaration of war was presented in Washington, but it was pretty close. See, we had a problem. We were on the edge of fighting a dirty and illegal war in a completely clandestine manner in a country that still had normal people and rules and a functioning legal system that might decide we were the bad guys. We didn't get to do shit like this with any sort of legal protections. This wasn't the bar at Mos Eisely where you could shoot first, throw a couple gold coins at the bartender, and tell him "Sorry about the mess." This was Regular Normie America and we just blew up forty-ish people two states away.

"Oh, shit. Morgan, get everyone and everything back here right fucking now. Cover your tracks on the way home."

On camera, he nodded. "You got it, boss."

"Hey, Fox?"

"Yessir?" Morgan turned the phone so she and I could see each other.

I took a deep breath and thought about it. "I probably shouldn't have said that out loud, but I did, and so it's on me. It was good shooting. I'll put you in for a Diet Coke with V device and oak leaf cluster, okay?" She laughed and grinned.

"You'll do better than that. I trust you guys or I wouldn't work here."

"Roger that. Morgan, get home safe." The call disconnected.

I turned to Dave and Jimmy. "Well, there's gonna be a war now and we fuckin' started it because I couldn't keep my goddamn mouth shut.

Jimmy shrugged. "It was probably coming anyway. Don't blame yourself."

Dave cackled. "Man, you've been pissing people off by saying stupid shit for twenty-five, no, what, twenty-six years now. What else is new?" I sighed. Longer than that, but that was where he came into the story.

Lee was sitting there off to the side, grinning like a possum in a full trash can. "I told you I'd make a fuse that worked."

I had to chuckle. "I saw the tests here, remember? I knew better than to doubt you. I can only credit the fine NCO mentoring you had early in your career."

He snorted at that. "Yeah, that's true. If you ever run into who did it, let me know."

Smartass. "Fuck you, Lee. Anyway, we got enough of 'em?"

He shrugged. "Hard to tell. Printers are still making more of the casings though."

Dave sighed. "Jokes aside, what did those videos tell us?"

"Chinese weapons?" I threw out.

"Look at the uniforms," he replied, with just the barest hint of smug.

"They were in boonie hats, not helmets," I mused.

Jimmy picked up on that. "Makes using NODs comfortably a real problem."

Dave nodded. "No helmets, no plate carriers, no nothing. Slick Chinese bullpups aside, they look like Brits set up for jungle school in the mid-1980s. That's gonna dictate a few things about how they operate. They're gonna be a daylight-only force and probably nothing too fancy."

"Lack of helmets doesn't mean lack of NODS," I protested.

Dave scoffed at that. "What, walk around with a set of PVS-7Ds hanging off your neck like binoculars and it's Panama in the 1990s? No fucking way."

Jimmy shrugged. "They could be picking up supplies elsewhere?"

"Nothing they actually trained with. We've been watching their rehearsals. They did the same platoon then company live fire every time. Shake out into a reverse wedge then do a three-abreast movement to contact. It's damn near World War One in execution."

I didn't want to be optimistic. "I still think they could, not that they will, displace and keep training."

Dave and Freddie both shook their heads. "It takes time to get good at night with all that stuff, and now that we blew up one of their buses and cut their timeline short, they don't have time to keep training elsewhere. Either they come now or they ain't gonna."

Chapter Twenty-Eight

The next major thing I did, the second Morgan got back from Florida, was get him into my office with Cash and Kara. With that unavoidable delay, I didn't have time to sugar-coat it. "We need to get you three the fuck out of here."

Cash just stared as she sat down on the couch, little sparks of defiance coming off her. "No way, sir. Not again. Not this time." She was still a little miffed about being left back that night in New York City when all this started rolling. Angel was a more skilled shooter, and I couldn't risk Cash catching a stray round since so much of the company's financial knowledge was in her brain.

Morgan wasn't thrilled either. "Why me? Why do I have to go? I just fucking got here. Can I at least sleep some first? I mean goddamn…"

I cut him off before he got warmed up. "Morgan, with Dave moving up into my old slot as the aide de camp, adjutant, chief of staff, whatever, you're now arguably the number two in Intel AND in IT. You know enough about what we do and how we do it, particularly with the offsite contractors, you can keep it going even if we lose this site and we get killed. If we lose, you get with Little John and Greg, use the people we hid at the backup site, and then get a new lineup put together. Your ability to do that outweighs any use you'd be pulling triggers in what's coming."

I'd hit his anger switch, and it started flaring up. "You're gonna put that shit on me? Fuck you, asshole. I didn't sign up to be in charge if you get killed."

"Morgan, it's you or Dave, and I need Dave here if we're going to win this thing and get you off the hook. You gotta be the 'Indian Outlaw' and get the fuck out of here. You have more life on the run experience than anyone else we've got, and," I pointed at Cash and Kara, "you gotta keep these two alive and uncaught."

"Fuck." He was still grumbly about it, but I could read his face. He saw the necessity involved in the duty.

I continued. "If you three get rolled over too, then we lose everything. And," I turned to Cash, "He's going to need you to know where all the money's hidden. The money downstairs in the vault is small change compared to the investment accounts and offshore deposits. There is a very good chance we lose this fight," okay, I was exaggerating but not much, "and your brain needs to be somewhere safe. That somewhere is not here." I looked over at her, and said "Kara, same goes for you."

Kara had been standing there quietly, then she looked at me with a lot of uncertainty on her face. "I can stay and help. I shot expert on my last pistol qualification."

I shook my head. "This isn't a pistol kind of fight, unless they get past us and get downstairs. If that happens, we already lost."

"But what about —"

I cut her off, knowing where she was going. "And it's not gonna be about your kind of intel. This is ugly tactical intel stuff. We can do tactical signal intercept without you, while if we do lose you we're fucked on the Fort Meade contracts. If we get you out of here, you and Morgan can reconstitute the capability."

Cash looked like she was going to cry. "Well, that's what the backup site is for, even if it's sketchy and under no official cover."

I nodded. "And we wouldn't have it if not for you." I refocused on Kara. "Last and most importantly, you, like Cash, know way too much to get taken. And you," I turned back to Cash, "repeating myself, they're going to need you to be able to pay for backup operations and life on the run."

Cash looked took a deep breath. "Okay. It's for the mission. The mission comes first. Fuck." She sighed and slouched back into the couch. I actually saw tears. "I fucking hate this. I don't want to be just another piece of mission essential equipment again. I want to stay here with my family." I just sat down next to her and hugged her. It sucked, but that's the job.

Kara then dug down into her deck and pulled that Uno reverse card on me. "Why the hell don't you get out of here too? Dave's arguably more qualified to command the defense than you are."

I wasn't just going to snarl at her and just tell her that was a stupid thing to say. It was an honest question and deserved an honest answer. "As much as I'd love to run like hell, it's my responsibility and I'm not going. End of story."

Morgan then skipped ahead to the next big question. "Where do we go?"

I looked at him and shook my head. "Not the backup site in 'Nooga. That's too many eggs in one basket at first, and running straight to it could compromise it. You can get there later. Past that, I don't know, and I don't want to know. What I don't know, I can't spill if I get rolled up alive."

Cash really looked upset at that.

I continued. "If we do get rolled up, they're going to want the money as much as the data, and that means they'll need to get her," and I pointed at Cash. "You guys get gone, and until you hear from us, you stay gone. Take one of the up-armored Yukons if you want, or call Matt and fly out. Either way, take some extra backup drives with you and anything else you'd need."

Cash sighed. "And we better take a bunch of money in cash."

I nodded. "As much as you can haul, but that means you gotta drive real easy and not get popped as an asset forfeiture case."

Morgan grumbled at that. The War on Drugs had given cops a license to steal, if you never noticed.

I thought about it more. "Morgan, as soon as Bradley finishes up with the Army, he's coming out here. You got his number?"

"Yeah."

"Good. Give it a week and ping him. He's got intel experience and he's overqualified to be a backup shooter here even if he showed up in the next five minutes."

Morgan nodded. "Can do."

"You remember that Goth chick of yours who was hanging on him in Vegas?"

"Shannon. She's at the Chattanooga site working economic intel."

I chuckled. "Bradley let me know he was quite taken with her, so use her as bait again if you have to. You know, your usual unethical shit." I didn't want to get between those two. Bradley and Shannon could work out Bradley and Shannon shit later.

Cash was somewhat out of it by then, leaving it to Kara to ask the real heavy question. "When do we come back?"

I thought about it. "I'll text you when it starts. Shouldn't take more than a day to win it or lose it unless we get shoved back into the mountain, and by then, we'll probably be the lead story on every network. That fight isn't going to be quiet, and everyone from Louisville to Nashville is gonna notice if it gets too far out of hand." I thought about it some more. "The all-clear signal will be 'Daybreak.'" Kara nodded. It had been the final episode of *Battlestar Galactica*, and I could tell she got the reference.

As Morgan and Kara got out of there, Cash lingered. She was visibly looking for her words, so I spoke first. "Babe, you understand why we have to get you out of here, right?

She nodded and attempted to smile a little. She was trying to keep it together, but she was still on the edge of crying with the occasional free-running tear, and that made it worse for both of us. "Like I said. I don't want to go. I know why I am stuck as mission equipment again; I just hate it right now. I should be here with you."

I shook my head. "You're my CFO and my beloved. You aren't my backup shooter, or at least you aren't supposed to be."

She pouted a little. "But Angel's staying!"

I nodded. "Because I'm putting Angel downstairs on the kill switch for the drive farm to free up the few ex-military IT guys who are still here to do other things. I'm not letting her outside. And Angel can't do what you do. The only chance we had to make another you was with Vivian, and we know she couldn't have stayed because of her own family responsibilities over there."

Her expression went a million miles away for a moment. "I love you. If you die, I will light every last dollar of the fucking money on fire just to burn them back." She hugged me. "I guess I gotta go, sir?"

I nodded. "I need to get you out while there's time. The Mustang is still at the house, right?" She nodded. "Take my truck then. I won't need it for a while." I handed over the keys and we kissed briefly. With that, she nodded and walked out with just the trace of a tear. Just as she left my office, Morgan then came doubling back with Fox. She looked as worn out as he did. Morgan was smiling a little. "Forgot to tell you one bit of good news."

I sighed. "We could use some of that right about now."

Fox was grinning. "We never called you back to tell you. I made one last run on the buses. There's a GPS tracker broadcasting from the roof of one of them. We can trace them all the way to wherever it's going."

I nodded. "That is good news. Morgan, Cash has my truck keys. Get the others and get the fuck out of here. Fox, you get some sleep. You and yours are going to be really busy again soon."

Chapter Twenty-Nine

For every goodbye, there was a hello. Angel and I were doing gear layouts in my office, and she was touching up all the blades. When my desk phone rang, it was the security desk topside warning me that Eric had just checked in. That gave me all of ninety seconds before the old man strode into my office looking like he'd climbed out of an old Special Warfare Museum display case in what I still remembered as Simons Hall on Bragg, even if that whole end of Ardennes Avenue had been rebuilt since I was last there.

Eric took one look at Angel, still head-down sharpening cutlery, shrugged, and dropped his rifle case on the floor. The late Vietnam War ERDL pattern jungle fatigues looked suspiciously original, and those green canvas boots were probably older than I was. Even the 'modern' touches in his gear like the plate carrier were twenty years old. He nodded. "So, you said you have a problem with some unwanted guests coming into town."

"Hi, Eric."

He walked over, and we shook then hugged. The old guy hadn't aged, looking not quite seventy for the tenth year in a row. Damn, I don't know how he did it. "Good to see you, brother. At least you were polite enough to invite me this time."

I shrugged. "What I really wanted to do was give you the option of sitting this one out. The numbers are not necessarily in our favor."

"I talked to your boy Dave, and made a few calls. We got some other friends coming in. Not many, and most of who I knew for heavy work are retired or dead these days, but not all the old timers were smart enough to say no to one last roll of the dice."

"How many more have we got coming?"

Eric shrugged. "Maybe six or seven we can really count on to get it stuck in, another eight or nine old-timers who are at least good for casual sharpshooting if they can get here quick enough." He looked over at Angel. "You're the one who can handle a Goose, right?"

Looking up from running my Chris Reeve 'Pacific' fixed blade along a Japanese water stone, she smirked a little. "Yeah, though finding more ammo for it was a bitch. I'd prefer something I can actually walk with."

He snorted. "Smart girl. Never carry a heavy if you can make someone else do it for you."

Then Dave's Black phone rang. He answered in English, then switched to... I don't know. Thirty seconds later he hung up. "We have more guests coming in. Don't worry, the kind we want." Still a little overwhelmed by the accidental bus bombing and the fact I'd been awake a while, I just sort of looked at him funny. He continued. "Some of my Polish friends were upset they didn't get to shoot anyone at that last little fracas they were in town for, so when I had mentioned this crisis of ours, they decided it was gonna be like Spring Break with explosions. They just landed in Nashville."

And everyone laughed at the idea when British Airways started that nonstop London to Nashville service of theirs. "How many of them are coming?"

Dave grinned. "An even dozen. All Afghan-experienced guys I've worked with before."

Well, that made a nice kicker in the force.

I figured I wasn't making it back to the house anytime soon, so I called one of my neighbors and activated her for dog-sitting duty. You have to think of that in this life. My neighborhood was mostly former military, so I could trust them to keep an eye on the place, more or less.

It wasn't just me stuck at the office. We now had a whole lot of guests, and no one was going anywhere. Everyone's personal cars were getting stashed fifteen miles away over at the mall by the Interstate, with one of the grandmotherly looking sorts from Intel detached to move them around so they didn't get towed.

Another buddy of mine unexpectedly called from Nashville Airport looking for a ride. Usually, he ran the National Guard marksmanship training office in one of the New England states I'm deliberately not naming. He'd used his State Police creds to get his competition guns cased up and onto the plane as carry-on baggage, and he arrived about the same time more of Eric's old timers showed up.

The off-shifts were sleeping on cots down on the seventh and eighth floors while a few brave souls slept outside in the fresh air while the weather was nice. Since people had to eat, we fired up the big kitchen in the picnic gazebo and some of our better amateur cooks started slinging meals out of what we had stored for parties. That turned into one major grocery run, and another, and another. Cooking at a time like this may seem ridiculous, but we couldn't exactly send everyone out to eat when we needed them here. Then since starting off with a stomach full of MREs is just a morale killer, that made it picnic time.

River and one of her Cajun buddies who'd turned up from somewhere decided it that feeding large numbers of people fairly cheaply was exactly what southern Louisiana cuisine was all about in the first place. She was taking charge down there, and that was making her original accent come back. I walked by as she was giving orders to her assistants and the big gas-fired flat top was heating. "Okay, de first t'ing you do is we gon' make a roux..."

Getting back up to the bay, I caught some of the temp help on the way out, the guys who weren't sticking around for the fight. Frank and I shook hands first.

"The filters are as stout as I can make them. Intake, overpressure, and exhaust."

"Alex still here?"

"Haven't seen him. He might well have split already. I know he had a long way home."

"You aren't exactly living next door either. Get the fuck out of here while you can."

*****

True to their word, the Poles had showed up on the next thing in from London. I had them hang around down there a little bit to pick up other stragglers flying in before they drove up, and then they arrived in a pair of rented minivans since we couldn't spare anyone or the time to make the run to the airport. Dave took them downstairs to the arms room, where with Sawyer's help they got into the rack of old Chinese surplus AKs and the boxes of loaner gear.

The senior of them, a hulking blond monster named Tadeuz, was loading AK mags when I came over. A couple of his guys were counting off frags and 'speed-balling' their Claymore mines for rapid employment. That involves ripping the bag, pre-coiling the wire, and so on. Ammo handlers and range safety guys hate it, so you never get to train on it and it's a bit of a lost art. Anyway, I told him, "I can probably do better than those AKs if you want something newer. I've got a couple SOPMOD conversions left, a couple FALs..."

He looked up with a grin, surprising me with nearly perfect English. "No, these are fine. These are what we carried until about twenty years ago, and sometimes the old ways are the better ones. Besides, these Chinese ones have the convenient 'Fuck You' spike on the end that ours didn't. Good in the woods. We did take a couple of your suppressed Sterling SMGs and Ruger pistols though. Best to begin quietly if we can."

I nodded, nearly a half-bow. "Use them in good health. If you need anything, just find me or Dave and we'll do our best. Missions like this really aren't what we were set up to do, but... yes, we're all doing our best."

"You know what I'm gonna say about doing your best, right?" Eric had just ghosted into the arms room and startled the fuck out of everyone. You know, as he does.

I turned and sighed. I was used to this kind of shit between him and Troy. "Yeah, and Connery said it in the movie too, so save it."

Eric wasn't really paying attention. He was looking around the arms room, slowly nodding. "Goddamn, brother, you did some cleaning up in here. I like what you did with the place, even though I'll never find anything now. Where did I leave my... ah, there it is." The unique antique, the suppressed M3A1 Grease Gun, the one I joked might as well have had PROPERTY OF ERIC engraved on it? Yeah. Property of Eric. He pulled it off the rack and locked the bolt to the rear, looking it over. "Hey, baby," he spoke to it. "Hope you got one more fight left in you." He paused, thinking. "I hope we both do." He turned back to me. "Where the hell did you hide her magazines?"

Sawyer handed him ten, already filled with .45 hardball rounds. "These were all I had on hand, sir." He then handed over a khaki canvas bag on a sling to hold them all. I think it was from '43, which made it older than my parents. They sure sewed to last back then.

Eric looked at me and looked at him. "The minion has minions now. You really are coming up in the world, man." He chuckled.

"The point was made to me that I'm supposed to be doing commander shit, not armorer shit, so we hired an armorer."

Sawyer looked distinctly nervous. Eric could do that to you until you got used to him, and then it only happened less frequently. Eric just smiled and patted him on the shoulder. "Relax, man, relax. If you get all tensed up, you'll turn into a walking stress grenade like your boss here, and that's bad for your health."

A *very* aged looking Asian gentleman walked into the arms room in a quite nice suit and tie, visitor badge in place, and escorted by another of Eric's old-timers. Eric turned and grinned. "Ah, General, glad you could make it in time."

He nodded and held it, making a shallow bow. "Wouldn't dream of missing it." He turned toward me. "And Eric tells me you are our host for this party?"

My eyes flashed to Eric in confusion, but I wasn't going to be rude to anyone Eric would address by their proper rank instead of 'dude' or "brother.' "Yes, sir, I am. Just call me Professor. Everyone else does.

Troy passed by, a crate of ammo in his hands. "At least we finally retired 'Lunchbox' as your handle!" He cackled on the way out.

"Fuck you, Troy!" I called after him. Okay, it's true, but there was a long story attached to it.

The old man was smiling narrowly, eyes twinkling a bit. *Goddamn this guy looked old.* Eric turned to me and said "Prof, allow me to introduce Brigadier General Nguyen Van Chi, former deputy head of special operations forces for the Socialist Republic of Vietnam."

Socialist. Republic. Of Vietnam. Wait a fucking second. I nodded and shook hands anyway. "Pleased to meet you, sir. Glad to have you here."

General Nguyen looked over toward the rack of AKs and smiled. "Ah, old friends. Let me grab one while there's still one left." He moved over and selected another one of the Chinese ones.

I stepped backwards, nudging Eric. "Eric, I gotta ask. Why is there a North Vietnamese general here?"

He shrugged. "First of all, there is no more North Vietnam — South Vietnam because they won. Yeah, I was on the losing team, but I still gotta respect that. Besides, I ran into him in Colombia twenty years ago when he was retired and contracting. We've been pals for a while, and he was over here in the States anyway visiting the grandkids. They're all in college here."

Shit. "And he wants in?"

Eric shrugged. "He says he wants in."

"Fuck me. He in the shape for it?"

Eric snickered. "He's in better shape than you are."

*****

223

Consulting Eric, I'd finally sorted out my heavier weapon issues. Two of the four Chinese surplus 82mm recoilless rifles had been put outside in revetments covering the open field past the picnic gazebo. I had another one around the back side of the mountain with a half-dozen of Eric's 'old but still good for casual sharpshooting' guys and my last pair of M60s covering our air intakes. I didn't want these fuckers getting clever on me since we still had to breathe. The spare recoilless and the spare Browning were in the garage bay to flex where I needed them. Not having much to do down here with us, Petey was hanging around up there with them. He had an excess M110 sniper rifle and high hopes he'd actually get to use it Eric also claimed a good number of the M60s and M79s for his old guys who were forming up, and even a few of the last unmodified M16A1s. Vietnam guns for Vietnam guys, I guess.

*****

I was back in my office with a bowl of River's gumbo when Alex walked in. I was shocked. "Fuck, dude, you're still here?"

He looked completely oblivious to all the turmoil and martial preparation. "Yeah, I was working on upgrading the wiring to the downstairs air handlers. I know Frank had to go home after he finished on the filters. Me and Tommy — that's his name, right? Tommy? Used to be a SEAL?"

"Yeah, that's Tommy. Was an electrician's mate on the *Ike* before he went to BUD/S."

"Yeah, he wandered off at some point. Anyway, yeah, I've just been busy working downstairs."

Oh, fuck. "Alex, I don't know how to tell you this, so I'm just gonna tell ya. I've got a crew of half-assed combat engineers about ready to seal the driveway with large concrete obstacles. You might want to get the fuck out of here while you still can."

"Is it that trouble you were worried about?"

"Yeah. About the worst goddamn kind, probably."

"Shit, my AR is in the truck. Figured I'd get some range time while I was visiting."

"Ain't your fight."

He shrugged. "I've never been in a real gunfight. A lot of paintball, some airsoft, a lot of flat range time, but never the real thing."

I shook my head. "Shit, man, I appreciate the enthusiasm, but it might get you killed."

"Nah, I doubt you'll let me be first one in. But I can be a backup shooter or flank security for somebody."

I couldn't fucking believe I was going to go along with this. "Okay. You want in, you're in. I need every hand I can get, to be honest. How many mags have you got with you?"

"Four?"

"Get more. You need a vest or anything, check the big closet on the first floor. We have some spares left, I think." Well, I hoped. We never had hired a full-time supply guy, and with shit like this I suddenly felt like we should have.

The GPS tracker on the ArmEx buses was popping loud and clear as it moved northward out of Florida and across Alabama. They were sticking to the Interstates, knowing buses are anonymous unless they stop and the people get off. Guess they were skipping Buc-ee's. They were probably keeping everyone on board the whole way, which was probably unpleasant as hell with only one small bathroom in the back, but they were hiding from normal people and the law as much as we were.

Chapter Thirty

The buses were coming up to around Nashville, at most a couple hours out. It was time to get everyone shaken loose and set up where they needed to be. The first ones out were my three three-man sniper teams. They'd been rehearsing for a few days and I hadn't seen them much. Fortunately, I had the chance to talk to them all one last time. I caught them in the garage bay all ghillie-suited up with their war paint on. Troy had wanted to get out there early into their hide sites.

We looked at each other, all feeling the acute tension of going back into mortal combat again at our age, and me feeling the guilt of being inside the mountain while they were going out. "Gentlemen, I remind you, your job is not to transmit except in the gravest of extremes. No routine check-ins or sending up kill counts. They may have direction finding gear and I am not risking your lives any more than necessary. I need you to surprise, kill, vanish, move, and then kill again, all with no electronic emissions."

That got nods all around. Surprisingly, it took me that long to notice the rifles. Rather than the long bolt actions with large scopes one thinks of when the word 'sniper' comes up, all three men were armed with shorty ARs with fat suppressor cans on them. I looked over at Paul. "Blackouts?"

He nodded from behind the grease paint. "Why the fuck am I going to carry the length and weight of a thousand-meter rifle into those woods where I'm not going to see more than a hundred at most? Besides, this is way quieter so we can get more work done. We'll start with subsonics. That allows us to get multiple kills before they start noticing, then we bump over to supersonics after things pick up." *And that's why I hire people even smarter than I am.*

Nichols grinned. "I never had so many options sitting on the rack to tailor for a mission before. I could get real used to this shit, man."

Their backup men were loaded heavier. I saw a couple more of our M79 launchers and at least one of the Rhodesian-painted FALs. I shrugged and continued. "The UAVs will handle the observing and reporting. You know the priorities of fire by the book. Key leaders, their RTOs, and then crew served weapons. Instead, there is another priority, perhaps highest of all."

I clicked on my phone screen, and up came a picture of a Chinese soldier carrying a bizarre, swollen looking thing that looked like a very pregnant sniper rifle. Nichols, the youngest of the bunch and the most technically astute on new things, nodded instantly. "Portable electromagnetic pulse generator. Supposedly an anti-drone gun for light infantry."

I nodded. "And it may be some AliExpress tier garbage, or it may actually work. Since the UAVs are the key to our defense, any potential threat to them has to get put down hard and fast. You see one of these things, and I need it taken out quick." There were nods and murmurs, and then they headed out. With that, I headed back downstairs to IT.

The drive farm was a backup data recovery facility run on a contract basis by us for a lot of governmental customers. It took up a long end of IT's floor, and had... I dunno, two or three thousand two-terabyte drives. Ask Petey. It was his job to know that so I didn't have to bother. I know that sounds like a lot of gear, but remember each one was only about the size of a deck of cards. Owing to whose data we were storing, there was a lot of stuff on those drives that couldn't be taken. The anti-capture protocol for that took some creativity.

Large electromagnets from decommissioned MRI machines had been an early idea we'd 'borrowed' from a really good novel from twenty years ago called *Circumference of Darkness*. You can get really cool stuff pretty cheap if you know the right scrap dealers.

The next idea was building an electromagnetic system into the door frame. Fire it up, and any drive carried through it would be fried. We stole that bit of inspiration from *The Cryptonomicon*. But in the interest of safety, we'd never connected all the MRI magnets to avoid a really unfortunate accident. That hour had come. Tommy put them in on their own circuit from the main electrical bay upstairs. Now there were a series of switches to flip, and then you *really* better not have any ferrous metal on you in that room or outside the containing wall. Hell, you might get slammed into the damn wall along with the furniture.

Unfortunately, as Tommy finished wiring it, somebody smarter than me among Petey's troops had realized the technology involved had leapfrogged that plan. The drive farm had, through cyclical maintenance upgrades, gone from what Petey called 'spinning rust,' old-school platter drives, to being about fifty percent made of the new solid-state drives, and those are way harder to destroy effectively with magnets.

Petey had reached out to one of the many mysterious 'friends of the family,' and they'd quickly come up with a High Energy Radio Frequency (HERF) system to back up the insanely overpowered magnetic field system. Made out of a whole bunch of two-kilowatt industrial microwave oven magnetrons we found cheap on AliExpress, and fed by spare server power supplies, each rack had one row of them shooting up and one shooting down through the drives. As I'd been told at install time, "Just flip up the safety cover and hit the switch, then everything in the racks will go *crack, pop, flamey flamey,* and be fully zorched."

And yeah, it was Angel's job to hit that switch when the time came. I couldn't trust anyone else to do it. Well, I could, but the others were going to be busy shooting bad guys in the face, and hopefully shooting enough of them that she wouldn't have to hit the switch.

*****

In one of the quiet moments before this, I'd been deciding which knife to carry for this, since it was a special occasion. To be honest, I couldn't make up my mind. Going out the gate in Iraq the first time, I usually carried three including the dinky little blade on my multitool. I'd wear a large fixed blade cross-draw on my load bearing vest, a smaller fixed blade off my trouser belt behind my right hip, and then the multitools. Since I'd retired those, a Cold Steel ODA and a SOG SEAL Pup for their sentimental value, and eventually the vest I'd worn that year, I needed to carry something else.

Really, I probably wouldn't need to. If I had to actually stab somebody today, something would have gone really, *really* wrong. Since I had no confidence that much of anything was gonna go right, I'd gone for some of the best steel I had at the office collection that I was willing to dirty up. My Chris Reeve 'Pacific' was in a nice piece of custom Kydex on my war belt. My Bjorn Bladeworks 'Element 225' was in an ankle sheath for just in case.

The same went for my gun choices. At the moment I just had a 1911 on my belt with two spare mags, and that was mostly so I was setting an example for everyone else to be carrying. My AR for today and the rest of my gear was still on the rack in my office where it was at least between me and the surface. Right now, my primary weapon was that collection of UAV feeds and EW data.

I went downstairs. I stopped on the second floor to check on Angel who was by herself in IT's space. Angel was hunkered down back by the kill-switch assembly in a plastic patio chair. T-shirt, shorts, and flip-flops. Her change of clothes and her combat gear were up a floor in my office. *All* her jewelry, her phones, and even her eyeglasses were upstairs. Again, she needed to be very non-metallic in the event she had to flip those switches. She was sitting back, reading a paperback manga I didn't recognize, just waiting to do her part if called upon.

I crouched down to her seated height and gave her a hug. She held on, and murmured in my ear. "Hey, baby. How are you holding up?"

Like I was going to give that an honest answer. A real good rule to stick to is that you keep your fears to yourself, but you share your courage. Sergeant Major Franklin Miller told me that back before he died, and the guy had the Medal of

Honor. I straightened and shrugged. "Shit, I came in here to ask you the same thing."

She chuckled. "I have nothing to do down here unless it really goes bad outside. That's your end of the deal, I suppose."

I nodded. "It is."

Angel continued. "And while I understand why you gave me a mission essential task that keeps me two stories underground and away from the action, I also understand why it's necessary to have someone you completely trust sitting near the switch, sir. Same reason you had to chase Cash out of here with the others."

I sat down for a minute. "Yeah. Quoting words that Web Griffin put in someone else's mouth, we do a lot of shitty jobs we regret are necessary. Wish they weren't." *Fuck, I did not have time to get depressed right now.*

Angel knew the symptoms. She knew letting me sit there scratching at the inside of my own head for more than a couple moments was a terrible idea. She gently started kicking me. "Get up, sir. You have shit to do. Go stay busy and stop thinking. I know you miss her. I miss her too. She and the others will be okay."

It was *way* more than just missing my other girlfriend. Most of it was the nagging worry I was going to get all of us fuckin' killed if this went wrong. I went back upstairs for another look around.

*****

The parking lot was empty. No sense providing something for the attacking force to hide behind as they neared the garage doors. The garage doors were blocked off with high concrete T-walls, double thick and tamped with dirt between. There was a protected space behind that wall where our two Chevy Suburban armored ambulances would sit, and we tucked a small side-by-side Polaris four-wheeler just in case.

Nashville's unusual geologic history worked in our favor this time. Despite being in the same county and no more than ten miles or so from downtown as the crow flies, way back here in the ridges and high ground of the 'Highland Rim,' we might as well have been on another planet.

The last front end loader closed the last of the driveway obstacles, then it was pulled way off to the side and parked.

Finally, the GPS tracking screen showed the buses pulling off the Interstate and threading the back roads toward White's Creek and past Union Hill.

Ready or not, here they come.

In those last minutes, a car pulled up at the gate, a nondescript gray Nissan. One of the UAVs banked around to get a camera on it. A blond-haired white guy got out, and then retrieved a GI duffle bag from the trunk. The car then drove off as whoever it was walked up to the gate control box, leaning in to examine it.

Him leaning in to the keypad box put him face to face with that camera as one of the intel kids clicked to put that one up on the big screen instead. In my confusion, I stared at the screen, getting a good look and also getting the shock of the decade. It was AJ. Seriously, fuckin' AJ. *Fuck me, the Ghost of Massacres Past had come to visit.*

Chapter Thirty-One

A s I hit the elevator and headed for the garage, I had a minute to mentally revisit everything I knew about the guy, since it had been a long time. Andrew J. Gustavson was the closest thing I'd ever met in the US Army to one of the Ninth Legion "Blood Angels" from *Warhammer 40,000*. Five-ten, compactly muscled, and so blond-Nordic-looking it hurt. Depending on the place, AJ was the guy you never wanted to go to lunch with. Great company, don't get me wrong, but because the guy was movie-star good looking it could be an issue. I went to our local Hooters with him once. I mean *once*. Forget having a chance to flirt with the waitress — I had to snap my fingers in her face and repeat my order three times just to order because she was staring at AJ, biting her lower lip, and breathing hard. No, this is not an exaggeration.

He was a kind and introspective soul, quite soft-spoken by infantry standards, and spent a lot of free time in his room painting and sketching. The only thing you had to watch was that he drank like a goddamned fish off-duty, even if he handled it extremely well. Like the fictional Ninth, there was the flip side of the coin. When his mental switch flipped, he was a savage and utterly remorseless killer, with probably the second or third-highest individual body count in our company behind Troy through that year of the Iraq invasion and opening counterinsurgency. As an aside, I'd tried getting the third guy in that mix to answer his phone, but he was way the hell up in Maine anyway.

Anyway, AJ's tool of choice was the M249 belt-fed 'automatic rifle'. He'd carried a triple load of ammo, twenty-four hundred rounds of linked 5.56mm, northward in 2003 and used damn near all of it in the three days of seizing and holding Karbala Gap. He'd stir-fried bad guys by the carload by day and still sketched landscapes before sunset. We did a second tour together in 2005-2006. He made a couple more spectacular messes then. Since he was here, I was already wondering if I could get another day's work out of him. To be honest, I needed the quality.

Grabbing the emergency four-wheeler, I got down to the gate and unchained it. I looked at him and blurted, "Jesus, dude, what the fuck are you doing here?"

AJ shrugged calmly. "Just retired. Suddenly have the time on my hands, so I figured I'd visit people I hadn't seen in a while."

"A while? Shit... I hadn't heard from you since, man, I'm not sure. Obama was still President, I remember that much. You told me you were going back on active duty. How the fuck did you know where to go? You didn't call, you didn't email..." This was unreal. As nice as it was to see him, I did not have the time for this shit today unless he was willing to pitch in, and I didn't exactly know how to breach the subject.

"Ran into CSM Michaelson when I was leaving Bragg. You know he's retired, but you still see him around post now and then. He and I got talking for a bit, and your name came up. He knew where to look up your work address, so I figured I'd drop by your office and surprise you."

"Saw the car drop you off. You fly in?"

AJ shook his head. "Nah. Mine broke down and I got it towed. Some engine computer bullshit. Rather than sit around the dealership in Nashville watching them work, I just caught an Uber out here. What's with the chained-up gate?"

Laughing grimly, I shook my head and took the opportunity to just throw all my cards down. "Man, you picked a hell of a time to show up after all these years. We're less than half an hour away from getting hit by a company-sized element of bad guys."

He didn't flinch. He just looked at me with the graven stillness of a Roman statue. "Really?"

Pulling him and his duffel through the gate, I nodded. "Fuckin' really. The odds are way too bad to want to make this shit up. To be honest, you may want to call that Uber back and get the fuck out of here unless you feel like getting in a gunfight today."

The trace of a smile ghosted his face. "How can I say no to that?"

I nodded. "Glad you're here, man." A handshake turned into a bro-hug. "Real glad you're here."

While I rechained the gate, Gustavson started scanning around. "Okay, your driveway barriers are good, but I think I see one of your Claymores though... Got any sniper teams out?"

"Yeah, three of them."

AJ had been in the snipers on that second tour, after the two-man sniper team concept had evolved after 2005 to three to four-man 'small kill teams' that added a belt fed and a radio guy. Like I said, AJ loved belt-fed stuff way more than he loved scoped guns.

"Anybody I know?"

"Troy."

He snorted derisively. "Third Platoon Troy? 'Killed more people than I did' Troy, but never so many all at once?"

I had to snicker. In the twenty-two years since our high adventure in 2003, I forgot that those two weren't exactly pals. Troy had been a sergeant then and AJ was over in First Platoon, so new he'd barely made PFC. "Yeah, that Troy."

He shook his head in disapproval. "Got anybody born this century?"

"You ain't exactly young anymore either, man. We got home twenty-one years ago from that first tour."

He tilted his head to the side just a tiny bit in thought. "I just age better than most people. I've only got a pistol with me. Got any quality loaner pieces?"

I nodded. "I think I can find you something. You doing this for free or am I putting you on the books for a day rate?"

He shrugged, as calmly as he did everything else. "I'm a terrible friend and fuck knows what that that new engine computer is going to cost me."

I didn't have time to haggle, so I opened big. "Ten grand cash for forty-eight hours. This shit will be over by then one way or another."

That perked him up. "Jesus Christ! Sold. Get me a goddamn long gun, quick."

Jumping into the side by side, we weaved past the obstacles and rocketed around the bend heading for the parking lot. We screeched behind the new concrete wall by the 'final' machine gun bunker, leaving it where I found it, and ran inside. I didn't even bother with getting him a visitor badge. AJ was just looking around calmly as we made it past the blast door and went down the elevator to the sixth floor. While we were riding down, he looked over at me with that slow-is-smooth calmness and asked "Does the President know you stole his bunker?"

I sighed. "It's a long story, but I ain't got time to tell it and you ain't got the time to listen."

We hustled into the arms room. Sawyer, bless his heart unironically, was still loyally holding his post until the last minute when he'd probably move to the sound of the guns. "Sawyer, what have we got left?"

"We're kind of picked over, boss. We got some of the old 1911s left, we got FALs, AKs..."

"Any ARs left?"

He shook his head. "Negative. Last one left maybe five minutes ago, and I was down to the Vietnam ones. Those old dudes were happy with those. I got almost all the Winchester twelve-gauges, most of the Thompsons..."

AJ wasn't listening. He pointed to an odd tan rifle hanging on the wall. "What the Kentucky fried fuck is that?"

I grinned. "Ohio Ordnance Works HCAR. That's my own personal gun, not the company's. Improved Browning Automatic Rifle, though that one's only semi."

"You using it today?" he calmly asked.

"No, got an AR."

"Okay, tell me about this thing then."

"Thirty ought-six, takes thirty round mags, up from the original GI twenty, and I killed about fifty people in Dallas with it about eight or nine years ago." Yeah, the so-called East Dallas Massacre was a long time ago. Damn, I wish Jeb Shaw and some of his cronies I'd rolled with that day that had lived were available for this thing. I knew some of them were working in South America these days, and that more than a few were dead since.

AJ took it off the wall, slowly balancing it, getting the feel. He frowned. "Too long and too heavy for a woodline fight, though the 'ought six would be nice for digging people out of cover." He turned back to Sawyer. "AKs, you said?"

"A couple left. Old Chinese ones."

"And Thompsons? Where the fuck did you find those?"

Sawyer shrugged. He had no idea. I don't think I ever told him the story, so I answered instead. "It's a long story. I've got one upstairs- wait a minute, I've got a couple ARs from my personal stash in my office I forgot about. Sawyer, hold tight."

"Yessir."

AJ followed me back upstairs to my office. "You can't have the one on the couch. That's mine for today." I quickly unlocked my refrigerator-sized floor safe. I had thirty or so long guns in there as conversation pieces and for personal emergencies.

He didn't even have the common courtesy to look impressed as he started looking through it. "No, no, this isn't World War One, nah, it's too old, no, no, Jesus fuck, that's an actual flintlock, how many Garands do you own, no, that's a distance rig, no... shit."

I sighed. "Take the one off the couch. I'll use something else if I have to."

He smiled a little as he picked up my 11.5 with the can, the same one I'd used in Oklahoma that night. "You sure?" I nodded, meanwhile he just looked at it and checked the Aimpoint optic. "Damn, a CompM2? How old is this thing? I had one on the first Iraq trip."

I sighed. "So did I, remember? That scope is old enough to drink legally. You want it or not?"

AJ shrugged. "It's the carpenter, not the toolbox."

"Fine. Take it and use it in good health, you sarcastic fuck. Battery in the Aimpoint was fresh two days ago, and you see the spare in the battery cap."

"You sure you don't have a 249 somewhere?"

"No. I don't even have any of its Knight's Armament grandchildren because I didn't want to have to stock belted five five six on top of everything else." I shook my head. "AJ, I'm damn glad you're here. Fuck it, take the chest rig too. I have another one. Look in the hallway closet for spare armor. Need anything else?"

"You got extra NODs if this runs past dark?"

"Yeah."

AJ shook his head. "I'm good then. Since we're partying in your yard, I trust you to get them to me. From there, my full war belt is in my duffel bag, so I'm good."

"Camo, anything?"

Another head shake. "I'm good."

"All right, get dressed quick. I know just the guy I'm gonna attach you to for this. He's got a scary gang of old-timers out there and they may need some younger blood in the mix."

That got a chuckle out of him. "How old is he? Older than you?"

"Way older. On his first enlistment, Eric was probably on the detail that nailed Jesus up. Joking aside, multiple Vietnam tours, Eagle Claw, Latin America, Desert Storm, and Afghanistan at minimum. Dude's ancient, but he still has moves."

AJ shook his head in disbelief. "Why did we all get old?"

Chapter Thirty-Two

"*You know what a Jewish optimist is? It's someone who believes that no, it really can't get worse.*"

~ *Ira Levine, former roommate of Hunter S. Thompson and friend of mine. I'm not Jewish, but pessimism works.*

The first of our big recon drones was up, eyeballing the four surviving charter buses pulling over on the side of the road that formed our northern property line. They'd used other cars to create a roadblock and make themselves a staging area. At least there was one less bus, so the enemy commander was starting twenty percent down. That hopefully counted for something.

Again, terrain would shape the fight. Fairly impassible ridges boxed us in along the north edge, west edge, and east edges of the property. South of us was a couple miles of creek-filled gullies then more ridges that you had to cross the hard way before you eventually hit another road. A clever enemy would have come that way, but it would take them a while before they even made it from a road to our rifle ranges. I figured we had some degree of eyes out even past our flanks. What few neighbors we had out here tended to be paranoid whackos and might get some warning shots off if pressed. Of course, since we couldn't rely on that, so that's what the UAVs were for.

Between the mountain and North Ridge, before you hit the woods, was the open field where the picnic gazebo stood. Knowing it was in the crossfire, we'd stripped it down pretty efficiently after that last meal we served. We could fix it later if we were still alive. Meanwhile I didn't want stuff like our deep fryer or the good refrigerators catching stray rounds. We'd paid a lot for that stuff. We'd even vented the propane lines for fire risk.

*****

The snipers were way out forward, three teams of three.

The fire teams were in the woods. Six teams were in the bunkers. They had preplanned sectors, keeping them interlocked. The snipers had cleared lanes to fall back through, and would check in at the bunkers. That would clear them to go hot.

Four more teams plus Eric's team and the Poles were floating behind the bunkers and covering the flanks. I'd gotten AJ pushed forward and linked up with Eric's crew. I wasn't sure what he thought of them or vice versa, and there wasn't much time to sort it out. I just needed the professionals to do professional shit and figure it out amongst themselves fast.

The mortars were at their primary firing position. I had the last two teams up close at the mountain. Everyone outside the mountain had no-transmit orders just like the snipers did. Nobody was supposed to make detectable electronic footprints.

The bad guys were doing about what Dave suspected they'd do. They really were playing the game just like they'd practiced. They were getting close fast using the paved road, then lining up to assault southward over North Ridge. They'd get through the woods, come down across into the open, and get across a couple hundred meters of open ground including our front parking lot to hit the doors. Their rehearsals we'd watched would dictate their plan.

Their plan sucked. I couldn't believe they were just going to try bull-rushing in the 'easy' way. Nobody with a lick of brains fights with light infantry that way. Frontal assaults went out of style with Pickett's Charge and the Somme. I actually felt good about this for a moment. They'd either really underestimated what I had on the ground here or they were just shitty overconfident. I was outnumbered, but *I* had a lot of firepower and *they* didn't have a lot of cover.

They had concealment, to an extent, but not a lot of cover. Then that made me feel worse because I refused to emotionally accept that this could go well.

A few of us were downstairs in Intel watching the UAV feeds on the big screens. Fox was the acting UAV boss, seated opposite Corey who was handling electronic warfare. I looked over at Dave. "No matter how pissed off you are at not going out there yet, I need your brain here. Now lemme call our friends at Langley and beg for help."

I probably should have done this a lot sooner, but I didn't expect I'd be believed until the situation was desperate, and "the need is immediate and extreme." Yes, I was mentally quoting the foundational Division general order that was Bill Lee's initial statement to the newborn 101st in 1942, but then I'd been there so long I was reverting to my base programming under stress.

I'd pulled that manila envelope from my desk and put it in my thigh pocket. Any phone would do, so I walked over to one of the side tables and ripped the envelope. It was one page of typed instructions, starting with a phone number with a Northern Virginia 703 area code. I kept reading as I hit the encryption button on the desk phone and dialed. There was a site code I was supposed to give to match my location to their index, and the code PRAIRIE FIRE EMERGENCY.

Even under the circumstances, I had to chuckle. That was an old MACV-SOG code to be given by a unit in the deepest of deep shit, like a recon team that was encircled and in need of every possible support to avoid capture or elimination. I knew several of those guys when I was younger. Cancer cut a hard swath through that community, but some of the lessons took before I lost my teachers. I looked down at Jerry Shriver's engraved memorial bracelet on my wrist that I'd worn for thirty years now. I could only hope whoever I was calling would get the true nuance of the phrase.

Ring.

Ring.

Ring.

A pleasant female voice answered with the last four of the number, and nothing else. Standard procedure when calling some people. As I have noted before, the CIA doesn't answer the phone "CIA", neither does the CQ desk at a Ranger battalion barracks, and neither do we for that matter.

"This is Professor at Site *redacted*. Am currently facing up to two hundred heavily armed hostile contractors. Compromise of entire site and contents is possible. Declaring PRAIRIE FIRE EMERGENCY, time now. Say again, PRAIRIE FIRE EMERGENCY, time now. Requesting immediate reinforcements." The site code was just a number anyway. How boring. I wanted a cool code name for the place. Site *Dwarrodelf* would have been cool. Maybe if I was still alive in two days, I could register a suggestion or something.

Her professionalism went out the window. "Uh, what?" She still sounded young and perky.

Grinding my back molars, I did my level best to sound way more calm and polite than I was really feeling. "Miss, we are one of your contract facilities. We have a LOT of your stuff in our basement that never, ever needs to see the light of day. We have a heavily armed hostile force knocking at the door, and we need a lot of fucking help, right the fuck now."

"Look, I don't know who you are or what you're talking about, but this is —"

I didn't have time for this shit, and my blood pressure was elevating. "Check my fucking scrambler codes. This is as serious as it gets. I get that you're probably some Langley desk type with an Ivy League diploma who didn't go through the Farm. But you're the phone number in my emergency instructions, and I need you to do X, Y, and Z. Z is probably call Fort Campbell up the road and kick me the infantry battalion that's on DRF-1." Or whatever they called it now, since I acknowledged my once-habitual knowledge of such things was twenty years out of date.

Even as I said it, I knew that was wishful thinking. The 82nd always got the emergency calls in the 1980s and 1990s because Air Force transports and parachutes can do a long-ranged forced entry operation when helicopters can't. Think Grenada or Panama, or the 1994 Haiti jump that aborted once negotiations succeeded. Packing helicopters up and moving them around the world in an extreme hurry is a major pain in the ass, and only one specialized SOCOM aviation unit does it well. Because of that, the Fort Campbell round-the-clock alert culture had atrophied into performative ritual even before the rotations to the Iraq and Afghanistan wars started in 2003. Because of the range limits of helicopters and the logistics needed to keep them operational more than a day or three, we just weren't all that portable a unit compared to our sister division, and I doubted that time had improved things. The 101 needs to stage within a hundred-fifty, preferably a hundred-twenty-five miles of the first fight. The 82nd could ride all the way from home to the target. That's why they were the worldwide 911 force for anything the Marines weren't a 24-hour boat ride away from.

The 75th's Rangers' recall system was intact, well-exercised, and their 'eighteen hours to be out the door' standard was well-publicized. Once they got the order, either one or maybe both of the two Georgia-based Ranger battalions could probably have a company here via parachute faster than someone in authority at Langley could call the Pentagon, the Pentagon call the 101st, the Pentagon probably have to get the SecDef or the President on the phone, have them give the orders, and then Campbell finally get the lead out of its ass and have a battalion an hour down the road to me. No way that was gonna happen either. The Rangers were the top of the line 'missions of national importance' option, so they weren't going to waste that shot on my problems. Even working downhill from there? There would be too many risk-averse lawyers, wobbly policy advisors, and other bureaucrats who'd say things like 'Title 10', '*Posse Comitatus* Act', or other magic words to keep me from getting the help I needed despite being a *de facto* government installation.

I didn't necessarily need ground troops. I'd have been happy with a flight platoon of Apache gunships, to be honest. That would have been easy enough to do if the right person got onto the phone to the right person. The damn things were right fucking there on the Kentucky state line, and it was twenty minutes of flight time if they kicked the birds in the ass. They could fly down, shoot themselves empty, call Winchester, and then fly back for more fuel and ammo. Hell, they could stop and eat lunch. I wouldn't give a shit. I just wanted help. I'd take the Avengers, Team Banzai, the X-men, the Justice League of America, whoever.

Meanwhile, while my brain was doing nervous backflips, she finally found her words. "I don't know what number you were trying to get, and I'm probably not supposed to tell you this, scrambled or not, but this is the Human Resources office. I've only worked here for a year."

Those words replayed in my head a couple times before it sunk in and that news finally hit me like a train. As that train passed by, it left nothing but a blank and hopeless space. *Leave it to one of those fucking morons at Langley to give me a memo with the wrong fucking number on it.* No one was coming. It was just going to be us, and we were in deep shit. The world was painting itself black.

In that sudden fit of depressive nihilism, there was still a streak of clarity to my thoughts that I held onto for dear life. Not just my life, but the lives of those who'd been dumb enough to follow me this far. *They're all gonna die. They're all gonna die, and it's gonna be your fault,* said the voice in my head.

I sighed. "Okay, cool. I'm about to have a very busy day, and you may see this on CNN in an hour or so. Hang on a second." Covering the handset's mike with my hand, I looked over at Dave. "Get my Black phone, or yours, and call Izzy. Tell him what's going on. He probably can't do much, but at least somebody with a brain there needs to know what's going on."

I returned my attention back to the nice young lady in HR at Langley, and *something* in my brain woke up and started giving orders. *Fuck it, man. You've been shot at before. Cope with it.* "You're Human Resources. Look up a Charles Stevens in the Directorate of Intelligence."

I heard keys clicking. "Uh... okay. I found him."

"Cool. Now I need you to fuckin' call him, and then tell him to get on the line."

"Hang on, I have to put you on hold to set up a three-way call."

In the first bit of good luck all day, Stevens was on the line in less than a minute. "Hey, Prof. I think somebody transposed a digit." He seemed way too happy, but then he had no idea what was going on yet. Time to ruin his goddamn day for him.

"Hi, Charles. Wonderful. You may notice that I have opened the emergency envelope. Meanwhile I have about two hundred hostile dismounts within a mile of my position, and I'm about to go to high explosives here unless you have a better idea."

His blithe happiness turned to disbelief. "You're shitting me."

"Nope. There's a reason I called a Prairie Fire. Nice historical reference on somebody's part, but appropriate in this case. Looks like African mercs smuggled into the country, and definitely working for a Chinese-controlled PMC called ArmEx out of Crystal City, Virginia."

I could hear him pause. "Wait, wasn't that Jim Shellington's company? We talked about them when you were up here and I was breaking your balls over that mess in Vegas."

"Yeah, emphasis on *was*. The Chinese-friendly clique of the New Zealand Army's retirees is running it now with Beijing's money. And this is going to make that mess in Vegas look like a rerun of Sesame Street just out of pure numbers and much better guns."

He sighed so loud I heard it over the phone. "I don't understand how you keep finding yourself in these fucked-up situations."

"Neither do I. Now unless you can wave a magic wand and get us some serious military assistance very quickly, maybe from up the road at Campbell, I have to get off the phone and go command the defense of the Alamo, so to speak."

"We're back to that problem where you really don't understand what 'discreet' means. Couldn't you just call the cops?"

I sighed. "I repeat, I have two hundred armed hostiles, repeat, TWO FUCKING HUNDRED, lining up outside my woods, and my mortar teams and machine gun crews are set up already." No sense mentioning all the other surprises. "This is not a 'call the cops' kind of problem. I'm going to have to take out their crew served weapons and key leaders early or I am very much going to lose this fight, then once they get past the doors, you'll have fuck knows who getting into downstairs and then your data goes fuck knows where. Am I making myself clear?"

"Oh, Christ." And then the bastard hung up on me.

Well, looks like it was just going to be us.

Chapter Thirty-Three

"*It has not occurred to you that your ancestors were survivors and that the survival itself sometimes involved savage decisions, a kind of wanton brutality which civilized humankind works very hard to suppress.*"

~ Frank Herbert, "God Emperor of Dune"

And now it began.

They weren't dumb. They had to know that breaching the gate was a low percentage move. That didn't mean they weren't going to try it anyway. That was fine, I couldn't blame them. It would have been irresponsible of them to *not* try it. Using a medium-sized dump truck they'd either bought or stolen somewhere, they crashed through the sliding chain link gate in the roadside fence. That was cool. That gate wasn't designed to stop much anyway. It made it another thirty yards up the driveway, tried to make the first turn, then abruptly slammed into the first of a half dozen large concrete cubes with which we'd corked ourselves in. *Ooops.* Well, when the sign at the road said 'No Unauthorized Traffic,' we fuckin' meant it.

The driver, surprisingly a white guy but also in their British surplus DPM uniform, stumbled out of the crumpled cab. He looked around, but then collapsed when his head came apart on camera. I had a feeling that was Troy's handiwork. Going down front and scoring first was his style.

Another one of our UAVs was covering their assembly area. Half a dozen of the mortar carriers were orbiting behind it. Part of me wanted to just drop multiple mortar shells on these guys right now where they were. But again... we live in a country with something resembling a legal system. That meant, when all this was over, I had to be able to articulate my thought process to somebody at the policymaking level to keep us all out of jail, let alone keeping the company active. The Florida 'accident' was already past our assumed margin of good luck. So... our side of the road was the tripwire. I wanted the woods to then be a roach motel for these guys. Let them come in. I was going to let as few out as possible.

There was one tall white guy walking around their assembly area, pointing and giving orders. Well... just *one* casualty off our property wouldn't make too much of a difference in the broader scheme of things. I turned to Fox. "Got a racer up?" I didn't like calling them suicide drones. Murder drones was far more accurate anyway. I suppose we could have gone with *kamikaze* out of semi-autistic historical interest, but I was gonna be practical for once in my life and not use four syllables when two would do just fine.

"Nope. They've got shitty endurance so we're keeping them on the ground rather than loitering them in the air. They're built for speed over everything."

"How long will it take you to get one into their assembly area?"

She shrugged. "Less than a minute at cruise speed to get close, then the burst for the final run into the target."

I pointed at the screen. "Send five of them. See the tall white devil out front in the mix?" Fox nodded. Something told me he was as foreign as his rank-and-file troops were. I was pretty sure it was one of ArmEx's Anzac officers. "Give him a really killer headache."

Fox did some dragging and clicking on her laptop. It would fly itself to 'close enough,' then one of the operators would take over to fly it into its target. Those operators were upstairs in the garage bay since they were also the ones pushing the new birds out as needed.

The recon drone sitting higher overhead caught the blur as the racer shot in and smacked Colonel Kiwi Fucker in the side of his head going about two hundred miles an hour. It was a hard enough hit that he did about a half-somersault and came down sideways on the blacktop. A mixed bag of his subordinates ran forward to check on him, but the awkward angle of his head with the red puddle beneath told me he was done for the day, to put it mildly. The platoon formations across the street from where he dropped were looking at each other, but they were still stepping forward and shaking out into files and wedges, as if they didn't have a worry in the world.

To be honest, I'd rather hoped that giving their commander a probably-fatal head injury where every last one of them could see it would inspire the others to break and run. Didn't look like any such luck. Goddamn it, I hate fighting hardened professionals, or even people who convinced themselves that they're hardened professionals. They don't quit. They stick in there and either you have to fuckin' kill them or they'll kill you. This sucked. I didn't want to have to kill anyone I didn't have to. This really wasn't what we were wanting to do today. We had other paying work from which this was a major goddamn distraction. Never mind the fact I didn't want any of my people to die. Their lives were far more dear to me than the other guy's mercs.

I turned back to Fox. "More racers... him, him, him, and... that fucker." She nodded, working the computer. I could just imagine the screaming whine of the overstressed electric motors. Then came four more traumatic head injuries to the guys who looked like the platoon level leadership. After that, those formations still went into the woods where the racer drones were infinitely less effective. We'd send more when they hit open terrain again.

While trees protect from some effects, they magnify others. When explosives go off in treetops, they turn pieces of the tree into additional shrapnel. 'Tree bursts' were another contributing factor in making 'The Green Hell' of the Hürtgen Forest into the death factory that it was in 1944. As the enemy force got about fifty meters into the woods, the mortars went to work. I wanted that formation broken and bleeding. I didn't put much faith in their chain of command to hold together as the casualties started piling up. I also had to be real careful about where we were dropping because the snipers were still out there. They knew where to be to not get stuff dumping on them.

The mortars shot three each, then over the treetops, came the half-dozen heavy homemade quadcopters carrying the airdrop-modified 81s. While not as super-murdery cool as all that slickly edited Ukraine War snuff video made it look, it was still a useful tool in the box if you were like us and didn't have a real air force. The improvised air-drop fuses on the UAV's 81s weren't smart enough to make airbursts or treebursts work. They just fell until it smacked something enough to make Haze's home-rolled creations blow, and blow they did.

When the half-dozen 'bombers' pulled off and went to reload, Freddie's guys put the tubes back to work. I wasn't an expert on mortar fire, but that's what I had him and his guys for. You couldn't hear anything down here, but the explosions were visible on the screen.

Then IT started flipping switches on their next innovation. There were direction-finding systems up on the cell phone tower looking for their FM radios. We had seen the antennas and numerous handheld communicators in use from the UAV cameras, so they had to be detectable. In less than a minute, we had their frequency and locations.

One of Corey's techs chortled in amusement, holding his headphones tightly. "Is it Amateur Night out there or what? They aren't even frequency-hopping, and they're in the clear in English."

I shrugged. "They might not have been up to doing anything sophisticated."

"It doesn't matter." Corey took a long drag off his brightly colored can of Monster and set it back down on the desk. His dark face split white with a self-satisfied grin. "They're going to pay very dearly for that oversight." He turned and nodded to one of his guys.

A couple mouse-clicks sent music pouring over the enemy command frequency. It was real familiar. "Are you really blasting them with Mia X Ally?" I asked in disbelief.

One of them shrugged. "Bagpipes and electric violin are soothing, man." It was the ladies' cover of Dragonforce's "Through the Fire and Flames." I don't know if that was exactly *soothing*.

"They going to be able to jam us back?" I asked.

That set off a round of insane cackling among the half-dozen techno-wizards at their computers. "Those handhelds push ten watts, tops. We're pushing ten *thousand* watts. And we have more on tap."

"How much more?"

Corey smirked. "Ignoring the lack of licensing issue, FCC maximum is a hundred thousand on broadcast band FM, which this technically isn't. Unless something on our side blows out and catches fire, I can probably push about one twenty directionally."

"A hundred twenty thousand watts? Won't that set the woods on fire?"

He looked at me like I was a moron, because on this subject I was. "First, vegetation makes a lousy antenna, so no. Second, it's the wrong frequency range. You couldn't even microwave dinner with this setup."

"Oh,"

"Now I might be able to zorch them hard enough to make some of their walkie-talkies catch fire. That would be kinda cool to see. Wolfman Jack had him a border blaster rig down in Tijuana fifty years ago that pushed a quarter million, and you could hear it way the hell up in Detroit at night. We can set up for that kind of power eventually, but we just aren't there yet."

A memory bumped loose. "Wasn't he working on the AM dial?"

Corey laughed. "Bossman, you're trying to think in technical terms and it's not your strong point. Stop doing it and just let us do what you pay us for."

Yeah, I had a feeling Corey and the other crazy fuckers would do this shit for free.

I looked over at Fox and pointed, then she clicked on her keyboard. First person view UAVs, what the drivers called FPVs, dove into the woods and swept through it like the speeder bike chase scenes in *Return of the Jedi*. It had that same gut-churning, stomach-flipping feel to it. Watching the drone feed as they zipped past our guests, there were holes in the enemy formation already. The mortars had taken a toll. Of the two hundred they'd crossed the road with, they had about 150 still moving with the formation. Some of the others could be merely be down and wounded, but that still wasn't bad work. Cameras aside, these weren't the high-speed murder-racing drones...

Boom.

Boom.

Another boom.

These were the grenade carriers. Right now, their piece of the air tasking order, assuming we'd ever bothered to write a formal one, was to find the forward edge of the enemy force in the woods and start making it explode. That would give warning to the fire teams in the blockhouses that the bad guys were close, and it was time to wake up the machine gun crews and get on the Claymores. The goal wasn't even killing them so much as it was keeping their formations broken so the blockhouse teams could do the real killing.

Meanwhile there was an opportunity. "Fox, get one of the recon UAVs to go double-check the buses. Look for a command post, reserves, a nuke with a timer on it, I dunno." She nodded and turned to one of the other operators to make it happen. If I had to, I'd take one of the fire teams I hadn't committed yet and go capture the buses.

One of the FPV drones sweeping through the woods watched as our machine gun tracers started cutting through the underbrush. Elsewhere, another got it on video as what was probably a big fat subsonic .300 Blackout from one of the sniper teams tore through a guy's head. And then the screen went black and it tumbled sideways. *Well, shit, I bet they got one of those EMP guns with them after all.* That was okay. We had enough to lose a few.

The OP on the back side by the air intakes called down that they were hearing machine gun fire and Claymores in the woods. That was a good sign. Meanwhile Fox was directing a bunch of the little grenade-carrying quadcopters to loop around and find the enemy rear. Staying up near the tree canopy and looking down, we were hoping to trace their line and plot it against where we knew our bunkers were. It wasn't going superbly.

Why was I having to rely on the UAV coverage to let me know what was going on in the woods? Everyone was still on no-transmit orders, remember? We still didn't know what these guys were doing for electronic warfare coverage, if any. I didn't want my force to be as visible to them as theirs was to me. But we weren't seeing their UAVs on the frequency scanner... unless they had done what we had and retuned them out of the FAA approved spectrum.

We were radio-scanning more broadly with the airborne detecting UAV, though we hadn't visually seen any of them either. Meanwhile, our small UAVs kept rushing in through the woods with more grenades, while the big ones lugging mortar shells circled above the treetops looking for things worth bombing. The mortars were on hold for now. Didn't want to bomb our own air force

"Corey, we got any signs of enemy electronic warfare gear?"

"Negative!"

Time to roll the dice again. Just as I was going to go for the radio mike to tell everyone listening *'Olly Olly Oxen Free',* the main frequency lit up. "Command, this is Bunker Two, say again, Bunker Two, they're getting past us on our left. Passing to our left, how copy, over?

I grabbed the mike and tried to be really, really calm. You never get to sound stressed as a command RTO, let alone a commander. "Two, this is Command. Roger, passing to your left. They get past your Claymores?"

"Roger, Command. We blew what we had out, took out their lead squad, but they ate those casualties and are bypassing between us and Bunker One. That gap wasn't as tight as we thought."

"You got any casualties?"

"Negative, Command. They suppressed the fuck out of us and flowed. Didn't waste effort knocking us out."

"Roger, break. All stations this net, all stations this net. Olly Olly Oxen Free, if you see them, call out."

"Command, Eric. They slid sideways, picked one breakthrough spot, and they went all in on it. We're moving to plug it. Nobody blow anything else — keep them mortars in 'check fire' until I call for 'em. UAVs too."

One of the smaller camera-carrying UAVs got there in time to watch the last ghosts of the Vietnam War arise from spider holes and hollow trees. Eric plugged three guys with that suppressed Grease Gun, and in the noise, it didn't seem like anyone noticed. One of his other old-timers bounced a guy from behind and cut his throat Hollywood-style with an old Ek commando knife, while others rocked their collection of M16A1s and M60 machine guns. One upped the ante when he pulled a Lagana tomahawk and buried its back spike in a forehead. I saw AJ, recognizable only by him having the only modern rifle of that bunch, smoke two of the ArmEx troops and then just fade into the bushes.

Trying to make a distraction for those guys to get their work in, some of the racers moved in to target who they could. Some made it, while some wiped out into tree branches. Another one went black and tumbled. I think it was that damn EMP gun again. The ones that crashed naturally generally still transmitted from their woodland graves. The EMP'd ones just went dead-dead.

"Command, this is *Polska* Actual. We are moving north on your East Ridge and moving to support Eric at the breakthrough," Tadeuz's accented voice came through the speaker.

"Roger." I looked over at Dave. "You wanna push forward and call the ball?"

He nearly snarled in feral joy. "Will bring you a couple ears." He headed for the elevator. I was pretty sure he was joking, but Dave does have his moods. Within a few minutes he called back. "I got with the Poles and we pushed on. We cut them up, but they're past us. We're reconsolidating everyone we got back here into a couple platoons' worth to take them from behind as they head toward you."

I wasn't sure how the fuck he'd gotten down there so fast. He told me later he'd gone straight east across the parking lot onto East Ridge then cleared up it northward until he met his, uh, Polish Legion, then they got past the bad guys on what we saw as their right side to get behind them.

"Dave, fall back off of 'em until you're absolutely ready. I'll get a couple more stonks of mortar fire on 'em before you push in, and I don't want you dudes sitting at danger close when the fire mission comes in, got it?"

"Roger. My forward trace is about two-hundred meters off it. We're back at the blockhouse line."

"Eric and all snipers, I need you off that woodline so we can hit it from here, copy?" Meanwhile Corey was waving at me as I tallied up the acknowledgments. I pointed at him and waved for him to say it, whatever it was.

"Don't mortar them anymore yet. We don't want them to scatter. We want them concentrated for what's coming."

Fuck "What's coming?"

"Something really kinda freaky."

I wasn't sure how many surprises I was still good for today. "What kind of freaky?"

He chortled. "Death ray freaky. Remember that big-ass radar antenna we put on the cell phone tower?"

"To be honest, no." I never looked at the damn thing. I had people to do that for me.

Corey was somewhat deflated that I'd failed to notice whatever he had been up to. "Oh. We bolted on a set of old Firefinder antennas we got out of the DRMO scrapyard." For those of you who don't speak the language, that's the Defense Reutilization and Marketing Office. "Three of them, with cameras mounted and mechanical steering added to them. Then we started building other shit. Some of the parts are Navy surplus, there's an Air Force piece, with some other odds and ends we scratchbuilt. It's all kinda kludged together. Remember what I said about not being able to microwave dinner with the radio jammers?"

"Yeah."

"This shit will cook a motherfucker half a mile off like he was a 7-11 burrito."

You know, part of me was sure this was absolutely a goddamn war crime. But Geneva was a long way that way, I never signed anything on the subject, and well, let's face it, it's only a war crime if you lose. Still, I had to ask. "You guys serious?"

Corey shrugged again, looking thoughtful. "Not really."

"Oh." I gotta admit, I was only a little disappointed.

Undaunted, he continued. "We've got some terrain masking issues from the tower and a lot of the math is theoretical based on the Navy electronics safety manuals. We were reverse-engineering the 'Thou Shalt Not Exceed' wattage numbers to get the desired lethality. A quarter mile is a much more realistic number. My math says four hundred meters at best for instant kills, but it's really kinda guesswork. Closer they get, the more efficiently the energy transfers. It's also a low humidity day which helps. Good thing we aren't doing this in August."

That was still really scary yet kinda cool at the same time. We were going to need a certain amount of cool shit to work if we were going to win this fight. He clicked, and a picture of the field came up. Like he said, there was a video camera on the antenna to help aim it, but the signal was kinda iffy from the amount of electromagnetic interference involved. Corey merely shrugged. "Still got some issues to solve." But as the camera panned to the right, stopped, and zoomed, there they were, massing in the woodline getting ready to assault across the field, pass the gazebo and parking lot, and head for our doors.

"Dave, keep everybody back. We got some unusual support fire coming in, so stay way back and get everyone down."

"Roger. Way to stick to the fucking plan, asshole."

I had to laugh. "We had a plan?"

Dave was laughing too. "Maybe next time we'll get it right. But we're holding."

"Mortars, be ready to fire that woodline concentration on my mark, but check fire for now. We're trying something else first."

Freddie called back. "Mortars, check fire, roger. What are we expecting?" I didn't answer, because I wasn't really sure.

Meanwhile the bad guys, maybe the hundred that were left, were all massing at the woodline, getting ready to assault across the field toward the doors. They had to know it wasn't going to work. *They had to know.* Unless they were just aiming for the garage and waiting on a heavy engineer unit to come help them crack it, they weren't getting into the mountain itself. But we couldn't exactly take that chance now, could we?

I turned and pointed. "All right, Corey, time to impress me." Corey's grin came back as the Spectrum King went to work.

At this point in history, nobody really knew what would happen if you deliberately shot enough radar into a person. Sure, there were some horrible military antenna accidents over the decades, but so far as anyone knew, nobody'd ever tried making a *deliberately* lethal electromagnetic gadget, a literal death ray. A human body is seventy percent water. That's going to heat up. How rapidly depends on how much power is involved. Enough power, that water would flash-boil into steam. Since steam expands sixteen-hundred times compared to the original volume liquid water, yes, one thousand, six hundred times, if you heat enough of that water, people don't expand and... *oh, holy fuck, that guy exploded.*

I heard one of the *Wayne's World* characters in my ears. "You ever see that scene in *Scanners* when that dude's head blew up?" Yeah, that was more impressive in the movie because we were a good distance off, and the special effects guy used a twelve gauge, but man, this shit was as real as razor blades. It wasn't like firing the Death Star cannon, but *oh, shit, there goes another one.*

Later, Corey explained the math, and enough antenna wave theory to get me very lost. A normal kitchen microwave pumps maybe a thousand to twelve-hundred watts unless you have a really old one or a really expensive new one to put you over or under that window. Commercial ones ran at twenty-four-hundred watts, or 2.4 kilowatts. The radar was pumping 'at least' a hundred-eighty kilowatts, so ninety times that. They were mechanically and electronically steerable, frequency agile, and so on and so on. That meant it could focus the beam down to the size of your finger and aim it. It couldn't do it for long, because that builds up a lot of heat, but even one-second bursts with that much power were more way lethal than bullets. The only thing I'd seen blow people up like that were 30mm rounds from an Apache's chin-mount gun. Corey confessed he'd gotten the idea twenty years ago from watching an errant seagull fly in front of a powered-on shipboard Aegis antenna off the California coast and instantly turn into a puff of smoldering feathers.

It seemed like no time at all when he said "Have to let her cool down some, boss man."

There were a bunch of really, *really* dead guys in the woodline, and the others didn't look in any hurry to try crossing that field until they figured out what was going on and why people were exploding for no apparent reason. I was impressed. "That needs some kinda cooling system."

He shrugged. "We were on deadline, and we didn't know what it would really do. I figure it will do ten seconds continuously, like tops. I'm going for one second bursts every five, but I'm still getting a high heat warning."

"Three antennas up there?"

"Yeah, but these guys are only coming in on one azimuth, so we don't get to spread the workload and let the antennas cool in sequence. We have 270-degree coverage until we find another antenna somewhere that actually works, but each one can only swivel in a limited arc because of the way they're mounted. We'll have to do something different for next time."

Next time? *Next time? FUCK a next time!* "Did it cool down enough to try again?"

Corey shrugged. "The warning light's off, but we know this bitch is preheated like an oven now."

Good point. *Time for Plan B.* I snatched up the radio mike. "Mortars, fire that woodline up, gimme a fast battery three, wait about a minute, then give me two more fast."

Freddie snickered. "Roger, but again, we don't call it that in mortars."

On the screen, the woodline started exploding again as the shells came down. I turned to the crowd. "Ladies and gentlemen, I salute you for your work down here, but this is becoming less a UAV fight and more an eyeballs fight. I've got to get upstairs and earn my paycheck. I got a handheld if you need me." Just to loosen up, I slowly jogged up the stairs. I didn't have time to go hug Angel again, so I went past IT and the glowing, blinking 'OUR MISSION' sign. Another flight of stairs later, thinking I might want to go while I could, I exited the stairway and headed for the first-floor bathrooms.

It may surprise you to know that almost all our bathrooms here at Athenaeum were gender-neutral. This was not out of social progressivism, but rooted in the fact that the original architect in the 1940s or 50s had designed this place for an all-male working staff back in the days when men were men and women were either just dates to the unit formal or home with the kids. There were three exceptions. There was a women's locker room off the garage bay that we'd put in since our female personnel used the gym too. There was the en-suite bathroom down on the fifth floor off Cash's old room, though of course I had used it when I was living in there. And there was a small bathroom right across from Big John's old office, now occupied by Dave, that had either been intended for female guests, the commander's secretary, or had maybe just been intended as a private spot for the commanding officer to take a shit in peace. Naturally Angel and Cash used it and it had a WOMEN sign on the door, leaving spare makeup bags and whatnot in there. You know, icky girl stuff.

Heading for the larger three-stall men's facility next door to it, I noticed a large hand-done sign taped over the WOMEN sign that said, in red:

WARNING: CONTAINS LIVE ANIMAL
DO NOT OPEN!!!!!!!!

No fucking way. Somebody was fucking around, and this was not the time for it. I pushed the door open. Somebody had thrown a big plaid flannel dog bed on the 1950s tile floor. There was an adolescent-size bobcat asleep on the dog bed. Well, he was asleep. In about half a second, Mister Murderbritches was up, furiously yowling and charging toward the door. Really, I was only guessing it was Murderbritches since it wasn't like we had ever been properly introduced.

After getting the door back shut, I went next door to the men's room and handled my originally intended drainage. Thinking I could spare a minute, I ducked into the break room, found a bag of leftover chicken tenders in the refrigerator, and just threw the whole thing into the women's room to calm him down.

From there, it was just a minute's work to get into my office and throw on my belt rig and plate carrier. Six AR mags, four 1911 mags, plus all the other necessary bullshit like medical, the commo pouch (shoving my radio into it), a quart of fruit punch Gatorade in the Nalgene bottle, and a couple granola bars and some beef jerky for later. *You're not you when you're hungry.* Just ask Murderbritches, who was probably happier for the chicken.

I pulled my 1911 of the day, my old Springfield Operator that had been stripped and rebuilt three times over since I'd bought it used a decade and a half ago. It had touches from John Harrison, Hilton Yam, and Stan Chen, though it hadn't seen the inside of any man's shop. Now I could have gone Glock today, but remember, we had so many surplus 1911s from the arms room out for use today that I would be just fine in terms of magazine commonality out there. If it did come to pistol work, I'd just have to be Johnny On The Spot with my reloads. As I have observed before, eight is less than eighteen.

Having given AJ the rifle I was planning on using, I was at square one and had to make up my mind up all over again what I was carrying out there. Most of the contents of the safe were laying all over the office. My match-modified 1903 Springfield, my Persian Mauser, my .303 Enfield, the .375 Holland and Holland... suffice it to say that all the bolt actions were out of the question except maybe my M24 sniper rifle. Forget about all that. I was limited to modern magazine-fed semiautos or better. I was even skipping over my M1 Garand today.

I wanted that Thompson like a junkie wants a needle of heroin. I really wanted a Tommy gun kill on my resume. But a Thompson rules a fifty-meter world. The far woodline was over four hundred meters away. I needed something with more legs. Realistically, with mags and pouches already set up, I was going to be sticking to another AR. I took my oldest personal one, the piece AJ had dismissed as a distance rig. sixteen-inch SPR barrel, midlength gas, etc, etc, etc, and a Swampfox Warhorse on top of it. I had more expensive glass on other guns, including the one AJ had just ganked, but this was what I had right now. If I had to be personally shooting, something had really gone wrong anyway.

While I acknowledged this thing might take a while, we were still eight hours from me needing night vision. I left my dual-tube goggles on my desk for safe, well, safe-R-keeping. I grabbed a last Mountain Dew as I went for the sugar and caffeine intake. I slammed it down as I went upstairs, and dropped the can on the top landing so my hands were free. I'd come back and get it later. You know, assuming I was still alive.

As I walked out into the garage bay, I stopped by the Notre Dame-style 'KILL BAD GUYS LIKE A CHAMPION TODAY' sign inside the door to the garage bay. For once, we were playing a home game, and we still might be the underdogs. I touched the cared-for varnish protecting the forty-year-old paint and sighed. Were I a better follower of any religion, I might have had the words, but if They were up there, and I mean any of Them since I wasn't exactly picky right now, They'd know what I felt right now.

Our Lady of Victories, pray for us.

A long time after, I went back and rewatched the movie. Yeah, I even got the line wrong.

Chapter Thirty-Four

*"*S*hoot until the target changes shape or catches fire."*
     ~ Sergeant Major Chuck Pressburg, US Army, retired. Though Chuck then told me it was the late Pat Rogers.

The garage bay was as busy as the hangar scene in the first *Star Wars*. It had that frenzied WWII war movie vibe to it that the young George Lucas had deliberately copied, only here the crews dwarfed the aircraft rather than the more usual other way around. I stayed to the edge of the action and cut around them.

At the door, I still had a full four-man team in the shack watching that doorway just in case, and I nodded at them as I passed. Yeah, they were my greenest new kids since they were at the least risk. If shit went bad, their job was to get everyone out of the bay and in past the big blast door before locking down the mountain.

I buckled my good helmet on, pulling the earpieces down. Integrated comms, electronic ear protection, etc, etc. We'd been spending a chunk of money on shit like that. Now if I could just find somebody who could make ballistic eye pro that could handle my fucked-up lens prescription. Shooting is a visual activity and my eyeballs have always been extremely substandard.

Heading out the personnel door to outside, I had to turn to the right and follow the barrier of concrete T-walls to the bunker that held the end. Ruiz's team was manning this one. There was already a stack of 7.62mm ammo cans stacked at the ready behind the bunker when I climbed into their position, with their junior guy Williams sitting on them. Being a 1st MarDiv sniper grad, Ruiz himself had one of our 7.62mm M110s the snipers had left behind, busily glassing the far woodline. He only came off the scope for a second or two. "Hey, sir, some of those dudes just fucking *exploded*. Like that guy's head blew the fuck up and I don't think we did it —"

I cut him off. "It was us. I'll explain later." I then switched to the radio. "Dave, I'm upstairs. You guys still down and clear? I grabbed the binoculars that no self-respecting machine gun team does without and scanned the woods myself.

Dave called back. "Still clear. What the fuck is going on up there? We aren't hearing anything except them yelling and screaming. It would be really fucking helpful if you guys were doing some shooting so we don't have to kill these fucking pricks all by our fucking selves, asshole."

"Tell you later. Break." I came off the button before rekeying. "Corey, hit it."

"Sending." There was no noise or light, no sci-fi special effects, but I counted off another set of bursts. "That's ten, gotta let it cool a while," he called back.

"You're doing fine. Mortars, fire that target line again. Gimme a battery three." Freddie was ready for that. "Roger! But remind me to reteach you mortar call for fire when all this is over!"

Now that I was up above ground, I could hear all the bangs and crashes involved in the mortar fire. Though I was trying to be a detached and calculating commander, it was kinda cool. *Crump, crump, crump, crump, BOOM, BOOM, BOOM, BOOM. Crump, crump, crump, crump, BOOM, BOOM, BOOM, BOOM. Crump, crump, crump, crump, BOOM, BOOM, BOOM, BOOM.*

Good, good. Back to the radio. "Fox, get a flight of UAVs ready with grenades to get in there under the trees. Maybe a dozen. Rock them a little bit while Dave gets that assault line ready."

"Roger, be a minute."

It hit me that much of the effort put into building the bigger mortar shell-carrying UAVs was a waste of fucking time. They'd be useful long-term, yeah. The one we'd pushed to Florida while Morgan and Fox were working, well worth it. But right now? We didn't need a half a dozen of the damn things when the four mortar tubes were doing the job. The six of them were up in what NASA would call a parking orbit, but we couldn't fly them into the gun-target lines of the mortars or they might get shot down by the incoming shells. Well, when you make shit up as you go along, this sort of thing happens. Better to have and not need, as Grandma used to say. Meanwhile, I turned to that bunker's main attraction, and Johnston's grinning face behind it.

Because of Eric's... unauthorized long term 'borrowing' of various small arms from 'Midwest Depot' forty years ago, you the reader remember I had these two M1917A1 water-cooled Brownings that someone had set up later for standard 7.62mm NATO link ammo as the world finally started to run out of WWII's massive piles of .30-06. You may also remember I had made those guns Johnston's problem.

See, sometimes when you need to make a real mess, it is best to use the implements of the past. For reasons of weight, shorter manufacturing time, and evolving tactical doctrine, machine guns stopped being heavy water-cooled beasts machined from forged steel billets and became, to paraphrase the late Ian Hogg, the stamped-out tack-welded sheet-metal contraptions they are today. In a mass-production maneuver war, the speed of and the cost of manufacture beat the previous emphasis on quality of manufacture and sustained fire capability from fixed positions. Everyone wanted a belt-fed they could pick up and walk around with. Remember when I told you about how the MAG-58, the 240, and its numerous foreign cousins were the last of the Browning guns? There was a practical point to that lecture, just as there was with my complaints for the record regarding the M60 receivers.

The point of all that is acknowledging the flip side of the coin, that if you need to continuously lay a lot of lead down for a prolonged period of time rather than merely popping off six to nine round bursts while running about, do it the way they did in World War I. Use something large, on a heavy tripod for stability, and with water cooling. And no, they really *don't* make them like they used to.

For those of you without the ambition to watch 'Forgotten Weapons' on YouTube, let me catch you up. Water cooled machine guns fell out of fashion after World War I. It took until the 1960s to really be rid of them because there were still so many of the damned things out there. We still used the '17s through the Korean War, and the British didn't give up their Vickers guns until 1968. So long as you have water and ammunition, the damn things basically run forever so long as you lube the moving parts occasionally. As I write this, there are still dudes getting schwacked right how in Ukraine with WWI or WWII surplus Maxim guns.

Anyway, you start by pouring a quart or two of water into the top of the cooling jacket. This doesn't fill the whole thing, but submerges the barrel. The water reaches 212 degrees, but no higher since past that it boils off down the exhaust hose into a condensing can. If you're clever, you have the end of the hose submerged in more water so it instantly condenses back to liquid water. It also hides any telltale steam cloud, and that's important when the other team is shooting back at you. You can then reuse that reclaimed water to refill the jacket, or if you don't mind a slight oily taste, you can play 'Old Breed' Marine and make coffee with it. If you have a Vickers gun, you must be a proper Brit and brew tea from it instead.

Despite having left the active Marine Corps inventory not long after the Korean War, its use in many of the Corps' most storied actions from Guadalcanal to the Chosin Reservoir made the water-cooled Browning a holy relic to Marine 0331s, the tool of their cult-specific saints like Basilone, Paige, or McKinney. That's why Johnston had taken this tasking to master the antique gun as seriously as any other religious obligation. Yes, I had suspected it would go like that. When you're in a mess like this, you gotta trust to skill and motivation more than numbers.

My thought process and historical musing was interrupted by the tiny roaring of small rotors behind us. Shocking the shit out of me, a stream of the small UAVs flew out the walking door and down the passage I had used minutes before. I had assumed they were using the big garage door for flight ops and I confess I hadn't expected to see that happen.

Johnston looked over at me and shrugged. "Yeah, it scared the piss out of me the first time they did it. I may be getting used to it now."

Ruiz snorted. "Bro, the first time was only what, half an hour ago?"

I couldn't pay too much attention to the snappy dialogue. I was preoccupied waiting for the UAVs to do their work, counting the booms. I needed them to drop their frags and get the hell out of the way before Corey could fire up that death ray of his again, otherwise he'd fry every circuit in the things. That would not be helpful, as I wasn't sure how many spares we had. Then the little stream of baby bombers came out of the woods, heading for the hangar bay to come reload. *We're gonna need to restock on frags after this.* Well, that was a 'later' problem.

We'd waited another minute, then Johnston asked "Can somebody cover me while I go take a shit?"

Ruiz looked at him. "Motherfucker, you gotta go now?"

"Fuck you, bro, I've been trying to hold it for two hours."

I waved for Ruiz to knock it off. "I got the gun for a minute. Johnston, go shit. I don't want you shitting yourself in here." Remember the men's locker room was right off the garage bay not even two-hundred feet away, so that wasn't a problem. He scurried off without a word. Exercising some privilege of rank, I took his place behind the gun.

I hit my radio button. "Corey, you ready?"

He sounded nearly joyful at the chance to fry more people. "Roger!" About ten seconds later he came back with "Shit, we lost something! Radar's giving me failure lights!"

Looking out the back of the blockhouse and up the side of the mountain, one of the antennas bolted to the cell phone tower high above us was belching flames from its front face. "Corey, we lost the antenna. No shit, it's on fire. Forget about it for now. We gotta finish this one the old-fashioned way."

Eric picked that moment to pop up on the radio. "My team's got the buses. Four live Chinese EPWs. Getaway drivers. Got some dead guys laying on the road, looks like blunt trauma to the head." *Goddamn right, it was.* Now those little gadgets paid off. We could probably rebuild the wrecked ones and reuse them over the long haul...

I hit my transmit switch. "Roger. Way to cut off their retreat. If any of you can push back south to rejoin Dave's element, do it."

Clearing my head, I slammed the gun all the way to the left limit on the traverse bar so the muzzle was to the right, I locked it down to keep me from traversing back into where Dave's command was. I set the tripod's elevation for a one-meter-high grazing fire across the field. That was really important. See, we were the anvil that Dave's force would push forward and upon which then smack what was left of the attacking force, but we had to be real careful not to shoot Dave's guys in the process. The machine gun tracers would keep the attacking force from walking forward into them, and make them hold still so Dave's guys could then kill or capture. Really, I didn't care which. Well, that was the plan, at least. This shit can get tricky fast. "Dave, you ready?"

"Roger, we're on line. Gimme one more battery three of mortars right on the woodline to count it down."

Freddie answered for me. "Roger. Time now?"

Dave told him "Send it!"

Crump, crump, crump, crump, BOOM, BOOM, BOOM, BOOM. Crump, crump, crump, crump, BOOM, BOOM, BOOM, BOOM. Crump, crump, crump, crump, BOOM, BOOM, BOOM, BOOM. The last set of explosions had barely faded when the woods erupted again with the sound of gunfire from multiple angles.

Dave called over the radio "We're moving!"

I grabbed my radio. "Fox, gimme some eyes in there! And send all the baby bombers."

"They gotta go in relays, but they're going!" Yeah, I knew that. There just weren't enough controllers to put all of them in the air at once, at least not under manual control. Shit, until a month ago we'd been in the surveillance UAV business and only owned six or seven of the damn things, never putting more than two up at once. Learning how to fight with these things wasn't a learning curve, it was trying to get up a learning cliff in the Himalayas.

Johnston was back and standing behind me. "I got it, sir."

I looked at him and said "Take my AR. I gotta try this thing while I get a chance." He laughed and took my rifle from where I'd leaned it against the wall. The problem was that we couldn't see through the woods to know where to shoot without shooting through them into Dave's guys. Therefore, we couldn't do shit unless Dave called for it, unless... then a clump of bad guys broke from the woodline, guns blazing, but right into the azimuth on which the gun was locked. I laid on the trigger, and the Browning started its deadly *chug-chug-chug*. Four hundred-fifty rounds a minute was dreadfully slow compared to the guns that came along later, but again, this beast was designed to do it all damn day before needing a barrel change. I didn't need all day — they got scythed down pretty efficiently by the hundred and eight year old gun.

While that was pretty fucking cool, loitering behind a tripod pulling a trigger all day was not the best use of my time. I stood up and waved Johnston back onto the little camping chair behind the gun. "Don't worry, man. We probably got more people for you to shoot." I looked over at Ruiz, who had just touched off a 7.62mm from his 110. "Get him?"

Ruiz nodded. "That near end of the woodline is only three-hundred twenty-five meters. Chip shot."

"Good work. Just make sure Johnston doesn't get crazy with that thing." I slapped him affectionately on the shoulder. "Hang in there. Oh, before I forget, you guys may know. Why the fuck is there a bobcat locked up in the first-floor women's bathroom?"

Matthews was kind of a redneck and knew about that kind of shit. "Miss Kara ordered us to trap and relocate as much of the wildlife out of the north woods over the last week as we could. She didn't want any of our animals getting killed when we started dropping HE on the trees. Never mind whatever the fuck that thing with the radar antenna was."

"Okay, makes sense in our weird way. Cool. Why the bobcat in the shitter?"

He shrugged, still scanning his sector. "Running the deer off was easy, most little stuff will hide in a den, but me and Mac from Hawkins' team only trapped Murderbritches really early this morning, so we had to stash him somewhere quick-like."

Shaking my head in disbelief, I unassed the machine gun position and headed back into the garage bay where the flight controllers were. I had to see what was going on in the woods, and short of running my old crippled ass across a most of four hundred yards of wide-open space and getting shot in the process, the small UAVs were the only way I was going to have visibility on the fight.

I leaned over Griffin's shoulder since he was at the closest controller. The drone he was running right now was zipping between trees, and he didn't look up. "Kinda busy right now, boss. Not tryin' to be rude."

"Nah, you're fine. Just trying to get eyes on targets."

I heard the Browning chugging away outside, but the screen had my attention riveted. The UAV camera pulled up over a branch then dropped like a roller coaster, catching a clump of bad guys trying to rally at the tree's base, using the thick old hickory for some kind of cover. Griffin slapped a red button on the homemade control box and laid a frag grenade into their midst then the screen went topsy-turvy again as the UAV banked and zoomed out of there. It broke out into sunlight and we got a great view of the mountain as it ran for home. I could see the antenna on the tower was still burning. *Fuck.* We might have to deal with that if the fire didn't go out on its own, or else we'd lose everything else on that tower.

He hit another button, which made another UAV launch itself off the floor and hover slowly out the door. "We programmed automatic return into these. Get them to where they can get home on their own on a preset course. We then reversed the steps so they can auto-launch. We just fly the mid-course portion and the ordnance delivery. Boosts our turnaround time by fifty percent."

"That's pretty cool. I still gotta figure out where the fuck the rest of those guys are." I got back on the radio. "Dave, talk to me. You need anything?"

"No, we're too close to them for mortars and we're even getting too close for grenades. We got this. Just watch for leakers. We're assaulting through."

Shit. I grinned, worried about my friends. "Good hunting."

Dave wasn't concerned, or didn't sound it. "Dude, shuddup and lemme work."

I turned back to Griffin. "I gotta see. Swing me a bird if you can."

He grinned. "Can do easy." The screen filled up with the end of the fight. Surprise, speed, and violence of action aren't just for fighting in buildings. Having been rocked by suicide UAVs, medium mortars, sniper fire, air-delivered grenades, a literal goddamn death ray, and then catching a close infantry assault by experienced professionals, what was left of them rolled over and put their hands up within about thirty seconds. *Shit, we didn't think about this.* Nobody had rehearsed the process of massing EPW search teams and prisoner handling at the platoon-ish level, but ninety percent of us had done it before.

Across the radio net, someone with a thick Polish accent uttered "*Venimus, vidimus, Deus vicit.*" Even without the accent, I would have known it was one of the Poles. Jan Sobieski III led the Hussars down off the heights overlooking Vienna and smashed the besieging Ottomans from the rear in 1683. Afterward, the Polish king one-upped Julius Caesar with "We came, we saw, God conquered." Maybe he was right? *Shit. I might have to start going to church.*

Now that the fight was over, it was time to secure what we'd held. I'd planned a little bit ahead for this. We had an industrial-size icemaker in the bay, and had prepped a dozen five-gallon buckets full of iced-down Gatorade bottles for 'during or after.' We had any color Gatorade you like, so long as it's either the red stuff or the green stuff. Letting my rifle hang on its sling, I grabbed one in each hand and waved at some of the excess UAV assistants to come help me.

I got back outside as quickly as I could move to help organize the capture effort. Nothing I hadn't done before either. A quick head count I heard over the radio as I moved told us we had twenty-one live ones at the final fight, and fuck knows how many of them left in the woods downed but breathing.

Chapter Thirty-Five

"*If it's a fair fight, you planned it wrong and your tactics suck.*"

   ~ Colonel Nicholas Andreacchio, US Army, former commandant of the School of the Americas. Miss you, Andy.

Few people are ever happy to have the boss show up, but when you show up with cold drinks after a midday gunfight, I figured they'd least happy enough to fake it. It was a little hot today for a Tennessee April, and none of us were exactly young anymore.

Speaking of 'not young,' the first of our combatants from the woods I'd run into was General Nguyen. I hadn't seen his transformation. The suit was gone, traded for an old set of American woodland BDUs, and like many of the others out here, he'd gone for full face paint. He limped out of the woods, slinging his borrowed AK as he came, and I moved to help him. He waved me off. "I'm all right, it's just my knee. I overdid it a bit back there, It will be better in a moment so long as I keep moving somewhat."

"You sure, sir?"

He nodded. "I am. Not a new feeling, I'm afraid. It's also why I had to give up playing tennis with younger people. Unfortunately at my age, that's mostly everyone."

"Understood. Aside from that. glad to hear you're well, General. Now could I interest you in a Gatorade?" Again, since this guy was someone even Eric was super-polite to, I was going to be really, *really* nice.

"What colors?"

"Anything you like so long as it's red or green."

He pondered that for a moment. "They make multiple sorts of red and green for different markets, but so long as it's the actual lemon lime and not anything unusual, I'll take a green, thank you." I passed it over, he cracked it open, and took a long pull. "Thank you. I asked for a green Gatorade once down in South America and got cucumber-watermelon. That wasn't what I was expecting at all. It wasn't bad, I suppose, it was just... jarring."

Andy came out of the woods between his two fire teams, also stumbling a good bit in the underbrush. He took his helmet off and popped the side releases on his armor for ventilation. I threw him a bottle of the red kind, then I handed the bucket off to one of his fire team leaders for distribution. It had enough left for his other eight men, which was good.

Once his bottle was half gone, Andy looked up at me, slightly whipped-looking. "I'm glad they didn't wait until summer. Glad I came, don't get me wrong, but after this, I think I'm officially too old for this shit." He then drained rest of the bottle.

General Nguyen looked over at Andy with a smile. "Young man, if you think *you're* too old for this shit, I have *extremely* bad news for you." I took a moment to introduce them, and Andy's socially gregarious streak kicked in. He's basically a human Golden Retriever. Damn, I was glad he hadn't gotten hit. Like I said, his girlfriend would have killed me.

Reconsolidating our force didn't take long. Eric's force of old-timers came out of the woods, rallying on General Nguyen. Eric was bringing up the rear, but none of them were moving particularly fast. Those guys had left it all on the field today, and I was learning firsthand it takes more to recharge your batteries as the years stack up.

Looking around, I didn't see AJ with Eric's force, so I asked him about it. Eric nodded. "He's thirty years younger than the rest of us, so he broke off after it was over and he's moving with Dave and the Poles. He's got some skills; that's for damn sure. He looking for work?"

I sighed. "I don't know. I am still wondering how he picked today of all days to show up after eleven or twelve years of not hearing from him at all."

He shrugged philosophically. "Don't overthink it, man. Fate does what it wants to, especially on battlefields. You do what you can to prep, of course, but like your friend picking today to show up, you just try to make the surprises work for you and not against you."

Sweeping the field, we were cleaning up a goodly number of enemy dead. There weren't many of their wounded still breathing. As we had observed, they hadn't been wearing body armor, and we'd been shooting the good non-Hague Convention-compliant ammo even before the Radar of Death opened up. Barnes Triple Shocks are expensive but worth it. If you can make one well-placed shot do the work of three or four, it prices out in a cost-per-round basis.

Another team of four was carrying a body in our gear out, but there hadn't been a call for the ambulance truck. No waving, no sense of urgency. *Shit.* That meant it was already too late. I hurried that way. Two of the bigger guys had locked hands and were carrying the body between them basket-style. *Shit.* It was Luke. He'd caught what looked like two bullets in the head, probably never knew what hit him. *Goddamn it.* Luke had tried to do the right thing at the end. He deserved better than that. Waving for his guys to set him down, I got on the radio. "Doc, Prof."

"Go ahead."

"We got one KIA down here. Too late for intervention, but we need a transport. Gonna need help as we find wounded, ours and theirs."

"Roger."

*****

We had a dozen wounded, most lightly and all walking. Miraculously, we only had one dead. While we'd mourn Luke, it could have been way worse. We'd accomplished this by blatant cheating. We'd stacked this deck long before the first card was dealt. I suppose that was the first lesson from all this. A long-retired colonel I'd known in my youth had coached me well on that point.

Dave came out of the woods, flanked by 'his' Poles. Tadeuz was grinning like he'd just won the lottery and banged Ana de Armas in the same day. Dave just sort of looked annoyed, but then that was normal for him.

I walked over, and we high-fived quickly. "How are you looking?"

He shrugged. "I got a dozen walking wounded so far like I called in, nothing bad. Snipers are on the way back in." He looked around. "We didn't really plan for prisoners, did we?" A squad or so of our guys were herding them. They all apparently spoke enough English to work with, which made it easier. They were all cooperative enough, though that wasn't any reason on our part to let them wander off or get stupid ideas

"We'll figure it out."

Dave took a long pull at his Gatorade. "Hey. There was one surviving 'officer' prisoner, a Brit. Ben's squad's got him zip-tied in the picnic gazebo. How about you go talk to him since you're calmer than I am, and I'll play first sergeant out here?"

"Can do." That was good news. Hell, I was just happy we could still use the gazebo. At first glance, it hadn't gotten anywhere near as fucked up by today's events as I thought it might. That was a serious practical consideration because everyone had a long day and we were gonna have a lot of really hungry people before long. Those really hungry people were heavily armed. "You good otherwise?"

He was thinking about it for a minute. "They came in stupid as shit."

"Remember, we killed a couple levels of their leadership by busting them in the head with UAVs. They just didn't have the junior leadership to jump up and hold it together."

"Decapitation works. Anyway, go talk to that asshole before he gets his wits about him."

*****

Lieutenant Digby Grenville-Bankes had a really, really pretentious up-per-crust accent that made him sound like an escapee from an old episode of

Sharpe's Rifles. After we got through the baseline pleasantries, I asked him "So, 'Leftenant'," pronouncing it in the British manner, "Why the fuck are you even here?"

He looked at me like a deer in headlights. "From the beginning?"

I sighed. Junior officers are usually predictable. "That would be an excellent spot from which to start, yes."

He took a moment to consider his answer. "I confess, I had the basic courses on how to behave as a prisoner of war while still in the British Army, but I confess I have absolutely no idea how those regulations and international laws carry over to the private sector security contracting industry."

I didn't have time for the philosophical musings of the English upper crust. "I, like you, have had a long and difficult day. Let's skip to the part where you start talking really fast before I lose what thin shred of patience I still have and just start cutting pieces off of you until I fuckin' feel better." I pulled my 'Pacific' from its scabbard and slammed it into the timber tabletop point-first.

He stared at it, swallowed hard, and replied "Very well, then."

I waved. "Well go on then."

"Having left active duty —"

"Where?"

"Public duties company, Grenadier Guards." *Well, that fucking figures. He has the wind-up marching toy look, so they park him with the best NCOs doing very little while keeping his dumb ass out of a deployable unit.* "I was new to the firm. I had just arrived in Namibia to aid in starting a recruit intake. We were to form a smallish battalion for a two-year deployment in the Solomon Islands replacing another of our units. My family disapproved, of course, but I wasn't ready to settle down and get into investment banking in The City, you know. But then our company was pulled from the battalion and given a new mission."

"I'll suppose you were smuggled into the States to a training camp in Florida instead."

He thought about it for a moment. "No, I flew commercial into Atlanta and rented a car and drove down to camp, as did the other officers before me. We didn't travel as a group since all of them were from New Zealand. The other ranks came in... you know, I don't know? They had got there before I did. A few older Chinese as operational advisors and trainers, which seemed odd, then the other ranks were mostly Rwandan."

"And that mission was this raid."

"We were told this site was full of Russian infiltrators preparing to launch false-flag terrorist attacks in the United States."

"That's interesting, who told you that? Your New Zealand colonel?

"The one you lot smacked in the head with a speeding drone and killed?"

I shrugged. "Well, in fairness he was getting ready to come shoot me."

The light bulb in his brain was sputtering to life. "So, you aren't Russians?"

I sighed. "Leftenant, were you naturally this stupid or did you have to take remedial courses in it at Sandhurst?" Other people's kids, man, I'm telling you. I don't know who his platoon sergeant had been, but I felt sorry for him.

He looked miffed, but stayed calm. Real easy to not act up when you're zip-tied into a chair. "I don't understand."

"ArmEx gets paid to provide security services, right?"

"Yes."

"Who was paying you guys to fight Russians in the United States?" He made sort of a "Uhhhh" noise while he thought about it, but I could see he was already in brain overload. I continued. "Better yet, who was paying you to fight Russians in the United States with Rwandan mercenaries, less than an hour down the road from one of America's biggest Army bases?"

I was getting a 'confused puppy' look out of him.

"Leftenant, you were lied to, it nearly got you killed, and it definitely got a bunch of your men killed."

It was starting to sink in, and he slumped in the chair as much as the zip ties would let him.

"So, with all the stuff you had available through ArmEx, why did you guys come light? I didn't see a single belt-fed machine gun, no jammers, no small UAVs, no nothing."

He sighed in frustration. "Because one of our buses blew up in the staging area in Florida, the one belonging to the headquarters section. All our UAVs and their operators were on that bus, as were the mortar section. We lost over thirty men and God knows how much equipment. The call was made to execute the mission anyway."

Damn. Either I was psychic and didn't know it or my dumb ass got really, really lucky again. It's better to be lucky than good. On a good day I was both, but good days are in short supply sometimes so you just gotta deal with it as best you can.

Then up above, we heard rotors and I stuck my head outside. A really nice late-model Bell was circling tightly past the picnic gazebo acting like it wanted to land in the field. The helicopter wasn't black. It was a glossy executive white with navy blue stripes, the sort you see coming and going from private helipads worldwide. I supposed that was the point. The 'Really, Really Dark Green' or the 'It's Not Really Black, It's Charcoal Gray' specials with all the antenna bumps and extra gizmos attract all manner of attention even when the machine guns aren't visible.

Stevens jumped out of the chopper, and walked over. Since he was at least two hundred meters away, it would take him a bit. I turned back to Leftenant Digby. "You got two choices. You can either deal with us or I can just give you to the VIP from the Agency whose helicopter touched down out here."

He went quite pale and said "I think I'll take my chances with you."

I looked back outside, and Stevens was getting closer. Looking back at the 'Leftenant,' I shrugged. "Probably a wise choice, but I make no promises. He kinda outranks me."

Going back outside, I headed his direction. I'd say Stevens was somewhat upset, but since he really wasn't in my chain of command, there was something of a limit to how many fucks I would give about that. It wasn't like he'd been particularly goddamned helpful in the last twenty-four hours so there was no fresh cushion of gratitude. I figured I had a second as he and I moved toward each other, so I pulled my phone out and I dialed Cash.

She picked up so fast I never even heard it ring. "This better be you, sir, or I'm killing whoever stole your phone."

"It's me, babe. The others there?"

"Yeah..."

"Put me on speaker." I heard the background noise change. "Daybreak, daybreak, daybreak. Y'all come on home. I have to deal with our Agency friend, so I gotta go. And Cash?"

"Yes, sir?"

"I love you. You did good. Gotta go. Oh, wait, before I go, Kara why the fuck is there a live bobcat in the first-floor women's bathroom?"

I could hear Kara screeching in the background. "A what! Those idiots put Murderbritches in the bathroom?" Smiling at that, I clicked it off as she spun up to an all-out tirade.

As he got close, I could confirm that Stevens did not look really happy. Again, I didn't care. He didn't say 'hi', he didn't say 'How are ya, are you okay?' No, he just laid on with the bullshit. "How the fuck are we supposed to cover this up? We needed discretion, goddamn it. How many people did you cowboys kill today, anyway?"

I sighed and put on as pleasant a mask as I could. "Nice to see you too, Charles. I'm fine. How's Laurie?"

He stopped short, thinking about it for a second. "Okay, I'm sorry I might have come off a little hard —"

Having made my point, I tried to be magnanimous. I waved it off. "It's okay, man. I'm way more used to this widespread violence shit than you are. Apology accepted. We'll be okay. As for how many? We can figure it out from the overheads and actual step-on body count. Under two hundred, I think. I

have my UAVs out hunting leakers right now and we're still walking the woods."
I waved toward the woodline and we began to walk around some.

He was starting to splutter. "Two hundred? I... I... I mean what the fuck. Seriously."

I calmly looked around, making a show of pointing and counting where we broke their assault line. I then looked back at him. "I don't suppose you can make some calls and get us one of those portable crematoriums from the creepy FEMA conspiracy stories to help us clean up this mess, can you? Otherwise, it's gonna be a very long afternoon on a front-end loader burying these guys." He didn't say anything. He just looked at one of the more, uh, *splattered* bodies the Microwave of Death had spectacularly done for, then abruptly threw up in the grass.

Maybe he and Laurie weren't going to come work here after all.

Down past the driveway, we heard police sirens at the road. I looked over at Stevens, still retching, and handed him my lucky bandana out of my back pocket. "Here, Charles. Wipe up. You're about to be on stage whether you want to be or not. Sell these guys real quick or we're gonna be roommates in the state pen."

Chapter Thirty-Six

"Death is just another path, one we all must take."
~ *That British lieutenant named Tolkien, via Gandalf the White*

It was a few tense moments dealing with the cops. Some of them were cool and had been out here to use our range before, but we had a lot of dead bodies lying around and 'We've been cool to this point' only gets you so much further with law enforcement at a moment like that. Stevens had to play the full-on 'Man From Washington' and make a couple phone calls to people even further up the food chain in order to disarm the situation. A little of that convinced them that no, there was nothing to see, and nothing was worth writing down. It seemed to work even more efficiently than bribery, which was really surprising. Cheaper, too.

The cops had just left when AJ walked up to me. "Hey, the dealership texted me and my car's done. Where do you want me to leave all this shit?"

I just looked at him. From his eyebrows down to his toes, he was completely smeared in either camo face paint or dirt. That layer had then been covered in a good bit of blood that didn't seem to be his. Every ammunition pouch was empty. He'd reholstered his pistol, but the filthy AR was hanging from its sling and he was idly twirling an expensive-looking custom sheath knife I didn't immediately recognize. "You know the rules. You shot it, you clean it. And where are all my AR mags?"

He waved toward the woods. "Out there somewhere. That angry guy from the Rangers has a detail going back and forth picking things up."

I don't know if he meant Dave or Ben. Really, it could have been either one.

I sighed, and he took that as an opportunity for quiet needling. "See, if you had loaned me a decent belt-fed, I wouldn't have needed your magazines and they wouldn't have gotten lost." He smiled a little bit, stretching. "This wasn't even four hours' work and we bargained for forty-eight."

"Lucky us. This could have gone a lot worse."

He pointed down at the AR. "You clean this thing for me and you can even keep your ten grand. You just owe me a good dinner sometime."

I shouldn't have agreed. Unfortunately, when I actually have the option, you can sometimes find my picture in the dictionary next to 'cheap bastard,' so I accepted his offer. "There's a locker room off the garage bay. I highly recommend you get cleaned up before you go pick up your car." He nodded wordlessly and headed that way without so much as saying goodbye. I thought I'd have a chance to talk more before he left, but he completely vanished in the ongoing confusion, leaving only a pile of filthy bloodstained loaner gear and a very dirty rifle piled up in the locker room. If it hadn't been for that otherwise unexplainable mess, I would have said that I hallucinated the SOB being there at all.

*****

We never did get the portable crematory. The bodies were hauled off by noon the next day in a commercially marked refrigerated eighteen-wheeler by some group of Maybe-Feds or Maybe-Just Really Weird Contractors that Stevens had called. They'd been a cheerful bunch, meant sarcastically, who somehow looked at us like all of this mess was our fault. Probably just as well they did it that way. I imagine the smell from burning a hundred and eighty-four bodies would have been revolting and completely spoiled the victory party River and the other underutilized medics were planning in the gazebo as it got put back together.

On that note, for your information, you can stack a truly horrifying amount of bodies in an eighteen-wheeler trailer. All those dead guys only filled it halfway. Think of that cheerful thought the next time a reefer trailer passes you on the

Interstate with that happy penguin or polar bear smiling at you with a caption inviting you to eat more frozen food. It may actually be full of piled-up dead people in black vinyl bags.

One of their now-abandoned buses was repurposed to make Leftenant Four Names, the four Chinese drivers, and the twenty-nine surviving Africans disappear. Stevens wouldn't let me keep Four Names, but assured me they were getting a plane ride back home, and not simply being disposed of somewhere as inconvenient witnesses who'd probably seen too much. Yep. I could believe that. Just like the dog you knew when you were little that 'went to go live on a farm' somewhere and you never saw again. Sometimes you just gotta accept what's probably a lie and live with it. After that, with the state and local cops having been backed off and us tucked back in under what I thought of as the National Security Security Blanket, Stevens had fucked off back to Langley.

It helped a whole lot that we had just enough rural real estate around us that nobody actually *saw* anything. The neighbors probably *heard*, yes, but lots of gunfire isn't that uncommon down here and the killer radar was, well, as silent as the grave. Mortar shells? *Naw, wasn't mortar shells. Just some Tannerite. Well, a lot of Tannerite. Got a little carried away on Range Day. Sorry.*

There comes a point after a military operation is over when you go to 'fifty percent security'. Rather than everyone still being awake, cocked and locked, ready to go, half the force can eat, sleep, change socks, whatever. You then rotate that role while everyone has the ability to get at least some recovery time in. Within 24-hours of the last gunshots, everyone had eaten a couple times, and gotten some sleep. Some of our own people had been able to go home, freeing up space for our out-of-town guests. To be honest, once they got that first really good meal or two in them and they got paid, our guest help were beginning to trickle out as well.

Once she'd finished helping in with the wounded, River was happily being Boss Mama in the gazebo. She'd put a couple of guys to work on the grills and was teaching her 'this is how you do a lot of jambalaya fast' method to some of the other kids. Troy walked past me with a big bowl of it and stopped. "Hey, man."

"What's up."

"Was I hallucinating or was fuckin' Gustavson here? I swear I saw him out there in the woods knifing people."

"Yeah, he showed up, helped out, and then he ghosted right after. He said 'Hi'." No sense getting lost in the details. It had been twenty years, why not smooth shit over between them?

Troy mused on that as he dug a good-sized shrimp out of the rice mix. "Huh. Well, hi back, I guess. This food is damn good though. We should have had some Cajuns with us last time." With that, he wandered off to eat.

Corey and his crew of lunatics, also lured by food, had come outside and were already planning repairs and upgrades to the... whatever you wanted to call it, now that that antenna had stopped burning. Somehow calling it a 'death ray' didn't quite sit well, but it still needed a name. Not a cringey one either. Calling it *The Eye of Sauron* wouldn't work.

*****

Cash was still somewhere around Dallas with Morgan and Kara, driving back in my truck. Angel and I borrowed one of the Yukons to get back to the house. I sincerely hoped nothing had gone wrong out there while we had been busy. There were no guards from the company left at the house, since I'd pulled everyone back to the office for the fight.

I went to the house next door with a two-pound bag of beef jerky, the good stuff. His kid loved it, and I figured I'd thank him for watching my animals. Also, I never knew if I might have to bribe his dog. His dog didn't like me very much sometimes, but then it was the dog's job not to like anybody, so I didn't take it personally.

Kevin was... imagine a human raccoon. Not in the fun CGI Marvel Universe Rocket Raccoon way, but dark-haired, dark-eyed, and you can't ever quite be sure if he's got rabies or not. He spent most of his time building loud, fast cars in his big two-bay garage and enjoying a surprisingly vast real estate portfolio. Never let some of these local rednecks fool you. They may not look it, but sometimes they can afford to buy you out in cash assuming they don't spend it all on expensive custom car parts first.

He was head-down in a welding job, so I kept my eyes away from the bright light and waited for him to finish before greeting him over the stereo's racket. After a few pleasantries, he got to the point. "Well, we had a little drama out here while you were gone. Got it done with quick-like though."

"Ah, shit. What happened?"

He considered his words with a shrug. "You did warn us there may be trouble at your place, and since my kid was watching Odin and the cats for you, I didn't want any problems. I knew your crew of gunmen was gone, so's I was walking back and forth across the yards with him, and of course I was carrying. So this carload of Chinese dudes pulls up, and they looked funny at JD here," he pointed at the massive gray pit bull formally named Jefferson Davis Hogg, "and he started barking at 'em. They didn't like that much. I think someone told JD they eat dogs, and he wasn't having that, you know. Lot of meat on JD." He patted that walking slab of muscle affectionately, which made JD give off some deep rumbly noise with lots of drool.

Sigh. "And then what happened?" I knew this wasn't going to be simple. I really needed some simple. Maybe I was just getting old, but the last few weeks had worn me out.

"Bottom line up front? It was easier to fire up the backhoe and dig a hole."

Oh, fuck. "What?" This was going to be harder to clean up than The Battle for Cell Tower Hill was, and I was gonna be on my own on this one.

"Well, them boys pulled up and tried that shit with the wrong hick, y'know what I'm sayin'? They pulled first, and I ain't gonna let somebody shoot at my goddamn dog if he wasn't doing anything to 'em. Let alone with my kid in the crossfire. I did all four of them, I think."

"All four of 'em, huh?"

"Shit, why leave witnesses?"

"What the hell were you carryin'?"

"Three-hunnert Blackout with a spare mag, the one you helped me with. Had the can on it too." Shit, leave it to him to walk around with a shorty AR just in case. Yeah, we sometimes go hard out here.

"Shit. Where's the hole?"

He grinned. "Man, this ain't my first rodeo. It's not buried on my land or yours. Down a couple miles toward the river where that holler takes a blind turn, 'bout a quarter mile off the pavement. Damn car's six foot under with all four of 'em still in it."

"The whole fuckin' car?"

"We shot the fuck out of it. Wasn't worth trying to hose it out and scrap it, so we just grabbed the guns and wallets and shit, then buried the rest."

"Wait, we? Who else?" *Ah, that's why the 'I think' part.* He'd had help.

"Well, Uschi," his German-born wife, "jumped in from upstairs and put a mag of six-five Creed in, and then one of the other houses got into it so we had a good L-shape ambush going from over on my left flank." Yeah, like I said it's that kind of a neighborhood. He then handed me a couple hundred bucks.

"What's this for?"

He grinned even wider. "You get a little taste of what was in their wallets as a finder's fee. Boys was carrying a fair bit on 'em."

I passed it back. "Think I still owe ya for welding."

He shrugged and smiled slyly as he pocketed it. "Pleasure doin' bizness witcha, as always."

Chapter Thirty-Seven

T here was a brief news story about a bus fire in Florida, and another news story about the FBI raiding a defense contractor in northern Virginia after allegations of contract fraud and money laundering. The news then moved on to sports and the drama surrounding the NFL's draft before some celebrity did something stupid and soaked up the spotlight. Welcome to life in the United States, y'all. This is the illusion of normalcy that we strive for and that we suffer to protect. Ignorance is bliss, and I'm one really unhappy person. My moods definitely went dark for a while after that despite Angel and Cash doing their best.

That mostly left our people to be taken care of. Only one was in need of final arrangements.

One piece of active duty paperwork I'd brought to the company was the 'In Event Of' sheet. If you got hit by a truck on the way to work, fried yourself in the generator room, fell down the stairs, or whatever, we had to have some idea what to do with the body and also know who got your death benefits. That was half a million, paid either in cash or into an investment trust. Which one was decided on by the next of kin. The fact this had only been paid twice before this during all my years with the firm, both times for death by old age, had made it seem comfortably imaginary for most everyone.

Now Luke hadn't formally been one of us when he died. He'd never signed a piece of paper, and he'd never taken a dollar in actual pay. He hadn't wanted to. I only got him to sign the 'in event of' sheet because I asked him what would happen if he flipped my front-end loader and died. Now I'm sure he would have been a formal member of the company eventually, but there just wasn't a good time to insist on it before the shooting started and there was never an after. That didn't matter. He would still be treated in death as if he had been. I looked up the address he'd given us, and it wasn't that far away, up the other side of Kentucky and across the Ohio River in southern Indiana. It was just some speck on the map out between Evansville and the Wabash River, surrounded by cornfields.

There are those who swear the US Navy recruits better from the Midwest than the coasts. The theory holds that kids who grew up staring at dirt or trees want to run away to sea. Of course, as I subscribe to the old line about shipboard life is all the fun of prison with the added risk of drowning, I did the reverse and traded my childhood weekends as a Chesapeake Bay boat bum for the infantry, much of that in deserts. But I've tried looking at the data, and the truth of it gets lost in anecdotes really quickly. For Luke, at least, it had been true. He'd left those cornfields, gone to the ocean, been a lot of places and done a lot of things, and all of it just to die in one last gunfight a three-hour drive from his hometown.

Some things you simply have to handle yourself. Leaving Angel back with Dave to help manage the two hundred things we had going with the cleanup and ongoing ops, I took Cash with me to play the finance professional. She would be needed if Luke's family wanted us to manage the money they didn't know about yet. I'd never done a next of kin notification before, but I felt I owed the family being there myself. Luke himself was at a local funeral home and wasn't going anywhere.

Casualty notifications are done in the military by a team in service or dress uniforms, so I'd elected to go suit and tie for this one, a black one I hadn't worn before, while Cash had gone with a dress far more conservative than her usual, also in a somber black.

We'd tried calling ahead, but the phone number dumped straight to voice mail. Four hours later, we were pulling into a driveway in rural Indiana. I would want to tell you it was the traditional white farmhouse shaded by hardwood trees two centuries old, but no. I could see a clump of trees and underbrush with a broken brick chimney in it. The house I'd imagined had once stood there, and now the ruins of its basement would trap anyone who passed the chicken wire fence around it. A somewhat battered double-wide stood up on blocks to the left of where the old house had been. Loud music poured out through the walls. There was a grandma-looking Mercury sedan in the driveway next to six or seven assorted flat-tired junkers that probably hadn't moved since the second Bush administration. A steel-sided barn and a whole lot of corn fields stood out past that.

Not sure what we would be walking into, I shrugged and suggested Cash wait in the truck. She shook her head. "No way, sir. That scary hick-hop stuff they're listening to in there suggests that," she flipped a page on her tablet screen, "Dorothy Burnham, mother," who he listed as the next of kin and beneficiary of his death benefits might not be home right now. So not knowing who is at home, I'm going up there with you, and I'll be the one with my hand in her bag on her gun while you stand up front looking polite and reasonable." She had a point. Mom could have been eaten by cannibal Insane Clown Posse fans or something. Maybe we had redneck werewolves, which would also be a problem, because I didn't have silver bullets, well, at least not with me. Never mind, I'll tell you later.

I took a deep breath, held it, and then sighed it out. "This is gonna suck. I've never done this before."

Cash rolled her eyes. "How do you think I feel, sir?"

We got out of the truck and walked up to the door. The doorbell button was snapped off. A couple rusted screws stuck out of the vinyl siding marking where it had once been. I knocked. The music played on. I knocked a little harder. Finally, the music stopped and the door swung open.

This wasn't Dorothy Burnham, unless she found a time machine and took thirty years off. Five and a half feet tall, maybe a foot wide, and with that scary-thin look people get from missing too many meals and doing *way* too much meth. Her bright pink 'Panama City Beach' T-shirt fit her like a tent now. I decided to get the first word in. "Good afternoon. I'm looking for Dorothy Burnham."

She sniffed, wiping her mouth with the back of her hand. Neither looked like it had been washed lately. "You cops?" Her eyes were too bright and she was scratching at herself.

"Do we look like cops?"

She sniffled. "You look like that FBI guy on the show with the flying saucers."

Maybe she was thrown off by the suit, but please believe me when I say I don't look a goddamn thing like David Duchovny. I was surprised she was even old enough to remember *The X-Files*. Maybe there was some other flying saucer show I hadn't noticed, but then my thought process was then interrupted by a bellowing male voice yelling "COPS? COPS!!!!" followed by a crashing noise of breaking furniture and broken glass. The bellowing turned to soft shrieks of pain. Pushing inward a little to see what happened, a large balding guy nearly old enough to be this one's dad was down on the floor lying in bloody shards of glass. He was covered in maybe thirty thousand dollars of tattoos... but no pants. It looked like he'd wanted to rush us at the door, but instead he'd tripped over then gone through a glass-topped coffee table. None of his injuries looked serious, no arterial spurting, so while he was still out of the equation I turned back to her. "No, we're not cops. We're looking for Dorothy Burnham."

I couldn't tell if it was a sob or the start of manic laughter, but after that incomprehensible noise, she blurted out "She died four, no, five days ago."

Well, fuck. Maybe during the fight. Ironic. "May I ask what happened?"

She shrugged. "Her heart had been bad for years. She dropped dead in the waiting room at the county hospital."

I raised my voice so the big man could hear it. "Either of you know a Luke Burnham?"

Big Guy moaned. "Yeah, my younger brother. Fuckin' war hero in the SEALs. I think he's the one who really killed Bin Laden, not that fucker you see on Fox News talking shit about it. Luke's a black ops superstar now, a big money contractor. If he were here, he'd be kicking your ass, man!"

I shook my head and walked into the squalor. I'd seen all this before in other shitholes both urban and rural. *Fuck, it smelled bad in here.* I crouched down next to him. I decided it was time to just be blunt. "Not anymore. He worked for me, and he's dead now. I figured the family deserved to know. So you're the brother. What's your name and who's she?"

He gritted his teeth as he tried to stand. Against my better judgment, I helped him up, being real careful to make sure he bled somewhere other than on me. I didn't know where he'd been. That task aside, he wiped some glass off, panting with exertion and pain. The edge was drastically scraped off whatever paranoid high he'd been on when we interrupted his day. He was sixty pounds past his prime, but in the mess of tattoos I saw old and faded Army jump wings. "I'm Jason. That's Cassidy. She's my girlfriend."

She shrieked "I thought I was your fiancée, motherfucker!" She was looking around looking for something to hit him with when Cash stepped further up the stairs.

In a cartoonishly thick Korean accent she was faking for the occasion, she interjected "I believe the magic words in your language for this occasion are 'Bitch, be cool.'" Cash didn't have to be threatening. The suppressed Glock did it for her.

The girlfriend, yeah... Cassidy, that was it, put her hands up and sat back on a stained couch next to an empty pizza box. "You two aren't going to steal our stash, are you?"

Jason went pale. "Bitch, shut the fuck up! That's our nest egg once I get it sold!"

I looked at him. "Trust me, we have no interest in whatever you're holding. Coke, meth, weed, whatever. Not our business. That's 'tween you, whoever you do business with, and the local law."

He turned back toward his old lady. "Yeah, well maybe I wouldn't have to still be cookin' and dealin' if this bitch here could keep her habit under control and could still earn the goddamn mortgage at the strip club over on the Interstate! She used to make good money off all them truckers when she still looked good. Look at her now! Then the stupid whore sold her engagement ring —"

"That you fuckin' stole from somebody else!" she screamed back.

I glanced back in her direction. Right now, Cassidy looked like what would have happened if Gollum had a Barbie makeover. I'm sure her glory days might not have been all that long ago, but the wrong drugs will do it to you quick if you can't handle your highs and don't watch your dosages. She'd need six months, maybe a year of rehab to be presentable again, let alone be a good earner on stage.

I looked back over at Jason and made a snap decision. I reached into the inner pocket of my suit jacket and pulled a bank strap of $10,000 in hundreds. "This is Luke's last month's paycheck. Unfortunately, there's no company life insurance in our profession. We'll leave you two in peace." *Yeah, in peace until the next time the sheriff's office gets called out here for a domestic.* They stared at the cash like I was a messenger from God. "Get this place fixed up, waste it partying, not my problem. Good luck." Cash and I turned and headed for the door. I probably should have asked them what they wanted done with Luke's remains, but they hadn't asked where the body was either.

"Wait," Cassidy said. "Y'all want a dog?" I turned back, and she was holding a German Shepherd puppy that magically appeared from somewhere. "His mama got her from the pound just before she died, only been a week now, but we don't know nothing about training a dog. I ain't got the heart to take her back to the pound neither."

I sighed and nodded. Cash was almost smiling at how predictably softhearted I was when it came to animals. People, not so much sometimes. "Yeah, we'll take the dog. What's her name?"

"We were kinda feeling her personality out to find one. She just had a number."

"We'll figure it out." I sucked at training dogs too, since mine invariably turn into spoiled couch ornaments, but another one of my neighbors was a retired Army handler and could probably help me out some. And Odin could use a stepdaughter to help him get around. Hell, a step-great-granddaughter at his age.

She handed the little dog over, and the puppy, whatever her name would eventually be, just smiled at me. I'd known smart Shepherds and dumb Shepherds over the decades, but this one was maybe ten or twelve weeks old and just looked confused by the world. "She eaten lately?"

Jason shrugged. "I split my McNuggets with her a couple hours ago. We're out of puppy food."

Cash raised a hand, keeping the exaggerated accent going. "Again, we'll handle it."

With that, we got out of there.

We were almost to the Ohio River bridge when Cash finally voiced what she'd been obviously thinking about. "So they aren't getting Luke's half million?"

I shook my head. "We won't pocket it just because his mom died. We'll find some other relatives if we can, or a good charitable cause like the SEALs' memorial association, but those two? Hell no. You give those two junkies half a million dollars, even in a trust fund where they can't get at most of it at once, and they'd be dead in a month. Giving them the ten grand I did give them might be the death of them anyway. Their 'friends' will figure out they had a windfall then rob them. They'll OD. He'll blow them up both up cooking more meth. I could go on and on. Giving lump sums of money to people who are already that fucked up is like dumping gasoline on a brush fire."

In the back seat, our new passenger gave a sleepy little bark and went back to her nap.

Epilogue

"Never leave one alive behind you."
~ Attributed to "Two-Two SAS"

A few weeks later, it seemed the magic broom of Uncle Sam really had swept the whole mess under the rug, and we were back to work. Things were about as normal as they ever seemed to get for us. It was getting late when Angel asked me if we were going to actually go home today. I looked at the clock, *shit*. Time flies when you're neck-deep in the world's numerous miseries. The laptop that was connected to the outside world beeped with one more email, and I naturally looked. I didn't recognize the sender, but that wasn't unusual. I clicked and read:

Professor... we both know that's not your name and you never did get your PhD, but since we are something like friends now, I'll respect your nickname. I just wanted to congratulate you on your victory, and wish your family well from myself and my family. See you around, maybe. It is a big world out there, and neither of us will ever retire.

"James," though you know that's not my real name either.

I stood, stretched, then got into the cabinet and pulled my 'For Emergency Use' bottle of Edradour single malt Scotch. I poured myself a finger's worth, neat, into a quite nice glass I suspect I'd acquired dishonestly, sighed, and then toasted my distant foe. As I sipped, I had a feeling I was going to regret letting him live that day, but like I always say, the world is a funny place.

Afterword

I think I have made a pattern for myself. Book Two was made out of a piece that fit awkwardly in Book One before being broken off, and now Book Three was made from Book Two. At least the first 38,000 of this one was severed cleanly off the end of a finished book, which made it easier. The original version of *Doubling Down* was already turned in for DOD review, sitting at 146,000 words. All the icky techno-murder bits for which I feared the security clearance process were at the end. So, people smarter than me suggested we bob it off and go forward so 114,000 words of Part Two could be on the street by LibertyCon in June. I was merely smart enough to listen to them, but not smart enough to get this fucking thing done fast enough for review to go quickly. I was told keep this around eighty thousand words... well, I kept it right around a hundred thousand. Good enough.

This one was born in tragedy. Right after pre-orders for the retooled *Doubling Down* began and I was enthusiastically pounding away on this one, word came that my friend Jack Clemons, the legendary cryptid of the Atlanta convention scene and the firearms world, had passed away on the 4th of May, 2024 after a brief illness. While this was mentioned in *Doubling Down*'s hastily amended afterword before its release on the 15th, I wanted to mention him again.

Though Jack, sometimes known as 'Bun Bun' for the homicidal switchblade-toting cartoon rabbit that John Ringo made famous (and John also redshirted Jack a few times) does not appear in these pages the way the even-longer-dead Justin 'Morgan' Sanders does, his very long and wide shadow still falls across it. He was a street *soldat*, a *ronin* of rare quality, and the humorous freebooter attitude with which the big man walked through life helped set the stage for all this. I remember walking around what would be one of the last gun shows at Knob Creek Range back in '18 with him, just gun-geeking, cracking jokes, and talking about Seth Bailey's latest novel that we were both in. Seth used us both in 2016's *Edge of the City,* which birthed The Professor and in turn led to what would eventually be *Door Number Three.* The cyberpunk-dystopia Atlanta story that Jack did in the *We Dare* anthology was magnificent and I wished he'd written more of it. We're all diminished by his passing.

Once again, laying grief aside for now, I continue. Now as with the earlier books, I had a good bit of help in making them happen.

First, my sister got on the Internet and found a Pepsi bottler up in Illinois that was selling twelve-packs of Mountain Dew Real Sugar off the loading dock for wholesale pricing. Me being me and therefore somewhat committed to living my act, I drove the five hours up just before LibertyCon '24. I bought thirty packs, and told the kid who loaded me up that I'd be back around Christmas for a resupply. I didn't even make it to Thanksgiving since I'd given, sold, or traded away two months' worth to my fellow addicts. Now the bottler can't get it anymore, and now I'm out again. If you have a hookup, let me know, but Pepsi allegedly doesn't make the stuff anymore at all which pisses me off. The modern corn syrup stuff tastes badly different.

Philip Schreier, now the director of the NRA's National Firearms Museum, showed me the thumb-lock trick to make a suppressed Ruger .22 even quieter when we were shooting his in the basement at his old house. Works great. Not like a .22 doesn't have enough recoil to hurt your thumb. Sealed-breech guns really are quieter. Get well soon, big brother.

My longtime friend and mentor Tom Kratman, who served here at Campbell in 2/502's battalion mortar platoon before his Panama years, helped out some with what I didn't know about indirect fire from mortars in general and 81mm M29s specifically.

My favorite Agency retirees gave me the inside story on the Director's dining room. Keeping that story in my back pocket for now, but it will happen.

My thanks in several capacities to the Clarksville (Tennessee) Civil War Round Table.

Another fandom buddy of mine, a truly demented polymath of extraordinary genius who knows who he is, checked some of the IT bits and did the radar antenna math for me since I'm just not that kind of smart. He was also the first one who suggested cutting *Doubling Down* off after Las Vegas, and using the run back into Amarillo as the cold open for this.

The idea for the company having an in-house medical operation came from my DragonCon buddy Adam Meyer, a former Marine Corps captain turned EMT, convention security lead, and proprietor of Usagi Medical Group. They provide medical coverage to fandom events in the Atlanta area. He was also tied for first with my first ex-wife in buying *Door Number Three* on the original fall 2022 pre-release. He also helped with some medical details, and since Jimmy was busy working, I hit up Demp at SoLaTac down in Louisiana for a second opinion on packing a skinny .22LR wound channel. He didn't think it was worth the effort, a difference of opinion alluded to in Jimmy's explanation.

I have to thank Jesse James Fain, who I met when we both got stories into the *Deadly Flames: Dragons In Combat* anthology, for coming up with the 'El Bajoon' nickname for our dead drug lord. Yes, it was a throwaway reference, but I still wanted it to look right. You should know by now I'm weird like that about details.

Of course that has its flip side of sometimes blatantly making shit up. You wouldn't believe the liberties I took with topography and land ownership 'somewhere north of Nashville' for the land around Athenaeum's mostly fictional office and the site of the final battle.

Alex Thomas was the LibertyCon buddy who put me onto Oak and Eden bourbon. The Saturday of con in '22, when I had sold what became *Door Number Three* to Holmes without it actually being completed, the realization I had to finish the last ten percent of the book in about a month had me in full-bore panic mode on the cigar deck. Alex, who I'd never seen before in my life, saw me puffing away and said "Man, you look like you need a drink. Try some of this!" That gesture was mentioned in the finished book, and about a year later he reached out on Facebook to say he was the guy with the bottle. He bought the Cannon Publishing "Red Shirt" at LibertyCon '24 along with signed copies of the first two books, so I owed him an appearance in this book even if he hadn't gifted me a fresh bottle at the autograph table.

Dave Bullock, the VP for sales at Rocky Patel Cigars in Florida, really did let me know that the Valedor lived on as the Sumatra in their Edge series. They're my go-to routine smoke. I occasionally cheat on them with Gurkha and Uppman, but then I basically started with Uppmans thanks to Web Griffin novels and those Gurkha Cellar Reserves they were giving out at NRA in Dallas last year were outstanding.

And since he will be officially retired by the time this sees daylight, I finally get to publicly thank Major Paul Jacobsmeyer, US Army, Military Intelligence (Retired), of the Pentagon's 'Defense Office of Pre-Publication and Security Review.' From when *Door Number Three* ended up on his desk in 2022, he's always been really easy to work with and he did a pretty fair job of teaching me what not to write. The original draft of *D#3* had over 200 required or recommended redactions, while *Doubling Down* had exactly one. I'd further argue that one was kinda bullshit, to be honest. But as the series got past the historical background and overly complex world-building into the wild ride it's become, there's less for them to complain about.

Now as for coming attractions. There is an all-new Athenaeum story in the *Cannon Fodder* sampler anthology that should be out and about by the time you're reading this. It's short, it's fun, and maybe it sets up some stuff you'll see later. Find it. Huggins and LaForce do have sequels coming to *A Cold and Mortal Spring* and *Hell's Belles* as I teased in Prof's off-duty reading. Enjoy them both, and then read those sequels when they hit.

Good news: The twenty thousand words of usable material for what would have been Book Three, tentatively *Unspeakable Cults* as an obscure H. P. Lovecraft reference, is now Book 4 in the chute.

Bad news: I won't commit to a deadline for it.

Door Number Three took about four years of inconsistent effort since it was a hobby. I never truly expected to publish it. With the immediate demand for a sequel, I got *Doubling Down* done in a year. Then I had to finish *Triple Play* in a year, and I also did five short stories in 2024-2025. The whole process was kinda painful and involved neglecting a lot of other things in my life, some of which needed to happen. Holmes has also put a novella for Cannon's *Fallen Empire* universe on my to-do list. Depending on what else I have to get written or what else goes on in my life, other projects might bump *Unspeakable Cults* back even further. That assumes I don't change the lineup and write *Dirty South* first, though it only sits at twelve thousand. I have a little time to think about it.

Fuck it, you'll have something from me by LibertyCon '26 unless I get hit by a bus.

More good news: I have scrapyard files for up to "Athenaeum Inc Book 8" on my computer, and thanks to my chaotic writing style, more stuff will accumulate in those piles. I might be able to keep this train rolling until the LLM/ faux-AI algorithms get better and put most of us novelists out of a job. Stay tuned on the social media and we'll see how it goes. Y'all know where to find me.

Now that you're done, don't forget to rate it and review it. Every little bit helps.

Dan Kemp Biography

Once upon a time I was a weird and nerdy kid with a taste for World War II history, JRR Tolkien, and Larry Hama's GI Joe comic books. Then I got into Tom Clancy, Stephen Hunter, Robert Heinlein, and so on. I still have a bit of a book hoarding problem.

To make a long story short, I finally finished up at Ole Miss then walked into a recruiting office and spent several years being much cooler than I am now, while abusing my liver and tearing up my knees. While sitting behind a desk partly crippled, I discovered John Ringo, Tom Kratman, and Larry Correia. Then I started trying to write books instead.

Writing is a combo platter of issues, ask the late Hunter S. Thompson or Anthony Bourdain if you don't believe me, but it's still cheaper than therapy. Authors are supposed to be slightly unhinged, and the all the 'troubled veteran' stereotypes give you so much maneuvering room in a space already filled with oddballs.

Pushed by friends, I was nearing completion on one really good manuscript. Then I ran into a guy on a rifle range at LibertyCon 2022, and we got talking while I loaned him a M1 Garand. It turns out he was a publisher. That sold my first novel. Thanks, John.

That turned into "I need the sequel in a year." A couple short stories besides, then "I need the sequel in a year." A few more short stories, and I know I have to have Athenaeum 4 done in just under a year.

You can find my latest ramblings on Facebook at "Dan Kemp Author" since Amazon has disabled author blogs.

****

More from Athenaeum, Inc!

The Professor has problems, and not just what decades of soldiering did to his back and his knees. His boss just died, leaving him as CEO of the extremely discreet intelligence contractor Athenaeum, Incorporated. His old buddy the Operations Director is a highly skilled Army Ranger veteran but his finance chief is slightly unhinged and spends her money on highly inappropriate work outfits. The surviving old men on the Board of Directors are stuck in the 1970s. Running Athenaeum out of an old Cold War bunker and keeping their roster of experts together is expensive, but the government contracts are drying up or going to bigger, flashier corporate players.

Door Number Three

Doubling Down

More From Cannon Publishing

Join the Crew!

Sign up for our newsletter for the latest news on new releases and more.

Follow our authors at their Amazon Pages!

Shane Gries (Dragon Finalist)

Lucas Marcum

Al Hagan

James Copley

Jason Kyle

G. Scott Huggins

Michael Morton

Charles Hackney

Jon LaForce

Jason Weiser

Kal Spriggs

Brian Gifford

More Books from Cannon Publishing

Irregular Scout Team One

In July of 2016 a plague swept the world, and the civilization collapsed and fell. For a lone National Guard sergeant, a veteran of the wars overseas who had settled down to a new life, the nightmare began on a hot summer evening at the barricades. Orders and chaos, gunfire and being overrun, his unit dwindles away in the face of the infected.Months later, living in the ruins, the thud of helicopter rotors followed by a crash and the rescue of a downed pilot leads Sergeant First Class Nick Agostine back into the arms of the US military. From his experience comes the idea of teams, military and civilians experienced in dealing with the undead and barbarism of the wilds. The first Irregular Scout Team leads the way for Task Force Liberty to advance down the Mohawk Valley in Upstate NY, making contact with survivors and clearing out the infected with stealth and firepower.

Volume 1

Volume 2

Volume 3: Civil War

Volume 4: Bad Company

The Line

When the world descends into chaos and anarchy with an unbelievably swift plague, turning victims into ravenous maniacs, the soldiers of America's storied 1st Infantry are asked to hold the line. From the brutal streets of urban combat to the bloodied, desperate defense on the plains of Kansas, they fight a war against an unrelenting enemy who used to be their fellow citizens. As civilization falls, can they hold the line?

The Thin Dead Line

Dead Storm Rising

The Big Dead One

Fallen Empire

What's a soldier to do when the war is over? When he's only known conflict his whole life? Since time immemorial the solution has been to find another war, this time for pay. Whoever has the credits and wins the high bid gets the experienced fighter. Sometimes, though, the credits aren't enough to cover the price.Empires rise, but Empires also fall. The Terran Union has spent five centuries under the control of the alien Grausians, like a barbarian tribe under the thumb of Rome. Now, after almost two decades of civil war and succession struggles, the formerly subject races have settled back in their ancient territories to lick their wounds and re-arm, leaving hundreds of settled planets to exist in a political vacuum.Into that space steps the free companies, mercenary units that fight for gold, honor, power and glory. Veterans who can't get the wars out of their souls, new recruits looking for adventure, corporations with their own agenda.Join us in a 27th Century that echoes history.

The Irish Brigade
Overrun
Silent Violence

Athenaeum, Inc

The Professor has problems, and not just what decades of soldiering did to his back and his knees. His boss just died, leaving him as CEO of the extremely discreet intelligence contractor Athenaeum, Incorporated. His old buddy the Operations Director is a highly skilled Army Ranger veteran but his finance chief is slightly unhinged and spends her money on highly inappropriate work outfits. The surviving old men on the Board of Directors are stuck in the 1970s. Running Athenaeum out of an old Cold War bunker and keeping their roster of experts together is expensive, but the government contracts are drying up or going to bigger, flashier corporate players.

Door Number Three

Doubling Down

Off World

When nuclear war erupts on Earth, the American colony in the Alpha Centauri system is left stranded. As the new day dawns, a furious attack by the native inhabitants threatens to overwhelm the colony's defenses. It's left to the thin red line of the US Army's 9th Regiment to stem the tide and ensure humanity's survival in this harsh new world.From two time Dragon Finalist and author of the best selling series "Irregular Scout Team One" and "Invasion" comes a new tale that tells of the struggle for survival on a brutal planet.

Offworld: Ragnarok

Offworld: Expeditions

Valkyrie

Humanity engages in a desperate struggle with an alien species for this side of the Orion Arm. Space ships die in instantaneous bursts of light and turn into vapor, but on the ground Marines scream and lie wounded in the mud and blood, praying for the Valkyries to come save them. They aren't wishing for death and a Nordic goddess to take them to Valhalla, the wounded are praying for the men and women of the '348th Field Hospital MEDEVAC to dive through fire and hell to come save them. Because they know that ...Valkyries never die!

Valkyrie
Valkyrie: Rebellion
Valkyrie: Attrition

High Caliber Awards

The Cannon High Caliber Awards are an annual contest for new writers. In it we ask them to submit a novella length story of Science Fiction, Military or Fantasy genre to challenge their skills.

2024

2025

The Wishkiller Saga

While on patrol Captain Aethal Paaling discovers evidence that an ancient terror has reached the rich soil of his home: the Lotus, a prolific growth whose addictive leaves devour their victims from within turning their hosts into horrible, terrifyingly violent mockeries of humanity. Created at the dawn of history by the twisted power of a godly relic called the Well, the return of the Lotus may be a harbinger of even more horrors to come. Carrying the fatal news to the capital, Aethal discovers that even in the face of death itself, the Lords Paramount of Verlaen will fight to keep their secrets and their power. With only the guidance of his legendary Greater Rifle and the aid of the Pheonix Lancers, the soldier must find his way through the halls of a forgotten holy order and into deep dens of crime seeking answers. He must find the truth as quickly as he can, because the Lotus may have already taken root among those he loves... and fighting it may cost him everything, including his soul.

A Cold and Mortal Spring

Hexen

When nine out of ten people in the world have died in a brutal plague, what do those who remain do to pick up the pieces? Does the creed, "Duty, Honor, Country" have a place any more if there's no country left? On his way across the devastated remains of Texas, Marine Corps veteran and survivor Eric Marten rescues a young woman from a vicious attack by men who have turned into savages. As Dani slowly learns to trust him, they try to stay alive in the deathlands that America has become, using all their wits to survive a post-apocalyptic nightmare.

90% Death Rate: A Post Apocalyptic Thriller
Angel of Death: A Post Apocalyptic Thriller
The Bloody Princess: A Post Apocalyptic Thriller

Hell Train

A single train carries what might be the last vestige of civilization through a hellish nightmare. A few hundred alive out of millions, lights going out all across what was once America as the possessed arose from the dead and murdered the living. A few hundred survivors travel across the country in an armored train, seeking some place to shelter in a fallen world. All that remains is a dystopian nightmare marked by rains of blood, impossible horrors, and portals to Hell opening in the skies. US Army Captain Jack Zamora is responsible for their safety, a self-imposed burden that wears on him every day. Fighting off undead, protecting the survivors, keeping the train running and supplied as his team desperately plans their next moves. Starvation and disease threaten. but it gets worse, because the ancient gods have sent their emissaries, horrific beings of myth and legend that walk the Earth. Things that can drain a man's very life essence or even that of an entire city.

Hell Train: All Aboard

The Path

Sometimes a hero isn't what you expect, and the one you need comes from the castaways of society. Nearly broken and at the end of his rope, former decorated scout pilot and prisoner of war, Red has finally accepted the inevitable. He and his kin have no future in the Human Confederation of Worlds, being gene mods and barely human themselves. With the help of his friend he flees Terra for adventure and fortune out in the reaches of the galaxy. Along the way he's dragged back into conflict that calls on all his piloting skills and he learns the deeper meaning of Kin, as his crew becomes his family.

Path to Freedom: The Path, Book One

Invasion

More than a decade after the Confederated Earth Forces were defeated, their commanding general, a boyhood protegee, lives in exile and disgrace. His life on an isolated farm is forever changed when two strangers show up at his homestead, and the war comes crashing back down on him. The problem though, remains the same. How do you fight an enemy that is technologically superior and holds the high ground?

Invasion: Resistance

Invasion: Day of Battle

Invasion: Total War

Military Sci-Fi/Fantasy Anthology

The military experience is timeless, and echoes down from our past and into our future. Along the way, not everything is as it seems. Thirteen stories from established and new writers in the field of Military Science Fiction and Military Fantasy bring you tales of the terrors of combat and the even greater fear of the unknown in Cannon Publishing's first Bi-Annual Military Anthology.

The Hundred Worlds

Fifteen classic Science Fiction stories from both masters of the craft and up and coming new writers!A tyrannical United Nations pulls the strings of its colony worlds, ruling with an iron fist. Corporate interests take precedence, and brushfire rebellions smolder on the edges. One system, home to the only alien species yet discovered, with human allies throws off the yoke and calls itself Independence.

MECHA

MECHA

Feedback from the slight pressure of a hand closing sends a powerful mechanical arm smashing into an opponent. A neural link hurls blustering plasma fire from your suit's shoulder mounted cannon. Your reactor levels scream with overload as return fire smashes into your armor, and damage alarms wail while you hurl your twenty ton body sideways for cover. You're a Mecha, a mechanical fighting machine with a human pilot. The guy that the infantry curse at in training and pray for in combat. The machine that the last hopes of your people ride on. The construct that strikes fear deep into alien hearts as they hear your turbines power up. The one able to pass through hell and come out the other side victorious, or die trying.

Under A Different Sun

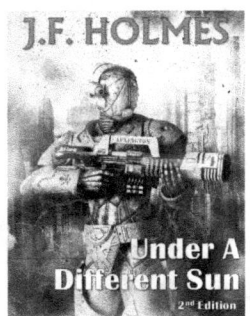

In the near future, massive empires rule the stars, and west of the Reach, they are battling for control of new systems. In the no-mans land between the front lines, Captain Nate Meric and the crew of the privateer Lexington fight for prize money, and loyalty to their ship and their friends. Beneath it all, though, runs a hidden dream. To see America restored, and take her rightful place among the stars.

Sea of Fire: Demonrise

Brian Corel, former slave, gladiator, ex-fiance to an Empress, exiled Captain of the Taland Royal Guard and now owner of the frigate *Widowmaker,* does the best he can to balance the lives of his crew with his own desire to live life as a free man.Skirting the border between being a privateer and an outright pirate, Corel stumbles into a war with a religious cult intent on corrupting the kingdom of an old friend and has to set things right while grieving over his lost love. Along the way he signs a dragon into his crew and has to risk everything to rescue his brother from the grasp of a demon that has destroyed an entire continent.

Chosen by the Sword

There are some things a PhD doesn't prepare you for, like running two feet of steel through the guts of a flesh-eating monster straight out of a nightmare, while ducking razor sharp claws. Or having the sword critique your fighting style while you do it. Dave Howard had a problem. Last week, he was out looking for a teaching job in the middle of a wrecked job market. This week he was neck deep in green blood and hellfire. Dragged into it by the very sword, his grandfathers' mysterious possessed blade, that was now walking him through hacking up a ghoul without getting his own head cut off. This wasn't exactly what he had gone to school for, and the University he had just taken a job with seemed to be anything BUT an academic institution. More like some kind of monster hunting bunch of weirdo nerds. Maybe his degree in Personality Psychology might be useful there, at least. The fighting though ... as he dodged another swipe of claws and awkwardly tried to follow the instructions the sword was screaming at him, he shot back at it, "Hell, I'm Canadian! Swordplay isn't in my cultural DNA!"

Beyond the Wall: A Novel of Post-Roman Britain

The legions are but a memory, the glory of Rome only a shadow of crumbling ruins and broken walls. A darkening tide of barbarism was washing across Britain's shores and the lights of civilization were slowly flickering out into darkness, only kept burning by the legendary Red Dragons cavalry unit. Led by their Tribune, Arthur, who serves no kingdom but goes where the fight is hardest and most crucial, they wage desperate battles to keep back the tide. The Red Dragons ride the length of Britannia to fight the invading Saxons, Scoti and Picts, wherever they show, from across the seas or down from the Highlands. At sixteen years old Peredur of Gwynedd has listened all his life to the stories of his father Pelinor fighting with Ambrosius Aurelianus. When word comes that his older brother has been slain in battle with the Saxons, his desire for revenge leads him to follow in his father's footsteps as a warrior, becoming a cavalryman with the Red Dragons. Along the way he may either find himself a warrior and leader worthy of Arthur or be left lying forgotten in the dust of history.

Hell's Bells: War & Love Downrange

Two souls collide in the middle of a deadly war.

Sergeant Sylvie Lyons of Her Majesty's Royal Engineers wishes she'd listened to her grandda's advice and stayed away from the military.

USMC Sergeant Hondo Cassidy wants nothing more in life than being a Marine and fighting. Hondo and Sylvie find themselves thrown together when his artillerymen are assigned to provide security for her engineers deep in the desert of Afghanistan.. Amidst death, destruction, cultural misunderstanding and the inevitable that happens when you mix an all male unit of Marines with an engineer unit that is mostly female, Sylvie and Hondo find in each other a reason to live. That is, if they can survive.

Semper Die

Semper Die

The dead rose expecting a feast. What they got was a firefight.

Sergeant Alex Slaughter and the Marines of Alpha Squad were on a routine training exercise near Quantico when everything went silent. No comms. No command. No clue.

What they find when they return to base is worse than anything they trained for: a bioweapon has unleashed a zombie virus that has shattered civilization, and now they must survive the Collapse.

But as the squad pushes deeper into hostile territory—through the death-choked streets of Arlington and into the rot-stained corridors beneath D.C.—they discover that the undead aren't the only threat. Desperate survivors, rogue military units, and darker truths buried beneath the weight of secrecy will test their loyalty, their mission, and their very humanity.

Written by USMC veteran Jonathan Shuerger and set in J.F. Holmes's brutal and unrelenting Irregular Scout Team One universe, Semper Die delivers pulse-pounding action, authentic military detail, and a terrifying vision of what happens when duty and apocalypse collide.

If you crave hard-hitting military thrillers, brotherhood forged in battle, and Marines who refuse to die quietly—this is your next mission.

Lock. Load. Semper Fi. Semper Die.

More from the Fae Wars!

Get the full series !

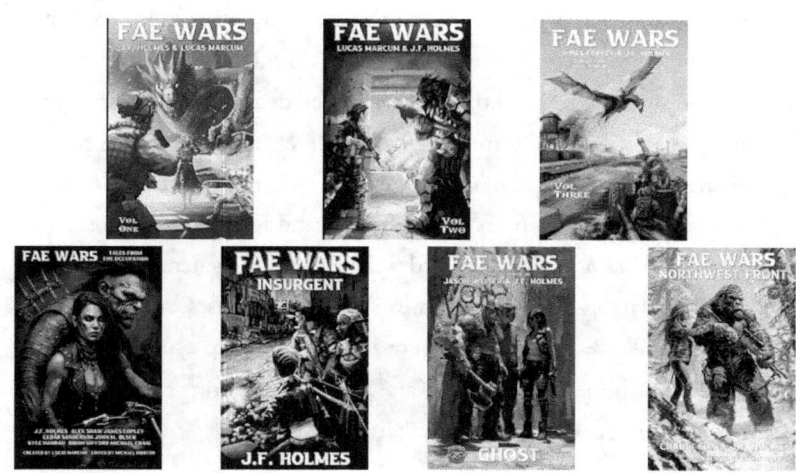

Onslaught

What would you do if America and the world were invaded tomorrow by a relentless and brutal enemy? In an alternate 2015, a US Army Special Forces Team, part of the legendary black ops unit "Delta", is in midtown Manhattan to take out a Chinese spy and his handlers, sending a message short of outright conflict. All goes smoothly until they find themselves in a full blown shooting war through the canyons of the City. Portals from another world have opened in Central Park, making a way for figures out of historical nightmare to invade. The Fae, creatures banished from Earth thousands of years ago and now only part of our legends, have returned with Dragon fire, spell and sword to conquer and take revenge. The first volume of The Fae Wars covers Team Three, G squadron, Special Forces Detachment (Delta) as they fight their way off Manhattan and then join the defense of the refugees as the Fae assault the bridges. The fabled 69th Infantry puts up an epic fight against superior weaponry and then the war descends into the asymmetric hell that the Delta Operators know so well. Along the way they find new allies and old powers that come to their aid

The Fall

For the first time in two hundred years an enemy has stepped foot on American soil and war has come to our cities. The US military is rocked back on its heels and driven into a fighting retreat as each defense line falls. The foe is unstoppable and ... Fae. Creatures from a legendary past who have come to reclaim the Earth in the name of magic and revenge. In the hills of Pennsylvania a ragtag, devastated army prepares to make a last stand against dragon fire capable of melting an Abrams tank and wizardry that stops fifth generation fighter jets in mid-air. Inevitably it comes down to shining steel verses human will, and Sergeant Oliva Acevedo transforms from a hospital clerk to a hardened fighter. Volume Two of the best selling "Fae Wars" follows the fighting retreat of the US Army as the Fae establish control of a shattered America.

Futures Past

Two thousand years ago the Fae were banished from Earth and they've spent that time plotting return and revenge. When their portals open around the world and start crushing the human's military with spell encased steel and dragon fire, it becomes a massive stuggle between technology and magic. When the Fae Invasion hammers the West Coast, Captain James Powers and his California Army National Guard artillery battery is caught on its way home from Annual Training. In a running battle the unit is smashed by combat with orcs and elves, leaving their commander struggling to keep his people together and alive. Along the way a dying priest with a strange ability to see the future manipulates people and events to bring Captain Powers to his true calling as a Seer. As they run and fight, the humans gain new allies, Fea tinkerers who love all things mechanical and hate the elves. With their help they begin to take the war to the enemy in a brutal mayhem of ambush and assassination. Book Three of the Fae Wars series following the bestselling "Onslaught" (set in NY City) and "The Fall" (Pennsylvania)

Tales From the Occupation: A Fae Wars Anthology

Wars end, enemies are defeated and territories are conquered and the combatants have to return to a life changed. America and the rest of humanity have fallen to the Fae, ancient mortal enemies of mankind. After building their strength for two thousand years, the Elves have claimed their vengeance and now rule Earth with an iron fist and dragon fire. Down but not out, a human resistance is building, but first daily life needs to be lived. An anthology of stories exploring life during the Occupation in the best-selling Fae Wars universe.

Insurgent

Wars come and wars go. Eventually even the most belligerent of combatants will arrive at some kind of living arrangement, either through exhaustion or slaughter. Kill enough, down to the last child, and there will be no more war ... until the next one, of course. In August 2015, the war started, portals opening up between their world and ours, allowing the Fae to return to our (or their) home world in blood, fire and magic. Conventional forces fought back as well as they could, but the invasion had been planned to hit us in the middle of our civilization. America's military was scattered overseas or concentrated in large bases that were quickly overwhelmed by forces that were dropped right in the middle of their units. The fighting was brutal and horrific, magic overwhelming technology. It took six weeks, and the President surrendered to spare the civilian population. A puppet government was put in place and the Fae started to divide the conquered lands into principalities run by their Great Houses, slowly turning America into a land of feudal slavery. Thing is, though, the Fae had lived in their exile for thousands of years, fighting wars among themselves and against various races that populated their new home. Pitched battles where there was a clear-cut winner and loser. They had never fought an insurgency and had no idea how bloody it could get. Major David Kincaid. United States Army 1st Special Forces Operational Detachment–Delta, soldier of a defeated but unbroken nation, was going to show them. If, that is, he can keep the faith. The follow up novel to the bestselling "Fae Wars: Onslaught" by J.F. Holmes.

Ghost

There are wars, and then there's War. The all-encompassing thing that is fought on many levels, and with many kinds of weapons, many kinds of warriors. Even ghosts. Alex was no one, a man just trying to get by at his paperwork job at the new Homeland Security. A man grieving for his wife, who had died in the Invasion. Someone just trying to keep his head down while the elves appointed him to do the paperwork of putting their boots on the necks of a conquered American people. Thing is, even a nobody paper shuffling clerk has a weapon, one that had lit the fires of revolution in America hundreds of years ago. His mind, and his words. The internet was still up and running, somehow and someway, and Alex takes to his keyboard. Inspired by his hero Patrick Henry, soon the words of the "Ghost" start inciting attacks on the Fae and the District of Columbia rings with explosions, gunshots and cries of Freedom. The Resistance notices, and Alex is soon assigned a bodyguard and a handler, an ex-police officer who is running from her own hidden past. Together they work to keep the flame of resistance alive and escape from the tightening net of the Fae. The consequences are, as always, Liberty or Death.

Northwest Front

Fae Wars returns on a new front as war rages in the Pacific Northwest! Corporal Erik Doherty isn't some kind of special operations super soldier; he's just an infantry grunt trying to get by in what was once the United States Army, now an enforcement arm of the Fae overlords. When orders come down from a chain of command more interested in boot licking their new masters than protecting American citizens, he has to make the choice. To serve and live, or run and die? Ashleigh Greene is a teenage girl with a price on her head, the Fae looking for retribution for the killing of one of their nobles. As her hometown burns behind her, she flees into the mist shrouded forests of the Pacific Northwest, her family killed by dragon fire and her world destroyed. On separate paths, each human comes face to face with a haunting legend that has lived for thousands of years. One that has been waiting, watching, and hating the old enemy that has finally returned. Together, they bring war to the Fae in a battle for honor and revenge. Book seven in the best-selling Fae Wars series!

Λ

www.ingramcontent.com/pod-product-compliance
Lightning Source LLC
Chambersburg PA
CBHW071248250626

47163CB00002B/370